PAST
THE
MIDWAY

SARAH HANLEY

EDWARD WAYNE PUBLISHING

First paperback and e-book edition July 2020

ISBN 978-1-7324442-2-5 (paperback)
ISBN 978-1-7324442-3-2 (e-book)

Library of Congress Control Number: 2020912070

Published by Edward Wayne Publishing
Maple Grove, Minnesota
www.sarahhanley.com

For Eve and Luke

Also by Sarah Hanley:

Matka

PAST
THE
MIDWAY

Jo

AUGUST, 1927

"I know of someone," Barlow says. His deep-set eyes are wide with fear under his caterpillar brows. His forehead furrows, a look I've come to recognize as thoughtful worry. My uncle sees a problem and fixes it. His years as a family man have at least taught him to sand down his words, cushion his delivery. "I've heard he does good things. We can go to him. He can help."

I'm on my knees next to the oven, against the wishes of Aunt Alice who had pleaded for me to stay in bed. The mushy air, the stagnant heat, the trembling moiré wallpaper that surrounds me, and the rancid smell of my own body all make my delicate stomach even more sick.

Aunt Alice and Uncle Barlow watch me. Neither move. Occasionally, Alice's eyes flicker to the two bundles of blankets balanced on the open oven door. Two swaddled humans. Girls.

Still fetuses, really, keeping warm with the help of the mechanical heat billowing into the room from the broiler. Keeping warm, though the kitchen swims in late-August swelter.

They shouldn't be here.

They.

Good God.

One was enough of a pinch. When the midwife called for a second blanket, and Alice's face went white, I thought…

I thought…

No, I didn't. I didn't think. At all. About any of this.

I look at the spindly purple beings nestled between the folds of flannel. Skin translucent enough that I can almost see their thin blood pushing through their veins. Their heads are elongated like those statues that Howard Carter fella brought out of King Tut's tomb. Their faces hold expressions of pain and confusion yet, at the same time, they look strangely aloof, as if they are so very disappointed in me.

Truthfully, they should be. I sure am.

Everything about them is miniaturized beyond what should be real. I look away and stare instead at a burnt bit of crust that crumbles in the base of the oven. I nearly hear it break to pieces. My aunt and uncle each hold their breaths in silence. The infants' immature brains don't yet know to cry. The quiet is too much.

This is my fault. I did this.

I close my eyes and will them to age weeks in only minutes.

"Jo." Barlow's low voice shatters me. "I read about this man in the *Times*. He's a doctor. He can help." He takes a breath, lets it out. "We don't have a lot of options. What do you say?"

I look up, but I don't answer my uncle. Alice taps her fingernail on the thermometer hanging near the oven door.

Touches the dial to reduce the flame. Adjusts the fan near the window that blows on us, relieving the oppression from both the oven and the summer, and also to clear the air of the deadly gas being released through the burner.

Though the room is still, my mind quakes with panic. Movement in the room comes to me only as a blur; sounds are thick as echoes. I try for a cleansing breath, but my nose is deeply plugged, rendered useless from hours of crying from pain and terror. Somehow, though, the odors of the day still break through, and I know that they'll stay with me. Smells always do. They lodge deep in the skin and cement into memory. Sweat. Blood. Bread still cooling on the countertop from this morning.

Fresh, parchment-thin skin.

Fear.

Barlow straightens his back, his gentle concern hardening to impatience. "Better than being cooked in the goddamn oven."

"Barlow, nobody's being cooked. The door is wide open." A click comes from Alice's tongue. She pats my shoulder.

I look up at my uncle. He waits with pursed lips. They all wait for me, the tiniest of them waiting to live or die. But I tell myself that's not up to me. None of this is. I have to keep rolling that over in my head. This isn't my fault.

But of course it is.

I swallow hard, "What if—"

"There's no '*what if.*'" Barlow's interruption bites more than he probably intends. He curbs his voice. "If we don't move now, we'll be digging holes in the backyard by midnight." He removes a toothpick from his mouth. "Jo, this is up to you. If you want this…" His eyes drop to the oven door. "If these two are your future—yours and Charlie's—then let's go. Trust me.

3

We'll take the Tin Lizzie. If we leave now, we can be there by," he glances at the clock on the wall above the back door, "eight, maybe eight thirty."

"Oh, Barlow," Alice picks up the bottle that sits on the table, a glass relic saved from her own children—my cousins—now grown. It is filled partway with warmed, fresh milk delivered this morning to the front door. It is doing absolutely no good to anyone, as useless in feeding the infants as my own body. The midwife tried bringing each little being to my breast, but babies who barely know how to breathe certainly won't know how to suck, especially at a swollen nipple that overwhelms their whole mouths. Alice rests the bottle down in the same spot, moves again to pick it up, but then stops herself. "Do you have to—"

"Yes. Yes, Alice, I do. This is life or death." My uncle looks at me. "This doctor works with tiny babies like these. He takes in weaklings, nurses them to health." Barlow slides off his cap, smooths out his thinning hair, then replaces the hat. "He works at Coney Island in the city. Guess he has these special machines. He's—"

"Coney Island, Barlow? The amusement park?" Alice's forehead wrinkles. She crosses her arms.

"Would it matter if he worked out of the town dump, if he keeps babies alive?" Barlow says.

I don't pay much attention to their squabbling because I'm stuck on the thought of Charlie. Our future. *Ours.*

This situation isn't *ours.* Charlie doesn't even know about this particular reality, the one warming on the oven door.

If he finds out, we're finished.

A pain shoots through my abdomen. I double over with a whimper. Alice presses her hand against my back and pushes my matted black hair behind my ear so the bobbed ends tickle my jawline. She strokes my cheek like a child's. "Jo, you need to rest. You shouldn't be up and about." She tries to pull me to my feet, but I don't move. My concern isn't with myself; these suffering little souls are each a piece of me. "Please, let me call Estella again," she says.

I shake my head. The midwife we called this morning has long since gone. Back home to feed her own children. Probably creamed, chipped beef and Velveeta sandwiches. Maybe a Hostess CupCake for dessert if they behaved well. There is nothing more Estella can do for me. For us. Her job's done. I look down at the purplish creatures peeking out from their swaddles, too weak to fight against the wrap of the cloth. Four arms that don't know their use, don't realize they're attached to anyone. I watch the movement of the ribcages that should imply breath. Honestly, I'm not so sure. A living, breathing being doesn't look like this.

I know who Barlow is talking about at Coney Island; I'd walked past the concession myself and even once or twice saw the man with the sleepy eyes who ran it. He mills around outside greeting people, dressed up like a doctor but talking like a showman. I never went in to see his spectacle. Had no reason to. The whole exhibit seemed like horsefeathers to me. Besides, Charlie has no desire to ogle over tiny babies, and Charlie's always the one who pays my admission.

Charlie. No desire for babies. Really, I'd thought the same about myself until only a few hours ago. Now every plan I had is unravelling in my head.

What the hell am I going to do?

I look up at Barlow through a fog of dried tears that burn my eyes. I nod my head, just barely.

"Okay." He claps his hands, startling me. "Alice, put some potatoes in the oven. I'll get a crate from out back."

"Potatoes?"

"They'll retain heat. It's a long drive. We used to put them in our pockets in the winter as kids. Kept us warm. We'll line the crate with them." He stops and pats me awkwardly on the shoulder. "This is going to work."

Alice and I just stare at him.

"Alice," he takes her gently by the shoulders and looks into her eyes with an intense, somber look that frightens me. "Potatoes. Now."

My breath catches as I turn back to the oven door. We'll have to move the babies, and I know Alice and Barlow will leave that to me. It's my job—they're my responsibility. My uncle and auntie never signed up for this, they'd only agreed to shelter me as my body bloated with too many lives inside it.

So, I suppose I should touch them first.

I lift my arm, spread my fingers, and gently rest my firstborn daughter's head in the palm of my hand. The velvet-soft feel of her goose-down hair in my hand tingles throughout my body. She's the slightly bigger one. The one I was expecting. Alice had placed her on the kitchen scale moments after her birth, saying something about how everyone always asks about a baby's weight. She didn't say the measurement out loud but gave away her disappointment with a click of the tongue as she scratched the number onto a notepad by the telephone.

She never bothered to weigh the second one, who came along as a surprise when we all thought we were through.

Mumbling something about potatoes needing an hour to bake, Alice reaches past me with four potatoes, each roughly twice the size of the head I hold in my hand. Starchy, bulbous chunks, heavy as rocks, grown deep in the ground. Tough and life-sustaining. Cut one into pieces and bury it, and it will grow again, sending green stems and leaves toward the sun, smelling of earth and life and fresh dew.

The simple potato. This is where we'll put our faith for the drive. Somehow, it's strangely comforting.

Cut me into pieces. Let me grow anew.

I never planned to keep any baby. But now, I can't take my eyes off of them.

Alice shakes her head. "These blasted spuds aren't going to cook with the door wide open like this. I don't know what that man is thinking." She rests her hand on my shoulder. "We better move the girls, Jo."

I withdraw my hand, not trusting my touch. Barlow had gone outside to prepare for the drive, and I see him out the window with his flivver's hood open, checking the fluids and tugging on tubes. After a few minutes when he's satisfied with his vehicle, he gives the front tires each a decent kick and then returns to the kitchen.

"It's time," he says.

Alice pulls herself to her feet. "The potatoes are barely even hot."

"We'll have to make do." Barlow wipes the summer sweat off his forehead with his handkerchief. "We can't wait any longer."

With a sigh Alice crouches and reaches for the potatoes, not even bothering with a potholder. She drops them into Barlow's crate, and Barlow pushes them out to the edges. Alice arranges a blanket in the middle.

They both look at me. I look at my girls. I lift the first

swaddled baby, careful to barely disturb her as I move her from the oven to the crate. Then I reach for the other. This baby feels like a wisp compared to her sister. Her cheeks are sunken. Her eyes, though they are squeezed shut and seemingly void of even the thought of an eyelash, are too big for the rest of her. She's as light as a petal, her velvet skin glowing just a bit more red than purple.

She smells of Borax and burning crust, freshness and a losing fight. Somewhere, though, I sense a tight bud, waiting to bloom.

"Rose."

I feel her name rush out of me in a breath as Barlow's strong hand guides my elbow toward the door.

We prepare ourselves for the sideshow.

2

Beth

The baby on the warming table is blue. I pull the oxygen mask toward him, ready to cover his mouth with it. Or rather, his whole face. Most of his head. I watch Layana. She leans over and suctions the baby's throat, lifts his chin with her gloved fingertip, tries to resuscitate a seconds-old human being that weighs barely two pounds and could fit easily into two hands cupped together.

Blue. Layana is probably coming up with some poetic bullshit about his blue being that of deep water, the air at dusk. Of things that slip so easily between the fingers of those cupped hands, no matter how hard you try to grab and hold them. *Slip away, baby blue.*

But to me, he's just the ashy, gray-blue of death. And it's my job to grab him and plant him firmly in with the living. I put the mask over his face.

Twenty-eight weeks. Twelve weeks early, by all practical measurements. Average, though, by NICU standards.

We need a neonatologist in the room; too bad Dr. Che has yet to answer his page. I'd even love the help of a nurse practitioner right now, but since we require an NNP to accompany all infant transports, Rita is currently in an ambulance on her way to Children's Hospital with a twenty-five-week-old preemie born forty-five minutes ago. We sent messages to our two other NNPs who aren't on call today. So far, we're on our own.

Thirty-seven minutes ago, while Rita was climbing aboard the ambulance, our current crisis was still tucked safely inside his mother while she lazily channel-hopped through talk shows from her bed upstairs, where she'd been sequestered for the past two weeks. There was no indication—other than the pretty consistent contractions that landed her here on bed rest in the first place—that labor would progress in mere minutes.

Well, here we are.

Layana and I lock eyes over the baby for a moment. I know she's the most capable nurse to assist, and she knows the same about me, but being capable nurses may not be enough. We also know that we are only nurses, and though we are capable, we are not fully qualified.

Our failure would not only mean the death of this baby, it could also possibly mean a malpractice suit. The loss of our jobs. Maybe even the loss of our licenses if the parents are especially hostile and out to place blame.

Layana's dark brown eyes narrow over her surgical mask, and her look tells me everything: *Hell no. Not again. Save him.*

I sense the respiratory therapist next to me with the endotracheal tube poised. I can't tell if it's Dillon or Raj. They both have similar builds and the same color hair. I don't look up to confirm. It doesn't matter—both are competent. Both know what we're up against.

We won't let this one go. We can't. Especially not after that nightmare a few weeks ago. Memorial Day. She was a nearly-to-term thirty-seven-weeker. The umbilical cord had wrapped around her neck three times. After Dr. Che called the baby's time of death and shot Dillon and me accusatory looks because we dared to allow a passing on his watch, I retreated to the staff bathroom with my stomach in my throat. While I cried in the toilet stall, I could hear the mother's screams echo down the hall long after she was left in the care of the postnatal nurses and the chaplain. The life she'd carried within her for the better part of a year was gone, and there wasn't a damn thing she could do to protect it. Those screams were all she had left of her little girl.

Like a wounded animal.

Those screams still haunt me.

No, not again. Not this one. A death in the delivery room throws a shadow over the whole department. Everyone feels it. We can't go through that again so soon. We should never have to, but life is messy, I guess.

I won't forgive myself for losing that baby girl. I never did find out if she was named.

Goddammit, Beth. Stay here. Don't wander. I shake my head to clear it. I can usually tune out the beep of monitors, the screams of the mothers, the smell of burning flesh as cesarean wounds are cauterized. But I'm especially distracted today.

I set my teeth, focus my eyes. Act like I'm a functioning nurse.

Above me, the screen is lit up in cute pastels: *Welcome, Baby! 2 lbs., 1 oz.* A few of those ounces are accounted for by the umbilical clamp, the tiny blue polyester hospital-grade hat that keeps falling off his head, and the sterile plastic bag we have him wrapped in up to his chin to prevent hypothermia.

Twenty-eight weeks is strong. He should do fine. Some babies at this gestation don't even need extra developmental help as they grow into their childhoods. And Layana and I know what we're doing. Still, we're not doctors.

"How is he? Is he okay?" The mother's voice is high-pitched and hollow as she calls from the delivery bed, her knees still in the air. I glance over to see the placenta ooze out of her body into a large stainless steel bowl, Dr. Whorton's eyes intently watching. The obstetrician's only concern is the mother; the baby is in our hands. Dr. Whorton doesn't make a move to help us, nor should she—plenty could still go wrong with a mother in the seconds after birth. The baby's father paces helplessly next to his wife, silent, chewing the nail of his thumb. I glance up at the dry erase board to remind myself of the mother's name.

"He's great, Gretchen. Just needs a little extra care." I always have to be careful not to sound too absent when speaking to the mothers, especially in the first few moments. The baby is delicate, but the mom is delicate too. I've seen this over and over. New moms are hyper-sensitive, feral—any warble in your voice and they can smell your fear a mile away. Still, my first priority is getting this baby to breathe. Addressing the mom without that tinge of distress in my voice is always second. A moment of fear and unknowing is worth it, if it means your baby survives.

"Beautiful boy, Gretchen. You did great. Just give us a minute to stabilize his vitals." Layana's voice is a gentle purr beneath her mask. I wish I had her bedside manner. She has a way of comforting even the most hysterical parents. She looks up at me again and says quietly, almost inaudibly, "Should I page Dr. Che again?"

I shake my head, careful not to roll my eyes. I'm looking forward to Dr. Che's retirement next year just as much as he is. "No, it's too late."

I cringe. I said it too loudly.

"What's too late?" Gretchen makes a move to climb off the table; her nurse holds her down. "Why isn't he crying? Is he dead? What's too late?" She's sobbing, and I can sense her primal screams readying themselves in her throat.

Layana's eyes meet mine. The baby isn't cooperating. I hear a throaty whine from the bed as Gretchen panics. Neither of us respond to her. Thankfully Frankie, the Labor and Delivery nurse holding her down, does it for us. "They're doing everything they can for your baby, Gretchen. Try to relax. Beth and Layana are excellent at what they do."

"Where's the doctor? Aren't they both nurses?"

I keep my concentration on the baby.

"Beth Roselli is the head nurse," Frankie says, "and very highly skilled. She assisted Dr. Che in saving our unit's first-ever surviving twenty-three-week preemie last year—"

"I don't want an assistant!" Gretchen is crying. "Where's the doctor?"

Good question. Where is the doctor?

Layana is still trying to get a response from the baby. I hold the oxygen mask steady over his face. The lungs are always the toughest on these little ones, especially the boys.

"Intubate," I say quietly. Raj leans in before I can blink.

Ah. Raj. Good.

Within moments the baby's lungs inflate, and I feel a

flutter under my fingertips. Raj calls for surfactant and begins administering it before he finishes saying the word.

The required minute ticks by. I keep one eye on the clock, waiting for the second hand to make its round, the other on the baby, watching his lungs try to catch up.

The child's face crumples as he attempts a scream around the tube.

The mother's voice has fallen to a raspy, defeated whisper. "What's wrong with him? Is he dead? Is my baby—"

Raj pulls the tube out of the baby's throat, and the room is pierced with a most welcome scream.

I glance at the clock on the wall. 9:25. Then I glance at the baby's monitor. *Time of birth, 9:21.*

Four minutes. Not bad. But we can do better.

The mother and father embrace, sobbing as joy and relief flood them. Layana smiles at them. "Gretchen, you can take a quick look at your baby boy," she says, her voice as smooth as caramel even as the sweat beads glisten against her hairline, "but we need to wheel him down to the NICU right away and get him into an isolette."

We wheel the radiant warmer to the mother, who holds out her hand towards the child. She touches the baby's reddish-purple fingers, which are only slightly larger than the metal tip of a ballpoint pen. "Carter," she whispers.

"You'll be able to visit after we get him settled, but for now we have to go." Layana is already pushing the wheeled warming table into the hall. She looks back at me. "Great job today, Roselli." Her voice is soft, careful to not reach Gretchen's ears. She's so much better at that than I am.

"You too." The door swings shut behind Layana and Raj,

and Raj shoots me a small smile and a nod as he goes. I start to follow them out of the delivery room, but the new father stops me.

"Will he be okay?" His face is still twisted with the horror of watching his wife give birth and then watching his child almost die.

"He's in excellent hands," I say. I give him a chipper smile. "Our NICU is one of the best, and the staff is incredibly talented, especially Dr. Che." That's bullshit; we're not even close, but we do okay. And Dr. Che's mind is squarely on his impending retirement. A parent doesn't want to hear that though. They want to hear about cutting-edge technology and well-rested, ambitious doctors and survival rates of 100 percent.

Gretchen's husband looks at his wife with a relieved grin, tears catching in the stubble across his cheeks, but Gretchen looks straight at me. "You saved my baby." Her voice is like gravel. The overhead lights reflect in the lines of tears that streak her face. "Thank you."

There was no first moment photographer. There will be no keepsake footprint unless there's a quiet night in the NICU and the nurses are bored and happen to remember. The colorful newborn hats knit by the elderly ladies over at the Community Center won't even fit him for a few weeks at least. By then, everyone will have forgotten that he never received one. He's destined to be sporting the hospital grade, powder-blue polyester like a 1973 prom date.

I watch Gretchen for a moment. Most mothers would be holding their child right now, giving the baby its first soft caresses, its first kisses. Gretchen's arms are empty except for the IV poked into her vein. Her face is streaked with tears and snot; her body is still reeling from the trauma of birth.

She'll be lucky to hold her baby sometime in the next few days. It could even be a week, depending. Maybe more. She's in for a long road. She and her husband both.

And Carter. Especially Carter.

I smile at her. "It's what I do."

AUGUST, 1927

I'm in a strange place. I don't register any scents around me; my nose is still clogged with the smell of burning oil from Barlow's car coupled with the emotion of the moment. The ride into the city had been silent, save for Barlow's cursing every time we hit a pothole, which was often, and the incessant creaking and clattering of the vehicle. Once we were parked, I remember the bunching of my dress against the leatherette seat as Alice helped me from the car and the quick clicking of my heels against a sandy concrete street. The sickening smells of sweat and cotton candy broke through. I thought we were at a movie theater; I could smell warm, sweet popcorn. A mosquito buzzed in my ear.

Now, a different kind of chattering noise fills my head. People, like spectators at a shutout Yankees game or moviegoers streaming into a Chaplin matinee.

"Miss."

I stand with the baby pressed against my chest. This is the reddish-pink one, the one whose name is Rose. I gave her a name, at least. She's the smaller one, the weaker one. I only see the top of her head, nestled under my chin and between folds of blankets. I try to warm her back to what should be a more human temperature. Her skin feels cool to the touch; the potatoes didn't do their job as we'd hoped. I'd held this child against my chest for most of the ride into the city, my other hand resting gently on her sister's back in the crate. I'd closed my eyes and allowed myself a breath every time I felt a tiny chest rise.

"Miss."

She'll warm up now. Any minute. Little Rose. We're safe now. You can breathe. You'll be fine.

I don't know where the other baby is, and the realization makes my stomach swirl and shake like a smuggled gin martini. I can't bear to look around, though; if I take my eyes off Rose, she'll be gone. Vaguely, I feel my auntie next to me. She seems a bigger presence than what I'd expect from my slender aunt.

A hand rests on my arm and squeezes gently. Alice's face fills my vision. She's holding something, which explains her girth. Something soft, white. It's a blanket. A nub of pinkish-purple peeks from within the fuzzy weave; two tiny slits for eyes, two tiny holes for a nose. Alice is surrounded by a crowd of people, all watching me. I don't know who they are or why they are here. A dull rumble comes from the crowd. The bored whine of a boy. The concerned cluck of a grandmother.

I'm so, so tired.

My body recoils as I feel the touch of someone else, notice a fragrance I don't recognize.

A stranger.

Don't take my baby.

"Miss."

"Jo." A different voice. Alice's. I relax; she's still here. My body leans into her. I feel the strong arm of my uncle around my shoulders. My face is wet, but I don't know why. Sweat? Tears? I can taste the salt in the air. Ocean?

"Jo," Alice says. "This is nurse Ida."

Ida, Sweet as Apple Cider. The song jingles through my head.

"It's time."

I drop my eyes to the reddish scalp I hold in my arms within the blanket. A fine swirl of black hair bends around the top of her head.

She hasn't moved for a while now.

"Rose."

The child feels as smooth and stiff as a porcelain doll. I see only swirls, blurs of color before my eyes. I feel the baby taken from my arms; it puts my body near collapse. I'm weakened, as if my life has been taken from me as well.

"Oh." I hear the nurse. Ida. Sweet Ida. She says something. I miss it, but I can tell she's troubled. Her voice is stern. So is Barlow's when he answers her, though I don't hear what he says either. Only mumbles cross between them. They're careful not to let their whispers carry; whatever it is, they'd rather I didn't know.

The commotion of the strangers around me bubbles. A child asks questions. A mother shushes her. The smell of corn and cigarette smoke. Too many bodies pressing in on me.

A pause, Nurse Ida's voice is uncertain but clear. "And her sister's name? The bigger one?"

"I…I don't…" My voice doesn't come, only shallow, wheezing breaths from deep inside my chest. I grip for something. My hand falls on Barlow's arm. I hear Ida cough. Another cough. It sounds like the Tin Lizzy's gears grinding.

"She's had enough," Barlow says.

"The baby needs a name…"

I only hear the rushing of ocean waves in my ears, the clanging of a freight train along its rails. More coughing. Sickness. Screams of terror or joy or both far in the distance.

Louder. The noise is too much. My body gives way.

It's done.

I don't wake until I feel a cool washcloth on my forehead, the warm summer sun across the blankets that cover me. It's day. I'm not sure which. I'm in Alice's bed. I'm back in New Haven, with the trip to Coney Island behind me. By hours or days, I don't know.

Alice strokes my hair. Her smile is careful, sad.

I know it's time to go home.

4

Beth

Mama Bear.

I force a smile at the woman wearing the gray printed T-shirt as she passes me in the hallway. She gives a shy grin then looks away. Two other ladies are with her, one of whom carries a big pink mylar balloon and a package of cupcakes. The third one doesn't look me in the eye as she passes, but I see her move her arm to hide the bottle of champagne that's sticking out of her bag.

I didn't see that.

The three women knock gently on a door down the hall and then all giggle and squeal when they're welcomed in.

My stomach is still in my throat from saving that baby boy; my surgical mask is still bunched in my fist. On my way to the nurses' locker room, I pass Gretchen's postpartum room. I can hear her crying. She's stuck here in the middle of the other

21

recovering mothers, all of whom have their babies with them. Not her. She has a cold, hospital-grade breast pump on a wheeled stand, and likely a lot of questions. I pause for a second outside her closed door, listening for her husband's voice to make sure she's not alone.

I don't hear him—or anyone else—with her, comforting her.

I have to pee, but I stuff the mask in my pocket and quietly knock.

A big sniffle and then, "Come in."

Gretchen is propped up in the bed holding a pump flange to each breast. Her eyes are red and wet. A box of tissues sits on her lap. I busy myself by reading her chart as she adjusts her body in the bed and tries to look like she hasn't been crying. "Oh, hi," she says cheerfully over the hum of the pump. "My husband went to pick up a few things."

I nod. Smile. "How are you doing?"

Tears bubble out of her eyes, all pretense gone. "I'm a mess."

"You just went through something traumatic. You *should* be a mess." I watch her eyes flood even more and realize that was probably taken the wrong way. *Soften your approach, Beth.* My past three performance reviews come to mind. I sit on the end of her bed. "But for the record, you're not. You're a perfect mom." That only makes her cry harder. *Dammit.* I force another smile like I did for Mama Bear, trying to center my thoughts so I don't sound phony. This isn't my job; I'm not her nurse. My responsibility is to her baby. Still, part of my job as a NICU nurse is to keep the parents somewhat sane.

"I know it's hard. I'm sorry," I say. "I just came to tell you that Carter is stable, he's doing great."

"When can I see him?"

"We're almost ready for you. Just rest a bit longer, then we'll wheel you down."

She gapes at me. "In a wheelchair?"

I shrug. "Liability. It's—" I almost say protocol, but experience tells me that's not a great word to use on a mom within an hour of giving birth. "It'll be more comfortable. You're still healing. The best thing you can do is take care of yourself."

She wipes at her eyes with her forearm since both hands are still busy holding the pump flanges. She flips off the pump with her elbow and then unhooks the bottle from the flange on her left breast. She holds it up to me. It's mostly empty, aside from a few droplets splattered across the inside. "This is it. This is all I got."

I feign some excitement for her benefit. "This is great! We'll put it on Carter's lips so he can taste it." I pause and then add, "And fall in love with you." There. Approach softened. I look at the plastic vial, and the colostrum drops have already dried. "It will get easier," I say. "I promise."

"Are you a mom?" She asks.

My forced smile eases into a real one. "Yes. My daughter Sylvie is almost three."

Gretchen nods and blows her nose into a soggy tissue. "This will all be worth it," she says. She pushes herself up in the bed, settling in against the flat pillows behind her. "Someday very soon, when he's home and safe and healthy, he'll look at me and he'll give me that wonderful baby grin." She looks at me hopefully. "That has to be the most incredible feeling, when you've gone through all the thankless shit and your baby finally smiles at you."

I don't say anything. My smile hurts again.

Her face pulls tight, fighting against the tears that gather in her eyes. "Right?" Her voice warbles.

"Yes." I answer. I wouldn't know, but she doesn't need to hear that.

She lets out a relieved sigh. I can validate her hopes. Actually, I can't. Though it's outside of my comfort zone, I lean over and gather her into a hug. I pat her back and rock her gently as if she were Sylvie with a bad dream.

As if Sylvie could tell me when she has a bad dream.

I stand up from the bed. "I'll come get you in a bit when Carter's ready for a visit. Meanwhile I'll..." I look at the vial of useless, dried colostrum in my hand. "I'll put this on Carter's lips. He'll love it." I let myself out into the hallway and drop the bottle into a garbage can. By the time I get to the locker room at the end of the hallway, I'm shaking.

Birth is a wonderful, beautiful thing. But when a woman gives birth, she is doing a wonderful, beautiful thing that is also one of the most vulnerable and violent things a human body can do. I've witnessed many births, and no one talks about the truth of it: the mother is out of control. She's in immense pain. She's having something that is connected to her, something that is sharing her blood, her nourishment, and even her emotions, removed from her body in the most chaotic, bloody of ways, leaving behind a mess of scar tissue and a cyclone of hormones.

Those mothers are grizzly bears. Their only concern is defending their birthed cub. And when that cub doesn't thrive—or worse, dies—the mothers' reactions are brutal. Savage. Devastated.

That turns quickly when a healthy baby lands in her arms. The mother forgets the pain, the struggle. It's all smiles and cuddles and tears of joy. Balloons and cupcakes and smuggled bottles of champagne. But when that healthy baby is never delivered to her arms, all that's left is a wounded, feral animal.

I suppose some portion of a mother is always feral. There is a real difficulty in caring for an infant on little sleep and possible post-partum depression, and there is true heartbreak when a child suffers or struggles as they develop. Sometimes that can be just as savage.

Always a Mama Bear.

I open my locker and pull out my purse. A picture of Sylvie dangles from my keychain. My beautiful toddler. Thick, golden hair. A beautiful, off-center dimple too high in her cheek that I very rarely get to see. Her birth was perfect—forty-one weeks, over eight pounds. She was that healthy baby, handed to me pink and chubby just moments after she entered this world. But I didn't know then what we'd be up against now. The hints that threw me over the edge during her first three years didn't all come together to make sense until just recently.

Technically, just yesterday.

Still, seeing what I've seen, I'm one of the lucky ones. I keep telling myself that.

I sit on a metal folding chair and pull my hair out of its bun. I dig my fingers into my scalp and massage away the tightness of my twisted hair, of my twisted thoughts.

My baby will never be normal. All those dreams I had—watching her stumble on her toes through her first dance recital, reading the Harry Potter series together and then comparing the books to the movies, commiserating with her that yes, algebra homework sucks, but then seeing the light bulb go off in her head when it starts to make sense—they won't happen. The weight of all of those milestones no longer there waiting for me in our future feels like a ten-ton stack of bricks on my shoulders. And the only time in the past three years that I've felt it lifted, was that horrible day last fall when I left.

I left.

Jesus. I'm a monster.

I pull my phone out of my bag. The internet search from last night when I was rocking Sylvie to sleep for the third time is still open: *healing autism.*

There has to be a way to fix this.

I switch from the browser to the phone app. I call Eddie.

"Hey, beautiful," he says. There's tension in his voice.

I take a deep breath. "I'm really sorry about the way I acted yesterday during that meeting about Sylvie. The team probably thinks I'm a wacko."

"I wouldn't worry. I'm sure they're used to it, Beth. They deal with this kind of thing all the time. I guarantee you're not the first mom to lose your shit after that kind of news about her child."

"It wasn't news though. We knew Sylvie would have problems, you know? I mean, it's been obvious she's…" I take a breath, force myself to say the word. "Autistic. Still…"

I hear his defeated breath through the phone. "I know. We didn't think it would be this bad."

"Yeah." I chew on my lip and stare up at the ceiling to will my eyes to stay dry. "And I guess I thought there'd be more help available to us."

To me. I need help.

No. I'm a nurse. I can do this. I can handle caring for my own baby.

"Well, there will be, once we get the medical diagnosis." His tone is very matter-of-fact. "We can't blame the team, they're just from the school district. An educational diagnosis is different than a medical—"

"Yeah, that's all bullshit. I mean, come on. Nadia is a psychologist, the other two are occupational therapists—"

"We can't control it, Beth." Eddie interrupts me, like I'd interrupted him. His voice is overly calm, careful. Like he's a zookeeper approaching a sedated tiger. "I know it's frustrating, but this is the process. We'll just get her in to a psychologist, and in the meantime, we can continue to have her see Nadia through the school—"

"Which is only free until she turns three next month." I try to keep my voice steady. "Then we're left in the lurch, paying out-of-pocket."

"We can afford it," he says. "And it will be worth it."

"That's not the point."

"You deal with insurance issues all day long. You know how these things go."

You're a NICU nurse, Beth. You know these things.

My stomach sinks as the words echo in my memory. I take a deep breath to settle myself, calm my voice. "It's different. None of my patients are older than a few months."

Also, none of my patients are my own child.

"I'm sorry. It's frustrating, I know." His voice sounds far away. I can tell he's distracted, or maybe he's just not in the mood for my meltdowns. I squeeze my eyes shut. There have been a lot of those lately, I know that. I'm a mess. I can't blame him for being wary. "This isn't about the services or the insurance, is it?" he asks.

I don't say anything. Of course it isn't about the services. It's about my girl. It's about how she's never going to have the future I've imagined for her. I bite my lip hard to keep the tears back.

"Did I call at a bad time?" I ask quietly.

"Nah, it's okay. I've got a client meeting in a bit, so I have to throw together some mock-ups, but I can't find my favorite X-Acto knife. Gotta go in a minute."

I stay still, willing the tears to dry and my stomach to go back to where it belongs. "I almost lost one this morning, Eddie."

"Oh, shit, Beth. I'm sorry. Are you okay?"

I nod, even though he can't see me. "Yeah. I'm fine. The baby's fine." I sniffle.

I'm not fine.

The distracted silence at the other end frustrates me. He's a million miles away. I take a deep breath and gather myself before I speak again. "I'll let you go."

"Hey," he says. "You saved that baby's life today."

"Yeah."

"You've been under a lot of stress. Your mom and all, and now this with Sylvie. Give yourself a break. You're a good nurse, don't forget that. You did awesome today."

The tears hurt behind my eyes. My throat feels like I swallowed a basketball, and I don't trust my voice to not give me away, so I stay quiet.

I'm a good nurse. But mother? I keep getting that wrong.

"You still there?" he asks with just a bit of impatience in his voice. I push away the feelings of resentment. He's at work. He's busy. I have to sometimes remind myself that advertising is not all ping-pong and free beer. He's being kind. Empathetic. He's one of the good guys. I can't lose him too.

"Yeah. I'm here."

"We'll talk more tonight," he says. "Love you."

"You too," I squeak out before I hang up, then I stare at my phone. I want to call my mom. I want to call my twin sister, Cara. Of course, I can't do either. I sit for a minute in the folding chair.

Diagnosis. We have a diagnosis. Yet, that doesn't explain everything, doesn't fix anything. That just pushes Sylvie into a group and labels her with what she does and doesn't do. It doesn't tell me anything about who she is, how I can connect with her, feel closer to her. Or how I can help her.

Or how I can even get through this.

Grief comes from more things than just death. Gretchen is grieving her birth experience right now, her child in distress. No one wants a premature baby. Grief can also come with a diagnosis. Answers don't take away the pain. Even though my baby is healthy, she's…not.

My purse sits on the chair across from me. Pinned to the canvas strap is a little silver rosebud. Mom's. I found it on top of her jewelry box the night she died. I stare at it, then I reach out and touch it to give my fingers something to do, to focus my thoughts on something else.

I have to harden past this—I have the rest of my shift to get through. I try to focus my thoughts on phototherapy, PICC lines, and heel sticks.

I take a deep breath, let it out, and twist my hair back up into a bun. It's a good day. I didn't have to send an infant to the morgue.

I drop my head into my hands and let myself cry.

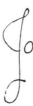

5

AUGUST, 1927

A roller coaster roars over my head, clanging and banging, the screams of the riders throwing me off balance.

So much is wrong with all of this.

For one, I'm here. Coney Island. And I'm wearing a fur coat in August. Jeez Louise. I'm standing on the hot asphalt amidst all of the lights and smells, the laughter and joy, pretending nothing happened. I can't believe I let Hazel talk me into this, but she has that way with people. Monday night, cheap admission. Celebrate my return to the city. I figure if I'd balked, she would have sleuthed that something was hinky, and I've got to keep up my line of lies, even for her.

I catch the shimmy of her beads out of the corner of my eye; she's wiggling in her dress, trying to adjust her brassiere without actually touching it or drawing any unwanted attention to herself. She sighs like an impatient six-year-old, snapping her undergarments into place. "Where are they?"

I shake my head. I should still be rotting up at Aunt Alice's in New Haven, sweating like a reefer rat in this August heat with my belly practically to my knees. But I'm not. I'm back home with Mama in the city. I'm *getting on with things*. That's what Aunt Alice said when she and Uncle Barlow loaded me up in the Lizzy a second time and drove me back to New York for good. "Give those babies each a kiss from us, and send Charlie our best," they told me.

"I will." I was trembling as I said it. That should have given away my doubt. Maybe it did, because Alice stiffened.

"You take care of those girls, and take care of Charlie." Her smile became brittle. "You've got a job to do now. Best to just get on with things." It took everything in me not to sob into her warm shoulder as Barlow loaded my suitcase into the automobile.

That was five days ago.

At that particular moment, I was sure I was giving the babies up. I was also going to give up Charlie. Be my own girl. Get a job, take care of Mama. Forget any of this ever happened. Or maybe I could keep them, and Mama could help me raise them. It would all be very modern and grand, just the four of us gals, making our way.

Except that I can't give up my Charlie. What would I do without him?

So, then I was going to talk Charlie into keeping the girls. We'd have a sweet little wedding, then vacation in the Catskills together while we watched the children play with their bird whistles and Flossy Flirt dolls.

That one made me laugh out loud.

The best idea I came up with was to blouse off to Paris by myself and escape all of this. Tempting.

I stand under this zipping, clattering coaster, the breeze from the speeding cars tickling the fur of the coat against my neck. I feel as stuck as a pig in thick mud. That's why I decided to just let Hazel call the shots for the evening. Now here I am, waiting for my beau, all wrapped up tight in Mama's girdle and Alice's fur coat so what's left of my figure doesn't cause any question.

I still don't know what I'm going to say to him.

I'm already losing track of who knows what. Mama knows one thing, Alice knows another. Hazel and Charlie each know something else. Nobody has any reason to believe anything different. Only I know the truth, but there are things even I don't know. Like, why my body failed me and labored so early. And what, exactly, is waiting for me just down the sidewalk, around the carousel, behind the pretend Samoan Village, and next door to Bernard the Master Magician.

And then, what am I going to do about Mama and Sergei?

A shiver goes up my spine. Mama's lover. I won't be able to avoid him forever. I take a deep drag from my cigarette holder and let it out in a long stream. Maybe I don't have to do anything. I can just leave it alone. Pretend none of this ever happened. That's what everyone wants, anyway.

Yes. That's it.

ClickClickClickClickClickClick.

The roller coaster climbs the fake hill that's hammered together out of studs and nails. Now that I've seen the illustrious, brand-new Cyclone for myself, there's no way I'm climbing aboard. I don't need speed and gravity to lodge my stomach in my throat; I'm doing a capital job of that myself.

Click...click...click. The train slows as it reaches the top of the hill. Time stands still for a moment before the coaster plummets, the riders' giddy screams following along a half a moment behind.

Even just watching this madness makes my stomach turn over. I drop my eyes down from the coaster train and follow the scaffolding to the little wooden bungalow that sits under the Cyclone. That's another thing that's wrong here. Through the window of the shack, I can see it's not a ticket booth or a mechanical room for the gears and motors. No, instead I see a man inside, sitting in an upholstered chair, sipping coffee. He turns the page of his newspaper as the Cyclone roars over his head. He doesn't flinch.

He's made his home directly under the tracks of the roller coaster. Or rather, they built the coaster right over his head. Either way, I can't make much sense of it.

I smell his coffee. Of course, that's impossible. His windows are closed, and the overwhelming smell of hot diesel from the thrill rides and cooking grease from the food vendors should overcome the aroma from his cup. Yet, there it is—toasted, nutty. Warm black pepper. Burnt walnuts.

A man brushes past me. He smiles and raises his Dixie Cup of coffee with a wink, and I realize I'm only smelling what's right under my nose.

The fella inside the house leans back, lifts his feet to rest them on a milking stool as he settles into an article about Rudolph Valentino's death or President Coolidge's tax plan or something else interesting or maybe just distracting. He's oblivious to the thundering trains barreling across creaking wood and steel over him. Oblivious to the hordes of revelers that cluster outside his window.

33

They say we are in a time of progress, progress, progress, but sheesh—give a man some peace.

Well, anyway, he seems comfortable. All cozied up like a baby nestled in his mama's womb, unconcerned with his mother's daily sweat chores and fast-paced, working-girl struggles.

I bring my cigarette holder to my lips, and the smell of burning paper and tobacco leaves overwhelm every other scent around me. Damn tobacco kills everything. I don't enjoy smoking, but Hazel says it makes a girl more appealing. I chomp down on the Bakelite with my teeth and let the warm smoke fill my mouth.

"Jo, do you have a light?" Hazel brings her own six-inch gasper holder to her lips. I fish a silver Ronson out of my pocketbook. She steps toward me and stumbles a bit on her too-high heels; out of habit I catch her. After this long of being girlfriends, we're able to anticipate each other a bit.

Dear Hazel. She's wearing that dreadful red flapper number she stole from the off-Broadway show she was in last spring. She was only an understudy for a chorus part, but when the show closed, she took the dress anyway. God bless her, she takes what she wants for herself. The dress holds the stink of the theater's backstage between the fibers—pancake makeup and mothballs, woven together with the clash of ambition and rejection.

It's just a costume, and all a costume does is cover. I should know—I'm standing here in a fur coat in August, certain I look ridiculous. My body is beyond recognition, even to me, so Aunt Alice thought the coat would help cover what's no longer familiar. Blur the lines, soften the edges. Make me harder to see. She cooked up this plan while I was still pregnant and insecure about my odd shape. But no one figured I'd be back in the city so soon, covering myself like this in the summertime. I wasn't planning to give birth until the air chilled and snow threatened the skies. The Fur Coat Plan would have worked perfectly then. Now I'm pretty sure I look like a sap.

Hazel's dress smells like moxie, like true grit. My fur smells like melancholy and regret. Maybe they're not costumes after all.

I loosen my shoulders and try to relax, but I'm uncomfortable. My breasts are sore and barely fit behind the silver beads of my beige dress. My hips ache from the months of burden, lifted so suddenly. I'm still bleeding. I can't keep straight what's true and what's not.

And now I have to face Charlie. Hazel had no idea what she was doing when she set up this little soirée tonight.

I'm not ready for this. For him. For him to discover all my lies.

My forehead sprouts a wave of heat at the thought.

I can either face Charlie or I can face Dr. Couney's exhibit down the street; I know I can't do both. I glance in that direction. It's down there, past the hordes of people. Past the carousel and the pretzel stands. Past the photographer mingling in the crowd, proudly capturing the unsuspecting with his tiny thirty-five-millimeter Leica. Past the midway with its clowns, its jugglers, its drunks.

I shift in my heels and wrap the fur tighter around my sweating body, cursing Alice for her harebrained idea. The photographer meanders past. Hazel lands a pose, giving a wink as his shutter clicks.

Crowds swish by me on either side, in front of me, behind me. I watch girls on the arms of their fellas, all dolled up in their glad rags and heels. Dressed to the nines to eat hot dogs and vomit in their beau's lap on the roller coasters. All fringe and feathers, polish and pretense.

"Never on time. Never. Goddamn you, Skip, and your lazy ways." Hazel slowly shakes her head, her cigarette holder hanging perfectly blasé in her hand. She touches her cloche hat, checking its position. She's a picture of Marion Davies, only with auburn hair. "Say, Jo, does Charlie ever keep you waiting?" I don't give her an answer because I know she's not expecting one. I stay quiet as she taps her gasper holder with her fingernail, annoyed. "Skip is always late. Always. Leaves me hanging. A guy shouldn't do that to a gal, you know? I don't know why I put up with it." She exhales deeply, the theater in her lungs coming out along with a thin stream of smoke. "Everything in my life is late. Would it kill someone to be early for once?"

Early.

"It might, Hazel," I say quietly. "It just might."

Hazel knows nothing about my past six months. I hid the pregnancy until I couldn't anymore, then Mama sent me to her sister's place in New Haven to wait it out. I played it as a summer out of the city, away from the heat. I made it sound very cosmopolitan to my friends; even Charlie was intrigued. Lazy days lounging by the wharf, picnicking in the park. An airtight idea; he said so himself. Wished he could join me, but alas, clients are calling.

Between me, Mama, Alice, and Barlow, the plan was that I would return to the city when the baby was safely adopted out to a good family. I would pick up my life where I left off, with no one any smarter.

Funny how plans have a way of never working out how you intend.

I look over to see Hazel studying me. I don't want to be a killjoy, nor do I want to give away anything eating me up inside, so I pull my shoulders up and jut out my hip. "No kidding, Haz. What do they think we are? A couple of wallflowers? We should just go. Teach 'em a lesson."

… And, scene.

I can be as much of an actress as she is. I hope. I'll be tested once Charlie actually gets here.

I should have told him right away. I could have convinced him it was some night when we'd had too much wine together. *Oh, Charlie, I can't believe you don't remember. Such a cheap drunk, aren't you?* A little giggle, a little flip of the bob. But now it's too late. It never would have worked, anyway; Charlie is detached, but he's not stupid.

I shift my weight between my aching feet as droplets of perspiration tumble down the skin of my back. A sharp, sweaty odor wafts to my nose. Is it me, or is it only scent particles trapped in the lining of the fur from the last time Alice wore it? Evidence of a previous owner, along with the smear of makeup on the collar and the lost glove in the pocket?

Nah, I'm just stinking up the joint. What a catch: a girl with a secret, all stretched out of shape, smelling like a coal miner, and dressed for the wrong season. I take a drag on my cigarette. The tobacco and a half a drop of *Toujours Moi* at my wrist manage to sweeten the air a bit from the stench. I guess there is a use for cigarette smoke after all.

ClickClickClickClick. Up it goes again, a new crop of coaster riders anticipating their playful dance with a death that is only for pretend.

The man in the house takes another sip of coffee and turns his page with the calm nonchalance of Buster Keaton. I have so many questions for him. I wonder if he lives there alone or if he has a partner, a roommate. Family to share the space, cramped as it is. Sometimes even the smallest spaces are shared with another. As close as close can be.

I wish I could ask him everything on my mind. He may have some answers.

Screams split the air as the riders fly by over his head, the wind tearing at their faces, their eyes wild with excitement. I can smell the feeble odor of vomit. The fella in the last car doesn't look so good. I tap my fingers on my pocketbook. The howls of an upset baby behind me makes my breath seize. I cough on my gasper.

"My girl," Charlie's voice cracks through the noise. "Wearing a fur coat in August. Always a bit of a kluck, aren't you, Ducky?" I feel his dry lips against my cheek. He doesn't bother to wrap his arm around my waist like Skip does to Hazel, but I'm relieved by that. He can't feel how it's all wrong around my middle. "Back from Newport early, eh?"

I catch my breath. "New Haven, Charlie." I kiss his cheek back. "Good to see you." I snag Hazel's eye as she knits her fingers with Skip's and immediately regret the shudder in my eyelid; she'll pick up on something amiss. She and I know each other like sisters, and Hazel has a razor-sharp sense to her. Once she's paying attention, she catches everything, and then she goes and figures it out like one of those Ford engineers.

But she never figured out I was knocked up. At least, I don't think she did. I feel the sweat come faster against my skin. I look away, hoping for a distraction. I watch the coaster train whiz along the greased tracks.

"Yes. Of course. New Haven." Charlie absently tugs on his bow tie, adjusting it under his chin. His hair is blonder than ever, his skin as pale as morning sun. Summer is evident in the rash of freckles across his nose and the glow of pink, sun-kissed skin under them. He'd spent time at the beach; likely he was entertaining clients, discussing trust funds, bond investments, and credit ratings in his striped bathing suit.

I have no fear that he spent his time with another dame. His eye doesn't wander to the ladies; he only notices the glint of a stick pin or the fold of expensive silk in an ascot. I give him a quick once-over while he looks around at the crowds, searching for some of his business associates or people more interesting than me. His eyes fall on the pockets of every gent that passes, assessing the thickness of their wallets and the shimmer of the golden chains that tether the man to his money.

Charlie's a financier, after all; he's just looking for new clients. Of course he would be sniffing out the dough. Every man he sees is only a dollar sign to him. He's deciding if it's worth following them to pass along a telephone card, a point of contact.

I give Charlie a good solid look to try to catch his attention. I miss the old days when I could keep his eye, when he seemed excited to be with me. Interested. Jeepers, that was only a year ago. Now he only ever seems bored with me. I'm doing something wrong. I gotta flirt a little more. "Missed you, Charlie." I smile.

He looks wilted in the summer evening heat—tall and lanky but not sure how to carry himself. Just arrogant enough to put on an appearance. He smells like stale Brilliantine under his cotton ivy cap, and though he smiles back, he doesn't make a move to touch me or slide any closer. He doesn't pretend to enjoy the view of other women as they strut past. Only the men, the keepers of the fortunes. His first and only love is a well-timed investment and the crescendo of its profits.

He doesn't want to be here at the Island any more than I do.

"Hazel, my chickadee. It's been too long." Skip swings Hazel back to plant a kiss on her lips. Hazel whoops loudly, her feet flipping into the air as she nearly lands on her rear. Hazel's the only dancer in New York born without the genes for physical grace. If there's something to trip over, she'll find it. Then she went and found herself a beau named Skip. A hoofer falls for a fella with a moniker like that, and suddenly her daddy's calling the florist and booking the church. A match made in heaven.

"Oh honey," Hazel giggles, "I just saw you this morning."

"Like I said," Skip helps Hazel upright, a grin eating up his face, "too long." Hazel and Skip handle each other with an easy intimacy. No charades, no mistrust. Just comfortable.

She stumbles, he straightens.

Bim–boom.

I look back at Charlie and wink to hide my jealousy. Charlie's not paying any mind. After a bit more searching around for fresh financial meat, he lights a cigarette and motions it toward me with a big sigh. "They wearing furs year-round up there in New Haven, then?"

Before I can answer, Skip jumps in, ever the comedian. "Must be a gift from a rich beau, huh, Jo? You have a little tryst up there over the summer?" Skip's smile is playful.

Charlie's arm slinks around my waist, his attention finally caught. The only thing he hates more than a bad investment is being made a fool. I work to relax my body against his. "You hook up with a Yalie up there, Jo?" he asks. His voice is louder than it needs to be, his arm pulling me tightly, almost painfully, against him.

A couple of girls in the crowd look our way; an eyebrow arches, a dimple leaks out of a cheek. Dolls are always waiting to watch trouble from a distance; if they can't be home listening to the Collier Hour on the radio, they take any chance they can to see an amateur drama reenacted right here in front of them.

I tuck a stray hair up under my cloche and turn my head to give Charlie a devilish smile. "More than one, Charlie." Hard to get. Mama always says that works best, though I'm not so sure about my guy. Jealousy gets him a little hot in the feathers.

"Enchanting." Charlie looks annoyed. At least he loosens his grip.

I pull another gasper out of my pocketbook. Now I have to do clean-up, thanks to Skip. "Oh, Charlie, don't get yourself in lather, it's just baloney I'm feedin' ya." I cuddle into his side. He still feels stiff as a bean-shooter, so I go on, sweetening the pot, my voice like honey. "There's no one for me but you, you know that."

"Mmm." He removes his arm from my waist, his eyes again wandering the crowd. He's already stopped caring.

I rearrange my pocketbook under my arm, taking the opportunity to allow a little fresh air beneath the fur. "New Haven was lovely," I say, changing the subject. "Aunt Alice says hello."

"Nice of her," Charlie says.

"So why are you back early, Jo?" Skip has a mischievous twinkle in his eye. He's just full of flim-flam tonight.

"Put a sock in it, Skip. She just missed us. Who wouldn't miss New York?" Hazel playfully punches Skip's arm, but she's got that bewildered look on her face that she gets when something just doesn't add up. She hadn't thought to ask before, but now I can tell—she wonders. *Why did ol' Jo come home so early from her summer holiday? And why on earth is she all wrapped up in a fur in the summertime?*

41

The coaster roars over our heads. Hazel's ginger hair flitters against her cheekbone under her hat. We all stand and wait for a break in the rumble. I stuff the cold cigarette into my holder to give my fingers something to do. Finally, Hazel speaks up. "So, are we gonna ride this thing or stand around chewing the fat?" She looks at me. "It's a riot. You'll love it. Skip and I've been riding it all summer, since it opened."

Charlie flicks his lighter for me. I force a fetching smile onto my lips and lean into him the way a girl should, careful as to how I position my body under the mounds of fur. I need to play the part—though, which part I'm playing, I'm not sure. I look to Hazel for inspiration—she's always playing one role or another. Though, she's usually memorized her script. I'm making things up as I go.

The flame from the lighter delivers a warmth against my nose, and with it I smell a tiny whiff of lighter fluid. For half a moment, I'm reminded of the open oven door, pulled down to a position only inches from the floor. A platform. A bed. The light smell of Alice's bread still lingering, a bundle of blankets resting on the open door. Tiny arms reaching towards nothing and anything.

Shivers climb my spine like the train of the Cyclone advancing its hill. I can't be here right now, pretending nothing has changed, when everything has.

I shake my head to clear it.

The four of us move closer to the Cyclone, but each step feels like my legs are half-melted Oh Henry bars. I've got enough of a windstorm inside me to make me feel like I'm falling without the help of this thing.

The cars fly past us, metal on metal groaning over a creaking wooden frame, the salty air from the sea already turning the white-painted boards to driftwood.

Old before its time. Like me.

*Click…Click…*I stop walking. Charlie's hand presses against my back as he leads me toward the ticket booth. Everyone moves forward except me. My head aches from the lights, the music. Movement everywhere. The smells of boiled corn and fried dough. My stomach twists into a pretzel that matches the ones hanging from hooks at the food booths.

I can't move.

The oven door.

Uncle Barlow.

Two tiny baby girls.

They are here.

Here.

At Coney Island.

In a goddamn sideshow.

I'm too close. I can't…

The Cyclone shakes the ground beneath my feet. The wind it creates whips the fringed hem of my dress up to reveal the tops of my stockings under the fur wrap.

"No." I guess I say it out loud, because they all stop and turn to look at me.

"Aw, c'mon, Jo. Don't you love a little thrill?" Skip's voice sounds far away.

I smile to show everything's berries, but it feels like it rips my face in two. The more I concentrate on acting "normal," the less I even know what that is. No matter how I position my body, it doesn't feel like mine. Everything's different. The vibrations through the heels of my shoes rattle my core. Lights. Movement. Music.

Playfulness. Flirting. Pleasure.

Joy.

I can't do it. I take another step backward. "I have to go."

Before anyone can stop me, I turn and run, melting into the crowd. They call my name, but I don't pause. I pull the coat up around my shoulders and escape my friends, my heels clicking against the paved road. Surf Avenue passes like a blur under me, flinging me forward in the direction of Stillwell Station.

6

Beth

The sun is just coming up outside the kitchen window, turning the dark backyard a sleepy blue. The sunrise glints off the dials on the grill, the swing set's steel brackets, and the small glass mosaic table on the patio. It's nearly five. I brush toast crumbs off my scrubs into the sink. The house is quiet, and it's nice to take a moment alone to enjoy the peace before I go in for my shift and before Eddie and Sylvie get up for the day.

Eddie left his sweaty baseball cap and sunglasses on the island. I pick them up with two fingers and wipe under them with a Lysol wipe. I move them over next to the pottery bowl where he usually leaves his keys, but of course the keys aren't there. A little hunting around, and I find them in his lunch cooler, along with his favorite X-Acto knife handle he was missing. No blade, thank God. I pile up his keys, sunglasses,

45

cap, and blade handle in the bowl on top of the twenty-seven cents, the paperclip, and the tangled mess of earbud cords that have been there since last September.

There. Clean. I glance at the cat's food dish to see if it needs a refill and find a little pile of torn paper scraps on the floor. Sylvie's new sensory fixation. I sweep up the pieces and check closely to make sure it wasn't anything important. It looks like a grocery receipt from last week. I toss the confetti-like scraps into the trash.

A scratching noise comes from the living room, so I take my coffee to see what's going on, thinking the cat got stuck behind the couch again. Sylvie is in the dark, lying on her stomach on the floor next to her dollhouse, her bed-head blond hair sticking out like rooster feathers. She has a plastic bowl full of little toy people, animals, and other odds and ends. She's laying them all in a straight line in what would be the front yard of the dollhouse. It's so orderly, it's almost calming.

"Good morning, Sylvie, my girl," I say. I set my coffee mug on the table and kneel next to her. I feel my body tighten, anticipating her possible meltdown, her emotional explosion. I gently rest my hand on her back so she knows I'm there, that I'm close. "Sylvie, Sylvie," I sing. "Good morning to my Sylvie. Mama's here. Mama loves Sylvie."

She doesn't look up, just continues with her sorting. Sylvie's Early Intervention teachers have taught us to use her name as often as possible, so maybe she'll be inspired to know it and respond to it. Same with Mama, Dada, potty, hungry, and other important words. So far, no luck.

"My best girl, Sylvie. Mama loves Sylvie."

She continues to ignore me, so I sit quietly on the floor nearby.

I had prepared for an outburst, but her indifference toward me is even more painful. I will myself to not take it personally. *It's not her. She does love me. It's her disorder.* Just thinking the word "disorder" makes my stomach drop. I watch her, the look on her face one of pure concentration. Plastic man. Plastic giraffe. Plastic girl. Plastic spoon. Wrapped tampon. Plastic mama. Scissors.

"Oh, no, no, Sylvie." I pick up the scissors, and she shrieks. "Owie to Sylvie," I say. "No, no, scissors make an owie." I put them on the table next to my coffee as she continues to scream. I try refocusing her attention. "Can mama play with you?" She's still agitated and giving me her angry grunts, but she stops howling for the moment. I figure the best course of action is to distract her. "Can mama play?" I move a bit closer, sit cross-legged next to her on the carpet. I hold out my hand. "Can I have a toy?"

She stands up and storms off to the other side of the living room.

My heart breaks, but I keep pretending to play in vain, hoping this time she'll come over, this time she'll want to share, to let me have a turn. Play with me. I pick up the plastic man. "Oh, is this Dada?" I put him in the dollhouse. "Does Dada sit on the chair? Nice chair. It's pink."

I steal a glance at her. She's not looking at me. She's curled up on the loveseat across the room, gripping the tampon tightly in her hand. I wish she would react to me, yell at me, even scowl at me in anger, but she doesn't. She just stares at the tampon's wrapper, tapping her finger on the word *regular*.

She hates me.

I leave the little toy man in his house and sit on the couch opposite her. I go through my mental arsenal of competing

47

information I've researched online. *It's her disorder,* I tell myself again. *She can't help it. She loves me. She does.* I have to keep reminding myself of that. "Sylvie, Sylvie," I sing, "Mama loves Sylvie." I wait to see if she'll react. Sometimes she'll just pout for a while; sometimes she'll lash out uncontrollably. Sometimes she's even fallen asleep, the tampon gripped tightly in her little hand. Any reaction has to be okay, so I wait for what comes next.

She rocks herself, quietly uttering, "oh, oh, oh." I can tell she's distressed. If she were any other child, I would scoop her up and give a big hug and kiss, but I know that can feel too aggressive for her. I sit and wait. I think about my cooling coffee on the table, but I leave it there. I look around at the clean, empty mantle over the fireplace, at the white basket in the corner of the room where I collect all of Sylvie's toys each night after bedtime, at the stark walls interrupted with only a few tasteful pictures here and there. Only a splash of color—too much would be cluttered. I shudder at what my sister Cara's house looks like: the boys' toys everywhere, Rocko's guitar propped up on a stand and his hockey stick leaning against the wall by the front door, and Cara's knick-knacks and dust catchers on every available surface. Ugh. If nothing else, if I can keep the junk around the house to a minimum, I can be at peace. Feel somewhat in control.

Though, I'd brave Cara's mess to just be civil with my sister again. To have my best friend back.

Sylvie's still rocking. I just wait.

I wonder what it would feel like to play pretend with my little girl. I remember the times my own mother would stub out her cigarette and get on her knees with me to play My Little Ponies, usually before Cara came crashing in with her giant, naked, pony-eating Cabbage Patch doll and destroy Pony Town.

I wonder if I'll ever be able to make memories like that with my own daughter.

After a few minutes, Sylvie slides off the chair to the floor and spreads her legs out in front of her. It's a move, and a good sign. I watch her, quietly singing her name over and over. She slowly pulls herself to her feet. Her lips are still pushed into a pout, but she slithers over like a panther and stands next to the couch, careful to not get too close. She stares at the floor and doesn't acknowledge me besides just being near.

Very slowly, methodically, I put my arms out. "Hug? Does Sylvie want a hug from Mama? Mama wants to give hugs."

She doesn't look at me, but I notice her lean just barely an inch toward me. That lean, though, feels like miles closing between us. Any show of emotion or warmth from her is a milestone. She finally gets close enough where I can carefully, slowly wrap her in my arms. I gently lift her onto my lap, and she rests her head on my shoulder. I cradle her and rock her, easing myself back into the couch.

I nearly cry from the beauty of it. My girl.

You left her. How could you?

Now I'm really crying. This always happens. I'm enjoying a moment with my daughter, allowing myself to believe she's breaking out of the shell that holds her captive, then my own conscience turns on me.

I did leave her. I can't deny that. I can't pretend it somehow didn't happen.

It's okay. I was just late picking her up one day. Not a big deal. I try talking myself out of the guilt, but I know the problem was never that I'd left. The problem was how I felt as I was driving away. That is the knife to my gut.

And that feeling is still there.

I put my face against Sylvie's hair and breathe in the smell of her. I have to take this moment with her, carry it with me. I can't ruin it.

My therapist suggested a sabbatical—just a week or two away to a spa or something. Some time for myself. That was when I stopped seeing her. Bullshit advice. Maybe that's good for others, but clearly, she wasn't hearing me.

I mean, wasn't she worried that maybe, just maybe, I wouldn't come back?

Those feelings I had—I still have—about motherhood, they're just not normal.

I sit and hold Sylvie for a long time, as long as she'll let me. I know my coffee's cold, and I'm running up on hitting traffic on my way to the hospital for my shift. Still, I sit. It feels good to hold her, to have her melt into me. I try to forget everything else.

I wonder if this is a breakthrough or if Sylvie just got cold in her nightgown.

7

Since I'm running in my T-straps, my hurried escape is littered with several Hazel-like stumbles. The clanging of the coaster and the shouts of my friends fade behind me. I don't look back. The fur keeps sliding off my shoulders, so I pull it tight, bundling myself against the balmy evening heat. I'm sweating even more now, the droplets tickling my temples and the sides of my neck. But I'm almost to the station where I can get a train back home to Manhattan. I just need to get past the rides, past the refreshments, past—

Of course.

I stop short, my breath caught in my chest.

This is where the freaks are.

I'm standing in front of a white building lit up against the evening sky. The lights here seem brighter than anything else on the midway, letters spelled out in incandescent bulbs embedded into the stuccoed concrete.

LIVE INCUBATOR BABIES

I don't fully remember, but something about it is familiar. It smells like a movie theater. Next to the building is a popcorn stand.

I've been here before.

Instinctively, I put my hand to my stomach. Empty.

I should have never been alone with that man those months ago. It wasn't my place to let him pull me toward him, into his warm arms, his exotic scent. Musk. Leather. Just a hint of dill. I breathed him in as he eased the strap of my dress off my shoulder...

My stomach flutters. No one knows. I dread the moment I'll have to see him again, pretend that nothing is amiss. I can't avoid it. I've already passed him once on the stairs of our building. I won't be able shuffle out forever.

"Tiny babies, kept alive in the most fantastic machines!" The barker's words stab me. I look up and meet his eye. "You've never known such small babies! The most adorable creatures you've ever seen! You must see it to believe it. I can hold one in the palm of my hand!" He smiles, a shimmer of fancy in his eye. "You there, Miss!" He points at me. "Come take a look! Each baby is alive, you might even want to take one home!"

Creatures that I can take home, like a goldfish in a bowl.

His smile grows wider, dimpling his cheeks, his chin. He's devilishly handsome, with a grin that crushes his face and brown eyes that can reach out and destroy a girl. A boater hat is tipped jauntily to one side of his head, revealing glossy black hair beneath. He wears a bright yellow vest over his white shirt and a red- and blue-striped bow tie at his neck. His gaze is penetrating. He's talking directly to me now. No one else. It's almost hypnotic. I gotta give it to him—he's damn good at his job. "Only a nickel for a sight you'll never forget."

I'm lost in his draw. My vision focuses on his eyes, his outstretched hand. The white wall behind him glows from the burning filaments of Mr. Edison's bulbs. He's like a shimmering ghost. An angel.

"Jo." A hand squeezes my arm, and Hazel's woody scent of *Tabac Blond* hovers over my shoulder. I turn my head, breaking the spell.

Hazel gasps when she sees my face. I didn't realize until now that tears dampen my cheeks.

"What's going on, Jo? Why'd ya dust out on us so fast?"

I don't answer. I open my pocketbook and dig for a handkerchief. Hazel's got one at the ready before I can find my own.

"Here, honey. Now, are you going to tell me what this is all about?"

"I…I don't…" I choke on my words.

She sighs. "Well, whatever it is, it's got you shaken like a pigeon in a flophouse. Here now." She puts her arm around me and pulls me into a hug. Then she holds me at arm's length. "Your dress is soaked, Jo. This can't all be from the tears, is it?"

I look down. The fur is open at the front. There's a large wet spot on the beige crepe of my dress, directly over my left breast.

"God. Haz…" I dab uselessly between the beads with the sodden handkerchief. "I can't get it to stop. I don't know…"

"Get it to stop? What are you talking about?" Her face twists in confusion. "Stop what? Are you leaking?" Her voice carries the curl of a joke, but as soon as she says it, her eyes pop wide, and her hand covers her mouth. "Oh, Jo."

I look up at her. I can tell she's just figured out the riddle of the Sphinx. Or part of it at least.

"Is this why you were gone all summer?" The concern in her eyes carries the sympathy of our years together, our secrets told to only each other, our greatest fears and worries whispered over dolls and under pink blankets. "I guess I shoulda known ol' Charlie got you in trouble." She shrugs, then gives me a demure smile. "Didn't know he had it in him, to be honest."

I press the handkerchief against my face, more to hide myself than to do any kind of sopping up. I feel my head move, but I don't know if I'm nodding at her question or just shaking from emotion. I hiccup. Hazel gives me a sideways hug, careful to not make the same mistake twice and get herself all damp.

"I could tell something was off back there. Now it makes sense." She lowers her voice into a calming coo. "Sometimes we get ourselves into a bind. But, it's over now, right? Best to forget. It's hard, honey. I know."

I look up at her through my watery eyes. Her sad smile is wistful. "You don't know, Hazel." I sniffle.

"Well…" her lips curl into a bit of a sad smirk. "I might."

We look at each other, seeing the other in a new light. I realize I likely don't know all her secrets, just like she doesn't know mine.

"It's hard to give up something like that," she says, trying to find words to comfort me. I suppose I appreciate the effort. "And it's hard to be reminded of it, especially in a place like this." She motions toward the exhibit. "The last thing you need is a baby thrown in your face right now. And at Coney Island? Posh. This is just bizarre."

She's quiet for a moment. I don't respond.

"Did you have the baby?" she asks.

I nod. I wait half a beat. "Did you?"

Her face pales in the incandescent light. "No."

Though we're surrounded by the bustle of the midway, the ballyhoo of games and oddities, there's a comfortable silence that surrounds us. Just two girls with their arms around each other, sharing a moment of grief.

"Did a good family take the baby?" she asks.

I don't look at her. That was the plan, but plans sometimes fall apart. "No."

Her frown shows her confusion. "So then...you've kept it?" She turns and looks at me. "Where's the baby, honey? Adopted, right? That's the only sensible option. Or..." She pauses. "Is the baby with your mother? Or...oh, honey, did the baby die?"

"No," I say. Her eyes are full, and I have to trust she'll keep my secret. I quickly glance at the barker, motion with my head toward the white building.

"Jesus. Here?" Her head pops up like an ostrich as she searches the exhibit for clues. "They actually keep real babies in there?"

I nod. Hazel's hankie is used up, so I search the pockets of the fur coat for one of Alice's wayward handkerchiefs or maybe even a wadded up, used tissue.

"Does Charlie know?"

"No."

"She lets out a long breath. "What are you going to do? You have to tell him."

"No, not now. Not yet."

"Why?"

"Hazel," I start slowly, deliberately. "It's a bit delicate with Charlie."

"Honey, you have to tell him. He has to know he has a—"

"Does Skip know?" I ask.

Hazel is quiet. She watches the barker collect nickels from the patrons one by one, his dancing eyes thanking each and every onlooker for their payment. "It was before Skip. Couple of years ago. The director of a show I was in." She looked at me. "He had a doctor friend. I got the feeling he took a lot of girls to see that doctor."

I squeeze her hand. "I'm sorry."

She shrugs. "Me too. But honey, Charlie needs to know."

"Charlie had nothing to do with it." I say it so quietly, I'm not even sure she hears me. But, she does. We lock eyes again, and I know by the look in hers that she understands. We've been friends for too long. Hazel may have a loud mouth and a sharp mind, but she has never betrayed me. She doesn't ask any more questions, and for that I'm grateful. She links her fingers through mine. She nods toward the handsome barker. "I'll go with you. I have a few nickels. Come on."

I pull away from her. Before I realize it, I'm running again toward the train station. Toward home. Stumbling. My shoes squeeze my toes, but the pain is satisfying. It feels right, unlike everything else. My body is all twisted out of shape, the bleeding deep inside me leaves only emptiness. My heart is shredded into confetti. My stomach heaves as if I were riding the Cyclone after all.

8

Beth

"You're quiet." Layana swipes her badge to start her shift. She sets those dark brown eyes on me, leans onto the nurse's desk, and pours on the compassion. "You alright?"

I shrug. "PMS."

"Ah. Need coffee?" She glances at the clock on the wall and shakes her head, her spiral curls bouncing. "Ten forty-five. Never too late for a cup o' joe."

I hold up my Starbucks Venti. "It's cold, but it works."

She pats my shoulder. "Good girl," she says. "You have Sylvie's weekly appointment this morning, right?"

"Yep. I have to leave in a bit."

She nods, fiddles with the bracelet at her wrist. "How are our guests today? Quiet morning?"

"Not bad," I say. "Carter's off CPAP and had several spells of apnea, one desat. Looks like his bilirubin is high too. Dr. Che will probably put him back on CPAP for a few more days." Carter is two days old. So far, he's doing as well as could be expected. I glance around the room at the eighteen isolettes that line the walls. "Noah struggled with the bottle for the last two feedings, so he may be back on the gavage tube. Oh, and Trinity had her first bowel movement."

"My girl! Poopin' like a lady!" Layana's smile spreads. She does a little dance and sings "Sisters Are Doin' It for Themselves."

"And this." I point to the monitor in front of me. The cranial ultrasound for one of the Miller triplets is on the computer in front of me. Baby C, the last born of the three and the smallest. Intraventricular hemorrhage. Severe brain bleed. Grade four, on a scale of one to four. As bad as it gets. I move the mouse to point at the area in question on the screen, rotating my wrist to absently circle the pointer against the picture. Clearly a grade four. I can see that, and from the defeated breath she lets out, I can tell Layana knows the same.

"Guessing little Patrick will be transferred to Children's before the end of the day." Layana whispers. "Shit, girl. Having babies in two different facilities is going to be tough on the family." She nods over to where Kate Miller is resting in a recliner with a blanket over her. Three identical isolettes surround her like bodyguards. There are four different wires and tubes coming from a barely noticeable lump under her blanket. Kate wiggles her nose like she has an itch but is too terrified to move. Right now, she's with Paige. Baby A. The first into this world by three minutes. In a moment, I'll help her switch to Phoebe, Baby B. She's the biggest by a couple of ounces. Patrick, little Baby C, will not be held for some time yet. Possibly weeks. Possibly longer. Layana absently taps her finger on the desk. "Does she know?"

"Yeah. Dr. Che called her this morning."

Having babies across town from each other will be tough, but what's going to be even tougher is Patrick's future. That baby will likely have problems all through life.

I know if Kate had the chance, she would have kept her babies inside her where they belonged for a lot longer than their twenty-six weeks. Nobody wishes for a preeclampsia diagnosis. Truthfully, twenty-six weeks isn't bad for triplets. Right out of nursing school I helped deliver a set at almost twenty-two weeks. In terms of human gestation, they were just past the midway point. Born by cesarean section, all within one minute of each other. They died after forty-seven minutes, one hour and four minutes, and one hour and twenty-one minutes, respectively.

That was the day I politely excused myself from the NICU, went out behind the picnic tables in back, and barfed my guts out. I'd like to say it's gotten easier, but it hasn't. My stomach's gotten tougher, that's all.

The fast-paced beeping of a monitor blares behind me. Layana's face hardens as she searches for the source. "Carter."

I pull on a pair of gloves as we race to his isolette. Inside, Carter lays motionless, overwhelmed by his immense preemie diaper and many wires. He's clearly not ready to go off CPAP, but we can't make that call without Dr. Che. Carter's face is pasty and tinted slightly blue. I reach my hand through the armhole of his isolette and lay my fingers on his torso. I give the gentlest of rubs to his skin. "Carter, honey. Deep breath, big guy."

Layana reaches up to silence the alarm. "Oxygen at 78 percent."

"Come on, sweetie." I stroke his abdomen. Tap my finger against his chest. Run my hand down his legs and rub a little harder. Flick at his toes with my fingers.

"Down to 71 percent."

"Carter." My voice is stern, though he can't hear me through the solid acrylic of the isolette. I rub more. Dance my fingers, tickle the top of his head, avoiding the spot where an IV is inserted into a vein in his scalp. My own scalp tingles as I flash back to the moments after his birth when he refused to breathe.

Finally, his body gives a little shake. I watch his chest rise. Then again. His color improves.

"Oxygen rising," Layana says.

"What's happening?" Gretchen stands next to the privacy curtain, disheveled in a hooded sweatshirt hanging open and yoga pants. She grips a small, nearly-empty vial of breast milk and the straps of her purse in the same hand. "Is Carter okay?"

"Carter's fine." I glance up at the monitor that shows 93 percent oxygen in his blood, and rising. "He just had a little spell."

"Spell." Gretchen looks like a zombie. "You mean an apnea and bradycardia spell."

"Yes." Good Lord, she's been on Google. Just about every mom does it to some extent. Gretchen's face is drawn, and her eyes are red, probably because she'd spent the first few nights of her child's life hooked up to a breast pump, Googling anything and everything about premature babies. I wish she'd just take this time to get some sleep, but new mothers are persistent. They want to save their babies, beat us to their diagnoses, educate us on the best treatments. I wish they'd give up the control and leave the saving to us.

Mama bears, every one of them.

"He stopped breathing, didn't he?" Gretchen's face is pale. "This one was worse than usual, wasn't it? What can you do for him? Do we just wait until he outgrows it? What if no one catches the spell in time to help him? Would he just die?"

"That's what the monitors are for," Layana says. "Someone is always here to help him." When Gretchen's face doesn't relax, Layana rests her hand on Gretchen's arm. Her voice gets even more silky. "We've never lost a baby to an A&B spell. They look much worse than they are."

"Dr. Che wanted to try him off the CPAP, but we'll likely put him back on after rounds this afternoon." I tell Gretchen. "I'm guessing we might also start medicating him once his weight is up where it needs to be."

"Medicating?"

Layana shoots me a look. *Soften up, Beth.*

"Very normal," I say, lowering my voice. "Many preemies of his gestation get it. It helps them remember to breathe." I smile at Gretchen. "It's actually caffeine."

"What?" Gretchen looks confused. Google didn't tell her that.

"Yep," Layana gives a little giggle. "Just like we need caffeine to get us breathing sometimes, right?"

Same old joke, told to every mother. Only a couple have ever said they don't drink coffee. Most other moms give us high-fives over that one.

Layana slides by me between the machines. "I'll record the episode," she says to me under her breath as she goes back to the computer.

"But, he's okay?" Gretchen's knuckles are white against the vial of breast milk.

61

"Oh, yes. He's fine." I step over to the storage closet to grab a new box of gloves. She follows me. "His bilirubin is high, too, so he'll go under the lights—"

"Bili-what?"

I pause. Too technical. I can't assume Google has answered all of her questions. *Ease up, Beth. Remember your reviews.* "Jaundice. Also normal for a lot of babies, even those born at term, but almost all preemies get it. We put them under special lights, kind of like their own little tanning machine. A day or two and all will be well."

"What's wrong with his head?" Her voice trembles.

I look over, not even realizing that an IV inserted into a baby's head could be troubling to a brand-new mother. "Sometimes a preemie's veins are easier to access in their scalp. It's completely fine, and very normal. I'm so sorry, someone should have called you and warned you about that."

That someone was me. *Nice fail, Beth.*

Gretchen lets out a little grunt, her eyes not moving from Carter's side of the room.

I take a step toward her and gently pry the breast milk from her hand. The vial has a label on it with Carter's name, and there's a smear of something yellowish along the bottom. A slightly bigger smear than last time. Gretchen is struggling. "I tried all night and this morning," she says. "This was all I could get."

I look into her exhausted face and smile. I muster as much excitement as I can for her feeble attempt. I know what it feels like to fail at this. "You did great! Let's give it to Carter." I walk back toward his isolette, and Gretchen shuffles along behind me. Her whole body is quivering; she looks like the last leaf on a twisted, winter tree. I pause my stride. She needs me to slow down. Okay. I see that. I stop, wait.

"It will get easier," I say to her in a low voice as milky as Layana's. "I promise. It's only been a few days."

A quick glance at the clock tells me I still have a few minutes before I have to leave for Sylvie's appointment.

She nods. Together we go over to Carter's isolette, and she lays her hands on the side as she peers in. Then she looks at me expectantly.

With a gloved hand I reach my pinky finger into the vial, but again the colostrum has dried. I can feel her eyes on me. I can't toss this one in the trash, can't tell her it's a bust. It will destroy her. I drag my finger across the dried milk and then reach my hand through one of the armholes of the isolette. I snake my finger under the CPAP mask and gavage tube, over the preemie diaper that has been folded down and cinched around his waist, between the wires and sensors to his mouth. I tickle his lip, miming spreading the imaginary breast milk along his tongue and gums.

"There." I try to sound encouraging. "Aww, he loves it. Keep pumping, and it will come."

"It's weird to be home now and not have a baby with me." Gretchen says. She watches Carter through the clear acrylic, and I recognize the look of distance in her eyes. Aside from brushing his hand with her fingertips, she's never touched her child. Never seen his eyes. Never felt his warmth against her skin. Those are the things that bond mothers with their infants, but she's yet to have those experiences. She can only see him through a spiderweb of wires and tubes, a CPAP mask covering most of his face, and strips of tape dotting his features and wrinkling his skin

63

with their medical-grade adhesive. The too-large preemie diaper covers him almost up to his armpits. At this point, the baby is really a barely-breathing tumor that was just removed from her uterus. It's no wonder NICU mothers look at their new babies in these industrial vessels with a sense of grief and detachment.

My grief and detachment come from somewhere else entirely.

Gretchen takes a big breath, and I wait. I wait to be asked when she can hold him, when she can take him home, when she can nurse him. When, when, when. It's the biggest question the brand-new mother of a premature child ever has.

"So, I guess Stevie Wonder was a preemie," she says.

I'm thrown off guard. This isn't the standard line of questioning, so my usual rapid-fire responses catch in my throat before they're released.

"Yeah. He was." It's all I can say. I reach for the thermometer, place a cover on the probe, and squeeze it under Carter's arm to busy myself.

"And that's why he's blind."

He's also alive. I bite my tongue before I say it out loud. This is exactly the kind of thing that keeps coming up in my reviews. I take a moment to remove the sarcasm from my thoughts. "There was a lot they didn't know about treating prematurity back then," I say. "We've come a long way."

"Oh, of course. I mean, you guys know what you're doing, I'm sure."

I force something that looks like a pleasant smile onto my face. *She's under stress. She's under stress. She's under stress.* It's human nature. People—mothers—don't like to give up control. We as humans want to fix things. When your doctor doesn't have the answers, Google certainly does.

"But," she continues, her voice small, "you are monitoring how much oxygen he gets, right?" Her face flushes. "I have to be an advocate for my child, you know?"

Carter's thermometer beeps so I put all of my attention on the readout instead of being insulted. I let out a breath. "Oh yes." I keep my voice light. "This is all brand new to you, I know. But Carter is in an excellent facility, and a lot has changed since Stevie—" I stop. Smile. "Since Stevie Wonder's time." My *Stevie the Preemie* joke has always fallen flat, so I leave it behind. Not worth trying to be funny and lighten the mood. *"Lighten the mood with compassion instead, Beth."* Item number three on last year's performance review.

There was a time when my superiors had to search for things to ding me on during my reviews. I guess Sylvie's undiagnosed problems used up all of my patience and made their jobs easier.

My cheeks burn. What kind of nurse am I? I need to balance myself more evenly. It's something that's required of me, both as a mother and a nurse. As a wife, too. Maybe it will help now that we have Sylvie's diagnosis. I can get some answers, figure out how to help her. Get my empathy back. I can do better. I have to do better.

I desperately push back that voice in my head that tells me apathy runs in my blood.

I'm a good nurse. I'm a good mother. I am.

"My baby shower is this weekend," Gretchen says. "I was supposed to still be pregnant." Her lip quivers.

I give a little nod and smile. "Make sure you get a good picture of him to have at the party," I say. "Maybe we can give him a bath today, that way you can get a nice one without all of the wires and cords hooked up."

65

"I want the wires and cords. This is him."

This is him. She's a brave woman.

Gretchen quietly watches her son. Then she smiles the soft, knowing smile of a mother. "When can I nurse him?"

There it is: *when.*

"First he has to learn to suck, and that might take a little while." First he has to breath on his own, but I don't mention that. "Given his gestation, it will be a little while before he learns the suck, swallow, breathe sequence. Maybe we can start trying in about a month."

Her eyes pop huge. "A month?"

Out of habit, I glance over at another monitor buzzing across the room. Two nurses hurry to that baby's isolette. "Possibly," I say. I flip the thermometer cover into the trash and turn back to Gretchen. "Babies learn those reflexes in the womb around thirty-four weeks, so it may be a month to six weeks before we can even start with a nipple. Right now your nipple is bigger than his whole mouth."

"Six weeks?" Her eyes nearly bug out of her head. "How long will he be here?"

No one has talked to her about this yet, and it looks like Google didn't give her a heads-up. *Shit.*

"Likely several weeks to a couple of months at least. It really depends on the baby."

Gretchen's face goes white.

"Listen," I lower my voice, softening it like how Layana would. "I know it sounds like a long time right now, but in the lifetime of your child, this is only a drop in the bucket." I put my arm around her and try for an awkward side hug.

Carter will be fine. I want to tell her that, but we've been trained not to predict the future. Honestly, we don't know he'll be okay, and okay looks different to everyone anyway. But he'll get through. And then Gretchen will be okay. Eventually the trauma of his sudden birth will blur and become less painful as more and more healthy birthdays pass and happy memories pile up. But the stress of that moment in the delivery room will probably always stay with her. She'll mourn that she can't look back on this day and say it was the happiest of her life.

She'll watch Carter grow and get stronger during his stay in the NICU, and there will also be days when he will take giant steps backward. These weeks will be difficult, but eventually he'll go home. He'll babble words and roll over and push himself up to sitting—late, most likely, but he'll do it. Her life tending to him in the NICU will be a distant memory. He'll be fine.

Unless of course, he isn't.

All those words Carter babbles—I hope he doesn't forget them later.

Gretchen stares at Carter, taking in his purple hue, the way his skin bunches at his knees, the pure primate look of his facial features. He has no eyelashes and can barely slit open his eyes. She takes another deep breath. I can hear the tremble in it. "I'm so thankful for all of this," she says, motioning to the machines around her. "I know there was a time when they would just let premature babies die."

I'm not sure what to say to that, and since I have a habit of saying the wrong things, I keep it simple. "That's true."

"Did you know they used to keep preemie babies in sideshows? Like, at Coney Island?"

"Yeah." The word falls out of me in a breath. My face burns as my stomach ties itself into a knot. I watch Carter's oxygen monitor wiggle between 96 and 97 percent.

"Isn't it amazing? I was Googling information about preemies and found the story."

"Yeah, it's…" I take a breath and let it out as slowly as I can. "Like you said. Amazing."

It was nearly a hundred years ago. That woman who abandoned my grandmother had nothing to do with me, and I'm nothing like her. That was long ago, before NICUs, before neonatal specialists. Before bililights and g-tubes and cannulas came along to help babies thrive. Before people even kept records of who was who and what was happening and why.

She walked away. And that was it.

I did the same. But I came back.

"I guess that's how these isolettes first came to be." Gretchen is still talking. I don't look at her. I have to get away from this conversation. I glance back to the desk hoping to catch Layana's eye, but she is talking to another nurse with her back to me. "Hospitals didn't want them. Can you believe it?"

"Good thing times have changed." My voice is flat.

"Well, they kept the babies alive and well, so—"

Gretchen and I look at each other. I must have some strange expression on my face because she stops talking mid-sentence.

"I'll let you be," I quickly leave Carter's corner and run into Dr. Che.

"Nurse Roselli, I need your assistance on isolette four," Dr. Che says and then immediately walks away, assuming I'll follow. He leads me to the baby in question. Patrick, triplet number three. Kate Miller is still sitting with baby Paige on the other side of the three isolettes. "We need constant surveillance on this infant," Dr. Che says over his shoulder to me.

"Of course." I glance at the clock on the wall. After eleven o'clock. "I'll assign a nurse to monitor him."

"And why won't you be doing it yourself?" he asks.

"My job is to direct the activities of the unit and delegate responsibilities." I lift my chin to him. That is word for word what my job description says, so he can't argue. "I'll be happy to supervise my team of skilled nurses."

He looks me up and down with his saggy eyes narrowed. Then he hands me Patrick's chart. "We need to watch for signs of labored breathing. His desaturations are happening with greater frequency, and I'm also monitoring for infection."

"Have you ordered blood work?"

His look slices me. "Of course, Nurse Roselli. Thank you." His voice drips of sarcasm. He goes over his concerns with me in slow motion, and I keep one eye on the clock. Minutes tick by. I'm going to be late. Finally, he thrusts Patrick's chart at me. "Page me with any changes in his status."

Dr. Che leaves the room. I turn and look at Kate through the tubes and wires. She's resting with her eyes closed.

I should stay. Dr. Che pretty much made it clear that I'm responsible here. It will just be one more of Sylvie's sessions with Nadia that I'll be missing. She comes twice a week, and I miss most of them. It's certainly nothing new. This baby needs an experienced nurse watching him.

But, all of my nurses are adept. That's why they work here. And this morning over her bowl of dry Cheerios, I promised Sylvie I'd be there. I don't expect her to remember that or to really even care, but I promised.

If I leave now and hit the traffic lights just right, I'll be late but I still might make most of the session.

"Nurse Beth," Kate is looking at me. She smiles. "I'm ready to hold Phoebe. Can you put Paige back in her isolette?"

"Of course. We can do that. Let me get someone over to help you," I say. I go out to the desk and assign Drea, a young but ambitious nurse, to monitor Patrick. While she's helping Kate and baby Paige untangle from cords and tubes, I scribble a few quick notes in Patrick's chart, clock out, and hurry downstairs to the parking lot.

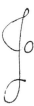

9

AUGUST, 1927

The apartment is dark when I get home, and the smell of borscht fills the air.

Sergei's here.

This is more than just passing him on the stairs, his purring accent teasing my ears. *"Josephine, back so early from your summer at the sea?"* I'd only briefly glanced at him and mumbled a *hello*. I kept walking with my head down, focused my thoughts on the patterns in the carpet to control my hammering heart. Tried with everything in me to keep my legs solid and my back straight. I couldn't reveal anything to him, other than my lack of interest in making those same mistakes again.

He didn't say any more, and neither did I.

And now, he's here. In my home.

I stand with the door open, listening for any movement in

the flat. Maybe he and Mama had gone to bed. I look toward her small bedroom and see through the darkness within the open door that her bed is still made, the round yellow throw pillow embroidered with her and daddy's initials arranged carefully on the white chenille bedspread. I know without looking that the pillow is purposely placed backwards, the initials demurely hiding from Sergei's jealous eyes, even though daddy is long dead.

I let the door click shut behind me, flip the deadlock and attach the chain, then begin the silent tiptoe to my room. I peek around into the shadowy corners, combing the place for any evidence of my mother's Russian lover.

Quiet. I don't see his shoes by the door or his hat on the settee. I relax. He's gone.

I hear an injured cat mewling in the kitchen. Only, we don't have a cat. I stop in my tracks and train my ears toward the sound. I call out, "Mama?"

Quiet.

"Mama, are you okay?"

When she speaks, her voice is strained. "Oh, Babydoll. You're home. How's Charlie?"

"Peachy." I set my pocketbook onto the coffee table next to Mama's stack of Photoplay magazines, wiggle out of Alice's fur, and drop it onto the green tufted sofa. I walk into the kitchen and stop short; she's seated at the table looking half dead, cradling her head in her hands. Her hair is a wreck, her makeup streaked. And she's as pale as…well, she's almost as pale as Charlie.

I slide into the chair next to her a little too easily. I don't have to shimmy past the old sideboard her grandfather built back in the seventies, the one with the inlaid mahogany panels and carved scrolls along the edges. The one Mama and Aunt Alice fought over when Mama was marrying Daddy.

I don't struggle past it because it's not there.

"What happened, Mama? Where's grandpap's sideboard?"

Her already pained face flashes guilt. She tries for a smile. "Sold it to the Hendersons down the hall."

"Why?"

"Well, Mrs. Henderson offered me twelve dollars for it." She tries to put on a show of indifference for me and waves her cigarette toward the empty space. "I never liked that big ol' thing anyway."

"Alice is going to kill you."

"Alice stopped caring about that hunk of rotten wood years ago."

"Mama?" I squeeze her hand. "Why are you worried about twelve dollars?"

She doesn't answer, and though my stomach is jittering from a new sudden worry, I don't press her.

"Oh honey." She stabs her cigarette into the ashtray longer than she needs to. "I'm fine. Just a little headache." She smiles weakly, wincing in pain.

"Little?"

"I just need to rest." She forces a smile and lets her eyes drop to the spindly potted azalea in the center of the table, a gift from her beau. She'd been preening and spoiling that plant for weeks, but no matter her efforts, it does nothing but shrivel. She reaches out, tugs a yellowed leaf, and lets it fall to the table.

"Mama, you should let that thing go," I nod to the plant, keeping my voice down. "It's dead. Spend your energy somewhere else."

"I can't give up on it." She rubs her thumbs into her temples. "If there's any chance it will make it, I have to keep trying."

"Sometimes," I say gently, "I wonder if it's best to quit."

"You're right, Babydoll." Her smile fades and her face twists against her pain.

"Where's Sergei?" My stomach falls as I whisper his name, but I can't let on that anything is out of place to mama. "Smells good in here, did he make you dinner tonight?"

She doesn't answer. Her eyes glaze over, and I know something is wrong. Something happened. I pat her hand and wait, my stomach in knots. What did Sergei tell her? My mind races to come up with a rebuttal or an excuse or maybe even just a confession. I work to keep my face neutral.

She takes a long time before she answers, and when she does, it's barely a whimper. "He's gone."

"I know, Mama. I didn't see his shoes by the door. Did you have a nice evening together?" I try to draw out her happier thoughts, wishing away her pain. Whatever is troubling her, it's certainly putting on the screws.

"Honey, he left. He's not coming back."

"Oh, Mama. That's not true."

"It is. He said we're finished. He took..." She holds her head. "He took the money. All of it."

"What?" For a brief moment I feel a selfish relief. He's gone. I'll never have to see him again. I can breathe easy. No more pretending nothing happened that cold night last February. No more false niceties when we're all three in the same room.

I won't have to carry that burden any more. Maybe I can forgive myself.

But that feeling lasts only a second as it's quickly replaced by the dread of our reality: Sergei was the only one keeping us afloat. Without him, Mama and I are a couple of lovely, single, penniless women without a skill between us besides killing plants and keeping secrets from each other.

Or maybe it's only me keeping secrets.

Mama's hollow eyes tell of her fear. She's a beautiful woman who had me quite young and married even younger. Sometimes she's even mistaken for my big sister. Her brown hair now has only suggestions of gray; her painted eyelids just slightly crease when she smiles, as does the funny little misplaced dimple in her cheek. *"God slipped when he drilled it,"* she used to joke, since it pierces her skin just to the left of her nose instead of at the corner of her smile where it belongs. I have the same wayward dimple, though it's often hidden since my smile doesn't come as easily as hers.

Shortly after daddy died, Sergei started in on Mama. Grief had made her headaches nearly unbearable, but Sergei seemed to have what she needed: Stop-Ake powders, a whisper of rosemary and eucalyptus oil, and straight-up European passion. Soon enough, Sergei had a deal worked out with our landlord that I didn't understand and really didn't want to. And he had everything he needed from Mama. So it seemed.

Her need for twelve dollars suddenly makes sense.

I drop my hands to the table and fold them in front of me to feign calm. "What happened, Mama? Did you have a fight? Maybe he'll come back. Maybe he just—"

"Honey," she sighs, tears welling in her eyes as she avoids looking at me. "I told him about the baby."

My heart stumbles inside my chest, skipping over itself, knocking around as if it doesn't know where to go or what to do. I see guilt pressing down on the pain behind her eyes, sandwiching the grief that only a mother can feel.

I unclench my jaw and try to speak, but it comes out barely above a whisper. "Mama, you promised."

"I know, honey, and I'm so sorry. He was surprised to see you home so early and asked why you came back. He caught me off guard, I didn't know what to say. I tried to cover it up, but he's just too damn smart, you know?"

I know.

"I really didn't think he would take it so badly," she goes on. "I thought he would understand. I know you were embarrassed that Charlie got you in trouble, and you didn't want anyone to know. I know all that, and I'm so sorry. But it's Sergei." A tear falls onto her cheek as she stumbles through her speech. "I thought he loved me. Us. I thought…" She trails off and dabs her eyes with a handkerchief.

I cringe. Last spring I'd begged her not to tell her lover. I said I was too embarrassed. I told her I wanted to spend the pregnancy in New Haven with Alice and Barlow, away from the city and everyone I know. I told her it was Charlie's idea, to save my reputation, and at the same time find a nice family who could adopt the baby. Mama became smitten with the idea of a baby and wanted us to keep it, to be a sweet little family together— me, Charlie, and the child. Of course, that could never work. I told her Charlie and I agreed it was for the best, even though Charlie didn't actually know a thing about my plans or the reason behind them.

I told her so many lies. And I asked her to lie to Sergei. Now he knows the truth. He knows I was pregnant. And he knows damn well it wasn't Charlie's doing because of my own loose tongue. A drop too much of vodka and suddenly Sergei knows all the details of my love life. Or the lack of one.

A shudder rumbles up my spine.

I watch Mama fidget with her guilt and her pain. A bitter laugh releases into my throat and dies before it reaches my lips. She's the one feeling guilty, after what I did.

What a real fine gag I've created here.

"Mama," I take a breath to calm myself, "it's okay. Really. I'm sorry I asked you to keep it from him. That wasn't right." I lean over and lightly rub her back. "What, exactly, did he say?"

I brace myself for the truth. The real truth. Whatever that is.

She only stares at the yellow leaf on the table in front of her.

My tongue goes dry. I wait.

She looks up at me, her face pained from all directions. "He was so angry. He kept muttering, 'Unacceptable. Unacceptable.' I'd never seen him like that before. He got real upset, Josie dear. It's not his business, only yours and Charlie's. I'm so sorry. I promised you. Now..." She draws in a slow breath. "Now I've sunk us."

I gaze at the dying azalea, hearing only parts of what she's saying. No number of Aunt Alice's embroidery lessons can tie together my relief at his being gone with the desperation of us being broke and Mama's heart being smashed with my own guilty lies.

"It's okay, Mama." It's not okay, but there's no use in saying anything else.

"I even told him about the family, but by then it was like he couldn't even hear me." Mama shakes her head sadly.

"Family?"

"Yes, dear. The couple."

Oh yes. The couple. The adoptive couple I pulled out of thin air for Mama's benefit.

She drops her head into her hands again. "I shouldn't have said anything. He said he won't ever come back." Tears leak from her eyes, carrying the gray remnants of her once-flawless makeup down her cheeks. "I just don't understand."

I take her hand and stroke it gently. The skin is just barely starting to loosen around the knuckles, pulling from her bones as her baby fat turns old and poor.

"He took all of the cash from the icebox. He said it was his money, and he wouldn't be supporting a couple of whores." I blanch at the description, and I see Mama does too.

I lean back in my chair, suddenly angry. Wasn't he the one who made us that way?

"Mama, we have a little saved up. We'll be okay." I'm lying again. Yes, there's a little bit in the bank that Charlie had counseled me on socking away for now, but it's not much. It would only prolong our poverty a month or two, if that. I watch Mama suffer across the table. This is all my doing. I have to fix it. For the millionth time, I'm sickened by what I've done. To us. To her. "Mama, I'll take care of you. Don't worry."

Too bad when it comes to making a living, I'm as useful as a flat tire. I can't type and can barely pour a cup of coffee. I try to clean our apartment weekly, but each time, I nearly pass out from the biting smells of Brasso, Absorene, and Lysol. Scrubbing toilets day in, day out would certainly kill me.

There has to be something.

"Honey, do you think Charlie will propose soon?" Mama very well reads my mind about my usefulness.

"Sure, Mama." I smile. "He'll take care of us. It will all work out, you'll see." Young as she is, Mama is old-fashioned at heart. She still needs a man to take care of her. But putting my marbles all in Charlie's square means I would have to give up the girls.

That's okay. That has to be okay. That was the plan anyway.

But that plan now feels like a knife in my chest.

"You know, Mama," I say, "a lot of girls are making it just fine by themselves these days. Maybe I could go get a job at Gimbel's or something. I could sell hats."

Mama forces a smile. "Such a sweet idea, my love."

She doesn't believe me, and I don't blame her.

I can't keep the babies and Charlie too. I can't get a job if I'm caring for infants. And leaving my babies behind rips me to shreds.

Oh, the savage mess of my own doing. My head is as tangled as that roller coaster. I'm starting to catch Mama's migraine.

"Josie, Babydoll," Mama gives my hand a weak squeeze. I know her pain is boiling inside her. "Tell me again about the couple."

"The couple. Yes." I'm too distracted to remember what I've told her. My thoughts are on our rent, our bills. Babies. Money. Charlie. Sergei.

Secrets.

Lies.

Everything is swirling, blurring in my head.

"I love hearing about how happy she'll be. You found her such a wonderful family." Mama leans forward, eager to be fed a fairy tale about her granddaughter.

"Well, sure. They're lovely people. Miranda and Henry live in—"

"I thought you said her name was Mirabelle?"

"Oh, yes." I blink and smile. "I'm just sleepy. Mirabelle. Of course. They live on the outskirts of the city, where there's lots of fresh air…" I try to remember the story as best as I can and keep the rest vague, but I can tell Mama is too tormented by her pain to pay much attention anyway.

I stop my story short when Mama moans, digging her fingertips into the back of her neck. Then she holds her fingers up in front of her, wiggles them, wills away the tingling numbness she's mentioned from time to time. She pushes herself up to stand and stumbles to the sofa, slides Alice's fur to the floor, and eases herself down into a fetal position.

"Mama, please." I follow her, waiting to catch her if she falls. I sit next to her on the cushion. "Let me help you. Your head—"

"It's fine, honey. Don't worry about me." Though she tries to lie still, her limbs pulse—climbing, thrashing. I can hear her stomach gurgling, pushing bile into her throat as a form of relief from the pressure in her head.

I leave her with a cold washrag on her head and hurry to my room where I pull a chair to the closet. I know I have something to help her. On my tiptoes, I reach towards the back of the upper shelf. Mama would die knowing there was vodka up there, even if my intention wasn't ever to drink it.

Lined up, hidden from the world deep in my closet, are eight clear glass bottles with mysterious contents: seeds, leaves, petals, all floating in alcohol. Next to them sits a pink, cut-glass perfume bottle, empty. Waiting. The stopper is carved into a delicate rose, with a gold ring around the lip of the faceted bottle. I pick it up. It's heavy in my palm.

Someday I'll create something wonderful, a scent truly worth keeping. When the vodka has persuaded the intricate scents out of the ingredients and my perfect combination has built itself into its fullest expression, it will go in that pink bottle. Maybe I'll even shop it around to the department stores. Maybe I'll make a name for myself. The next Coco—like Sergei said. I'll show him. But it will have to be something incredible.

Something truly special.

Rose.

I feel dizzy. I reach out to steady myself against the wall to keep from topping from the chair.

A bit more rummaging and I return to Mama with a tiny vial, one of the few store-bought scents I have, one I've yet to successfully recreate.

I open it and hold it several inches under her nose, letting the aroma comfort her. At first she flinches, but then I see her muscles calm, the straining grip on her face loosen. "Oh...But, Sergei? It smells like...the time he..." She says no more.

"He taught me a few things." I keep my voice soft, soothing, leaving behind all the worry he's also given us, at least for the moment. "Just relax. This will take it away."

"What...?"

I don't speak, only shush into her ear like the ocean I saw out past the Cyclone only a couple of hours earlier. The ocean that is nothing more than a tease: it calls people to line its shores on the hottest days of the summer, lulling them with the promise of brisk waters and gentle breaks. Then the beachgoers arrive to the reality of standing shoulder to shoulder with sweaty, smelly strangers, hoping for a chance of a cool breeze against their faces. The ocean that smells nothing of the vial in my hand, but instead of salt, rotting seafood, and wet sand. Sometimes, I suppose, even death.

After several minutes, I see Mama's body go soft and her breathing deepens. I wipe my hand across her damp forehead and turn the washcloth, easing back the hair that's matted to her sweaty face. "Sleep, Mama," my whisper barely reaches her ear.

I slide back onto my heels and carefully pull myself up. I glance at the label on the front as I cap the vial. *Yardley's English Lavender.* I tiptoe silently down the hall to my bed like the cat we don't have.

10

Beth

JUNE, 2017

I run up the walk to Bitty Babies Daycare Center and nearly bowl Nadia over on my way.

"Oh! Beth!" She jumps, startled. "I wasn't even looking where I was going, I'm so sorry."

"Hi. Am I too late?" I slow to a stop. Nadia was assigned to us from the school district to get Sylvie on track in time for kindergarten. Part teacher, part psychologist, part physical therapist, she comes to Sylvie's daycare a couple of times of week to work with Sylvie and give her all the help I don't know how to give.

And she's leaving. Of course I'm too late.

Nadia gives me that sad, sympathetic look that grandmas give little kids when they scrape their knees. She takes off her turquoise glasses and lets them dangle on a beaded chain. I

83

notice actual feathers woven in between the funky hot pink and orange beads. "I'm sorry, Beth," she says. "We cut it a little short today. Sylvie was having a tough day, so we just did some quiet activities. Gentle physical therapy, sang her favorite song, things like that. She said a couple of words, but I really had to draw them out of her."

"Oh." I feel my face heat as relief fills me instead of disappointment. Someone else is dealing with my daughter's disability. It doesn't have to be me.

But I promised Sylvie. And I failed.

"She was up several times last night," I say, to show I'm an involved mother. "I'm sure she was tired."

Nadia smiles, adjusts her purple fringed scarf, flips her long, gray hair over her shoulder, and swings her several canvas bags full of binders, folders, and developmental toys to her other arm. "Yes, she went down for a nap right after our session."

"Well, that's good. She needs that," I say.

"Whew! Don't we all." Nadia chuckles warmly.

Something buzzes in my pocket. The pager app on my phone. I look at it, but it's blank. The thing has been going haywire since the hospital started implementing a smartphone system last month. I stuff it back into my pocket and try to keep my emotions at bay. If Sylvie's sleeping, there's no use going in now. "You sang her favorite song? That's nice." I try for a smile, but I don't think it works well. I should know my own daughter's favorite song, but I didn't even know she had the capacity to have a favorite song.

Nadia reaches out and pats my arm. "The song about the hippopotamus on the bus." Her eyes are patient. "It's a fairly new thing, maybe from just last week. We noticed completely by accident that she loves it." Her tone tells me it's okay that I didn't know. Still, the "we" that noticed didn't include me, her own mother.

"Can I help you carry your bags?" I ask, turning to go back down the walk. She always carries so much with her, and her cluttered and messy style of teaching makes me anxious. She's suggested sensory activities at home like playing with shaving cream and spreading uncooked rice all over the floor that make my head explode. She's great with challenged kids, not so good at keeping the carpet white.

"Oh, no, I'm fine." She readjusts the totes again, and we walk back to where we're both parked on the street. She tosses everything into her back seat. "I'm scheduled to come back and work with Sylvie again on Tuesday at eleven thirty, but if you want to be there and another time works, just let me know and I can adjust my schedule."

"Thanks," I say. "I'll try to make it."

Nadia's voice is soft. She looks at me with compassion. "Some moms make every meeting, and some don't come to any. It's really fine either way. Whatever works for you."

I know she's trying to take some of the pressure off, but it only makes me feel worse. Some moms make it every time. Some moms make their child a priority. Some moms don't want to run away.

"You take care," Nadia says. She gets into her car and waves as she drives away. I look back up at the daycare building. A few older kids have come out to play on the jungle gym.

I should be here every time Nadia visits Sylvie. No excuses. I have to be here. How can I know what I'm doing if I'm not even present for her therapy? But I can't. I have a job. Patients who depend on me. Other co-workers who also deserve lunch breaks.

Which reminds me, I'm starving. I'll pick up tacos or something from a drive-thru on my way back to work.

When I get in my car, I check my messages.

A call back from clinic scheduling, for Sylvie's pediatrician appointment.

Eddie, texting to say he'll be late for supper.

Three different emails from different departments at our health insurance company, telling me the same thing in three different ways. "Please contact your healthcare provider…"

A phone message telling me that two prescriptions are ready for pick-up at the pharmacy. I don't remember what they are or for whom. My migraine meds? Something for Sylvie? Did Eddie call in his Adderall and forget to tell me?

My phone vibrates again. I look down. This new smartphone paging system is still buggy. Looks like the message was sent ten minutes ago, but it's only reaching me now. It's from Drea, who I left in charge of Patrick, the delicate triplet.

Beth Roselli. Return to NICU ASAP. Infant in distress.

Fuck. Patrick.

Drea's first call would have gone to Dr. Che, so he'll be there waiting for me. In fact, he was probably the one who told Drea to page me.

I speed back to the hospital, hurry through the sliding doors and past the Emergency Department, gripping my purse over my shoulder with white knuckles. I take the stairs two at a time, but when I get to the top and turn toward the nursery, I stop hard. I feel an ugly heat rise through my chest, up my neck, and toward my face. I'm planted to the terrazzo floor.

Walking ahead of me down the hall with his slight Desert Storm limp is Reverend Dooley.

Occasionally, the family of a child who is not dying or already dead will ask to speak to the Chaplain. Occasionally. Not often. There are other explanations, of course. There are always other explanations. But the most likely one right now is that Patrick died while I was gone.

I pull out my phone. The paging app is flashing at me, again too late.

Beth Roselli. Infant death. Return to NICU ASAP.

I'm still standing at the top of the stairs, my hand on the railing. I could leave. Go get Sylvie, take her home. I could call in to the NICU and leave a message. Or I'll ask to talk to Layana; I could tell her I'm horribly sick. Puking all over. Or a car accident. Flat tire. That's it. I was rushing back and hit some glass on the road. I'll be there as soon as I can. And then I can just not show up. Call it a day.

I very nearly turn to bolt down the stairs when I see Reverend Dooley stop short, pat his pockets, and turn to look for whatever he thinks he dropped. Though I'm at the end of the hall, he sees me when he looks up. "Nurse Roselli." He starts coming toward me.

I could run. I can always run. I could say I felt nauseous. Or that I had a horrible headache. I could say that. Instead I just stand there. I stare at him.

What the hell am I doing?

His forehead creases in confusion—I must have a look of horror spread out across my face. "Terrible news, about that baby. And we were all so jubilant when those triplets were born." His eyes are welled with empathy. "Those girls will never know their brother as they grow up." He shakes his head, and I notice fine slivers of silver weaving in and out of his sandy hair. "As much as I believe that baby is now comfortable, it's still not fair." He pats his pocket again, this time locating the keys he thought he lost. "I was with a cancer patient and her family right before lunch, but I got here as quickly as I could."

"Me too," I managed to squeak out over my dry tongue.

"Lunch break?"

I nod.

His voice softens. "So you weren't here when it happened."

I shake my head. I can't say anything. My lips only squeeze together and slide back and forth against each other like I'm smashing fresh lipstick. They don't open to let anything out.

He holds out his hand to me. "Let's go together, okay?"

No! I can't! I'm horribly sick, and I have a flat tire! I can't go in there. I can't face what's waiting for me in that unit.

I lick my lips. "Okay."

None of this is making sense to me. The baby wasn't supposed to die. And I don't respond to infant mortality like this. I'm a NICU nurse. I've worked in neonatal units for sixteen years. I've been through the death of an infant before. It's never easy, but it's also never this hard. I've never felt like I wanted to run away.

Maybe with Reverend Dooley escorting me, Dr. Che won't hand me my ass. Maybe Kate Miller won't realize I'd left her delicate child with a less-experienced nurse. Maybe my staff of nurses won't resent me for running off for an appointment when we had an urgent situation.

The reverend rests his fingers on my elbow to lead me.

We walk together down the hallway, past the large sepia-toned photographs of fat, healthy babies snuggled in baskets and blankets. With each step we take, I calculate how many weeks Dr. Che has left before he retires and if he'll think any disciplinary action toward me would be worth it.

I wonder what in the hell I'm going to say to Kate Miller, the grieving mother.

The NICU is quiet when we get there. Layana is at the desk, soberly reading over a document. "Beth." She looks up and immediately wraps her arms around me in a hug. I return the embrace, but my eyes search the unit. They glance over to the corner where the triplets were. Three isolettes are still there, and so is Kate. Her husband is holding her. Dr. Che is standing at Patrick's isolette talking to the parents while Drea, who looks destroyed, rubs baby lotion into Patrick's spindly, lifeless legs. There are no more tubes and wires coming off the infant.

"I got back as soon as I could," I say. My body is trembling. "I didn't get the page until after several minutes; the app is messed up. I'm sorry. It's all wrong. I missed the appointment with Sylvie. I didn't mean to be gone so long." I'm talking too fast. My voice is still carrying on, but my brain stopped keeping up. "I... Oh, God—"

"Hey," Layana grabs my shoulders and looks me in the eye. "What's going on, Beth?"

I look at the clipboard she'd rested on the desk and concentrate on the hinge that keeps the paper secured. Something simple and useful to take my mind off the tears that want to fall. I don't know what's going on. I've never felt this level of panic at work. "It's just...I should have been here..."

"You did your job, Beth." Layana arches an eyebrow.

"We all know Tuesdays and Thursdays are when Sylvie has her appointments. You have every right to be there for those."

I nod. She's right. I did my job. I delegated responsibility. I took my legally-mandated lunch break. I did nothing wrong. Or, I did everything wrong.

I'm the head nurse. I'm responsible. And yet, my instinct was to run away.

"Hey. Beth." Layana squeezes my shoulders and brings me back to the here and now. "You okay?"

"Are we ever okay when a baby dies?"

Layana nods and hugs me again. Dr. Che pats Kate and her husband on their shoulders and comes over to the desk. I wipe my eyes and square myself to him, bracing to take the brunt of his storm. I go over my resume in my head and wonder what the commute to Children's Hospital downtown would be like, if they'd even have me.

"Nurse Roselli," he looks up at me. His droopy eyes are even more tired than usual. I look straight at him and lift my chin. At least I'll take his rage with dignity. "While Reverend Dooley is with the family, make sure you go through the death checklist and log all notes in the system. I'd prefer you do it personally, but Drea will have the details you need."

"Okay." I wait.

"I've already contacted the bereavement photographer," Layana says. "She's on her way."

"Good. Thank you. Page me if you need anything."

He says nothing else. He pushes through the glass door of the unit and leaves.

I let out the breath I'm holding.

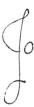

11

AUGUST, 1927

He's gone.

I lay in bed and strain my ears against the New York City night noise filtered from the street below. I listen for Mama's pattering footsteps to the bathroom or maybe a faucet filling a glass of water. But there's only silence. At least she's sleeping.

He left Mama with a broken heart and a broken pocketbook. I should hate him for that, but I have my own reasons to hate him. Like what he could do to me with a simple wink or brush of a finger.

Unable to sleep, I sit up in bed and reach for my deck of Luckies. I concentrate hard on snapping the lighter to the end of my cigarette, not bothering with a holder. I've got no one to impress here, all alone in my bedroom at night.

If I'd been stronger—smarter—I would have easily chased

him off. Called him out, spilled his tendency for wandering fingers and other things to Mama. Together, she and I could have given him the boot. I could have saved my self-respect. I could have avoided those two too-tiny creatures I have nestled up in a sideshow. I could have gotten a job and done something more useful than rubbing flower petals together and coaxing oil from smashed leaves.

Chasing a damn dumb dream. Well, I suppose I've never been the brightest lamp in the fixture. And who put that crazy idea in my head in the first place?

It was him. Of course it was him. He taught me everything.

I flick my ashes. We're better off without him. Broke, but better off. I wave away the cloud of smoke around me. I hate smoking. But I hate Sergei more.

His lips on my neck…

His fingers brushing my shoulder…

Brushing my—

Fuck-a-doo. I take another deep drag and hold it until the tremble up and down my spine stops.

I'm glad he's gone. We don't need his money. We certainly don't need his games.

I lay back into my pillow, cradling my gasper near my lips. I stare at the cracks in the ceiling above me, lit up orange from the neon signs three stories down from my bedroom window.

We'll be just fine without his dough. There's got to be more than one way to skin a hog. Okay, so we lost our bankroll. So what? Sergei's not the only jack-jobbie in town.

Charlie.

I sit up on my bed and stab out the cigarette in an ashtray. Charlie's got a good job down on Wall Street. He can handle cash and cares deeply about his nest egg. If I can get myself in as Charlie's wife, I'll be set. And Mama will be okay.

And the girls…

He'll forgive me. He'll take them in as his own—I'll talk him into it. He's a good man. He'll do the right thing. It will all work out. He'll forgive me. Maybe he'll learn to love another man's children.

I cough on the smoke still thick in my lungs. More goddamn lies.

I flop back into my bed and run my hands down along my breasts, still swollen from motherhood. Has Charlie ever even looked at them? He's gotta be thinking marriage soon. He's moving up in the firm, and I know those spinach-counters love to see a nice, stable missus behind their advancing brokers. If he doesn't want me as a lover, Charlie needs to at least see me as a rung in his ladder. And what can level out a young man even more than a wife? A child, of course. Even better, how about two?

He will never stand for it. Unless…

Unless…

I could tell him I found these twin girls in an orphanage. So sweet, so adorable, and wouldn'tcha know it, they need a home. *Honey, sweetie, please, I want to adopt them.*

Well. This story is getting more and more knotted up.

I stand up. Pace the floor. I glance out the window at Fredrick's Jeweler's clock across the street. Four fifteen. I reach for another cigarette but don't actually light it. I just keep pacing, bouncing the cigarette off of my thumbnail with each step I take.

Probably the best option is what I'd planned on all along— giving those girls up to a good home, a family who can love them, care for them.

Afford them.

My body heaves and twitches. Just the thought of it squeezes my heart.

My girls. How can I walk away from a piece of me? I'll always wonder where they are, what they're doing. Are they fast runners, good painters? Do they smile at the smell of a lily or cry at the sound of a crashing wave? Do they prefer lemon drops to bubble gum? Peanuts to chocolate?

I'm their mother. I can't leave them. I may, at the moment, be terrified to visit them, but I will. Soon.

I sigh.

As a distraction, I go to my closet, dragging my chair with me. I climb onto it and switch on the light bulb. The bottles are all lined up like little soldiers, the lavender slightly askew from when I pulled it down earlier for Mama. I straighten it, then reach back to the pink cut-glass vial, the empty one. I run my fingers along the angles and facets of the glass, the delicate curves of the cut rosebud.

Someday.

I set it back on the shelf. I pull the other tiny apothecary bottles towards me, all of them slightly different and still holding their original labels: Citrate of Magnesia, Aspirin, Cannabis Extract, Quaker Bitters. I'd drawn a sharp black ink line through each word, no longer the contents. I lift one bottle and hold it up to the faint light from my lamp, swirling the clear liquid inside. A single leaf floats, browned and curled. I remove the cork and the sharp, acid scent of vodka mixes with the pungent smell of fresh tomato vines. It smells like rain.

A series of these bottles sit, undisturbed, waiting—just like Sergei taught me. Orange rinds, lilac blooms, and fennel seeds float in either clear vodka or grain alcohol—whatever I could get—their contents now lifeless, the alcohol stealing their colors, their scents, their very personalities. They'd bathed for months, long before I even knew I'd be leaving for the summer. The scents had to be just right if I wanted to one day mix them into perfume.

It was good to leave them untouched; releasing the essenced liquids too early, while they're too delicate, could be catastrophic. That is what Sergei said as he led my fingers, a butter knife balanced between them with the tiny droplet of hazelnut extract on the tip.

"Measurement is vital, Josephine. Never too much, never too little. Exactly right, every time." The droplet fell into the bottle just as his lips fell to my shoulder, tickling my skin as the extract disappeared into the waiting liquid.

I grind my teeth as my body responds to the memory. Heat spreads inside me like a blooming thundercloud.

Scoundrel.

I reach for a bottle originally labeled "Epsom salt," but the words are crossed off and writing in my hand spells out, "heliotrope." A handful of tiny, faded purple flowers float in the liquid inside. I pop the cork off the top and wave a whiff toward my nose.

Vanilla. Sun-kissed grapes. Warm, baking pie.

Alice's oven.

I quickly close the bottle and reach for another.

"This is the real work, the real magic, Josephine." The exotic way Sergei said my given name, like the purr of a panther, always made my knees turn to butter. I watched him add a tiny drop of fig extract to a jigger of vodka, the brown droplet hitting the clear

liquid and swirling like slow-moving smoke. Mama had gone out to the butcher, so we felt safe experimenting with the hidden alcohol. We didn't drink it—well, sometimes we did steal just a nip.

Sometimes a bit more. Sometimes too much.

Even now I can still smell the thick sweetness of the extract, the sharp slap of the alcohol. Here in the closet I look at the bottle I have gripped in my hand. "Camphor" is crossed out. "Fig, cherry, walnut. Hint of orange," is written in pencil.

This is the bottle. This is the one that led to two girls born too soon.

"If the alcohol is quality," he said, "it will take on the scent, create a personality of its own. You can add more essence to it, weave this together and blend that, but you must be careful not to overwhelm the fluid."

I brightened and went to the trash can where I'd thrown out the orange rinds from earlier. "What about this?"

"Brilliant, Josephine." Sergei's smile spread, creasing his eyes. Those brown eyes, so warm. No one looked at me the way he did. "Citrus and fig. Lovely." He paused. "Like you."

I felt my cheeks heat. "How did you learn all of this, Sergei?"

He waves it off. "I had an auntie who liked to play with the nose. Plus," he put his hand gently on my arm, "a little trust in my own desires."

My arm sizzled where he touched me.

"It's magical," I said, swirling the liquid in the glass, concentrating hard on the orange rind and not the heat of his skin.

"Mesmerizing, yes?" I only smiled. "You can mix your own."

"Oh." Now my face was burning. "No, I…you…"

He laughed. "I'll teach you. You'll see. The pleasures of fragrance pull you in." His eyes lit onto mine. Warm, gentle. "Close your eyes for a minute and take in the aromas around you."

I did as he asked.

Oranges.

Alcohol.

I felt him move closer to me, the hairs on my arms standing on end, reaching out to him.

Tobacco, laced with spice.

Warm rye bread punctured with fennel.

Skin.

Sergei...

Oh...

I nearly fall off my chair in the closet. I set the bottle back on the shelf, resisting the temptation to throw it out the window.

Damn you, Sergei. Good riddance.

I step down from the chair and switch off the light. I start pacing again.

There has to be something I can do. I could wait tables, maybe connect telephone calls. How hard can that be? I can learn.

I learned scents once before. Maybe I can learn fabrics, colors, the shape of a good haircut, the perfect mix of flour and yeast for bread. I can learn anything. I can do this.

Tomorrow I'll go for a job, and then I'll go to work on Charlie.

12

Beth

I rest my head against my steering wheel, squeeze an empty pack of Belair cigarettes in my hand, and hold it to my nose. The smell is faint after all these years, but it's there.

Mom.

I'd found the crumpled old pack stuffed in a corner of the trunk when I cleaned out her 2003 Grand Am to sell it. That was last summer. We knew mom wouldn't be needing a car anymore.

_We._ Jesus. Cara and I were still speaking then. I miss my sister as much as I miss my mother.

At the time, I also knew mom couldn't possibly be sneaking cigarettes—Belair had been discontinued years ago, and that was her final inspiration to quit after I'd begged her for years. She'd been tobacco-free for a long time when I found that empty pack. She also could barely take a breath on her own without oxygen support, so smoking was mostly impossible anyway. This was likely her celebration pack from when she bought that car new years ago, discarded and forgotten with the picnic blanket and jumper cables.

I watch the clock in my car switch over the numbers. 5:56. 5:57. I'm parked across the street from Sylvie's daycare, but I still have three minutes until they start charging their late fee. Three minutes until I have to go into that chaos of a daycare and be hit with a wall of wails and shrieks, the vortex of smells that mix baby shit, Desitin, and French toast sticks.

Only a moment of peace. I mean, come on. I deserve this after the day I've had. This doesn't make me a bad mom. I'm only taking three minutes for myself.

I turn the cloud-dotted, sky-blue cigarette pack over in my hand. The cellophane wrap is flaking off, the foil inside worn soft. The minty, musty smell of menthols clings to the paper just like I cling to it. It reminds me of her seat covers when she picked me up from school, of her favorite sweater when she hugged me, of her pillowcase when I climbed into bed with her after a bad dream. The best reminder I have of Mom right now is her goddamn cigarettes. Her executioner.

Kate Miller won't have hardly any reminders of Patrick. A picture. Maybe the identification tag that was on his ankle. That's all.

She lost her baby today, and I blame myself. Just like Kate is probably blaming herself. That's what we do as mothers. She did everything right, but still, it turned out all wrong.

That's not what nurses do though. We do our jobs. But today, I didn't. I wanted to run away.

I know what a stay in the NICU can do to a mother—to a

family—even in the best of circumstances. I see parents fall apart every day. And every day I tell those moms and dads that they are doing a great job. They are good moms. Good dads. They all end up taking their babies home after a week or a month or several months, and they bring us cupcakes and leave the unit with big smiles and tears of joy. Some come back after a year or two to show us how strong and smart their active toddlers are after such a difficult start, and we nurses *coo* and *ahh* and finish the day with smiles all over our faces.

You're a great mom, I tell every single one of them. *You're doing a good job.*

But no one ever said that to me.

I was supposed to know everything. Everyone commented at how simple it would be because I was a NICU nurse. *"You do this for a living; you've got it down to a science. It must be so easy."*

It wasn't. It was hard. Every second of it.

Everyone told me I was a great nurse. But no one ever told me I was a good mom. Because I wasn't.

I'm not.

And now I'm not even sure if I'm a good nurse.

Sylvie was a healthy baby. A perfect eight-pounder, removed from my womb and placed on my chest, just like a newborn infant is supposed to be. We were discharged the next day. All kinds of opportunity for bonding.

But it didn't happen.

I knew how to care for a baby. I got all of her shots on time. I recognized a fever before the thermometer told me. I monitored her poop, her sleep, her ounces of food. She never had thrush, she never had RSV, she never had reflux or colic. Mom came to help several times that first year, when she was still healthy and could handle it. I had nothing to complain about.

It wasn't Sylvie's fault I couldn't nurse her, that my body failed to make enough milk to sustain her. It wasn't her fault I'd get death looks from other mothers when I loaded up on formula at Target. As a nurse, I should have been able to look past it. As a mom, I couldn't. It wasn't Sylvie's fault that I would spend her naps sobbing in my bed, in the shower, in my car in the garage. Everything felt wrong. I couldn't rise above it.

She would cry, because that's what babies do. Healthy, normal babies. Even healthy, normal toddlers. They cry. Good moms don't cry. They just deal with it and smile and remember how lucky they are to have a healthy, normal child.

But she wasn't a healthy, normal child. Of course, I wouldn't know that for a long time.

I look at the clock again. 6:01. I'm late. Still, I can't move.

It's okay. I've been late before. I've been really late before.

So late that I'd actually left.

No, I didn't leave her. I went back for her. Of course I did. I would never leave her. But I'd gotten as far as the turnoff to St. John's University in St. Cloud before I came to my senses. Actually, before my phone started buzzing like crazy. It was November, and the screen lit up the whole interior of the car against the darkness that had already settled outside. Phone calls. Texts. I didn't look. I didn't have to. I knew who it was. If I didn't answer, Bitty Babies Daycare would go down their list of emergency numbers. Then Eddie would get a call. He'd find out what I'd done.

My face flushed hot as I glanced down to my phone. *"Answer,"* or *"Ignore."*

Jesus Christ, this is my child, my daughter. A living, breathing piece of me.

I pulled over, my thoughts going in slow motion. I was

sobbing. Mom's cigarette pack was squeezed tight in my hand, just like it is now.

I sent a text to the number that kept calling: "Something happened. On my way. Hang tight."

That text is still somewhere on my phone, never going away. Too far back to scroll and delete now. It's like a virus that lies dormant in my blood, haunting me though I can't even see it.

I turned around and drove back. I bawled the whole way, but not because I was late picking up my daughter, not because I took an hour to myself to drive all the way to St. Cloud, and not because of the huge late fee that was piling up. None of that really mattered, and I knew it.

What upset me was how I felt.

As I drove away from her, I felt a relief wash over me, a lightness in my shoulders that hadn't been there for years. Then, as I returned to get my girl, despair washed over me. I felt nothing but sadness, emptiness.

How I feel right now.

What the hell is wrong with me?

That cold night last November, more than two hours late, I parked at the curb outside Bitty Babies. The same spot I'm parked now. I took three deep breaths before I went inside. I quietly paid the two-hundred-dollar late fee with my head throbbing and my eyes burning red, and took my daughter home without so much as an apology to anyone. Sylvie slept in her car seat all the way home. Thankfully Eddie was working late on a TV spot and wasn't home to ask questions, so I gave Sylvie a quick supper of crackers and cheese and tucked her into bed with her favorite bunny. I kissed her forehead. Got up with her again that night at eleven. At two. At three thirty.

Later, Eddie told me he had gotten a strange message from the daycare, and he asked me why I was so late getting Sylvie. I told him I had car trouble. I told him I'd take the Civic in to Midas to get checked out, which of course, I never did. Because there was nothing wrong. With the car, at least.

I was never going to leave her. I just needed a break. Still, that smoldering feeling of despair and emptiness inside my chest terrified me. It scares me still today because it hasn't gone away.

I unfold myself out of the car and drag myself up the walk. A string cheese wrapper flitters past the spot where Nadia and I spoke earlier. Earlier, while Patrick was dying.

The door to the daycare is busy. I squeeze past moms and dads who have already collected their kids and are leaving, everyone chattering about picking up a pizza for supper or whose turn it is to walk the dog or *mama, mama, mama, look at the picture I drew, the words I wrote!* Every day I watch these kids run, cannonballing into their parents' arms, their voices at full volume talking all at once about how they got pudding for a snack or how they went potty all by themselves or how they want to wear a pretty scarf on their head like little Zahra.

My Sylvie won't even notice I'm here. I'll take her hand and she'll obediently follow, without a word or even a smile. I'll be the one doing the chattering, trying to draw out her words, trying to get some glimmer of emotion from her.

Today is not the day for me to offer up some joyful chatter.

"Hi. Sorry I'm late," I say to Zoey, the young woman managing pick-up. I stretch a smile at her and hope my red eyes and smeared makeup don't expose my weaknesses.

"Oh, hi there, Beth. No worries, I understand. It's only four minutes." She grins, and I flinch. I know she's not necessarily referencing that day last November when I was a lot more than four minutes late, but it still feels like a knife to my gut. "Sylvie seemed tired today," Zoey says, adding the twenty-dollar late fee to my bill on the laptop near the door. "We checked her temperature, but she was fine. She had a tough time when Nadia was here."

"Yeah, I spoke to Nadia about it," I say, trying to make myself sound like I'm more engaged than I am.

"Poor little thing." She smiles. "We'll have her out in just a second. She was still asleep last time I checked on her."

We stand for several minutes in awkward silence. I don't have the energy for small talk. I just want to get my girl and go home and be done with this horrible day.

Another woman is hunched over near us, stuffing a too-big blanket into a tiny backpack. She stands up. "Sarasota," she says.

She appears to be looking right at me. I frown. "What?"

She motions to Zoey, behind me.

"Oh yes, that's it," Zoey says. She looks at me. "I'm sure you heard about it, since you work in a NICU. We were just talking about that baby."

My stomach sinks. Have they already heard about Patrick? What the hell does *Sarasota* mean? My expression must look as bewildered as I feel because Zoey pushes her hair behind her ears and leans in. "Someone abandoned a baby in a NICU in Florida."

"Sarasota," the backpack woman clarifies again.

"Now the baby is about to be discharged from the hospital and she has nowhere to go. Not a single visitor the whole time she's been there. Poor thing." Zoey shakes her head, her long, straight hair coming loose from behind her ears. "Has that ever happened where you work?"

I'm careful to keep my voice steady. I don't want to think about work anymore. I just want to collect Sylvie and go home. "No. No, we've never had a baby abandoned. Not like that."

Not like that.

"Well, that's a relief," she says. "I wonder how often it does happen."

Now that I think about it, I know the child she's talking about. I tell myself it doesn't happen anymore, but it does; every once in a while, a story of an abandoned NICU baby surfaces. San Antonio. Vancouver. Connecticut. Montana. I take each of these stories personally. A child left behind, a delicate baby abandoned.

"It's rare," I say. My mouth feels sticky, dry.

"Oh, thank God," the backpack mom says. "What the hell kind of crazy lady walks away from her baby?"

"Right?" Zoey says.

I stay quiet.

"I mean, it's sick. Just horrible," the other mother says.

I don't want to get involved, but they're both looking at me. I'm the professional, I'm expected to have an opinion. "Well, when it happens, usually the moms are addicts." I decide to keep it clinical, not take a side. "There are safe haven laws in place so they can make sure their child is cared for, but people in those positions don't always understand the resources available to them. Plus, having a preemie is a scary thing all around. A NICU stay is tough for anyone."

"We just need to better educate people then." The woman gives me a thin smile and then, thankfully, turns to leave.

Zoey nods, looks at me. "Fear can make a person do crazy things, I suppose."

"Yes," I say.

Zoey steps away to check on Sylvie. I'm left thinking about what would drive a mother to walk away from their child.

What drove me? Fear?

I feel my lungs contract and my pulse stumble on itself.

Is that why my great-grandmother left?

"Here's our girl!" Zoey leads Sylvie out by the hand. Sylvie is carrying her favorite bunny and her little backpack.

"My sweet girl Sylvie!" I say with as much enthusiasm as I can pull together. Sylvie doesn't respond. I say goodbye to Zoey and lead my daughter outside to the car. "Did Sylvie have a good day today? I heard you were very tired. Me too. Will feel good to sleep in our beds tonight." I lift her up and strap her into her car seat. "I missed you today, Sylvie. I'm so happy to see you."

She doesn't look me in the eye, only stares out the window. I situate myself behind the steering wheel and try to guess what she's looking at: other kids jumping and dancing and proudly carrying their art projects under their arms? The shadows of her teachers beyond the darkened windows, cleaning up and readying the playroom for the next day?

I look ahead out the window, silently willing Sylvie to talk. To scream. To tell me she wants to go home, that she's tired, hungry. Something. Anything.

I left my girl. I drove away, and it felt good.

I could call it post-partum depression, except that Sylvie was two years old at the time.

I could call it a mental breakdown, except that I never felt clearer as I was driving away. I knew exactly what I was doing, and it was exhilarating.

I could call it genetics. Blame my great-grandmother. It's

in my blood, skipped generations until it landed on me. Except that I'm a nurse, and I know that's not how genetics works. I can't blame that woman from so long ago for who I am today. That's all my own doing.

Sylvie is everything to me. I'd never just leave my girl. Never. *But you did. You're the coward. You always walk away when things are hard.*

"Sylvie, Sylvie. Sylvie in the pink dress," I sing to distract myself. The cigarette pack is still on the passenger seat. I put it back in the glove compartment and pull away from the curb.

Gretchen was right—the smile makes it all worth it. I waited for that smile, just like every other mother. Someday soon, I thought as she learned to hold up her head, to roll over. Two months. Four months. There was no smile. I kept waiting. Now, at nearly three years old, Sylvie has smiled at me a total of three times in her life. They're fleeting moments, but those are what keep me going. Maybe before the end of the day, I'll be up to four. Maybe, if I keep working, if I do and say the right things, today will be a good day.

13

AUGUST, 1927

My eyes are puffy from lack of sleep. I pull a tunic dress over my head and stuff a couple of dollar bills from under my mattress into my pocketbook.

Sergei didn't take everything.

I have to find a way to fix this. Somehow, I have to find a way to keep the girls too. I'll get a job, support an apartmentful of women. Three generations, all together. Just us gals. The thought makes me smile—it could be a keen setup. We don't need a man around. We can do this.

But I can't give up Charlie. Where would that leave me?

The stink of vinegar and vegetables from Sergei's borscht lingers in the living room. Mama is still on the sofa—I know it will be another long day of debilitating pain for her. The lavender only subdues her headaches long enough for her to sleep, but when she wakes the pain is there, waiting for her like a thief eyeing a wealthy man's watch. I bend to check her forehead before I leave, making sure it's not too hot. The pillow on the sofa smells like Mama's rouge and, of course, Sergei's soup. It's infiltrated everything in the apartment—the couch cushions, the pillows, the window dressings. Even my clothing.

Sergei's gone, yet he lingers. He has a way of leaving too much behind as reminders.

"Mama," I whisper, "I'll take care of us. Don't worry." I'm still not sure how, but I have to figure it out. Maybe Mama would be well enough to watch the babies while I work. She's not that bad off.

I stand and look at her, curled in a ball on the sofa. She doesn't stir. Since I've been back in the city, she's spent four of the past six nights folded over in pain, barely able to get herself upright to use the bathroom. Twice I had to practically carry her to the toilet after her groans and shrieks woke me in the other room.

But maybe she'll get better. She has to.

I go to the kitchen and reach for a pen in the drawer of Grandpap's sideboard before remembering the hulking piece of furniture is not there. I hunt through the kitchen and find a pencil under Mama's pocketbook. I leave her a note saying I'll be back later.

The sky is barely starting to lighten outside the kitchen window. I stand for a minute, watching birds swoop in and out from under the eaves of the building next door. I quietly let myself out of the apartment. I need a plan—wandering the streets before dawn isn't going to help my cause. I pass the hall telephone and stop. Pick up the earpiece. Ask the operator to connect me.

"Hello, Hazel Johnston here." Her voice sounds unreasonably chipper for this time of day.

"Haz. It's Jo."

"Bushwa." Her voice cracks with fatigue and sinks back into a groggy moan more fitting of the hour. "Only producers call this early. You trying to give me a brain hemorrhage?"

"Sorry."

"Honey, are you okay?" Her voice is slow, and I can imagine her rubbing her eyes beneath her sleeping mask. "I was worried about you last night after you ran off."

"Sergei's gone."

"Your mother's boyfriend?"

"That's him. Bloused off, and not coming back."

"Dammit. His vodka was top-o."

"Hazel, we're broke." I stop. Let that sink in. "Sergei was keeping us afloat." I don't tell her what else Sergei did.

"Oh shit."

"I need a job."

"Sure you do." I hear bedsprings creak. Lucky girl, sporting a telephone right in her bedroom. She calls it a business expense and would rather go without eating for a week than give up her telephone. "I think I have some leads; let me look. Hold on to your bloomers for a sec." A bang, a crash, and several loud taps cut through the static as she knocks over her mouthpiece, and in a minute her voice comes back on. "Jo, honey, there's a cattle call this morning at Stellamann's. Glove counter. Ask for Mrs. Vandernoodle."

"Vandernoodle?" I grab the pencil that hangs from a string on the wall and scribble notes on a scrap of paper.

"Let me know how it goes." I hear her yawn. "Say, what

does Charlie think about this? Is he gonna have a beef with you getting a job?"

I swallow hard. "Charlie doesn't have a whole lot of say just yet." I fiddle with the corner of my paper scrap.

"You're not going to tell him," Hazel says. "Am I right?"

She's absolutely right. Charlie hides things. I can certainly do the same. I lift my chin, giving myself confidence against all my lies. "If Charlie doesn't like it, then I suppose he should go ahead and propose. Right?"

"That's right. Make an honest woman of you—" There's an uncomfortable pause where I cringe, and I'm pretty sure she does too. "Damn. I didn't mean it like that, Jo. You know that."

"I know, Haz." I rub the toe of my shoe against the worn floorboards. "Well, if that happens, I can always scram out of the counter job. For now, though, I need cash."

"Well, good luck. Or break a leg. Or, hell, pluck a chicken. Whatever's gonna make it work out for you."

"Thanks. You're a peach." I hang up and hurry for the stairs.

The morning sun glints between the buildings, stretching the shadows of commuters and newspaper boys into long, thin black lines along the ground. I stop at Sweeps for a pack of Lucky Strikes, then count the change the clerk dumps into my hand. Eighty-five cents. Enough for a light lunch and subway fare.

My next stop is Lincoln National, where Charlie suggested Mama and I open the bank account. I get there minutes after they turn over their "open" sign, and the teller reports back our current financial situation of fifty-nine dollars and twenty-two cents.

Jesus. Rent is sixty-three dollars, due in a week. Guess we'll be living off the earnings from Grandpap's sideboard after all.

I eye the teller behind the cage and take in his black vest and bow tie. I wonder if a girl could get a job like that. I glance down the line of tellers, looking for finger waves or strings of pearls.

Not a one.

I leave the bank, keeping the money safe and sound in the account. Another few cents of interest could mean a sandwich or a cigarette. Back out on the sidewalk, I take the folded scrap of paper out of my pocket. Stellamann's. Vandernoodle. I make my way down the street, pushing away all the thoughts in my head that tell me this will never work. I don't think about babies' schedules, Mama's illness, Charlie's strong dislike of working women and children he never fathered. I'll worry about all that once I land the job and get us at least a hope for an income.

I pull open the glass door to Stellamann's lobby and enter a space hanging heavy with a mishmash of perfumes settling on a crowd of well-dressed young ladies. They're all assembled just past the doors, each holding a paper application in their gloved hands. I look down at my own hands. No gloves. My fingertips are stained red from crushing tea rose petals and smell faintly of turmeric and vodka. What's worse, all of the other ladies are dressed smartly in suits and matching cloche hats. My tunic dress is wrinkled, and my own cloche was picked up second-hand and is at least three years outdated. Still, I push through the crowd, tossing a casual *"pardon"* over my shoulder as I wade through the sea of elbows and pocketbooks. One woman sits at a table with a stack of papers, so I move toward her. She looks official enough.

"I'm looking for Mrs. Vandernoodle."

The woman looks up at me. Her eyes travel to my t-straps and back, taking me in—the whole mess of it. The contempt is clear on her face. I know immediately that this will be a waste of time. "Perhaps Mrs. Vandernohl? Is that who you mean?" She puckers her lips. "That's me."

"Oh. I'm sorry."

"Do you have experience selling gloves?"

"Well, no. But I can learn."

Her eyebrow arches. She makes no move to hand me an application; instead she stands and claps her hands. "Ladies. Attention. Attention." The buzz and chatter in the room dies down. "Thank you for your interest in Stellamann's. As you know, we are a very upscale department store. We expect our sales ladies to be of the highest caliber." I slink back away from her, trying to blend in to the taupe-painted brick wall. She holds up a pair of burgundy driving gloves. "If you know at a glance the type of leather from which these gloves are made, then you've just passed the first step of the interview, and please follow me. Otherwise, if you don't know your calf skin from your cordovan, then I thank you for your interest." She marches around a corner, and a good three-quarters of the women follow her. A few other ladies are left in the lobby with me, each of us pretending we dropped a handkerchief, or that our fingernails were much more interesting than the job prospect we just lost. One by one, we pass back out onto the sidewalk. I step on a discarded application on the tiled floor as I make my way to the door, just as empty as mine would be had I gotten one.

I stoop, pick it up, and stuff it into my pocketbook. At least I could read over the questions, practice filling in the empty lines and spaces.

Outside, the sun is in full force now, blasting me with a blinding white light that makes my eyes tear up and shrink to slits. I smell bread. I wonder if there will ever be a time that I can smell freshly-baked bread and don't think of my girls, hanging on for their dear lives on Alice's oven door. I shade my eyes from the strengthening sun and look around to find the source. Before I know it, my stomach is leading me across the street to where the scents of sizzling bacon and percolating coffee join with the baking bread.

A "Waitress Wanted" sign is propped in the door.

Maybe the smell of bread is what's reeling me in, telling me that this is right. Maybe my girls are showing me the way. After all, in the end, I'm doing this for them. All babies need a home. I can give them one. Somehow.

I concentrate on the scents that contrasts sharply around me: coffee and chocolate, mustard and pastrami. I forge ahead to speak with the proprietress, a robust woman in a stained, gray smock. She's more friendly than Mrs. Vander-this-or-that, but is even more pressed for time. Since I've never carried a platter or taken an order, she is less than excited about hiring me, but she very nearly does. Then she asks if I have any hurdles to working days, nights, weekends, every day.

"I need to know I can count on you to be in for you shift. I won't tolerate last-minute excuses or requests to leave early." She looks up. Catches my eye. Waits for my answer. When I hesitate, she leans back in her chair. "You have a little one at home, I'm guessing? *Opa*. That's a tough spot." She taps her pencil on her notebook. "You have a neighbor who can help watch your child?"

A breeze of hot air from the kitchen sends a strong message of fresh bread to me, overwhelming me.

I wouldn't trust our neighbors to water Mama's dying azalea.

I thank her for her time.

Back on the sidewalk and now hungry, I shoulder past a small group of young women chattering with each other. They each clutch a stack of books to their chests. One wears a cloche hat, the other two are in berets. Their Mary Janes click the sidewalk. Each is wearing a sweater vest; one has a large S and J embroidered on it.

St. Joseph's.

College.

Also, I realize, quite strangely, my namesake.

I turn my head and watch the girls amble down the sidewalk. Is St. Joseph calling to me? With a college degree, I could work at a better job. Less hours for more pay. Education; isn't that what Mama always wanted for me? Papa?

"Education will never fail you, Josephine. Always take a chance at learning something new."

The Russian roll of the tongue in my memory reminds me of who said that, but I decide to forget it was Sergei. Maybe it was my father, before he died. Yes, that's good. The thought that Daddy gave me such sage advice when I was young excites me.

This whole idea excites me.

I could be a college girl. It could lead to something really meaningful. Something that would make a lot of dough without a man calling the shots.

With almost a Charleston in my step, I follow the gals as they flitter like leaves down the street. They turn down Clinton Avenue, and as I pass the big brick building heralding St. Joseph's College in engraved letters above the door, I stop.

I'm here, I might as well inquire.

I pretend to be Hazel and march up the steps to the front door, lean against it and let myself in. There is no reception desk inside, so I just stand there looking dumb. A woman swishes by in a harsh dress and spectacles. Before I can stop myself, I reach out for her arm. She startles as she looks at me, a cross of fear and curiosity flashing in her eyes.

I force a bright smile and clear my throat. "Who can I talk to about attending classes?"

She points a pencil down a short hallway. "Admissions. Room 115. Mrs. Frye." She's off before I can thank her.

Room 115. It's barely a room, more of a closet. Inside, someone thought it was a grand idea to cram a desk, a coat tree, piles and piles of folders and papers, and a stocky, older woman in a drab brown suit with glasses sliding down her nose. The room smells of the need for a bath. I knock gingerly on the door frame and the woman looks up, adjusting her glasses as she does.

"Can I help you?"

"Mrs. Frye?" I thanked the great God above that her name was fairly normal and held no Vander-s or noodles-s. "I'd like to look into attending college."

"Well, that's what we're here for, lass. Classes start on Monday." She pulls a few papers out of a filing cabinet and slides them across the desk toward me. "Teaching?"

"I'm sorry?"

"Are you interested in teaching?"

"What else is there?"

"What's your words-per-minute?" Her voice is thin with a slight lilt. She sorts her paperwork and barely looks up at me.

"Excuse me?"

She pulls her glasses off of her face and drops them on the desk. She wiggles her fingers in front of her as if she were seated at an Underwood portable. Her expression looks annoyed. "Typing."

"Oh." I shake my head.

"Okay." She shuffles a few more pages around. "Nursing?"

My stomach jitters as I think of the women caring for those

preterm babies, and especially the one who took Rose from my arms. My memory is distant from that day, but I can see her.

Ida, Sweet as Apple Cider.

My face must pucker and turn a hundred shades of red because the woman sighs. "Great. A queasy one." She leans forward and puts her elbows on the desk. "Honey, you're going to have to figure out what you want to study before you register for classes. We need some kind of direction to send you in."

"Oh. Well, thank you." I feel my shoulders slump, but I pull them up, determined to keep my dignity long enough to make it out the front door before I let myself fall apart.

I don't know what to do with my girls.

I don't know what to do about Charlie.

I don't even know what I want to study in school.

And I don't know the which, where, and how, about getting a job.

What a useful doll I've turned out to be.

I wander out to a bench in front of the building and sit. I pull a handkerchief out of my pocketbook to dab my leaky eyes but then cough when the smell of vinegar and beets hits me again.

Damn that Sergei. He's even gotten into my hankies.

Everything.

"You never know, Josephine. You may be the next Chanel."

"I doubt Coco Chanel mixes her own perfumes." I carefully measure half of a droplet of anise oil and release it into my dish of alcohol. I swirl it around, breathing in the smell just like he taught me. Just a pinch of hyacinth, maybe, and this will be perfect.

I steal a glance at him, and he smiles. "I suppose you're right. Then, how about the next Madame Curie?"

117

I can't resist letting a giggle escape. "Madame Curie? Say, now, did she make a perfume out of radium?"

"Chemistry, my love," he says. My stomach swirls like the small dish of scented vodka in front of me. He's not so much as talking anymore; his words come only as a breath. He leans in close, our lips nearly touching. "The beauty is all in the chemistry. Scents are only molecules, and the way they join, it's like making love."

On the bench outside of St. Joseph's College, my fingers have twisted my handkerchief into a sweaty wad in the palm of my hand. I can feel my body giving way, going limp as I think about him. His tenderness. Our chemistry together.

Chemistry.

I suck in a quick breath and stand, pushing Sergei out of my thoughts. I run back into the building and down the hall to the admissions office. Mrs. Frye has her coffee cup to her lips when I burst in and practically shout at her, "Mrs. Frye, I want to study chemistry!"

Her only movement is to set her coffee cup down and wipe up the droplets of coffee she spilled onto her desk blotter. I stand awkwardly in the doorway, not really sure if she'd heard me. Finally, I step forward. "Ma'am? I said I—"

"I heard you." She dabs at her blouse. "That's not an option."

"Not...what?"

"Miss," she lets out a heavy breath, as if a dozen young women have already come in begging to be scientists and she's had to turn them all away with the old explanation of a woman's place. She continues wiping up her coffee. "You can study teaching, secretarial, or nursing."

"But..."

"Sorry, honey. I appreciate your pluck, but chemistry is only available to the male students."

"But…Madame Curie—"

She glances up at me and gives an amused smile then returns to searching her skirt for spots of dropped coffee. "Goodness. If you flapper gals aren't pining to be Mary Pickford or Gloria Swanson, then you're cheesing to be Marie Curie." She laughs to herself. "Oh, Betty."

"Josephine."

"It's an expression," she says, her face hardening. She wipes her hands with her handkerchief. "And with classes starting soon, I'm a bit busy for chit chat, love."

My cheeks burn, but this time I felt as if I'd been slapped. It takes me a few moments to realize my mouth is hanging open. I close it and lick my lips. "Isn't this the land of opportunity?" My voice is so calm I don't even recognize that it's mine. "And this is New York City, right? Where anything is possible? I'm not asking to be Mary Pickford or Marie Curie. I'm only asking for an education. And I want to study chemistry."

Mrs. Frye's eyes lift from searching for wayward droplets of coffee, and she finally looks straight at me. She narrows her eyes, and I wait for her to give me a good reaming for my pluck. With a brisk clearing of her throat, she puts on her glasses. "Well." After a pause that feels like ten years, she continues, her eyes still on me. "Fine. Not my business. You can take it up with the professors, I suppose. Tuition for the year is due before classes start on Monday. That means either today or tomorrow."

I'm stupid. I'm a stupid, stupid girl. I didn't even fathom the fact that college carries with it a hefty cost. My heart sinks, and I brace myself, smiling like a mannequin. "How much is tuition?"

"One hundred and eighty-five dollars per year."

Fifty-nine dollars and change in the bank. A buck eighty-five in my pocketbook. Twelve dollars or so from the sale of Grandpap's sideboard. And rent due next week.

"I've heard of scholarships," I say. "Is that an option?"

She looks at me with real sadness in her eyes. "Not for a young lady wanting to study chemistry."

"Okay, I'll be a nurse, or a secretary—"

She shakes her head. "Not for a young lady wanting to study anything."

I recognize the regret etched into the lines that crease her face. I wonder if one day long ago she had aspirations to be something besides and admissions secretary. "Yes, of course. I understand." I move backward toward the hallway, nodding as if everything makes sense. "Okay. Thank you so much, Mrs. Frye." I close the door behind me as I leave.

It's not for me. There's only one line my life can follow, and that's drawn by Charlie.

I step out onto the sidewalk, my mind racing to come up with other options for a job. Something that Charlie wouldn't find out about, something that I could still do if my daughters come home. Something that won't make my senses sick.

Out on the street, I watch the other aspiring nurses, secretaries, and teachers hustle around the lawn, discussing their books and schedules. I won't be a chemist. I won't be a nurse, a teacher, or a secretary either.

I'll be a wife. Soon, I hope. It has to be soon. And somehow, I have to find a way for Charlie to let me be a mother too.

14

Beth

JUNE, 2017

"Beth."

"Yeah?" I step into to the living room when I hear Eddie call me, and I immediately regret it. My sister's husband catches my eye through the front picture window, and he gives a crooked, awkward smile through his beard as he comes up the front walk. He's carrying a Blue Moon beer box.

"Rocko's here."

"Thanks, I see that." I take a breath. "Shit."

I know what Rocko's carrying, and it's not a case of beer. I look at Eddie. He shrugs. "Sorry, beautiful. Pretty sure he saw you." Eddie nods toward the window. "You can't run away."

Eddie knows me too well. I steel myself and open the door, letting in the sweltering summer heat that crawls under my scrubs. "Hey, Rocko."

His black Under Armour hat is on backwards, and his tight, red t-shirt shows dark stains under his arms. His hair looks damp. Why men wear beards in the summertime, I'll never understand. "Hey." He forces a smile. "Is this a bad time? You going to work?"

"I work at one. After lunch." I hesitate. "So, I have a minute."

"Okay. So, ah, Cara and I finally got around to cleaning out your mom's house last week." He shifts his weight then pushes the box toward me. I take it from him, though I don't want to. "Anyway, we found some things that you...that maybe Sylvie might like. Someday. You know."

"Cara couldn't bring them herself?" I cringe as soon as I say it. I wasn't going to bring it up. God damn my mouth, flapping before my brain catches up. I look around for help from Eddie, but he's slipped into the kitchen. The only other person in the room is Sylvie, who's lining up wrapped tampons at the coffee table, oblivious to us.

Rocko looks even more uncomfortable. "Yeah, well, I was going to be in the neighborhood anyway, so Cara—"

"It's okay, I get it. Sorry. I didn't mean anything by that." The box is heavy. I move my hand for a better grip, and something clinks together inside. I catch a glimpse of a ceramic giraffe I painted for Mom when I was in third grade. She always displayed it proudly on her dresser, even when I'd moved away to college.

Oh, my God. No. I can't do this. Not now. I feel my hands sweat against the printed cardboard. I clear my throat. "Yeah, so, thanks for taking care of my mom's stuff. I've been, you know..."

"Busy. I know," he says. It sounds a little less sarcastic coming out of Rocko's mouth than it would Cara's.

"Yeah."

Rocko shifts his weight between his feet. "So, ah, Eddie

told me at the funeral that you guys were going to start doing some testing with Sylvie…" He stops as if he wants to say more but thinks better of it. He takes off his cap and runs his fingers through his hair. He flips the hat back on. "How's that all going? You get any answers yet?"

I nod and swallow the knot in my throat. What else did Eddie tell him? That I miss my sister? That I wish I had the courage to call her? "Yeah. Autism is confirmed. I mean, we knew that, but now we have something official."

He stares at his feet. "God. I'm sorry. That's rough." He looks at me; his eyes are kind. "But now you can get her some help, right? A diagnosis makes that easier?"

Nothing about this is easy. I soften a bit and shift my own feet. It's nice of him to ask, I guess. "She has a great care team. So far, the diagnosis is only educational, but it does help. We're working through it all."

"Eddie said she's not even talking yet." He shrugged. "I mean, Brody was a late talker, too…" He trails off as if he just realized it's not nearly the same.

"Yeah, well, Sylvie's mostly nonverbal. Maybe a word here or there, but it's really hard to understand." I keep my voice gentle. Rocko is only trying to be nice. "It's frustrating, but we're doing the best we can."

More shuffling of feet. More flopping of his cap on and off. Why doesn't he just go? "So…you know," he looks up the street and squints into the summer sun. "You and Cara should really get together, or something. All this fighting…" He drops off and shakes his head.

"Well, we're not fighting. Just…I don't know. Not speaking."

"Still, you're sisters."

These questions were mostly likely planted by Cara; I know Rocko doesn't understand or care about this petty drama between his wife and her sister. And why should he? It is petty, I guess. She's my twin sister. Still, I went to her for help, and she practically shoved a knife in my gut. My sister is more able to break my heart than anyone else in the world.

We stand for a moment, awkward in our silence. Finally, he speaks, his voice changing back to something more upbeat. "So there's a lot of Christmas decorations we cleaned out, too, if you're interested in any of that. An old silver tree that Cara said you might remember. Bunch of other random Santa shit." He shrugs. "You know how your mom loved Christmas."

My stomach flips, and his face reddens a bit. He just caught what he said.

Mom died three days before Christmas. I tried to put on a show for Sylvie's sake—Santa and presents, the whole bit. I'll never know if she even noticed any of it. The overstimulation of the holiday threw her into a rage, and that, paired with my own grief, worked up a migraine for me that lasted until New Year's. "We don't really have room for any of that stuff, Rocko. Our basement's packed to the ceiling with junk. Sylvie's stuff. You know how it is. Toys she's not ready for and all that." Toys she may never be ready for. "But, uh, thanks."

"Okay." Rocko stuffs his hands into the pockets of his shorts. "Well, I've got boxes of her clothes I'm taking over to Goodwill." He waves towards his Pathfinder. "You want any of that?"

"Nah. Get rid of it." I lean against the storm door; I feel a bit like I'm talking to a door-to-door insurance salesman who won't take a hint. "So, I'd invite you in for lunch, but I don't have much time before work..." I half-heartedly motion inside with my head, the box still heavy in my arms. I try to smile but have a feeling it looks pretty forced. Just like his does.

"Oh, no. Thanks. I gotta get going. Stop at Goodwill, then pick up a pizza for the boys. But hey, we'll see you soon, okay?"

I knew we weren't going to see any of them soon—at least not until Cara decides she's ready to sell mom's house and she needs my signature. "Okay. Sounds good. Thanks for the…stuff."

"Sure thing. Say hi to Ed for me." He jogs down the walk back to his SUV. I let the storm door slam shut and return to the cool comfort of air conditioning.

I stand there and watch him through the window. I don't realize I'm shaking until I hear the items inside the box clatter together.

Eddie sneaks up behind me and takes the box from my arms. "Painless?"

"Not that you were any help." I shake out my cramped fingers and lean against a chair to regain my balance.

"Your rodeo, baby."

I take a deep breath. Hold it for a count of three. Let it out. "You're my husband. You could have at least hung out for a minute, you know. Backed me up."

"Oh." His face goes a little white. I get the feeling he legitimately didn't realize that would have been a good idea. "Sorry."

Another deep breath. My body somewhat stabilizes against the dizziness. "It's okay, I guess. Rocko's a good guy."

He puts his free hand on my arm and looks me in the eye. "I know Cara misses you, Beth. Neither one of you should have had to go through your mom's death alone. I don't know what this beef is all about, but you guys really should—"

"I know. I know." The wounds from Cara still feel fresh, even if they're months old now. *"You don't fucking leave your child. What the hell is the matter with you?"* I can still hear the crack in her voice, the angry waiver. *"Quit being a goddamn entitled little bitch."*

Any other time, I would have just taken it. I'd certainly endured worse from my sister over the years. But I went to her for help. I was a mess. I showed up on Cara's doorstep because I needed someone to tell me I was a good mom, that I was doing the best I could, and that sometimes it's okay to fall apart. I needed to believe that I still deserved to be Sylvie's mom after what I did and how I felt. I was at my lowest, but somehow Cara pushed me even lower. I'm not sure if I've climbed out yet, even now.

I look up at Eddie then down at the box he holds in his hands. Resting inside are tchotchkes and trinkets that flood me with grief. The giraffe. A little green coin purse that belonged to Grandma Vee. Mom's old roller coaster snow globe that lost most of its water sometime in the 1970s.

This was mom's stuff. These are her memories. Our memories. Happier times. I feel heat rise in my cheeks. It's still too new. I can't think about it or I'll be a babbling mess, and I have to go to work.

It's junk. Just junk. Not worth it. My eyes burn. All I have left of her is junk. I've been using an old, crumbled cigarette pack as a substitute for my mother. But of course, nothing can replace her. No box full of little dust-catcher items that Sylvie will probably break someday anyway. I turn away from Eddie before the tears form. "Just put the box in the basement. I'll deal with it later." *Like, maybe in ten years. Or never.*

He balances the box on his thigh and peers in. "There might

be something good in here. Something worth some cash."

"I'm sure Cara and Rocko set aside anything worth money. This is all just the junk they didn't want to throw away themselves. But if you have time to put stuff on eBay, then fine. Go right ahead." Another glance at Sylvie tells me she's okay for the moment, now stacking blocks on the coffee table next to her lineup of tampons, her body poised on her tiptoes. She doesn't acknowledge we're in the room.

I follow Eddie to the kitchen where he sets the box down on the granite island. He reaches in and moves a few things around. "Wow, this is great stuff. Look at this."

He's entertained. I'm annoyed. He's not hearing me. "You know, I just don't want to see that stuff right now, okay? I'm not ready."

"It's been six months since your mom died, Beth."

"I'm not ready, Eddie." There's a bitterness in my voice. The little souvenirs of my mother's life are only salt in the wound of her death—I don't care if it's been six months or six years. Sylvie hiding them and losing them around the house would make it even worse. I imagine her lining everything up execution-style in front of her dollhouse. "I don't want that stuff around, okay? Not now. Just get rid of it." I feel a familiar tightening inside me.

Out of nowhere, Sylvie is at my feet. She's reaching her arms up, grunting. I bend to pick her up, but she whines. I set her back down but she continues reaching, only now with more frustrated grunts.

"I think she wants to see the box," Eddie says.

We both watch her. I'm torn between the awe and wonder of my daughter actually communicating a want for something and the frustration at the thing that she wants being something I don't want to give her.

"Goddammit," I say under my breath.

"Beth, this is huge."

"Yeah, but she can't have it."

"Why not?"

I don't answer. I know these sensory items would be good for her. I know she needs to learn that the best way to get what she wants is to ask. Still, I can't do it. "No, sweetie," I say gently, "not for you."

Sylvie grunts more. Her face darkens.

"Didn't Rocko say this stuff was for Sylvie?" Eddie says. "What does it matter if she plays with it."

"Rocko doesn't know shit—" I stop at the bite in my own voice as Eddie's face turns to stone. I know I'm being unreasonable. "Sorry. I'm just…I don't know. I don't need this stuff spread out all over the house." It would kill me to see these things that belong on Mom's nightstand, in her jewelry box, beside her purse, instead reduced to debris from a toddler who doesn't understand or respect them. I don't need more pain right now.

There's only one thing that I've found comfort in, and the really ridiculous thing about all of this is that it was what ended up killing Mom: her cigarettes. None of the things in this box will carry her smell like that box of Belairs does. "I'll go through that stuff later and find some things that Sylvie can have," I say, "but not now, okay?"

Sylvie is still reaching for the box, her pink shirt pulling up as she stretches. Her whining becomes more desperate. "Her therapist said to encourage her when she asks for something," Eddie says. He arches his eyebrow. "Right?" I can hear the impatience in his voice. Eddie would give Sylvie a set of steak knives if she made the effort to ask for them.

He thinks he knows more about Sylvie and her issues than I do. I'm the goddamn nurse. I give him a look, narrowing my eyes. "She can't have everything she wants. She has autism, but that doesn't mean we spoil her."

Eddie drops his eyes to the box, rummages around listlessly. I can tell he's deciding not to make this into a blowout argument. "Yeah. I guess." I see him keeping one eye on Sylvie, and I know he's going to sneak her something when I'm not looking. "What about this? Can she have this?" He pulls out a flashlight and switches it on and off, which makes Sylvie screech. "It's fairly harmless, Beth, and the battery is good." He hands it to her, careful to show her where the button is and how to push it. She copies him, pushing the button over and over, flashing on and off, on and off, on and off. That satisfies her for now, and she takes it to the living room. I can hear the button from the kitchen.

ClickClickClickClickClickClick.

"Fine." I pull a package of raw chicken legs and a bottle of barbecue sauce out of the fridge so I don't have to look at my husband or the box he's so interested in.

Let it go, Beth. It's just a box of junk. Don't get worked up.

"Hey, maybe Sylvie would like this." He holds up a little cut-glass perfume bottle. Pink, with a rose carved into the stopper. Some of the petals are chipped off, and the gold banding is worn and tarnished to a mottled patina. "Someday, you know." I give him another look, but he's studying the bottle and doesn't see me. He hasn't heard a thing I've said. I'm seething. "There are two of them," he says. He picks up another bottle from the box. Holds it in the palm of his hand. "This one's pretty plain, just square.

129

Looks like something's in it." He shrugs, squinting. "Maybe that inside tube thing for the spray part. Looks moldy."

"Moldy? For Christ's sake, that's gross. Just throw it away." I concentrate on the raw chicken in front of me to calm myself.

"You know, some of this stuff looks older than your mom's time. Wonder if it's your grandma's?"

My temples throb. Arguing with him will only make it worse. "Maybe." I didn't help clean out Grandma Vee's house either, when she moved into the nursing home. Busy.

He lines up the two bottles on the counter. Then he shakes the pink bottle with the rose stopper. "There's something in here too. Like dirt. Sand." He holds it up to the light. "Maybe someone went to the beach and got sand as a keepsake. Might be a story there."

I dump the chicken pieces onto a plate and cover them with the sauce. I take a deep breath, hold it, and then let it out to try to get over my anger. Why can't he just respect what I need? Why isn't he hearing me? *He's only trying to help, Beth. He's trying to be nice. You can be nice too.* "Cara probably played with it in the sandbox as a kid." I have no memory of either of us playing with perfume bottles as kids, but then Cara had a way of finding old junk around the house and using it in her art projects and pretend play a lot more than I did.

"Perfect." He turns." Sylvie!" She ignores him, so he takes the pink vial to her.

"What are you doing?" I wipe my hands on a dishrag and follow him to the living room. "No, no, honey, those aren't for you. Not toys." I look at Eddie. "I told you I don't want her to have this stuff."

"You just said Cara played with it as a kid."

"I don't know, Maybe she did, but she was probably a lot older than Sylvie. And they probably weren't gross and moldy then. And—" I stop.

"And Cara wasn't autistic, right?" I sense the grate in his voice.

"What if she breaks it and cuts herself on the glass?" I try to wrestle the pink bottle from Sylvie's grip, but she's squeezing it tight.

"Then she'll learn an important lesson. Besides, these are solid. They made everything to last back then. This glass has got to be a quarter-inch thick."

"And chipped. And broken. And sharp."

"It's not sharp. I don't think she'll break it any more just by playing with it." Eddie lowers his voice. "Beth, it would be great for Sylvie to play with something other than a box of tampons." He pats Sylvie's shoulder. "Sylvie, honey, do you want to play with this in the sandbox?"

"Pin," she says, looking at it. "Pin."

Stunned, Eddie and I look at each other. I kneel down to be on her level. I try to get more from her. "Pin? Like a sharp safety pin? Or a pen, that we write with? Sylvie? Pin?"

"Pin," she says more forcefully, so I know she's telling me I'm wrong. "Pin." She points to her shirt, pats her tummy. "Pin."

I'm bewildered. I'll never understand my child, and this breaks my heart. Other kids her age are talking like politicians, and she can't even say one word.

"What are you saying, honey? Pin?"

"Pink?" Eddie says to her. He holds up the pink vial.

"Pin." Her voice softens. She doesn't smile or even lift her eyes to either of us, but the way her voice suddenly changed, we know. Eddie got it right. The excitement I should be feeling about my daughter's word—a descriptive word even, which should be making me do cartwheels—is overshadowed by my failure.

Defeated, I stare at the carpet.

Why do I make this a competition? Just because Eddie figured it out doesn't mean I never will. It doesn't mean I'm a bad mother.

Maybe it does. My head continues to ache.

Sylvie turns the bottle upside down and dumps the sand out onto the carpet.

I'm shaking from wanting to cry, scream, swear, or everything all at once. I'll have to wait until I'm alone in my car. "Eddie, honey," I say very carefully to my husband. I'm talking especially slow so I can control the tremble of frustration in my voice, but at the same time to make sure that he knows that I'm livid about this. "Please take our daughter outside and watch her in the sandbox. Okay? Can you do that for me, please? And maybe turn on the grill, too, on your way?" I drag the vacuum out of the coat closet. "And please, get rid of that box. I don't want to see it. Throw it in the trash for all I care."

Sylvie and Eddie both retreat out through the patio door while I vacuum the sand. I'm so angry. No one listens to me. I'm angry at Eddie. I'm angry at Rocko and Cara. I'm angry at Sylvie. I'm angry at Gretchen and Carter and Patrick and the loathsome world.

Most of all, I'm angry at myself.

Sylvie's the one who can't talk, yet I'm the one no one hears. Of course, it's not my place to care about that. I'm here for those who need me. I'm selfish for wanting anything for myself.

That goddamn pink perfume bottle. It couldn't have been Mom's; I don't think she ever wore perfume. Maybe it was

Grandma Vee's, like Eddie thought. I take a few deep breaths. If I know my Sylvie, that pink perfume bottle will end up in the bathtub with her tonight—that's where all of her treasures go, sometimes before I can stop them from being ruined. I've had to fish entire boxes of bloated tampons from the water before. Maybe then I can trade her for some light sticks, and give the bottle back to whom I think it belongs.

15

AUGUST, 1927

"Charlie!" Mama had run down the hall when she heard the telephone ring, leaving our door wide open. "Oh yes, very well, thank you. Much better today." She's quiet for a minute, then she laughs, her voice tinkling as Charlie charms her.

I slowly ease off the sofa where I'd spent the evening paging through a chemistry book I'd picked up at the big library across from Bryant Park. I was having a hard time concentrating, though, because every confusing alkaline and complex isotope made my mind wander to the two confusing and complex little infants I had waiting for me. I cast a longing glance at the Harper's magazine on the coffee table in front of me; I don't have time for that kind of mindless luxury anymore.

A sudden fear shudders through me: what if Mama says something to Charlie about my pregnancy? I quickly slip through the door to the hallway and hurry beside her by the telephone. Mama's smile is as wide as Fifth Avenue as she talks to my beau. She takes a moment, laughs again, and then excuses herself. "Oh, Charlie. So great talking with you. Here's Jo." She hands the telephone to me with a wink.

"Hiya, Charlie," I say into the receiver. Mama keeps standing there next to me, listening. I wave her away, even hiss silently to go back to the apartment, but she doesn't. She just grins and flutters her eyelashes.

Charlie clears his throat. "Ducky. How are you, my girl?"

"Swell, Charlie."

"Great. That's just great." He sounds distracted. I look at the clock above the phone; it's six in the evening. He's calling from work, burning the nighttime oil. I'm one more thing to check off his to-do list. "So Jo, I have a potential client I would like to take out for dinner this weekend, on Saturday. I'd like you to join us."

"Oh, well…Saturday?"

"Is that a problem?"

I sigh. I should have known he'd forget. "No, Charlie. No problem. What time?"

"I'll pick you up at seven. Wear something nice. Not too… flapper-ish. Okay?" I hear his lighter flick through the line, and his next words come mumbled around his cigarette. "The fur's probably okay if it's a cooler evening as long as you leave it in the check."

"Fine." It comes off a bit harsh, and Mama squeezes my arm. I give her a look, but still, I soften my voice. Truthfully, I'm annoyed with Charlie. No birthday dinner, just schmoozing some rich rubes. "So, anything else about Saturday?"

"Just let me do the talking, okay? Like always. You sit there and look pretty, like you're so good at."

I nod to myself, though I know he can't see me. At least I'm good at something. "Say, Charlie," I pause. Watch Mama. Try to shoo her away again.

"Yes?" He sounds impatient. He needs to get on to the next item on his list.

Though I probably know the answer, I want to bring up college with Charlie. I don't want my hopes to just be one more lie I keep from him. He loves me. He should love what I want for my future, too. And besides, no one knows a thing until they ask. Maybe, just maybe, mentioning it now will plant a seed. Maybe he'll come around. I can even turn it to make it sound like it's his idea. He could think the idea so grand that he'd even offer to pay for it. I feel my heart lift. "How would you feel about me taking some classes?"

There's a moment of silence. I hear him writing something, the scratching of the fountain pen mixing with the static on the line. He's still distracted when he speaks. "You mean, like a knitting class?"

"No, Charlie. I mean, college. Chemistry."

Mama's eyebrows shoot up on her forehead. Charlie laughs through the telephone. It's a good, hulking, cleansing belly laugh. I haven't heard him laugh like that for a long time.

I have my answer.

"Oh, never mind, Charlie."

"Jo, you're a hoot. Say, see you on Saturday. Be ready and waiting, I don't want to be late, okay?"

"Sure, Charlie."

I hang up and look at Mama. "So, a date? On your birthday?" she asks. Her excitement for a date with Charlie takes priority over her questions about my education.

"Business dinner, Mama. He's entertaining a client. He

didn't even mention my birthday." We both look up to see Mr. and Mrs. Gillum, our neighbors from down the hall, pass by. Mrs. Gillum's smile is tight, forced. Mr. Gillum's is wide and relaxed. Mama and I both tense, but they pass without incident.

If Mrs. Gillum hadn't been with her husband, Mama and I both would be wedging ourselves against the wall to avoid a hallway groping. We look at each other, a knowing relief passing between us. "Still," Mama says after the neighbors are out of earshot, "it's a date."

I shrug.

"What is this business about chemistry?"

I wave my hand in the air. "Just a thought. It's nothing."

"I think an education is a great thing, Babydoll, but chemistry? Like that scoundrel Sergei?" She tuts her tongue, grimaces. "Always going on and on about the right mix of this and that. Compounds and molecules and nonsense. Did he put that idea in your head, with all of his potions and mishmash?"

"No, Mama," I lie. "I guess I never took much interest in what Sergei did. I just thought I could teach or something. Help pay the bills."

She watches me, her eyes squinting. Either she was figuring things out, or she was getting another headache. "Josie Dear, that's what Charlie's for, once you're married. That's what you should be fussing over. Not those silly textbooks."

"Yes, Mama." I fidget, the walls of the hallway closing in. I have to get out of this stifling hallway.

And I know where I have to go. Where I've still not gone. I have to do this.

I lean over, hug her, and kiss her forehead. She relaxes. "Mama, I'm going out for a little while." I say to her. "I'll see you later."

16

Beth

His dark eyes of no particular color are open, but I know he doesn't see me. We dim the lights in the nursery at night, but I still notice just a tinge of bluish-gray here and there around his pupils. Eventually they'll find their color, find their sight, be useful, but right now all they see is what they shouldn't be seeing— light, blurred movement. He should only be seeing darkness, still only be feeling the warmth of Gretchen's body surrounding him, hearing the sounds of her heartbeat and her muffled voice instead of the constant buzz and dinging of monitors and equipment. He shouldn't even be breathing air yet, but here he is, struggling to do so.

He cuddles into my shoulder, and I caress the downy blond hair that has sprouted on his head. If I've learned anything as a

NICU nurse, it's that babies have a way of knowing when they're ready to be born. Carter was ready. He'll be fine. He will.

I spend just another moment with him, nuzzling him, before I return him to his isolette. It's a new thing to hold him—he's five days old, and this morning was the first time he was allowed into Gretchen's warm arms. Now I look forward to his feeding times, when it's encouraged that the nurses hold the babies to soothe them when their mothers and fathers can't be here. Carter has a way of coiling himself into me while breast milk—donated by overabundant strangers—filters through the g-tube, into his nose, and down his throat. It's a good time to bring him the safe feeling of a warm embrace, even if it is only from his nurse.

Carter hiccups as I lift myself to standing, and I smile. He's a little angel. Sweet little heart-shaped mouth, and he's even starting to get some shape to his cheeks. He's a gentle, old soul. I look into his sleepy face as I nestle him back into the isolette. I know he'll never remember me. Maybe in time, I won't remember him. The point, though, is that we're giving him a chance to remember something. He will go on, survive, thrive.

Not like Patrick. A jolt goes through my body, landing a sick feeling in my stomach. To my left, there are two isolettes where there used to be three.

I think about what Gretchen said, about how preterm babies in my grandmother's time were usually left to die. Some, unfortunately, still do. But Grandma Vee was saved. Maybe her mother did something right.

Survival of the fittest. I guess some are just unfit.

I think about my Sylvie. She's at home, cozy in her bed. She's not unfit. She'll be okay. I have to find a way to believe that.

I watch Carter's eyes blink slower and slower as his body

relaxes. Dinner will do that to a person. I run my finger along his cheek, and I swear he smiles at me.

He's not unfit either. Only little.

At the nurses' desk I chart the milliliters he consumed and the weight of his diaper. I give the rest of his chart a quick glance and see that we are still waiting for the results of his routine cranial ultrasound that was done earlier today. Radiology is notoriously slow around here.

Time for my break, and I'm starving. I close the cover on the isolette and swipe out with my badge. Layana is on with me tonight, so I wave at her on my way out. She's sitting at the desk, tapping out a beat with a pen, moving her lips to some soundless, invisible lyrics that float through her head. She gives me the finger-gun point and winks.

I creep down through the dark, lonely corridors of the hospital.

Next time I work an overnight—which I think is tomorrow—I'm going to strap my lunch box to my head so I'll remember it. Right now, the very lovely chef salad I'd portioned out in the very special salad container I bought at my neighbor's very expensive Tupperware party is taking up very precious room in the fridge at home, doing me absolutely no good. Instead I hit up the vending machine since it's the only thing open at this hour.

Doritos.

Skittles.

Funyuns. I can't believe they still make these. I can't believe I'm going to eat this garbage. I wish they'd leave a few things out in the cafeteria for us night nurses who have too much on our minds to remember something as silly as lunch.

I take my dinner to the seating area behind the cafeteria. It's dark and quiet, the only light coming from the emergency exit sign at the doors and the streetlights outside the tall windows. Sometimes on my night breaks in the summertime, I'll go outside to the picnic tables and enjoy the cool night air and the quiet, but these past few days the humidity and the mosquitoes have been brutal, so I've opted for the climate-controlled indoors instead.

In the stillness of the empty cafeteria, the bag of Doritos sounds like the Fourth of July as I open it. I pull out my phone for company. The lineup of browser windows show my thoughts over the past days:

Ketosis and autism.

Benefits of vitamin B.

Detoxing heavy metals from toddlers' bodies.

Early Intensive Behavioral Intervention.

Is autism hereditary?

I close the entire cascade of browser windows, but that last one stings with guilt; I was trying to pin it on Eddie. He's struggled with ADHD since he was a kid. He's a little scatterbrained. He doesn't take much of anything seriously. His priorities can sometimes be out of whack. But, none of that puts him on the spectrum. If anyone is, I suppose it's me with my sensitivity to smells and my need for order and control.

My fault.

Unfit mother.

I sigh and look into the bag of Doritos. The smell of powdered, processed cheese hits me in the face and turns my guts. I wish for my chef salad or even the leftover spaghetti I left in the fridge for Eddie and Sylvie.

I turn off my phone and stare out the window. My stomach growls. Some lunch break.

The Skittles go into my purse for my four o'clock, middle

of the night slump, and I gather up the Funyuns and Doritos for the trash. That's when I feel someone's shadow fall on me, the very faint smell of warm lavender reaching my nose. I stay sitting at my table.

"Hey, Rita," I say before I see her. We're not supposed to wear any fragrances at work, but Rita carries a tube of Crabtree & Evelyn in her purse that she always slathers on the minute she clocks out on break. It's subtle, lovely, and lavender is actually a calming agent, so no one complains.

"Ach. You caught me."

"You're not so sneaky, you know. Even for a nurse practitioner."

"Heavy-footed, I guess. Shoulda been a surgeon." Rita laughs and sets her lunch down onto my table. "Delicate fingers, feet like clompers." She slides into the chair across from me. "Everything okay?" Her gravel voice is always so soothing to me, like she's Frida Kahlo reincarnated. If that was what Frida sounded like. Seems like it would fit.

"Sure." I shrug. I glance at the clock by the exit: two-fifteen. Rita keeps watching me, the crinkling at her eyes deepening as she studies me.

"I know you had a hard time with the triplet death," she says. "Always so heartbreaking, no matter how long we've been doing this."

"Yeah."

She eyes me, my silence giving away my pain. Finally, I give in and talk. "Oh, it's Sylvie. She had a little sniffle today. I'm just worried about her."

"Ah." She nods in a way only a mother can. "Or, rather, worried that Eddie is taking care of her the right way while you're at work?" She arches her eyebrow. I know she's not buying the sniffle story.

"Oh, he's fine." We're quiet for a minute, and although Rita is never one to make anyone uncomfortable, I feel a bit fidgety. Something is off about her demeanor, and I wonder if something is wrong. I guess we can both read each other well. "Missing my mom too."

She nods. "That was when I missed my mother the most, when my children were sick." The corners of her mouth flex. She's humoring me. "It always reminded me of my childhood in Chihuahua and how my mamá would make me cinnamon tea with honey. Sometimes she would add onions if I had a particularly bad cold." Rita shrugs. "I was never able to get the mix quite right. Ended up giving my kids plenty of Robitussin instead."

I smile. "As a good mother does." I play with the Dorito's bag, folding it over, unfolding it, watching the silver catch the red light of the "exit" sign behind me. "You heard about Sylvie? I'm sure the news has gotten around."

Rita nods, the empathy heavy in her eyes. "Yes, that autism is confirmed. Bittersweet, yes? Now you have a direction to go in to help her, but you also know that it's not going to be easy, and it's not just going to go away." She smiles and pats my hand. "That's what we always hope for our babies—that they'll magically get better. It doesn't always go like that, does it? Still, she *will* get better, it just won't look like you probably hope. She'll learn to cope with her unique mind, and so will you. You'll give her everything she needs to thrive, I'm sure of it." She leans back in her chair. "Sylvie will be just fine, in her very own special way." She says it with an air of confidence that makes me think she may be absolutely right.

"Thank you, Rita." I look up and catch her eye just in time to see something is definitely wrong. That deep, sympathetic look of a favorite auntie that Rita is blessed with is now laced with trouble around the edges. My stomach sinks. "Hey, what's up? Everyone okay in the unit?"

She's quiet for another moment then bites her lip. When she speaks, it's a doozy. "Carter's cranial scans came back from radiology a couple of minutes ago, they must be working a late shift tonight." Rita shakes her head, pulls her glasses off of her face, and lets them fall onto the table between us. She rubs her eyes, the loose skin of her face stretching beneath her short nails. "Intraventricular hemorrhage."

"Fuck." It comes out as a breath. I'm allowing myself this language in the middle of the night in the abandoned cafeteria. "Grade?" I hope for a mild classification, grade one or two.

"Three."

"No." I jump to my feet. "Rita, that can't be right. He's…" I stop and lower myself back into my chair, embarrassed. Too much emotion for a nurse of my experience, even if the wounds of Patrick's diagnosis and death are still fresh. "I was just with him before my break. I never would have guessed a grade three brain bleed." I know there would be no way of knowing that. Often intraventricular hemorrhages don't present with symptoms any different than normal prematurity.

She shakes her head. "You know how these things sneak up on us without any warning. Alas," she lets out a deep breath and lifts her hands palms up with a slight shrug, "there it is."

"Shit." I say. "I can't take two severe IVH diagnoses in the same week."

Rita puts her glasses back on. "Such is life. We can't control;

we can only treat. Still, I've been in seven different NICUs over the course of thirty years, and these IVH diagnoses never get easier. Such a blow."

"Do Gretchen and her husband know?"

"Dr. Che will see the scans in the morning." Rita shakes her head. "He'll be the one to tell them."

I let out a defeated breath. I prepare myself for my next shift tomorrow evening. By then Gretchen will have lived with the news for a good ten hours, and she'll be deep in some different level of grief by then. Still, I'm glad I'm working nights this week. Layana and Rita are both much better at comforting families when bad news hits. No matter how I try, I always sound cold and clinical. Telling a parent that their child will likely have lasting brain damage is the second worse thing we as NICU nurses have to deal with. The first is obvious. I close my eyes and wish for Gretchen to have one last good night's sleep before she knows the truth.

"You're crying." Rita says, purposely not looking at me. She opens her lunch container. "And I don't blame you." She picks up her fork, stabs a darkened avocado slice. "I'll be honest, I cried too. Carter is *mi cielito*."

My phone buzzes. So does Rita's. We both look; she puts on her glasses first. Severe thunderstorm watch until nine in the morning. We both instinctively look outside, where there appears to be no wind. The only movement is the weaving of moths and mosquitoes in and out of the glow of the streetlights.

"Summertime in Minnesota," Rita smiles. "If we're not battling mosquitoes, we're waiting for the tornadoes."

"I used to be terrified of them," I say, trying to get my mind off of Carter. I smile. "The tornadoes, not the mosquitoes."

"Mosquitoes are terrifying too." Rita pushes her lunch over

145

to me and hands me an extra plastic fork from the bin behind her. "My papa had malaria when I was little." She waves toward her lunch. "Didn't you eat? Please, share mine."

"Rita, I can't eat your lunch. Besides, I don't have any appetite right now."

"You can, and you will. You need your strength for the rest of your shift." She smiles with a glint in her eye. "I force-feed humans every day, I'll do the same to you."

"With a gavage in my nose?"

"If I have to."

I give her an annoyed smirk, but I scoop a forkful of rice and beans anyway.

"It was probably the *Wizard of Oz* that did it for me," I say. "I've heard plenty of tornado sirens, and I've even ended up crouched in a basement a few times, but I've never seen a tornado. Still scared me shitless as a kid." I swallow my forkful of food. "You ever go through tornadoes, growing up in Mexico?"

Her eyes were knowing. Rita had seen it all. "Not in Chihuahua," she says, "But once we were in Texas, yes. And I tell you, you have every reason to be scared shitless."

17

AUGUST, 1927

An hour later, I'm back at Coney Island. It took everything in me to pony up the subway fare and bring myself here. At least this time, I'm alone. Charlie's working late, and Hazel has an audition. I can take my time, go at my own pace. I can do this and not have to answer to anyone.

It's been eight days since I gave birth to the girls. I have to see them. What kind of mother am I, avoiding them for more than a week? Actually, I'm terrified of what's inside that exhibit. My stomach wrings like Mama's laundry. Will I ever bring those babies home? Will I ever be a mother?

I have to see them. Maybe it will give me some clarity. Or, it could make it harder for me to walk away from them. Which I will have to do.

This was a mistake. My legs wobble, so I look for a bench

to sit, but nothing is vacant—the seats are all filled with tired families, gray-haired ladies leaning on each other, and young couples looking for petting parties. I reluctantly stay standing, staring ahead.

The things I know now—the pain of childbirth, the scent of a newborn—I shouldn't. I should still be with Alice, learning her blasted boring needlepoint, collecting ideas from her dresser full of aging perfumes, and deciding who, if anyone, would adopt what was growing inside me.

I look past the bright, lit-up sign spelling out INCUBATOR BABIES. The fantastic light bulbs, a wonder unto themselves, lead the way to another marvel inside. My sight settles on the dark door.

They're in there. I'm so close.

Words painted in a black arch above the door emphasize all of the adorable delights waiting within:

All the world loves a baby!

Sweet. Cute. And each of those babies inside are on the edge of death.

Deep breath. C'mon, Jo. Take a step. Just hand the barker the coin and go in.

A crinkling to my right jars me from my thoughts. I look down beside me. A girl, barely four, is licking her fingers. Her shiny, dark hair is held back with a blue ribbon; her dress is a breezy yellow cotton that falls straight from a wide collar at her shoulders to the top of her knee socks. She holds crumpled paper in her hands and has a smear of chocolate on her cheek—the only evidence of the chocolate cookie she just devoured.

The rumbling roller coasters don't faze me, nor do the groups of young men passing on the boardwalk with their jokes and catcalls, yet this tiny sound from a tiny person catches my attention. Am I suddenly so sensitive to youth?

"Do you like babies?" Her voice, like a little bell, cuts through to my ears. I look down and feel an easy smile take over my lips. So beautiful. My hand lifts and gently pats her hair. I reach to take her hand, not caring about the sticky sweetness that lingers on them.

But then I realize what I'm doing. I freeze and pull my hand into a tight fist. She's so small, so innocent. But she is not mine. What was I thinking, reaching for her hand?

Was I looking—or rather, hoping—into the future, seeing her as one of my own?

I open my mouth to say something that I don't even know yet, but nothing comes.

Another woman's hand lights on the girl's shoulder, the nails short but shiny, a diamond ring encircling the third finger. Her mother, of course.

Her mother, who is not me.

My cheeks burn as I consider my thoughts, my purpose, here today. I'm only here to see for sure what's in that building. Then I can have my peace and, hopefully, so can they. Those delicate, tiny little girls. I look up toward the blinding whitewashed walls, the bright lights…a quiver of tears hurts my eyes.

I shouldn't be here. I should have left well enough alone and *gotten on with things*, as Alice suggested. Yet, here I am. Again. I can't help it; I'm drawn to this concession. This freak show. Where inside, nestled in the heated steel and glass coffins…

"Quite a thing, isn't it?" The woman with the diamond ring

says. The girl leans back against her mother's solid legs, entwining her sticky, crumb-covered fingers with hers.

Here is a woman with a strong, healthy girl, and she's come to be entertained at the expense of those poor children inside. I feel my cheeks grow hot, anger bubbling inside me.

She has no idea.

"It disgusts me," I hear my voice say. The words commit themselves before I give them any thought, though I know deep down they carry the truth. It does disgust me, the idea of it. It tortures me. It disturbs me to my soul. Just like this woman and her lovely daughter do.

I wonder if I meant to say, "*You* disgust me..."

The woman's head swings sharply toward me. Her eyes sparkle like the lights strung throughout the park. "I suppose you're one of those who believe weaklings should be left to die." She crinkles her nose, her voice rising. "Then go and enjoy the Better Baby Competition down the boardwalk. Nice, fat babies with blond hair and blue eyes, passed around and cooed over, only so they can die of tuberculosis in the fall." She pulls her daughter protectively closer. "This place—the nurses, Dr. Couney—they perform miracles. Just look at her." She pats her daughter on the shoulder. "The doctor said to leave her be, to let her die peacefully. He told me I can always have another. He told me there was no chance for survival. Well, I told that doctor to go to hell. I wouldn't give up. I wouldn't just let her go to God without a fight." She's a bear protecting her cub, and her words bite. "You have no idea about having a baby too early, about being told all you can do, all you *should* do, is watch your child die."

My head swoons. I feel my knees buckle, my ankles loosen,

my grip on the ground giving way. "Oh, but I do." I say. My voice is barely audible, yet it is resolute.

From the periphery of my vision I see the woman's shoulders lower. "Oh, honey," she says quietly, her voice melting. "Have you lost a child?" When I don't respond, she steps closer and puts her hand on my arm. "I'm sorry, honey. I get a little chopped up about this whole thing. I should learn to hold my tongue." I try to offer a smile, but it hurts. "Do you have someone in there?" she asks.

My eyes fill. I feel my head give a very quick, very tiny nod. Just one. More would suggest I'm fine with it. I'm not.

"You're one of the lucky ones, believe me. Come," the woman says to me as she nods her head towards the exhibit. "I'll pay your admission."

At that moment two nurses tumble out of the infant exhibit, laughing as they pull at their sweaters and cigarettes, presumably happy to be off their shift and into the freedom of the warm night air.

"Goodness, Mae! Is that little Beatrix?" One nurse does a double take toward us. She rushes to the girl, the other nurse in tow. She hugs the woman and then crouches down to the girl. "Hello, Beatrix. I knew you when you were smaller than my pocketbook." She looks the child over. "Oh, Mae, she's beautiful. So grown-up." As the nurse moves, I notice her scent: antiseptic, fresh paint, and something that smells like a cheap knockoff of *Shalimar*. Still in a crouch, she turns her head to the other nurse behind her. "She's a graduate from before you started. One of our very own!"

Mae's expression changes from protection to pride. "Not even two pounds when Dr. Couney came for her. Now, look at her!"

"My name is Trixie," the little girl spits out with more than a little fierce annoyance. Mae smiles with pride.

The new nurse studies the girl through her cigarette smoke. "Well, hello there, Trixie." A smile spreads on her lips. "So wonderful to see a success, especially after the day we'd had." The two nurses meet eyes and nod solemnly to each other.

My stomach drops. Mae notices my reaction and puts her arm around my shoulders. Her voice continues to be bright as she speaks to the nurses. "We have a new mother here. She has one inside."

They both look at me with pity in their eyes, but also something else—like they are welcoming me to a very exclusive club. The first nurse stands from Trixie's level to look me in the eye. "Welcome, dear." She takes my hand. "We'll take good care of your baby; you can trust that. This is the best place, really. Would you like to go in?"

I don't hear anymore. I can't. I run, as fast as my feet can take me. Away. Again. Not toward the subway station, not toward anywhere. I'm just running to get away. That's what this concession does to me. Like a magnet it pulls me in, then suddenly turns the wrong way and all I can do is leave.

I need to go inside the exhibit, but I also need to be alone, inconspicuous. I have to make my peace in my own way. My heels click against the street as I maneuver the thinner weeknight crowds, dodging and swerving around strolling lovers and cranky children. I see concerned glances, I hear people calling to me, but I don't stop. I pass the Cyclone, still spinning up its melodrama of a spine-tingling tragedy every four minutes, the man in the little house serenely turning the pages of his newspaper.

I feel caught in a Cyclone myself—lights rushing by, wind

gripping my hair, my feet barely hanging on to the ground. My steps transition from hard cement to creaky wooden boards, then to soft sand. I keep running, stumbling through the unstable grains as they give way under me.

Darkness is falling across the city, and the deserted beach stands in contrast to the hot days when a gal can hardly move from the crowds. Packed in tight, too many individuals in too little space.

My girls.

I push ahead toward the rumble of the Atlantic Ocean spitting waves up onto the beach. My run reduces to a trot as my lungs ache for breath. The noisy racket of Coney Island is left behind me, and I approach the lapping waves of saltwater, my shoes full of sand. I close my eyes and breathe in the scents of right now: sand cooling in the moonlight and rotting seaweed washed onto the beach have overwhelmed the reheated hot dogs and burning exhaust belched from the coasters' motors.

To my right, the Steeplechase Pier towers against the darkness. The air is heavy; there's a storm moving in from beyond the pier. The billowing, black clouds with their flashes of lightning threaten to swallow the bright moon whole. The wind kicks up and knocks the smells out of the air, bringing with it only a whiff of wet, electric rain just minutes away. It's a scent so alive that it can't be bottled, can't be contained.

Rose.

Is she still alive? Are either of them?

Their tiny, elusive scents couldn't be contained, either, but they will stay with me forever. Warm. Sweet. Their shivering lungs struggling to bring in a breath that would exhale a scent I'll never forget. The smell of love.

153

"Better than being cooked in the goddamn oven." Only Uncle Barlow was quick enough to think about options. And now, here I am. I'm a mother, but I'm broken. I have to save myself and hopefully my own mother who is broken in her own way. I have a direction, a line through life that will set everything in the right order. Love. Engagement. Marriage. Babies come later. That's the only way.

Yet, back behind me, just past the popcorn stands, the juggling shows…

It's all broken.

I slip off my shoes and take a step towards the water. The waves wash up around my ankles. I feel the coolness of it.

I'm a useless mother. I'm a disgraceful daughter. I can't keep the interest of the man I love, so I went behind his back—and my mother's—and betrayed everyone. I've created my own mess, and now I don't know how to clean it up.

Even if I did, I wouldn't have the courage to follow through.

Like now. I take a step back from the ocean. The idea of the incoming storm taking me far away feels like a relief, but in truth, I'm terrified of drowning.

Yet, in a way, that's what I'm doing.

I take another step back. Sand sticks to my wet feet. I look up to the sky and the storm clouds. It hasn't started raining yet, but I feel droplets against my cheeks.

"Don't, sweetie. Please, come back." The voice calls out to me, startles me. I turn and look; three women and a child stand at the edge of the boardwalk, watching me. Two nurses in matching sweaters, a mother, and a robust and stubborn child born weighing less than two pounds.

Each of them, stronger than I am.

154

I pick up my shoes and turn toward the pier. I walk carefully, resolutely, and it feels like I'm walking through honey in a bad dream. Still, I keep going, away from the dark figures calling to me. Near the pier, I turn and make my way back to the wood and cement of the park.

Those tiny babies all lined up in that incubator exhibit have someone to watch over them. They have nurses, doctors—piles of people to coo and cluck over them. Not one of them needs the likes of me.

I push my way into Stillwell Station and watch the cold, metal tracks vibrate with the incoming trains. I wait for the cars to stop, and then I board to go home to Manhattan.

18

Beth

It's impossible to sleep midday in June. The sun is bright through the blinds, and my mind keeps racing, thinking of Sylvie. Patrick. Carter. Gretchen.

Cara.

Mom.

"Family is forever, Beth." Mom's words are imprinted in my memory. I can see her now, younger, her hand moving deftly through the cream cheese as she smears bagels for breakfast. Her brown eyes glance up at me, soft but not without warning. Her voice is rough from smoking paired with a weekend spent cheering us on at some high school tournament. *"You and Cara will always have each other. You'll always be sisters, no matter what. Don't let something silly get between you."*

Cara had made a dumb move in our quarterfinal basketball

game. Or it was my dumb move. Or maybe it was a track meet. I don't remember what it was, but her words stuck with me. I'd always been able to forgive Cara, for everything. Until now. My heart won't let go.

I look at my phone next to my bed: six minutes before noon. I get up and pad down the hall. Sylvie's at daycare and Eddie's at work, so the house is quiet. Even the cat is out and about. I don't work until late afternoon, so I have a few hours to myself. A day of quiet. No one to bother me. Just me and my thoughts.

Oof. That may be too much. Just me and maybe no thoughts. Just coffee.

Down in the kitchen, the box of stuff that Rocko brought over is still sitting on the floor next to the patio doors. Of course it is. Eddie can't be bothered to put anything away.

I yawn and press the "on" button on the Keurig on the way over to the box. The coffee maker gurgles to life. I crouch down next to the box and stab through the items, my curiosity getting the best of me. A veil of sadness folds over me, a tingling that starts at my scalp and falls over my face.

This was Mom's stuff, Grandma's stuff. They kept it for this long for a reason. Maybe I'll just put it in the basement for now. Maybe someday I'll be able to go through it or at least be ready to toss the junk in the trash. Maybe someday I won't be so triggered by these trinkets of my past.

"I love you, Beth," Mom had said as she lay dying in the hospice bed. *"You and Cara take care of each other."*

It was the last thing she said to me. Of course, Cara and I already weren't speaking. Our confrontation had happened several weeks before. Mom never knew.

In the box, stuffed under a chipped ceramic dish, is the soft, curled edge of old, thick paper. I pull it out carefully. It's a USO identification card with Grandma Vee's picture as a young lady and her full name that she never went by. Looks like she'd spent some time as a "Junior Hostess."

Grandma Vee was lucky—someone was there to rescue her when she was abandoned, to give her a good life. I wonder what happened to the woman who walked away when Grandma was only an infant. Grandma never really talked about her. I don't know how much she even knew.

Squinting at the faded photograph, I notice something pinned to her lapel. It's sort of cut off in the picture and a little hard to see, but it looks like a rosebud. In fact, it looks identical to Mom's rose pin, the one attached to the strap of my purse.

The pin. The perfume bottle with the rose stopper. Vee must have loved roses as a young woman.

I toss the card in a drawer. It's probably worth keeping, since it's something of a World War II relic. Maybe there are more curiosities in that box. I peek deeper inside, and I'm bowled over by the musty smell of mold. Probably *not* worth keeping this junk if it's going to make us sick. I go grab my coffee from the Keurig, but the moldy smell stays with me, fighting past the warm, cheerful smell of the coffee. It's almost as if the odor is stuck in my nose.

"She had a lovely scent to her that seemed to hang in the air long after she was gone." Grandma Vee waved her hand. "That's the only thing Mama ever said about her, the few short times she saw my real mother. Her perfume lingered, but she certainly didn't. Nothing but a ghost as far as I'm concerned. And that's all I have to say about her."

Grandma Vee seemed certain she hadn't died but knew very

little else. What made my great-grandmother a ghost? What made her walk away from her own child?

What made me walk away from mine?

"Fear can make a person to do crazy things, I suppose."

So, what was that woman so long ago afraid of?

To try to escape the smell that's now trapped in my senses, I take my coffee and the box outside to the shady front step. There's a light breeze, but I can tell the day is heating up to be a sizzler. I sit on the front step in the small swath of shade, put my coffee next to me, and set the box of Mom's stuff by my feet. The sun is centered in the lunchtime sky high overhead, blocked only by the overhang that shelters our front door.

I squint down the street and see a moving truck parked several houses down. A man and a woman struggle a sofa out of the back, while another woman in a tank top moves a floor lamp out of their way. In the front yard, three little kids chase each other. From this far away, I can't make out any faces or distinguishing features, but they look young; in fact, the littlest seems like he should be in diapers. But he isn't. He's naked.

My eyes drop to the box sitting on the step. I can't help but look inside; every time I do, I notice something different. This time, I see a scratched-up shot glass with Lincoln National Bank etched into it. Ancient. A promotional item from years ago. Maybe Eddie was right—some of this stuff might be worth something.

I pick up the clear, boxy perfume bottle with the moldy tube. The label on the front was probably at one time white, but now it looks like a piece of dirty parchment.

Chanel No. 5. I run my fingers over the black letters of the label. Wasn't this the perfume Marilyn Monroe wore? I take off the lid to see if it still has a scent. I'm surprised that the lid is actually a stopper that tops off the open bottle, not an atomizer like I'd thought.

I sniff.

Nothing.

Perfume. I laughed to myself. What an old lady thing. I don't know anyone under the age of sixty who wears perfume. I toss it back into the box. It clinks against the shot glass.

I see movement out of the corner of my eye; a child is running down the sidewalk toward me. As she gets closer, I notice she has a jelly smear across her chubby face, and she's wearing nothing more than a pink Tampa Bay Buccaneers T-shirt and Batman underwear. She's sprinting at full speed, and she looks absolutely feral with wild, blond curls sticking out like they've never been combed. The woman in the tank top is chasing her. I try to melt into the cement steps. I'm not awake enough yet for socializing; I came out here for the quiet of a neighborhood where everyone else is at work. I discreetly touch my messy hair, consider my yoga pants and lack of makeup.

It's too late to run away; she sees me.

"Hi there! Ooooh, Bindi, you little monster. Come here you." She finally gains on the child and swoops her up in her arms. The girl squeals as the woman showers her in kisses and flips her around. I smile hospitably, hoping now that she's caught the kid, she'll go away. The woman stops in front of our house, the giggling girl upside down in her arms. "I'm Kirsten. This is Bindi. She's a slippery one."

"I see that." I give her a wooden smile and wish I were feeling more social. Kirsten seems nice enough. "I'm Beth." I wonder if I should apologize for still being in my pajamas. Then again, yoga pants count as real pants, and Kirsten probably doesn't notice anyway—her own children are running around in various states of undress. "Nice to meet you."

"Same! We're just moving in. You've got yourself some new neighbors." Kirsten sets Bindi on her feet and shoves her gently in the direction of the moving truck. "Go on, Bindi, go to Mom."

I look down the street and see the woman who was moving the sofa is waving and holding out her arms for the child. Kirsten watches the little girl retreat back down the sidewalk but doesn't make any move herself. She looks back at me, a glowing smile on her face. She's ready to make friends. I'm not. "That's Olivia, my wife."

"Ah. Gotcha. Well, welcome." I say it in a way that should be the universal way of saying, *"Great, good, now please go."*

"Thank you! And that's Olivia's brother. He's helping us move. Really, he's just in it for the case of Mich Golden I offered. And of course you know Bindi; she's got a couple of brothers running around here somewhere too. Dane and Ezra." She twists her ponytail into a top knot and stabs it with a pen I didn't know she had in her hand, expertly securing it. "You'll meet them soon enough. We're potty training Ezra, so he's doing the naked dance today. Bad idea to potty train a little one during a move." She gives an exaggerated eye roll.

"Ah. Yeah, you're probably right."

She keeps going. "Olivia starts her new job in a couple of days, so we need to get all this moved in quick." She blows a stray, sweaty strand of hair off her forehead. "I hate moving. Hate, hate, hate it!"

"Yeah."

There's an uncomfortable silence. If she has a ton of work to do, why doesn't she go do it? I wait. Then I start to feel like an ass for not holding up my end of the conversation. I can at least try to be friendly. "So, what's her new job?" I ask.

"Boston Scientific. Medical devices. She's a researcher."

"Cool. I've heard it's a great place to work."

"Oh, good." Kirsten says. "I'm a teacher, so I'll be looking for something for this fall, hopefully. Early childhood, preschool age."

"That's great."

"What do you do?" she asks.

"I'm a nurse."

"Awesome! Nurses are the best." She puts her hands on her hips, then looks at the box at my feet. She cranes her neck to see inside. "Cool stuff. Antiques?"

"Oh, just some junk from my mom's house. She, uh… doesn't need it anymore."

Kirsten takes a few steps forward and peers into the box uninvited. Then she reaches in and touches the Chanel bottle, making me flinch. "Oh, cool! This is *Chanel No. 5*. Are you selling this stuff?"

"Oh, I don't know yet. Maybe?" I pick up the box and set it on the landing next to me, away from her grip. This stuff is none of her damn business. God, she's got nerve.

"My aunt in South Carolina collects old perfume bottles. Let me know if you're selling it, I'll tell her."

"Okay. Thanks." My head starts to pound from the humidity, the lack of sleep, the brightness of midday, and the stress of meeting new neighbors. I raise my eyebrows at Kirsten as if to say, *"Well, I'm super busy, so you know…"*

"We're hoping there are a lot of kids in the neighborhood." Kirsten is not getting the hint. I wonder if Olivia and her brother are annoyed at Kirsten's tendency to talk too much and leave them with all the work. I look down the street, but both adults and all three children have disappeared. Maybe they've gone inside for lunch. "We're kind of 'free-range' parents. Kids have to get out, get dirty. Go exploring. You know? Do you have kids?"

I pause. I don't want to lead Kirsten on in thinking that my daughter will be a playmate for her children. Under other circumstances, she could be. But not my girl. "We have a daughter," I say. I leave it at that.

As if the magical grace of God himself came down to help me out of this awkward social situation, my phone starts to vibrate next to me. "Oh, and that's her now," I say. "I've been waiting for her call. Sorry, I have to take this."

"Eek! Kids with phones! Is she a teenager? Whooboy—can't wait for those days." I don't correct her. I just smile. "Well, I'll let you be. Talk to you soon!" She jogs off down the sidewalk. I look at the phone.

Then my heart sinks.

Bitty Babies Daycare.

It actually is a call about my daughter.

She has a fever.

Fell and broke her arm.

Got frustrated and punched some other little kid.

Swallowed a grape whole and choked.

She's dying.

Oh, my God, she's dead.

I couldn't save her. I'm a goddamn nurse who tosses her kid into daycare just to get some sleep, and then she dies.

I answer the call terrified, stumbling over my words. "Hello? Yes? This is Beth."

"Hi, Beth. It's Nadia. I'm over here at Bitty Babies with Sylvie. Is this a bad time?"

It's always a bad time to tell a mother her child is dead; I know that from being on the other side. "No, of course not." I try to keep my voice steady. My head pounds harder.

"Sorry to bother you. I could have just sent a text, but I had to share this with you." Her voice sounds shaky, emotional.

For a minute, my mind scrambles. Why would she text me that my child is dead? I take a deep breath. "Uh-huh. Okay." It's only then that I realize I'm missing another of Sylvie's appointments. I meant to sent my alarm. I should have been there.

Nadia continues. "When I got here today, I just watched Sylvie for a few minutes before I jumped in to her therapy. She was playing alone, which, of course, is pretty normal for her. Stacking blocks, like she likes to do. One of the other little girls was playing nearby and she left her toy on the floor. Sylvie picked it up and brought it to me." Nadia sounded practically in tears by now. "She held it out to me; she was asking for help playing with it. It was a little caterpillar flashlight. It had buttons for the lights and music to turn on and off. She knew I was there to help her! I showed her how it worked, and then she pushed the right buttons. She did it! It was amazing, Beth. We all gave her lots of hugs, lots of encouragement. She looked so proud of herself! You should have seen her face."

Yes. I should have seen it.

A flashlight. Like the one Eddie had given her. Buttons to turn on and off. Eddie had it right. Sylvie asked for help in her own way after Eddie showed her the same thing this past weekend.

Sylvie has never asked for help from anyone. She rarely asks for anything. All things considered, this is a huge milestone for my daughter. I need to be happy for my girl, not sorry for myself that I missed this important step or resentful that Eddie had it right with the flashlight.

I especially should not be angry that I'm having to get excited about something my daughter should have been doing as a baby years ago.

"Each kiddo is different, Beth." I hear Mom's voice in my head. *"Sylvie will catch up when she's ready. Let her go at her own pace."*

Thinking of Mom's words, spoken to me while she was dying in hospice, shreds my heart into pieces. I take a deep breath and feel it shake within me. "This is really great news, Nadia." I bring as much joy as I can into my voice, but I can hear the flatness in it.

"Oh my God, did I wake you, Beth?" Her voice changes, thick with apology. "I know you work nights sometimes; I didn't even think of that. I'm so sorry—"

"No, no, that's fine." Guilt takes over. "I was up. I'm just a little tired, but I'm fine. I'm so glad you called. Thank you, Nadia. I'll see you later."

I end the call and then stare at the phone. I don't know what to do next. I very nearly open a browser to Google this, to find out if Sylvie's actions are a step from which I can build, if there's still a chance to save her, and what we can do next.

But then, I don't.

I miss my girl. Just like I miss my mom, my sister.

Tears prick my eyes. I wish I could call Mom; she would know what to say, what to do. Mom always got it right. Even with twin girls pulling at her attention, she was able to give us each what we needed. Mom made every effort to spend time with Cara and me each separately when we were little. She'd put us into alternating swimming lessons, and while one of us was swimming, she'd take the other out for ice cream. It was our thing, and Cara and I each made our own memories of it without the other one fighting for her love.

Maple Nut ice cream. It was what Mom always ordered, every time. We'd sit in the cool air conditioning of the food court in the old mall that was torn down ten years ago. 33 Flavors. Just Mom and me. I remember counting to make sure they had that many. I wanted to try every flavor, but Mom always got Maple Nut.

I'd forgotten about those ice cream dates.

Now I'm hungry for Maple Nut.

Mom was always there for us. I'm sure there was plenty of fear in her life, especially after her and Dad's divorce, but she never would have thought to abandon her children. She always called us the Three Little Kittens. We were a tribe.

So, why does running away feel so right to me? It must come from someplace deeper.

I look down to the box, to the shot glass and the pink perfume bottle with the rose stopper. I turn the bottle upside down. A piece of tape is stuck on the bottom with tiny writing in pen: *Coney Island.*

This was the bottle from which Sylvie dumped that sand. Coney Island was famous for its beach. Grandma Vee was originally from New York City. Things are starting to make sense—this was very likely my grandmother's memento. But why a perfume bottle? If someone was going to save sand from a beach, wouldn't a Mason jar work just as well?

Something strange catches my eye at the bottom of the box. I move the shot glass aside to get a better look. It's a small watercolor illustration: a cat wearing a flowery bonnet, standing upright in a Scarlett O'Hara dress and carrying a purple basket full of baguettes. I pull it out of the box. It's a greeting card. I open it. A message is written inside in a very rigid and uniform script:

A blessed 18th birthday to you.
So happy to know such a tiny baby has
grown into such a wonderful young woman.
All the best,

M. Couney

Coney Island, New York

M. Couney. This was someone who knew Grandma Vee as a baby and kept in touch, at least until she turned eighteen. Could this have been from Vee's mother? Maybe she didn't abandon Grandma after all. Maybe she came back.

Maybe she wasn't what I thought she was.

Maybe that means I'm not either. Maybe I'm okay. Maybe I *am* a good mom.

I need to find out more about Vee's mother. Her real mother.

The sun is coming around the house, roasting the skin on my feet. I stand and go inside, leaving the box of Mom's stuff on the front step.

19

Charlie bobs up and down beside me in the restaurant's curved banquette. We may as well be going around and around on a carousel, with all of his see-sawing and back-and-forth-ing, talking to no one but himself.

"I see them."

He stands.

"No, I guess that's not them."

Sits again.

"Oh yes! Julian!"

Raises his hand in a wave.

"Ah, maybe not."

Drops his arm.

I try to get a word in. "Charlie, I—"

He cuts me off, standing again. He cranes his neck toward

the entrance. "The maître d'hotel doesn't even see us. I should go wait up front.

"Ach." He sits. "Maybe that would look too eager."

Every time he plops back down, I'm pushed up, ejected with a poof of air under the leatherette seat. Up. Down. Rises, falls. Always moving. I stay stationary, aside from the bump I get when he drops.

I'd like a sip of my seltzer, but I'm afraid with all of his ricocheting up and down, I'd time it just right so I'd only get a paper straw up my nose.

"Any minute," he says. "Oh, there they—ah, shit." He looks at me as if he'd forgotten I was even there. "Oh, crabapples. Sorry for my language, Ducky."

I wave away his apology. No need. Instead of sipping my seltzer, I stab the straw into the ice and watch my beau's reflection in the sparkling mirrors that line the walls of the restaurant. Just like a carousel. Up and down, round and round. Bad music and too-bright lighting.

A carousel. Like our first date a year ago. Charlie had grabbed a golden ring on only the third time around on those shiny black carousel horses. He presented it to me on one knee like a proposal. It was a cute act, at the time. We had a ball together all summer, drinking root beer, riding the Spinning Disk, and hamming it up for the midway photographer. We both loved Coney Island back then. Jiminy, that seems like a lifetime ago. So much has changed.

"Charlie," I lean over to him. "He'll see you when he gets here. You told the maître d' to bring them over, and he will. You have to trust him; that's his job." I touch his arm, try for a little flirting. "We can take a minute, you know? Just us. Come on over here and chin with me." He's not looking at me. I don't think he heard a word.

God damn. I sink my cheek further into my fist.

"They must be quite late," he mutters. "Wait, he sees us. Over here! Julian!" Charlie stands once more and waves his arm like a little boy at a parade. A couple is slicing through the diners like a hot knife: a man in a smart suit and dark mustache follows a woman in an elegant green silk gown with an actual train. They appear to be in their middle twenties, but their sophistication adds potency to their years.

I feel suddenly underdressed in my little blue frock—as sexy as I dared without upsetting Charlie. I glance down at my open décolletage; I was hoping it would be enough without being too much. I was hoping he'd steal a glance at some point in the night. I was hoping I'd see a little fire in his eyes, catch a tiny curve at his lip.

I had a lot of hopes for tonight.

A proposal from Charlie has become my biggest priority, and to get that, I have to play his game, whatever that is. Charlie's thick on appearances. Fine, I'll dress the part. Charlie wants to put on certain airs. Great, I'll toss my head and flick my gasper. At this point, I have to use every trick in my bag to snag him.

I straighten up in the banquette and smooth out my dress. I pine for Alice's fur to add a little elegance to my look but, unfortunately, I'd stuffed it away in the coat check near the door like I was told.

"Charles. Splendid." Julian reaches out to shake Charlie's hand. Then he swings his hand to the woman as if he is presenting tonight's desert. Which, maybe he is. "This is Mrs. Shaw. Darling, this is Charles Pritchard."

"Please. Mona. Lovely to meet you." The woman rests her hand in Charlie's. Then she looks at me. "You must be Mrs. Pritchard?"

"Oh, no." Charlie jumps in a bit too fast, and Mona looks taken aback. "This is Josephine Westley."

I frown for only a second. I'm only me. Nothing to him. Not his *"his."* But anyway, I rise to my feet and flash a smile. That's my role tonight, and I better play my part well. "Charmed. Please, call me Jo—"

"Josephine," Charlie says, cutting me off. He prefers I use my full name with his work acquaintances, a fact I generally prefer to forget. Charlie spitting out "Josephine" sits in my craw in stark contrast to Sergei's whispering "Josephine" in his Russian-tinged purr. I can't help but register the difference.

And now I'm torching for Sergei again. Cad.

I pull a big smile on my face as I pass my greetings to the couple and try to discard any thought of that man.

Charlie lifts his iced tea in a salute to Julian as he and his wife take their seats—Mona next to me and the men on the outsides of the curved banquette. When Charlie sits, he pulls his bow tie, adjusting it. It's his tell. He's nervous. I catch his eye for half a moment and try to give him a wink and a smile, but his look doesn't linger. I silently forgive him for the "Josephine" thing. Julian is a new potential client at Charlie's financial gig on Wall Street, and snagging him could move Charlie up the ranks quickly at his firm.

Good for us all.

"No wife yet, Charles? What's the hold up?" Julian orders an iced tea of his own with only a finger and a nod to the waiter. He again waves his hand to his wife, who gives a one-word answer of "cognac."

"I'm sorry, Madame, but cognac is prohibited by law."

"Do what you can."

The waiter nods and backs away.

"Just not ready for the handcuffs yet, see?" Charlie says, putting on his best schmoozing voice. "Besides, it wouldn't be fair to Josephine, what with all of the long hours I'm spending working on my clients' accounts." Charlie's fingers go to his bow tie again.

"All work and no play, my good man," Julian says. He pats Mona's hand on the table. "You gotta move fast, before the good ones get away."

Mona rolls her eyes, but I can tell she's playful about it. "Oh, please. I'm no good, and you know it." She looks at me. "Are you one of the good ones, dear?" She smiles wickedly and winks. "Or one of the naughty?" I nearly spit my seltzer through my nose, and Mona giggles. "Oh, I kid, honey. It's all static." She hands me a napkin as Charlie shoots me a severe look.

Once I regain my composure, I can't help but laugh. Mona is so comfortable to be near, and she and Julian have a rapport that feels alive.

This was us, not so long ago. Wasn't it? Wasn't Charlie just as much fun to be with? Or is that something I've always just hoped for?

Mona continues, "Tell me, Jo—you did say you prefer Jo, is that right? Tell me, what is it that you do?"

"You're not one of those flapper girls, are you?" Julian offers with a wink of his own.

"Good God no," Charlie says, tilting his iced tea to his mouth.

I take another sip of my seltzer and wonder if any of them will let me answer for myself. I see that Mona is watching me, ignoring the men, waiting for my reply. I have to appreciate that. I relax my shoulders. "Jo is fine." I look at Charlie. He looks away. "And I wouldn't feature myself a flapper. I'm usually home in bed by nine in the evening. I'm not at all naughty." I try to keep my cheeks from burning. *Not at all naughty.* Though, ten days ago my illegitimate children were born in secret. I still haven't seen them. I haven't been any kind of mother to them. I straighten myself out; I have to keep up the bluff. "Though, I do love jazz."

"Oh honey, who doesn't? The music in this place is positively stifling." Mona leans into me like we're old friends. I try to avoid her question of what I do since I don't know myself, but she doesn't let me. "Are you an artist?"

I tilt my head, intrigued. "What makes you say that?"

She shrugs. "I always see artists in those jazz clubs, and I—"

"When are you in jazz clubs, kitten?" Julian says with a big grin and a lot of sarcasm as if he doesn't want to admit he often tags along with her.

She waves him off. Then she takes my hand, squeezes it lightly in her own gloved hand, and turns my fingertips up. "I noticed the color at your fingertips. Thought maybe it was paint, that you'd been working on your masterpiece."

I look at my fingers. I'd been crushing lilies at home before Charlie came to get me, and the pollen had gotten all over my hands, staining my skin orange.

She's right. I was working on my masterpiece. Something for the pink cut-glass bottle. Lilies and ginger and a hint of lemon peel that I scraped my knuckle trying to zest. I look up into her striking blue eyes, and for a minute I consider telling her my fragrance dreams. I consider telling her all of my dreams, about my interest chemistry and my dear sweet baby girls tucked

173

away at an amusement park. About my affair with my mother's lover and my own lack of affair with my own beau. How every memory I have becomes a scent, how I see things in top notes of lemon and base notes of leather. About how Sergei taught me all of this, opening up my world and for the first time having it all make sense.

I straighten my back, look at Charlie. His expression is stoic. His eyes tear a hole right through me. I know he's silently telling me to shut my trap, to be the demure little thing he needs me to be. A fancy atomizer for his own important bouquet.

Still staring at my stained fingers, I open my mouth, not sure of what will come out. "Actually, I—"

"Josephine won't be working at much of anything, once we are married," Charlie says. He passes a cigarette to me with a look of warning. I take it. "Except tending to the children, of course, when the time is right." He smiles, his drink poised before his lips.

"Well now," Julian leans back into the banquette, a cold gasper poised, waiting between his fingers. "You won't even allow your girl a hobby, Charles?"

"Certainly." Charlie flicks his lighter and leans forward to light Julian's cigarette. A cloud of smoke billows between them. I nudge Charlie with my elbow and he fires his lighter for me, too. "But the notion these women get lately that they can take over the workforce…" Charlie chuckles, slides the lighter back into his breast pocket, and shakes his head. "Just the other day, Josephine asked me what I thought of her taking chemistry classes. Can you imagine?" He looks at me and lifts his drink in a toast to my uselessness. "Not my girl, that's for sure."

I see Julian's face turn stony, and Mona, who is still holding my hand, goes rigid. I open my mouth to defend myself, to remind

Charlie of Madame Curie's Nobel Prizes in both Chemistry and Physics, but I quickly change my mind. The last thing he needs is me, his dame, embarrassing him in front of his wealthy clients. "Oh," I laugh, "It's nothing, really. Just a lark."

"Girls, pretending they can think like men." Charlie smiles at me and pats my leg. "Ol' Josephine here is just fine sticking to being the beauty she is."

The silence stays thick. Mona mumbles, "Indeed."

Julian clears his throat. I hear the shuffling of feet under the table. Charlie reaches up and pulls on his bow tie.

The quiet is broken when the waiter brings over Julian's iced tea and sets a small rocks glass filled with brown liquid in front of Mona. "Madame, a small taste of our house-brewed cola. Many say it competes with Coca-Cola. I hope you enjoy."

"Oh, thank God." Mona brings the glass to her nose and smiles. I can easily smell the cognac from where I sit.

"A few more minutes," Charlie tosses off to the waiter, who wrinkles his nose as he nods briefly and walks away. Julian bristles further, his face hardened into a chiseled mask. Beads of sweat bloom across my forehead. I know Charlie is sometimes awkward in social settings, but jeez—he's sinking his own nickels here.

Not sure of what else to say, I watch Julian, our reason for the evening. He's looking around the room, possibly searching for a way out. Mona doesn't seem quite as offended, but then, she's only along as decoration—like me. She forces a smile and takes another sip of her drink. "Chemistry, dear?" she says, swirling her glass before setting it down on a cocktail napkin. "Is that what interests you?"

She won't let it go; she's one of those kinds of girls—won't rest until she gets what she wants. Like Hazel. I wish I could know her better without the shroud of Charlie's business dealings and outdated beliefs clouding over us.

"Oh, I don't know." I blow it off, trying to be sweet and lovely and charming like Charlie wants. But Mona's eyes drill mine. She's looking for more. I recognize the tilt of a question on her face, and I realize something: she's looking for a reason to respect me. Suddenly, desperately, I want to give her one. "To be honest…" I glance at Charlie. He's watching me. I blow the smoke out of my mouth in a thin line toward the ceiling, wiggle my stained fingertips in the air, and take a chance. "Lilies. The pollen stains like crazy, everything it touches. Makes a real fine mess." I look at each of them; Julian and Charlie both arch an eyebrow, likely for very different reasons. I shrug. "I like to mix scents."

"Like, perfume?" Mona sits up, her voice rising in interest.

"Sure." I glance at Charlie, careful to avoid the machine gun stare he has pointed at me. "Just a hobby." I shrug, grasping for the words that Charlie would want me to say. "Something I enjoy jingling with while my beau is out doing the important work around town."

"Good for you, Jo," Julian finally speaks, and his face has turned pliable again. "That sounds plenty interesting. Perfume. My, my." He leans back into the banquette. "Sometimes a hobby can turn into a booming career, especially if it's something that holds your passion. You just never know." He pulls the cigarette out of his mouth and taps the ashes off the end. "We may have the next Elizabeth Arden in our midst. I say, bravo."

"Well, now, I don't know about that." Charlie says, still with a chuckle in his voice. He tugs his bow tie.

"Well Charles, I, for one, am thrilled about the women

of today. Independent, headstrong…" Julian drags hard on his gasper then points it at his wife. "See? I married my Mona, didn't I? When I met her, she was managing a pool of secretaries over at Farkley and Thomas. She coulda been running the whole firm, with her head for business." He looks at Charlie. "An educated dame isn't such a bad thing, old man."

"A secretary is one thing, certainly," Charlie says, his tone still telling me he's irritated. "But the sciences…" He stops and shakes his head in his cloud of smoke.

"So, is your girl any good at this hobby of hers, Charles?" Julian winks in my direction. "Will her fragrances grace the wrists of the finest starlets in town?"

"She smells wonderful from where I'm sitting." Mona says. "What is that?" She turns her eyes heavenward as she leans toward me. I fidget. I don't want to look at Charlie, but I also want to keep an eye on him. The table seems to be ganging up on him, and that never bodes well for Charlie's temper. "Oh, I smell… grapefruit? And maybe, orchid? But something else too. Spice, maybe." She leans back and her dark eyelashes flutter. "Reminds me of Havana in April. Lovely."

Charlie watches me. I keep my face stable, serene. Humble. I try to tell him silently with my eyes that I'm only attempting to save his business deal, save him from himself. Just like he was telling me silently to keep quiet. I don't know if we actually have that kind of connection, or if I'm just downright perceptive of him.

His eyes are like switchblades. He's angry. The last thing we need is for him to pop right now.

"Like I said, it's nothing." I fold my hands in my lap and keep my eyes down. "I don't bother Charlie with silly things like this. It's just something to putter away the time."

There's another moment of uncomfortable quiet. Then Charlie readjusts himself in the banquette and speaks. "Her scents are wonderful. Jo is such a delight, in every single way." He smiles. It looks sincere, though I know it's horsefeathers.

He doesn't know my scents. Never smelled them. Ever. At all. Charlie can't smell a thing.

He's told me that; it was one of our first "getting to know you" conversations. Occasionally he'll notice the sharp smells of burnt toast or a backed-up sewer, but the diminutive odors that surround us daily evade him. He's never smelled a rose, or griddled flapjacks, or the piercing sweat of a girl in a fur coat on a hot summer evening. I used to have a little fun with it and hide a stick of Wrigley's in his pocket to see if he'd notice, but he never did.

At least now he's picked up my message from across the table, and his business mind is sharp enough to play along. "Quite a talent, my girl. I'm lucky to have her. In fact…" He leans back and extracts a small box from his jacket pocket. He places it on the table between us but keeps his hand on it.

No. This can't be.

He wouldn't propose marriage to me during a business dinner with his clients. He wouldn't. I look up at Mona, and beyond the shock on her face, I see pity in her eyes. She's thinking the same thing. What a place for a proposal.

I hang back for a moment, unable to move, but I don't want to get Charlie even more riled up by my reaction. I smile and reach for the box.

Charlie catches my hand and holds it gently. He doesn't let me near the gift. The box stays on the table between his iced tea and my sweating seltzer.

20

Beth

The hallways of the nursing home smell like cold cream. I turn the corner from the blue hall with the framed pseudo-Monet paintings to the green hall with the pseudo-Renoir paintings and then make my way to the community room just past the nurse's station. I search the sea of elderly for my grandmother. Bookcases line the far wall, but I quickly look away—books are just stuffed here and there on the shelves, not according to size or color. It's distressing. I tell myself there must be some alphabetical sense to it.

I find Grandma Vee sitting in a wheelchair, aimed toward the television with three other gray-haired ladies. One of them is snoring loudly.

"Grandma?"

She looks up at me, and her eyes spark in recognition. For a moment, I have hope. "Oh, Andie, dear. You came."

179

My stomach falls. "No, not Andrea, Grandma. Beth. Andrea's daughter." I take her hand. "Do you remember me?"

She smiles and shakes her head. She looks back at the TV. It looks like *The Fugitive*, the one that came out when I was in high school. I wait. Sometimes she'll give it another try. After a minute or two she looks back at me. "Oh, honey. Something to drink, please."

"Of course, Grandma, I'll get you some water."

"Cider, honey. Apple cider. Please."

"Sure, Grandma." I try the same technique with her that I do with Sylvie—if I keep calling her "Grandma," maybe she'll remember that's who she is. I get up, get a little plastic cup of cider from the cafeteria, and come back. I hand it to her, wrapping her fingers around it so she doesn't drop it.

She holds the cup in her trembling hands. I can see the sleeve on her sweatshirt is twisted so I fix it for her, straighten it out, smooth it. She gives me a little smile. "That poor man." She motions to the TV. "He's in such trouble. He didn't kill his wife. Oh, I hope he doesn't get sent back to jail." She looks at me, real worry in her eyes. "They were going to give him the death penalty, but he didn't do it. I know he didn't. He's a doctor, you know. A very good man."

"Grandma, it's just a movie."

"Mmmm." She's engrossed in the TV, not hearing me. "You know, he's an archaeologist too. A very busy man. But he's so good to me." She looks at me and clamps her hand onto my arm. "We have to help him, dear. Can you call that gentleman there?" She points to Tommy Lee Jones on the TV. "He's with the FBI. Tell him that my husband didn't kill anyone. They'll listen to you." Her voice rises and she's almost yelling. The snoring woman shifts in her sleep.

I coo quietly into her ear to calm her, like I would with Sylvie. "It's okay, Grandma. It's not real. Just a story. That man is safe." Grandma has come to believe that Harrison Ford is her husband. While, sure, many of us have had that fantasy, she actually believes it. That's what dementia has done to her. I lose what little hope I have of getting any useful information out of her today. Maybe if I can get her mind distracted from Han Solo, she'll pay attention enough to spark something real in her memory. Sometimes, for her, seventy years ago is clear as day, while yesterday's events are long forgotten.

She pushes away from me a bit, wary. She slits her eyes. "Why are you calling me Grandma? Who are you?"

"Grandma, I'm Beth. Do you remember me? Andrea's daughter. I'm your granddaughter." Her eyes are suspicious, but she doesn't argue. "Grandma Vee, can you come with me, back to your room? I'd like to visit with you. Maybe we can look at some pictures together."

Her face brightens. "Are you a nurse?"

I don't want to confuse her further, so I just smile. I'm dressed in real clothes today instead of scrubs—capri pants and a sleeveless top. I'll change later before my shift. "I'm Beth, your granddaughter. Andrea's daughter. I've come for a visit."

She looks around. "You didn't bring those boys, did you?"

"Boys?" I think for a minute. She's confusing me with Cara. It reminds me of high school, when teachers would make the same mistake. "That's my twin sister, Grandma. Cara. She has three boys, your great-grandsons."

"Well, I don't like them one bit. They're loud. They always turn the channel to some Japanese cartoon that hurts my eyes."

"Yeah, well. Kids can be like that, I suppose."

181

She sips her cider, the boys already forgotten. I pat her hand and glance at the TV. A commercial. If I can get her away before the movie starts again, I have a chance. "Come with me, Grandma Vee. Let's go somewhere quiet and talk."

I wheel her down the hall to her room. She pulls herself out of the wheelchair and plops down into a wing-back chair by the window. I hold my arms out to help, but she bats me away. Next to her is a dresser covered with an ivory-colored doily. An Entertainment Weekly from earlier this year is propped up between a glass bud vase and a dying African Violet plant. Harrison Ford and Ryan Gosling are on the cover of the magazine, but the lower half of Harrison's face is worn away, the bottom of the page wrinkled and bubbled. Grandma holds her cup of cider to his face and pours a few drops onto the magazine. "He gets so thirsty. You know, I keep telling these nurses to bring him a meal, but I don't think any of them ever do. Poor man must be so hungry."

I don't say anything for fear of choking up. The state of her mind is heartbreaking. I know the nurses try to humor the patients' delusions as much as they can as long as they're not hurting anyone. Some patients get downright violent when you try to tell them their fantasies aren't real. Grandma's marriage to Indiana Jones has been deemed harmless by the staff.

"What's your name, dear?" Grandma turns to me, listing a bit to the side.

"Beth."

"Beth," she repeats, almost as a whisper. She's looking at her "husband" on the magazine cover. I move closer to the window, so when she looks at me, the picture isn't in her line of sight.

"Grandma, I have something of yours. Do you remember

182

this?" I reach into my purse and fish past a handful of tiny paper scraps from Sylvie. I pull out her USO card.

She takes it and smiles. "Yes, of course. This was around the time I met my first husband."

Her only husband. I smile encouragingly. She remembers something. It's a start. "Tell me more," I say.

She stares at the identification card. Then she launches into singing "The Boogie Woogie Bugle Boy" loudly. I let her sing— she looks happy. When she finishes, she laughs. "Oh, he was a good man, my husband. He was president once, you know. Such a brave man. Nearly died in a plane crash."

My smile falls. Harrison Ford again—she's thinking of *Air Force One*. She's even more confused than the last time I saw her. I resign myself to just spend my visit chatting with her. Her mind is far too gone to offer any glimpse into the real past.

I lift my bag to hang it on the back of my chair, and Vee lets out a little gasp. She leans forward, squinting at my purse. Her face turns sour. "You're a thief!"

"What?"

"That's mine." She points at the strap of my purse where Mom's rose pin is attached. "It's my pin. It's been gone for years. Have you had it this whole time? You took it!"

She recognizes it. I smile. "I found it for you, Grandma. Would you like it back?"

She leans back in her chair. "Yes, please."

I take it off and give it to her. She holds it between her fingers, admiring it. "Would you like to wear it?" I ask. She nods, so I pin it to her shirt. "It's beautiful."

Her fingers rest on it, and she seems at ease. "Oh, yes. I thought it was gone for good. Where was it?" she asks.

"Andrea had it. Your daughter, my mother. I found it after…" I stop and smile around the painful memory of the night my mom died. "Did you give it to your daughter?"

"I don't know. She probably stole it from me."

I see her face crinkle again in distress so I try to turn the course of our conversation. "You must love roses, is that right?"

She looks bewildered. "Not particularly."

"Oh," I frown.

She flitters her hand as if brushing the thought away. "In fact, I don't like most flowers. Too strong, they smell up the whole room. Same with perfume. That one nurse always wears that horrible stuff. I've told her to stop it, but she still stinks. Too sweet." She waves a hand in front of her nose.

I know the nursing home, much like the hospital, has a strict "no-fragrance" policy. "I can talk to someone about that, if you'd like."

"I would. Thank you." She relaxes.

"Tell me more about that pin, Grandma. Who gave it to you? Do you know?"

"Oh my." She shakes her head, fingering the rose. "I don't remember. Probably my mother. Maybe one of her friends she'd have over for those silly games with the tiles."

I nod. Great-grandma Jane. "Do you remember this at all? Was it yours also?" I pull the pink perfume bottle out of my purse and hold it in front of her, hoping to go three-for-three.

Her face twists. "Oh, no. I don't like perfume. In fact, one nurse here is always wearing it. Smells terrible—"

I cut her off before she tells me the whole thing again. "Well, this one is empty. It had some kind of sand in it. Do you remember it at all? Is it yours?"

Vee studies it. "No." She adjusts herself in the chair and sips her cider before offering Harrison another drink. "No, no. I've never seen that before."

"Oh." I slip it back into my bag. I had hoped that by warming her up with these trinkets of the past, she'd be better suited to remember what I came to ask her about. So far, it's not going well.

She leans back into her chair and starts singing again, this time quieter, with less chutzpah. Almost sadly. I don't recognize the song.

> *Ida, sweet as apple cider*
> *Sweeter than all I know*
> *Come out in the silv'ry moonlight*
> *Of love we'll whisper, so soft and low...*

I let her finish, then I reach out and take her hand. "Grandma," I whisper. She looks confused. "Grandma, do you remember anything about your mother?"

"Oh, yes, of course. She was a nurse. She cared for babies."

I shake my head. "Not great-grandma Jane."

"You asked about my mother. What other mother do I have?"

"Your real mother."

"Dear," she looks at me questioningly, and I know she's already forgotten my name. "I only had one mother. Her name was Jane." She laughs some more. "In fact, Jane was a nurse at a circus." She knits her brow. "How that worked, I haven't the slightest idea. Why would there be babies at a circus?"

"They kept premature babies in incubators—heating machines—to keep them alive. Hospitals didn't want the machines, so they set them up as sideshows at carnivals. That's where your mother worked, at Coney Island. That's where she found you."

"Found me?"

"Grandma, you were adopted. Do you know anything about the woman who gave birth to you? Who gave you up?"

Her face falls. "My goodness." She looks out the window and stays that way for a long time.

I hand her the card with the bizarre cat on the front. "Is this yours?"

She looks at it, and at first her expression is baffled. She opens the card and reads the writing inside, and expression turns warm. "Oh, my. Where did you find this?"

I know the answer doesn't matter, so I press her further. "Who was M. Couney? Was that…" I swallow hard. "Was that your mother?"

She frowns. "Oh, no, honey. Martin Couney was the doctor my mother worked for. My mother's name was Jane."

My shoulders sag.

"Mother was a beautiful woman," she continues. "She was so good with children." Grandma Vee looks at me and her voice softens. "She was good to me. Beautiful blond hair, soft as a cloud. Golly, I miss her."

This is real. She's remembering real things. It's a start. I squeeze her hand. "She was a good woman, and beautiful. What else do you remember?"

She looks confused for a minute, but then her face blanches white. "Oh, my God. Is Mama alright? The car… Did Papa get the car fixed?" I see tears in her eyes. "He said it was an accident, and it was very bad. Honey, do you know anything? Where did they take Mama?"

I've gone too far. She's remembering, but she's remembering the pain. Her mother, Great-grandma Jane, died in a car crash when Vee was a teenager. Shortly after, Vee and her father moved to the Midwest.

"It's okay, Grandma." I stroke her hand. "It was a long, long time ago. You don't have to remember. Just take a deep breath. You're not alone."

Still, she's agitated. "Mama never said much about her, just that she'd left me. And she was sad. A very, very sad woman. But she always had a beautiful smell surrounding her."

"Who?" I ask, straightening. I work to calm my voice. "Your birth mother?"

She shrugs and stares into space.

I'm losing her. I'm so close, but it's not worth upsetting her further. It is, after all, my own selfish, macabre fascination that brought me here. I only wanted to know if there was anything redeeming about the woman who'd left my grandmother for dead. Maybe she had good reason. Maybe she could be forgiven. Maybe I could be too.

"It's okay, Grandma. I smile, but I'm disappointed. Looks like any information I could have gleamed from Grandma Vee died with Great-grandma Jane. "Did your father tell you anything about her?"

She chuckles. "Oh, honey. Papa wasn't like that. Quiet man." She rubs her forehead then turns to smile at her magazine. Her eye catches a baseball-sized mylar balloon that sits in the bud vase. She reaches for it, pulling herself out of the chair as she does. She nearly tips her cider all over Harrison's magazine, but I grab it before it falls. "Would you mind, please don't bring those boys around anymore. They're so loud."

I look at the pink mylar in her hands. *Happy Mother's Day.* Cara remembered to visit Grandma Vee and probably brought her that bud vase with a flower that was promptly thrown in the trash, but at least she came to celebrate Grandma on Mother's Day. Where was I?

Working. I was working.

"Those are Cara's boys," I say. "Have they come to see you recently?"

"Oh, yes." She says it in a distracted way that tells me she has no idea. She meets my eye. "And who is Cara?"

"My sister. Your granddaughter."

"Granddaughter." She spins the balloon around between her fingers. "Cara is your sister? She's a nice girl." She leans forward. This time she's the one who takes my hand. "I hope you two are close. I always wanted a sister." She sighs and presses her other hand to her chest. "Seems like I always had a big hole in my heart where a sister should have been."

I don't say anything. Grandma didn't have any siblings. My eyes sting. I'm lucky that I do.

"Are you Andie's daughter?"

"Yes, Grandma."

"Where is Andie? Why doesn't she come see me anymore?"

I pause. "Andrea's dead, Grandma." I say it quietly. "She was sick for a long time. She died last Christmas. She always wanted to come and see you, but it was hard for her to get around. She missed you so much."

"Oh." Grandma keeps staring at the balloon. I wonder how much of this, if any, is registering with her. "You're Andie's daughter?"

"That's right."

"Do you have any children?"

"I have a daughter," I say, dropping my eyes.

I feel her hand on mine. "What's wrong with her?"

"What?" I look up, suddenly terrified that she can see right through me.

"Why didn't you bring her to see me?"

"Oh." I take a deep breath to steady myself. "She's little. She's almost three. Children that small are too fidgety and impatient." I pat her knee. "I wanted to be able to have a nice visit with you."

"Bring her next time, dear."

"I will, Grandma." I lean over and give her a hug, hoping the movement will stop the tears from forming in my eyes. I gather my purse. "Grandma, I'll see you soon, okay?"

"That's fine, honey."

I make my way down the orange hallway to the main doors. I dig for my keys in my purse as I push open the glass door. There's a flurry of activity as the second set of doors in front of me opens to a lot of movement and noise.

I look up, but don't register anything until I hear a familiar boy's voice. "Aunt Beth?"

21

SEPTEMBER, 1927

Mona and Julian fidget in the banquette. Mona stares at the little box on the table, while Julian averts his eyes and looks around the restaurant. Charlie pulls at his bow tie, his lip curled into something that looks more like a snarl than a smile.

"May I take your orders?" The waiter appears again at Julian's elbow.

No one answers.

"Ah," the waiter says. "I'll return in a moment." He disappears as quickly as he'd arrived.

I stare at the box. I taste empty bile in my throat, which is just another reminder that we haven't eaten yet. I don't think I could now, anyway.

"Jo was gone for a good part of the summer, visiting her auntie up the coast," Charlie says. His smile turns easy and inviting. I'm not so sure. "I missed my gal." He's looking at me, but I can't quite read him. Is he upset with me? Overwhelmed by the importance of the moment? Annoyed that I decided to leave the city for the summer without getting his approval first? "Sure is nice to have you back home now, though, Ducky." He squeezes my hand, just a bit too hard. "And just in time to celebrate your birthday."

He remembered. I hear a gasp catch in Mona's throat.

"September third," he says, smiling. "I was planning to surprise you up there in New Haven, but I'm happy you decided to come back early instead."

"She must have missed you, Charles," Julian says. "Gotta say, it's the best feeling in the world, knowing there's a dame out there pining for you." He catches Mona's eye. She looks away.

A shiver tingles through my spine and nearly shakes the chilly smile right off my noodle. If I hadn't given birth early, he would have seen me looking like I'd swallowed a basketball. I suppose there's a silver lining to all of this after all. "Well, that woulda been swell, Charlie. But here I am now."

"It's your birthday?" Mona lifts her drink. "Cheers to you!" Though she's trying for cheerful, she sounds ruffled.

"Cheers, indeed. This is a celebration!" Julian tips his iced tea, finally a wide, relaxed smile on his lips. "You can't be a day over eighteen, Jo."

"Twenty."

"Ah. Welcome to the decade. My girl Mona here matches the year." He puts his arm around her shoulder. "Twenty-seven in '27."

"Julian. Dear. You never talk about a woman's age." Mona's voice drops. I see a bit of pink sidle up inter her cheeks.

Julian lowers his eyes, pats her knee. "Sorry, kitten."

If it had been awkward before, we've managed now to take it to a full-on flop. I search for something to say that won't offend anyone, but that seems impossible at this point. "I can only hope to look as good as you do at twenty-seven, Mona," I say. Her smile back at me is crisp, and I doubt those words were the right ones.

"Charles," Julian says, "we could have met for dinner on a different evening. This day should be all about your gal." He glances at the little gift, sitting like a grenade on the table between us.

"Oh, no. Josephine doesn't mind." Charlie says.

My cheeks hurt from the smile I push up onto them. I wonder if my misplaced dimple, the one I inherited from Mama, is flaunting itself. I wonder if it comes out even when my smile isn't real. I wonder, for just a moment, if my own children will have the same wayward dents in their cheeks.

Oh.

"So…you were gone for the summer, Jo?" Julian says. We all look up, anxious to talk about something—anything—else. "Do anything fun?"

All eyes are on me. I try to relax my anxiety into a calm flirt. "Sat outside, enjoyed the air," I say. "So much cooler in Connecticut. Did a little needlework. My Uncle Barlow taught me to play Mahjong."

Charlie reaches the bottom of his iced tea, gives a final suck on the straw, and pushes it aside. The waiter sweeps by and takes it, then disappears again. He never did return to take our order; he must have noticed that none of us have lifted our menu.

More silence between us. Mona takes a sip of her drink. Julian fiddles with his cigarette. Charlie seems unaware of his ineptitude at socializing. If he wants to be good at hob-knobbing with the business crowd, he needs a lot more practice. And probably a girl with a better gift of gab than myself. Or one with fewer secrets to keep quiet.

"My sister was sent off to our auntie's one summer, quite a while back," Julian says to split the lull. "Vermont, I think. It was years ago."

"Oh Jules, that was a whole different situation," Mona says. She leans in conspiratorially. "She'd found herself in a bit of trouble with her beau, if you know what I mean."

"Poor girl. Spinster now." Julian shakes his head as he pops another cigarette between his lips. Charlie's quick with the lighter, if not the conversation.

I look down at my seltzer and watch the bubbles rise against the glass.

Poor girl.

There's another pause. I look up, and all eyes are on me. I feel my forehead tingle. I schlep my bobbed hair behind my ear to give my fingers a cause. "I suppose she was a flapper?" I give a wry smile.

"Ha! That's a girl." Julian says with a laugh. He picks up his menu, but then sets it down again and looks at Mona. "My dear, I think we should leave these two kids to their dinner, to celebrate Jo's birthday properly." He taps his cigarette against the ashtray. "Charles, lovely of you to host us. Call me on Monday; we can discuss the details of my accounts."

"Oh, you don't have to go—"

Julian holds up his hand. "No, no, I insist. It's all jake, Charles. We'll talk next week."

He stands up and holds his hand out to Mona. Before she slides out of the banquette, she gives me a friendly squeeze on my arm. "Happy birthday, dear. Hope to see you again soon." She stands, and her expression turns thoughtful. "Do keep us in the loop about your perfumes. I'd love to be able to say, 'I knew you when.'" She tickles her fingers in the air as a wave, then the couple turns and sashays toward the front door.

Charlie watches them go over the top of his menu.

"Well, that was nice of them," I say after a moment.

Charlie looks at me. Something in his expression jabs me in my stomach. He folds his menu like Julian did, only slower, and sets it down on the table. I follow his lead and do the same. Guess we're not eating just yet. Good. My stomach's in knots.

I wait, but he doesn't speak. After a bit of silence, I say something. "He said he would call. That's good news, right? Sounds like he wants you to handle his accounts?"

"I suppose so," Charlie says. He takes a deep drag on his gasper, lets it out, then smashes the butt into the ashtray. "Yes. Sounds like good news. I suppose I have you to thank. I'm not much good at socializing. But they both seemed to like you and all your little notions."

I'm not sure if it's a compliment, but I thank him anyway, feeling like a rube.

He leans over and takes my hand. It's sweet. He strokes my fingers. I let myself relax a bit. Maybe we can salvage the evening. Maybe he's even up for a little romance.

"I want to make one thing clear, though." He squeezes my fingers. I flinch. He keeps squeezing. I feel the blood pulse in them and watch my fingertips turn nearly purple.

"Charlie!"

He doesn't let go. His hands shake from the pressure and the rage. He looks up and slices me with his eyes. Finally, he clears his throat threateningly. "You are to never do that again. Do you understand?"

"Let go." It comes out as barely a whisper.

"Do you hear me, Josephine?"

I manage to wriggle my hand away from him. I'm rooted to my seat; even if I were to run away, where would I go? My eyes drop to my warming seltzer. I nod as I rub the circulation back into my fingers, though I'm not exactly sure what it was that I did.

"You are only here as my charming date, not to impress our guests with your piss-brained ideas of chemistry or silly perfumes or whatnot." He smiles but only with his lips. His eyes stay narrowed, almost sad. "Women have no place in the working world. I don't care what people like the Shaws say. I won't sacrifice my morals for a fickle client."

I don't say anything, but he's watching me. He's waiting for me to answer, to agree. I nod again, but it's not enough for him. "Fine," I say. It comes out a bit sharper than I anticipated.

I'm quiet while he sips the new iced tea our waiter had covertly placed in front of him without either of us noticing. "Jo," he says, leaning back and adjusting his blazer, "I know someday, with maybe a little training, you know, you'll make a good wife."

My eyes drop again to the little box that sits untouched. This is a hell of a proposal.

"Gee thanks, Charlie." I stir the melting ice in my seltzer.

"And if we have children, you'd probably be a good mother too."

That tiny word slices me right down the middle.

"*If*, Charlie?" I strain to keep my voice level. "You don't want kids?"

He shrugs. "Don't know. Don't especially care for them. Maybe, maybe not."

I flip open my pocketbook to search for another cigarette. "Well, it can't always be helped. I mean, babies come—"

"Oh, there are ways around it." He narrows his eyes. "You're a modern, independent woman, aren't you? I'm sure you know about these things."

I watch the sneer slide across his face and decide to stay silent; that seems the safest. Though, I know from my experience this past year or so that his favored method for preventing pregnancy is likely avoiding any of the more intimate marital relations. In other words, no whoopie with the wifey.

I bite my lip. I know who he was watching as our guests left the restaurant, and it wasn't Mona's shapely backside.

"Speaking of," he causally spanks the tablecloth with his menu. "Funny what Julian said about his sister."

"I don't suppose there's much funny about that."

"No. You're right. Damn shame," he says.

"Sure is." Mona's scent of *Tabac Blond* lingers next to me. It's the same fragrance Hazel wears. I tap my finger on the table next to the small box that still sits between us, the sweat from my seltzer dampening the tablecloth and threatening the gift. "So are you going to let me open my birthday present, or—"

"You know," he laughs to himself like he just thought of the funniest joke ever, "if I didn't know better, I'd think you were in trouble yourself, and that's why you left the way you did. But that couldn't be. We both know that, right?" He winks, but his tone makes me shift on the banquette. The leather seems suddenly hard against my rear. "I've been nothing but honorable with you, haven't I?"

He stares at me. He actually wants me to answer.

He thinks I'm a whore.

Which, I suppose I am.

"Just what are you getting at, Charlie?" I pine for another gasper, but didn't come across any more in my pocketbook. I will myself to not drop eye contact with Charlie.

"Well, I'd hate to be one of those fellas whose dame was going around behind his back."

My body recoils, which I realize is a terrible mistake. I consider for a moment telling some story of us getting drunk and he doesn't remember the deed, but I know that would be a jump. Charlie's no sucker. I try to turn my body to look like I'm furious he'd even suggest such a thing. Which, I guess I am. Furious I could get caught. "You think I'm that kind of girl?" I let the anger flow through my voice. "Jeez, Charlie, I can't get away for the summer? The city is too damn hot." I reach my fingers for my glass, nearly dumping it all over the table. I notice a darkened drop of cognac coating the bottom of Mona's glass. I wish I could make a move for her leftovers.

"You've never had a problem with the heat before, Jo. It all just seems so suspicious."

I take a drink of my seltzer. I feel the sparkle of bubbles in my mouth melting against my tongue like the pierce of a thousand pins.

I have to somehow turn this back on him. I give him a stern look. I have to show him I won't take his accusations, no matter how true they might be. I need to know that even if he can't love me, he has to have some respect for me. Like Julian and Mona. Their regard for each other was clear. After all, Charlie still needs a wife, and I need him. I can give up on those exciting, electric moments of lust; it's childish, really. I've had my fun with that, and look where it got me. I still need a husband, though.

I lift my chin and place my bets. "Well, maybe Alice invited me, and it sounded nice. What's it to you, anyway? It's not like you've proposed or anything. I don't belong to you, Charlie." I lean back, pouting. "Why would you even think something like that about me?"

He's quiet for a moment before he speaks. "Well, that's not really a denial, is it?" His face scares me. My heart races as I think of how he squeezed my fingers.

I just glare at him, silent.

"I need the truth," he says, raising an eyebrow. "You know, you were putting on a few pounds last spring."

"How dare you, Charlie!" I pick up the menu and concentrate on it. Caesar salads. Seared tenderloin. Well, I better stick to the salads so Charlie doesn't get the wrong idea. I can smell someone's Chicken á la King, which makes nausea grind in my stomach. Though I'm terrified, I have to double down. I have to force his hand. I have to leave tonight with a proposal, or mama and I will be in deep trouble. My insides are twisted as I look at him over the menu. I keep my eyes stern, angry. Horribly hurt.

It seems like an hour goes by. It can't possibly, because I can still feel the bubbles in my mouth and smell Mona's perfume.

Charlie sighs loudly. He runs his hands over his face in exhaustion or frustration or who knows what. Then he taps his finger on his closed menu. He lifts his hand, and for a moment I think he's going to call for our check so we can end this awful date, but he doesn't. He reaches for the small box and slides it toward me. Then he takes my hand in both of his. I bristle, but this time he rubs my fingers gently. "You're my girl, Ducky. And I guess I have to believe you." He lifts his arm as if he's going to wrap me in a hug, but instead he only pats me on the back. "I know you've wanted this for a long time."

My stomach twists even more. I hold back the sickness that washes over me. The simple, clear seltzer still bubbles in my stomach, threatening to return.

Will I always remember this proposal with this blasted lump in my throat?

The box is wrapped in pink paper, and after finally getting a good look at it, I see it isn't the right size or shape to be a ring. I hate admitting to myself that it's a bit of a relief. Puzzled, I unwrap the paper.

Though Charlie may not be the one I yearn for, and he may be awkward and jealous and downright dumb at matters of the heart, at least my guy knows me.

It's not an engagement ring.

It's a bottle of *Chanel No. 5.*

22

Beth

JUNE, 2017

Three young boys crowd into the small space between the glass doors, but I don't register them because I'm looking in shock at their mother following behind. Cara seems equally stunned to see me.

"Beth," she says, collecting herself. "It's good to see you." She doesn't smile.

For a moment I don't say anything; my stomach is clenched into a fist. I smile at my nephews, but they hardly notice me—their constant movement, punching, and wrestling reminds me of a cartoon fight that's just a swirling cloud of stars and fists. They're five, seven, and eight years old. I understand Grandma Vee's annoyance—they're the perfect age to drive a sensitive, senile old lady even more out of her mind.

"Aunt Beth! What are you doing here?" Ian, the seven-year-old, yells at me. They're all three yelling and giggling. "Hey, watch this!" He gives Brody, the eldest, a roundhouse kick to the kidney, which seems impossible in this cramped space, but still, it happens.

"You little shit!" Brody grabs him in a headlock. Chase, the youngest, jumps on Ian's back.

"Language!" Cara yells into the void. None of them hear her. "All three of you, outside, now. Go climb that tree." She holds the door open and motions to a grassy spot next to the parking lot. Brody and Ian take off, racing, and Chase goes after them, living up to his name.

"It's good to see you too, Cara." I'm not sure what else to say, but that seems like the best thing. "Uh, thanks for cleaning out Mom's house."

"Mmm." Her face cracks a slight, bland smile.

"The boys look well," I say.

She shifts her purse up higher on her shoulder. She's as uncomfortable as I am. "Oh, yes. Well, you know how it is." Her face reddens. Maybe she realized that I don't actually know. "So, uh, Rocko told me about Sylvie. Sorry to hear. It must be hard." Her face stays indifferent, without any whisper of the empathy that her words would suggest.

"Yeah. Thanks." I'm careful not to say too much. I remember clearly what happened the last time I confessed my struggles to her.

We both shuffle our feet. "Well, still," she says, "I mean, she's healthy at least. It's not like it's a death sentence. Autism is so common these days. I have several friends…well, you know. There must be a lot of help available."

I try for an awkward smile, even though my insides are

boiling. She's still as self-righteous as ever. I'm careful about the words I choose; I decide it's better to humor her rather than kill her right here at Grandma's nursing home. "Yes."

"Come inside, Beth," Cara says, reaching for the inside door and motioning to the lobby just past it.

"Come inside," she said from her front porch, her coffee steaming in her hand and concern painted across her perfectly made-up face. I stood in her driveway, feeling cold against the early-winter wind. Sylvie was strapped in her car seat. I couldn't bear to take her to daycare after what had happened the night before.

I just stood there, staring at my sister until she set down her coffee, bounded down the porch steps in her bare feet, and undid Sylvie's straps. She lifted my daughter onto her hip. Sylvie didn't protest. "Come inside," Cara repeated. "I can be a few minutes late for work, but I do have to be in by nine for a meeting." She put her free arm around my shoulder. "Whatever it is, let me help."

Her warmth dissolved that morning, once she heard me out.

"Oh, I was actually leaving. I have to get home. My shift starts in an hour." The tiny space between the glass doors closes in on me. Even with the boys gone, it's too small for the heft of what's between us sisters. "It was good to see you," I know I just said that, but I'm at a loss for what else to say. "Grandma Vee is pretty sensitive today. You might want to just keep the boys outside."

Her face changes to annoyance. She squares her feet toward me and juts out her chin. "Vee loves the boys."

"Of course." I'm not getting into it with her. Not now. Not here. "Didn't mean to offend…"

But Cara has a different idea. Her eyes flash at me, her eyebrows held in an angry arch. "I suppose you're waiting for an apology from me for last fall."

I'm surprised—I didn't think she'd bring it up. I don't look her in the eye. It was eight months ago, but I can nearly smell the strong, toasted scent of Eggo waffles in Cara's kitchen from that morning. She'd flittered around, cleaning up crumbs and empty orange juice glasses and dumping them into the sink. Her movement and lack of attention that day made me even more uncomfortable. I felt so exposed, overwhelmed. I wasn't used to that awful feeling of being out-of-control.

I wasn't used to making mistakes.

"No, Cara. I don't want anything from you," I say. "I was wrong to come to you that morning. I regret confiding in you."

"You were wrong to leave your daughter."

"I know, Cara. I know." Cara is the one person with whom I've always had trouble keeping my anger in check. As my twin, she was my first love. We were born practically hugging. I love her with everything in me, even now. But she also knows how to bring out the worst in me. We are the best at pushing each other's buttons. This time, we pushed too far. "Thanks for your insight. As if I don't already feel bad enough about it. And by the way, I didn't leave Sylvie. I came back."

"You drove an hour to St. Cloud! And you only came back because you were afraid they'd call Eddie and you'd be found out."

"It wasn't quite an hour." I take some breaths, count to four, employ the calming strategies that Sylvie and I have been learning from *Daniel Tiger's Neighborhood*. "And I went back. I went back. I told you that. I would never leave her. It just got hard."

"You poor thing. Life got too hard." Cara's tone is sarcastic, condescending. "You know what was hard? Trying to raise three high-energy boys while your mother is dying from lung cancer. You came to me that morning while I was trying to get ready for work, bitching about how hard it was, about how you ran away from your child and it felt good. And then you wanted my sympathy." She shakes her head. "Unbelievable."

"I didn't leave her." My voice has fallen to a whimper. I do everything I can to keep the tears intact, to not let them fall. All my life, Cara was the one I went to when I needed support. She was eight minutes older but decades wiser. I told her everything—how I lost my virginity to my loser boyfriend at fifteen, how I spent all night puking vodka in a frat house bathtub my sophomore year of college. How the night before I was supposed to marry him, I still wasn't really all that sure about Eddie.

I guess I assumed she would always have endless patience with me, but that day I learned that she had none left. "I came to you for help. I felt like a failure, Cara. It was just so painful."

"The pain is what tells you you're a good mother. It's supposed to hurt. You don't run away from that." Cara leans against the glass door of the nursing home entrance, her face reflecting my fears: in her eyes, I have failed. "You know, I put Mom into hospice, alone. You didn't help. Too busy, right? I did it all. But you had plenty of time to run off to Winnipeg for a fun weekend with your girlfriends, didn't you?"

I look at her, shocked.

I was the one who talked Mom into quitting smoking.

I was the one who researched local hospice facilities when it got to that point.

I was the one who went to the weekly meetings with Mom's oncologist because I was the "medical person" in the family.

And I drove to Winnipeg, alone, without any girlfriends, to try to get her medication without putting us all into bankruptcy.

Cara doesn't remember any of that. Or she never knew. All

she can see was what I didn't do. I wasn't there for her when she needed me. I didn't talk to her. I only ever dumped on her.

I was in a spin that morning before I went looking for peace at Cara's house. I woke up with the screaming noise of a freight train in my ears; I'd left my baby behind. The signs of her disability were multiplying, but the process of testing her and getting her help was daunting. As a scientist, I yearned for evidence. As a nurse, I needed to anticipate her needs to help heal. As a mother, I just wanted to know my daughter would have a future. I wanted our family would have some resemblance to the idea I'd always carried in my head. I needed to know that Sylvie would be okay.

I needed to know that I would be okay, too.

Leaving her wasn't the answer, but it was the only thing that felt right. At that moment, I was failing at everything. I was failing her. What kind of mother would leave her child and just run away?

Stop it.

Get help.

Find someone to talk to.

I'd been seeing my therapist long enough by then to know the routine. *Find someone who will understand and listen.*

Cara.

She'd always been the one to straighten me out, kiss me on the cheek, and send me back into battle. I knew she'd have the right thing to say. She'd recharge me, and I'd be able to face another day with a challenging toddler.

But that's not what happened.

That morning, in her kitchen, I took a chance. I told her everything. I confessed the vicious truth about the day before.

I told her how I almost left Sylvie. About how I hated myself for it but also how I felt a sinister relief as I drove away toward North Dakota.

About how I was afraid I might do it again.

"I just can't take it anymore, you know?" I heard my voice get *filmy, pleading. I hated the way it sounded. "I mean, you understand, right? You have kids—"*

"And as nutso as they are, I've never considered leaving them." Cara's voice held the sting of something sharp. She wiped at a sticky *spot of syrup on the counter, still not looking at me.*

My stomach flashed with nauseous anxiety. My speech sped up; my tongue tripped over itself. "Sometimes I just can't, you know? I mean, there are times when it gets to be too much—"

"No, I don't know." Cara bit off. *"You know what you do when it gets hard, Beth? You do it. You fucking do it. Then you wake up the next day and do it again. You pick those kids up and you kiss them and hug them and listen to their stories and feel their pain. You look every time they say 'Mama, mama, watch this!' But you don't leave them. What the hell is the matter with you?"*

She was right. And she wasn't done.

"I mean, Christ," she went on, wiping her hands on a rag. *"Mom's dying and she's still only worried about you and me. She was actually apologizing to me last week for being a burden. What kind of bullshit is that?"* She pushed her finger into the granite countertop to make a point. *"Mothers give up everything for their children, and when it gets hard, they keep going. Our mother and grandmothers did it. And their mothers. And theirs before them. They all did it through war and poverty and illness and probably abuse and a host of other bullshit. They did it. They didn't complain when it got hard. They just fucking did it."*

They didn't do it, though, and Cara knew that as much as I did. She'd conveniently forgotten about how our great-grandmother didn't do it. She'd left, and she never came back.

"Children are helpless, but you're not." Cara continues. *"You're the grown-up. You're not helpless. You are everything to Sylvie. Act like it. Quit being a goddamn entitled little bitch."*

I watched her eyes glaze with anger that day as my own filled with tears.

I turned and gathered Sylvie from the living room where she had just settled in to watch *Paw Patrol.* She screamed, but I didn't stop. My mind was blank, like Cara was a tornado that had flattened every thought I'd ever had. I struggled Sylvie into her coat, then walked past my fuming sister and out the front door. I never returned.

Is Cara right? Is motherhood supposed to hurt this badly?

I came back for my daughter. *Of course* I came back. Sylvie's my sweet love bug, and I can't bear life without her, even if this life is crushing me. I made a bad decision, but I fixed it. I came back, even if it didn't feel good. Even if it hurt like hell. It wasn't her fault; it was mine.

I look at Cara now, leaning against the door to Grandma's nursing home. This tiny vestibule is getting unbearably hot with the afternoon sun. My shirt sticks to me. I can smell the sharp sweetness of my deodorant doing its magic under my arms.

"I'm sorry you were grieving mom," I say. "I was too. I'm sorry your children are hard to raise. Mine is, too" My jaw tightens. "You know, I would have been there for you. You never talked to me about any—"

"You wouldn't have listened, Beth," she says. "It's just always about you. You, and your stressful job, and your stressful family, and your stressful life." She crosses her arms. "Why are you here visiting Grandma Vee, Beth? Does she have something you want?"

She's right, and it takes my breath away like a gut punch. I came here not to visit Vee; I came for answers.

I push open the outer door to the parking lot and hurry outside. The hot summer breeze feels cool after the stifling vestibule. I rush to my car where I search through the glove compartment for the empty Belair pack.

Oh, Mom. I'm so sorry, Mom. I really need you now.

With the cigarette pack still clutched in my hand, I peel out of the parking lot.

For the second time, I run away from Cara, leaving her behind without another word.

23

SEPTEMBER, 1927

"Honey, that's a hell of a birthday gift." Hazel yells at me as she taps her gasper against the ashtray.

"What?" I yell back and point to my ear.

"Birthday gift. A hell of a birthday gift."

Hazel had to park us right in front of the stage, like always. The trombone player winks at me every time he thrusts his slide in my direction. I smirk around my cigarette and try not to catch his eye as I slide the *Chanel No. 5* bottle back into my jacket pocket. Wonderful to have pockets again—with September upon us, a light jacket is finally appropriate in the evenings.

My hand cups the perfume protectively in the pocket. Any other day I would have loved receiving an ounce of Coco's perfume as a gift from my beau. But it's not a ring. It's not a promise. Not even a hint.

I think about Mama, giving up her cabinet to the neighbors for pocket change that will help pony up our rent and our food. I squeeze the bottle in my pocket. Would someone buy it from me? Would they consider it used? How much is a secondhand bottle of *No. 5* worth?

Hazel's eyes narrow. "Jo. Yoo-hooo?" I look at her and smile, probably a bit too big. The band hits their last stinger note, then announce a break. "Oh honey." She's able to bring her voice down to a normal talking level now. "You were expecting a ring and a proposal, weren't you?"

"I can't wait much longer, Haz. Without Sergei around, I either need to find a job or find a husband. We're running out of time and money."

"And as soon as that baby is well enough to come home, you're going to have another mouth to feed."

"Two."

"What?"

I choke on my cigarette. It doesn't matter how many babies I have waiting for me, I can't bring any of them home. I cough to clear my throat. "Two?" I smile innocently. "Is that what time this place closes?"

She gives me the eye. "How should I know? I thought it went all night. Besides, it's barely nine now." She waves at a clock toward the entrance.

"Well…" I lean back in my chair, resting my cigarette holder between my fingers. "The short of it is, I need money, *tout de suite.*"

"Here's an idea," Hazel says, leaning one arm over the back of her chair and crossing her legs. "You should sell your perfumes. You're good at it, and you're already *parlay-ing ze Français, ooh la la!*" She giggles. "I loved that scent you showed me, with the vanilla and the hints of cinnamon. Go talk to someone down at Gimbel's."

I shake my head. "I can't even sell driving gloves. They'll laugh me out of the store."

Now it's Hazel's turn to shrug. "Well, anyway, I'm not sure how you'll be able to keep a job once that baby comes home." She jabs her cigarette into the ashtray, which pushes it in a way that it tumbles to the floor with a clatter. She ignores it. "Babies have a way of disrupting a girl's schedule." She sighs and looks around the room. "Guess you're right, honey. Charlie's your best bet. He's a good guy, just a bit awkward, that's all. He's sticking with you through all this, and that's a sign of honor, if nothing else." The expression on my face must look like I'd bit a lemon because she leans in and pats my arm. "He'll propose soon, I'm certain. He'll want you two married before that baby comes home."

"Well, that's the crop, isn't it?"

She studies me. I try not to give myself away, but my eyes are heavy as they lift to meet hers. When they do, tears sting. Hazel's face is heavy with empathy. A man passing our table crouches to pick up the ashtray, and then opens his mouth as if to start a little flirt with us. As soon as he sees our faces as somber as mobsters, he places the ashtray on our table and keeps moving.

Hazel's eyes narrow. "Jo, there's something you're not saying." She pauses. "You've told Charlie about the baby, right?"

I look away and stare at the trombone now sitting discarded on the stage, its player sitting at the bar guzzling sidecars between sets and winking at the heavy-lidded flappers lounging sideways on their stools.

"Jo. Jo?"

"Charlie's never going to stand for it. You know that, Hazel."

She chews on the end of her empty cigarette holder, tapping the Bakelite mouthpiece against her front tooth. "Could you convince him that it's his? Maybe the timing worked out—"

I give her a long look in the eye.

"Jeepers. It's like that, huh?"

"Oh Hazel, I tried." I slide a stray hair back under my cloche. "Once I figured out I was in trouble, I tried everything I could think of. Remember when I borrowed that little white dress from you?"

"That one that's nearly see-through? I remember that." She says. "I was terrified to give it to you. You were so sick, and that dress is hard to clean." She drains her champagne. "It didn't work?"

I shake my head. "I tried it all. Nothing but an icy mitt."

"Damn," she says. "So, what are you going to do? Your baby will come home sooner or later. Charlie's going to find out."

I let out a big exhale to cleanse my body of the pain inside. "You know, survival of such small babies is low…"

"You're saying your baby is dead?"

I stay quiet.

"You've seen her?"

I only stare at the ashtray.

"Jo. Do you hear me? You've seen her, right?"

"Well, after I gave birth—"

"No, I mean now, while she's in that baby place. What do they call it?"

"Infantorium."

"Jesus. What a name." She tries for another drink before she remembers her glass is empty. "It sounds like something from a Lon Chaney horror film." She leans back in her chair, her eyes intent on the saxophonist, who's quietly wiggling his fingers across his keys, warming up for the second set. He's playing "Ida! Sweet as Apple Cider." The song stings me and makes my stomach swoop to my throat like I'm riding the Cyclone.

Nurse Ida.

"Haz," I say, "I'm scared. I'm afraid of—"

"Mothers are always afraid. That's what motherhood is all about."

"Well, most mothers know if their child is dead or alive."

She leans forward, on her elbows, her empty cigarette holder stabbing the air. "Don't tell me you haven't even been to visit your baby?"

I bite my lip.

"Shit, Jo." Hazel stands and tosses some coins on the table. "Come on, let's go. Right now. I'll go with you." She grabs my arm and pulls me to standing. I have no choice but to follow her as she stumbles through the crowded tables, bumping chairs and stepping on feet.

The subway is a good block down from the Pearl Club. Hazel bubbles on about something or another while she pulls me along. As we wait for traffic to pass, my eyes are drawn to a dime store window. A bag of bread flour, cigarette papers, an assortment of miniature trains. A sweet little beaded purse.

Baby shoes. My heart skips.

Then, on a shelf all its own, some tiny, colorful bottles. *Mystikum*, *Le Jade*, *Djer-Kiss*, a couple of fragrances from Corday. There are a few other bottles that I don't recognize, so my imagination bends the smells of lilacs and sweet peas and coriander to construct what could be their scents. I don't realize I'm pressing my nose to the window until Hazel's arm slinks around my waist.

"Yours will be there someday too, Jo. Right up there next to Coco's."

Dear Hazel. I give her a brave smile. The only place my scents will ever be is on the top shelf of my closet, getting dusty and going rancid.

Not thirty minutes later, that same handsome barker from before leers at me. Hazel soaks in his gaze; her loyalty to Skip doesn't stop her from flirting with everyone else. But this fella makes me uncomfortable. He adjusts his stance in his spit-shined, spatted shoes so he faces us, his mouth curling into that welcoming smile. His dimple deepens—at least his is in the right place. Hazel moves herself into a performance pose. The two face off while I'm hovering nearby, awkward as a bangtail in a boiler.

Hazel said she'd hold my hand, though now her hands are filled with a hot dog and a cigarette, and her attention is on the handsome man reeling us inside. Ketchup spills from her hot dog bun and onto the sidewalk. She doesn't notice, or at least she pretends not to. I hope she doesn't slip in it when she takes a step.

"Hazel, let's leave, okay?" I say. "We can come back another time. Let's go to Jessop's. It's nearby."

She glances at me and purses her lips. Her eyes go back to Mister Handsome Barker. "Jessop got pinched last night. Closed down her whole joint and hauled her off to the hoosegow. Frank Shady's is open though." She elbows me with her cigarette arm. "We'll go put down some hooch once we're, you know…" She motions toward the building with her hot dog. "Done."

"His vodka isn't any good."

She shrugs. "Don't I know it. Damn, I miss Sergei and his mix."

"Well, he's gone," I bite back.

Hazel turns to me. My cheeks heat as her eyes narrow. She's

214

got that look again that something's not adding up. "Jo, do you know what happened between your mother and Sergei? Why'd he blow like that?"

I don't answer. I'm overcome with thoughts of that evening— the purest vodka I'd ever known. That night I was introduced to the scents of the East, combinations I never knew existed. Saffron and Cedarwood, Jasmine and Eucalyptus. Chemistry at its most intimate and so much more. Sergei told me everything a girl ever longed to hear. All just a line? Maybe. Still, I felt liberated and beautiful. But he's gone now. And he wants nothing to do with what he put inside me.

"I...I guess...not? I don't know." I try to keep my face stoic. I fail. My lip quivers.

"Jo. What happened?"

"It's—it's nothing." I glance up at her. "Hazel, it's nothing."

Hazel's eyes widen and then fall into defeat. "No. Oh, no no no Josephine. Don't tell me." I try so very hard to keep my eyes from welling, but they do anyway. She sucks on her cigarette. "That goddamn Russian. *He* did this?" She lets loose a sigh of exasperation. "What does your mother know?"

"That Charlie got me knocked up. And that the baby went to a good family."

"Well, that's all hooey. She doesn't know about you and Sergei?"

"No."

"And obviously neither does Charlie."

"Obviously." I shift in my heels.

"Charlie will never take in someone else's child. His pride wouldn't allow it. Jealous ol' mac, isn't he?"

"That's right."

"So what are you going to do?"

215

I shrug. I don't have the energy for any more thought.

"Christ on the goddamn cross, Jo, you're in all kinds of applesauce here." I'm grateful she doesn't scold me about my behavior with Sergei as much as I deserve it. She knows better than anyone that there are many reasons a gal can get knocked up by a fella, and very few of them have much to do with her own decisions. Hazel pulls a tiny flask out of her pocketbook, no bigger than Charlie's bottle of *Chanel No. 5* that still weighs down my pocket. "You need a shot before we go in? Might settle the nerves. New batch that Skip got ahold of."

I stare at the flask. Maybe it would help. A little nip might calm my stomach and flatten the cyclone that swoops through me. I take it from her and let a few drops slither down my tongue. I gag. It tastes like rotten peas.

"Jesus, Hazel, what the hell?"

"What, no good?" She smells it and makes a face. "Ugh. Sorry, honey. Bad stuff." She pours it onto the ground, and I watch the liquid seep into the cracks in the cement, intoxicating or probably killing the weeds that push through the stone.

"Come on in, ladies! Only a nickel. All the world loves a baby." The barker has those words arched above his head memorized. There's a line of people queued in front of him. Workmen in overalls, their hands as big as the babies they wait to see. Housewives and young mothers in their summer cottons, pining to visit infants a fraction of the size of their own at birth. Sticky toddlers and energetic children who should already be in bed, chasing each other in circles while they wait to watch what they don't understand.

All the world loves a baby.

My stomach sinks to my knees from anxiety and bad booze.

In the distance I can hear the Cyclone rumbling, the people on board screaming in delight. I wonder if that man still sits in peace beneath it, paging through his paper while his coffee gets cold.

Dusk sets in and electric light bulbs flitter to life around me. I squint from the brightness as they flash, chasing each other like the children in line.

"Come on." Hazel shoves the rest of her hot dog into her mouth and follows it with her cigarette. She brushes off her hands, the holder clamped between her teeth. "Let's go."

I dig in my heels, but I'm no match for Hazel on a mission. She pushes me to the front of the line, past the ladies who dole out impatient smirks and their children who outright yell their complaints. "Oh, go chase yourself," Hazel says. "She's got someone in there." She shoves me toward the barker, who reaches out to catch me as I fall toward him. "She's one of the mothers," Hazel yells at him over the uproar. "She has a baby in there."

"You do? Well, little lady, I'll let you in this time free of charge."

Such a concession.

He pulls back the curtain with his hooked walking stick. We move into the black abyss that stands as a door, and Hazel trips over the threshold. Inside, the walls look like they're supposed to be white, but the greenish light of the mercury vapor lamps mixes with a few incandescents to give everything a sickly yellow cast. Along one wall, a row of large stainless steel boxes with glass windows stand, each propped up on solid metal legs. Incubators, like what farmers use on chicken eggs. A baby in each. All that separates us from the babies in their pods is a waist-high railing made from a couple of iron pipes and a length of rope.

Leaning against the rope are the gawkers. Mostly women. A few kids. Several bored men and one or two who look genuinely concerned. Daddies.

The silence of the room knocks me over. We'd gone from the bustle of the midway to a sterile, respectful hospital quarters in just a couple of steps.

Nurses buzz around behind the incubators like bees. A couple of them hold babies, but not in the comforting, tender way a mother holds a baby in the crook of her arm. Instead, they hold them with one hand gripped around the back of the baby's neck and the other hand under the diapered rear like they were holding up the Kentucky Derby trophy for all to see.

Spectators pack the room, laughing and pointing, ooh-ing and ahh-ing.

The too-small infants are all decked out in lacy dresses, big blue bows, tiny hats, and suspenders the size of rubber bands, as if they were adults dressed for Sunday services. One starched nurse with stern glasses sits in a compact rocking chair. She holds a baby wearing tweed knickers and a blue shirt. He's propped upright on her left knee as if he were already a bouncing two-year-old, though the child still carries the purplish hue of early birth and looks barely a week old. The nurse holds a long tube. She bends the tube to the child's nose, and slowly pours in the contents.

I cover my mouth, horrified.

"Do the ring trick!" one little boy says a bit too loudly, eliciting a hiss from his mother but a few murmurs of agreement from the crowd. A nurse with light blond hair in the center of the room smiles and retrieves a tiny baby from an incubator and a diamond ring, probably—hopefully—fake, from her pocket. She rests the baby on his back on a small, blanketed platform and holds his arm up for all to see as if she's demonstrating the fall's newest fashions. Then she slips the ring over the baby's hand and wrist. It's now the baby's bracelet.

How is it that these tiny humans can even survive? Some look to be smaller than the cobs of corn they sell for a nickel further down the midway.

I watch one woman move past the rope barrier. The nurse welcomes her and then brings her to a small room behind the incubators. I strain to make out what looks like three rocking chairs in the room. By the movement of shadows in the room I know that the woman has sat in one of the chairs. The nurse retrieves a baby—decked out in a little blue sailor suit that looks several sizes too big—from one of the incubators and disappears into the room with him.

"Nurse? Nurse!" Hazel boldly waves her cigaretted hand at the nurse with the ring. I want to run, but Hazel has a vice grip on my arm. She pushes us up through the crowd, her voice bouncing off the antiseptic walls. "Nurse!"

"Ma'am, please. We do not allow cigarettes in here." The nurse with the ring recoils away from us with the baby.

"They're closed up tight in those boxes. They're fine." Hazel motions her thumb towards me. "She's got one in here. Which one is hers?"

The nurse looks at me with a raised eyebrow, skeptical. "Your baby's name?"

I can't speak. I only look at her. Then I swallow hard and force myself to form her name. "Rose." I stop. I don't recall the name of the other. Did I not name her? What monster doesn't even give her daughter a name?

"We don't have a Rose here," she says impatiently. "All right then, what's your name?"

I only stare.

No Rose.

Oh God.

"Jo." Hazel answers for me. "Josephine Westley."

Her face brightens. "Yes, yes. I just fed the Westley baby and put her down. Over there. Number eight." She motions down the row but doesn't allow me past the rope barrier.

I feel dizzy. I can't move my feet, but Hazel drags me along. The smells of cleaners and spoiled milk mix with the taste of Hazels' rotten alcohol. I swallow several times to rid myself of the vomit that pushes up into my throat.

Incubator number eight looks just like six and seven and nine and fourteen. All identical. Tiny coffins, trying to keep the inhabitants alive instead of burying them in death.

Through the glass window of the incubator, I see a baby nestled into folds of purple silk. She doesn't move. There's a label on the side, under the large figure eight.

Violet.

I feel cold. My teeth chatter, and I grip the iron railing support for stability, but the smell of my sweaty palms against the flaking metal makes me sick all over again.

Did I give her that name? Or maybe, did Alice? Who did?

"You're okay, honey." Hazel wraps her arm around my shoulders and tries to calm my trembling. "Hey, Violet Number Eight! You can name one of your perfumes..." She trails off, probably realizing her joke is falling flat. She clears her throat. "It's a lovely name."

I look around the room. "The nurse," I say through clenched teeth, "the one with the glasses..."

"I'm sorry?"

Ida, Sweet as Apple Cider. "Ida. She was here when I…Where is she? Where is nurse Ida?" My words stumble out of my mouth like pops and scraps from a rusty engine.

The blond nurse looks at me. "Short, rotund woman?"

I nod. "Yes. Ida. I need to talk to her. She was here. She would know…" She would know what happened. What happened to Rose. I just need someone to tell me that they held Rose, comforted her. I need to know that my daughter wasn't alone in her last moments.

"Ah, Ida. Terrible thing. Her heart gave out. Died just a few days ago." She bit her lip. "Wonderful nurse. Smart as a whip."

"She's gone?" I try to get ahold of myself.

"We miss her dearly. She had a soothing way with the smallest ones." The nurse shakes her head, her grief obvious.

"Was there…" I have to ask. I force the words. "Was there another baby brought in that day? Another girl?"

The nurse frowns. She steps to the back of the incubators and flips through some pages on a clipboard. "I have Violet's chart here, but she's the only live baby admitted that day."

Live.

I look at the nurse, then at the incubator that houses my surviving daughter. The tiny girl inside the incubator remains motionless. The crowd churns and jumbles behind us, pushing me into the rope that holds us back. The chatter of the gawkers turns into thunder in my head.

"This place is pretty homey, for a sideshow," Hazel says, tapping off the ashes of her cigarette. "Fancy rugs on the floor, little knick-knacks up on those shelves. Clowns, dolls…" She blows out a line of smoke as I follow her eyes around the room. They do have it set up to look something like a nursery, but it still has the feel of a hospital room painted onto a circus.

"Please, miss. Your cigarette."

"Oh yeah." Hazel drops it and crushes it with the toe of her Mary Jane. "Say, nurse," Hazel says as she points to a shelf on the wall. Between a porcelain doll and a propped-up copy of *The Velveteen Rabbit* is a line of small flour sack bags, each about the size of a drawer sachet. "What are those little bags? Medicine for the babies?"

The nurse's face casts gray. "Oh no, ma'am. Those…" She trails off.

"Yes?"

"Well, we have an excellent survival rate. We take good care of our babies. But there are some who are just too small, too delicate. Some, unfortunately…" She trails off.

"Some die." A boy of about ten finishes for her, looking up at Hazel with wide, knowing eyes.

Hazel's arm twitches on my shoulder. "So, those hold… ashes?" she whispers.

"We keep the remains," the nurse says quietly, her eyes drawn downward. "In case the family returns."

"What do you mean, in case?" Hazel's frown is harsh. "Are you telling me there are mothers who don't come back for their child's ashes?"

"Yes. Some don't." The nurse shakes her head. "Sometimes a baby is already dead when they bring them in. Maybe they don't know the child is dead and they are holding on to their prayers, or maybe they don't know what else to do with the infant's body. Maybe some think we can actually revive them." She looks at me, and I must have a look of horror on my face because she pats my arm. "Oh, honey, that's nothing to worry about." She brightens a little too much. "Violet is doing splendidly. I'll admit I was beginning to worry a bit, but you're here now. You will be able to take your daughter home before long." She folds the papers back over the clipboard and sets it down on a stool. "That's good news, especially with autumn coming on. It reminds us that November is approaching faster than we may realize."

"What happens in November?" Hazel asks.

"Coney Island closes on November first. All the remaining babies will go home then."

"Home?" My stomach squeezes into a tight ball. "But, what if they're still sick or too weak?" *Or don't have a home to go to?*

The nurse looks down at the baby in incubator number eight and smiles softly at little Violet. Either she didn't hear me, or she's ignoring the question. "Isn't she beautiful? She'll be a real looker one day." She doesn't make any motion to open the incubator or remove the baby inside.

I let my eyes drop to the ground. They well up.

"So even if they're still too weak, they go home?" Hazel has the gumption to repeat my question. I'm glad someone does. "What happens to them?"

The nurse looks puzzled. "Well, most do just fine, I'm quite sure."

I don't know how she could possibly know that, but I don't say anything because I really don't want to know the truth. What can be done? With the park closed, there's no one to hand over their nickels for a peek. There's no way to pay the nurses or to buy the powdered milk and the soap to wash the diapers.

"Jo, you should hold her." Hazel puts an arm around me and motions me toward the incubator.

"No, thank you." I step back.

"Oh, Jo, you need to. You can't bring her home if you've never even—"

223

"No, Hazel…" I press my hand to my mouth. I turn and shove through the crowd piled in behind me. I shimmy past shoulders that hold up overalls and aprons straps, repeating "excuse me" over and over.

The black curtain of the door floats in front of me, and I push through it. I see only a flash of the barker's colorful vest, his voice booming as he draws in a new crowd of onlookers. Trying to keep just a little dignity, I lift my head and slowly walk down the steps to the street. I make my way across to a bench and sit, resting my elbows on my knees and my head in my hands. Hazel is hot behind me and plops down next to me.

"Ladies," we both look up as the barker shouts to us. His smile spreads wide, as if it were to take over his whole face, body, and all of the space around him. A Cheshire Cat. "Come again," he says with the twinkle of stacking nickels and dimes in his eye, "and next time be sure to bring your friends."

24

JUNE, 2017

Sylvie's small cup of vanilla ice cream is melting into a warm puddle. She sits, turned in her chair with her back to me, looking out the window.

I kept thinking about Mom and her ice cream dates. My visit with Grandma Vee only strengthened my want to be closer to Sylvie. We can make our own new memories, just us girls.

It's not working.

I encourage her to try the ice cream and model it for her with my own spoonfuls, but she doesn't. Once in a while she'll move the spoon around in the cup and watch it melt, but mostly she has no interest.

She touches her fingertips together which tells me she's upset that she's sticky, but she doesn't cry. She just stares outside. I thought her attention was piqued by a plastic grocery bag caught on the wind, but when I follow her line of vision, I see that's not it. I squint past her shoulders. The reflection of the sky in the puddles? Maybe she sees a heat mirage coming off the parking lot? I don't know what she sees, what she's thinking. I guess I'll never know.

There's a family on the other side of the shop. A mom sits at a table with a little girl and a little boy, a bulky infant stroller at her knee. The boy and girl are toddlers and seem to be close in age. Maybe twins, maybe Irish twins. Hard to tell. They look to be about the same age as Sylvie, but they're years more advanced developmentally. Both shriek with joy over their ice cream. Both are covered in chocolate. The mom looks exasperated. She occasionally barks at the children to sit down, use their spoons, stop hitting each other. At least the baby seems to be sleeping through it all.

Mom looks like she's had enough. Still, I get the idea she's doing better than I am.

"Water? Sylvie? Does Sylvie want a drink of water?" I push a plastic cup toward her across the table, careful not to spill it.

Sylvie doesn't respond. I poke at my ice cream and watch it melt into its own puddle. They didn't have Maple Nut, so I figured Butter Pecan was close enough. It's not. Too sweet. It's nothing like the samples Mom would let me steal from her cone. I remember the smoky, nutty taste of true Maple Nut, a contrast to the early-eighties flavors I would always try: Bubble Gum, Mint Chocolate Chip, Peppermint Twist, Tutti Frutti.

The saccharine smell of this place is making me sick.

The little girl across the shop shrieks, screams, and lashes out at the boy. The boy screams back then cries. Sylvie's attention is caught by the commotion. She looks over at them. She stares.

She doesn't cry, but I can see by the creases across her forehead that she's agitated.

"Oh, honey, it's okay. They're little kids, and little kids sometimes get mad or feel sad. It's okay." I try to take Sylvie in my arms but she pushes away. She looks back out the window.

I glance at the mom; she's staring at Sylvie. When she notices me look at her, she turns her attention back to her kids, her cheeks flushed.

I stand, dip a napkin into a water glass, and kneel next to Sylvie. I turn her face toward me to wipe the stickies, but she's clean. I gently pull her fingers to me. She tugs them away and touches them to each other. I show her on my own fingers.

"Wipe. See? Wipe clean. Make stickies all gone. Mama make it better."

She stares at her fingers. She doesn't offer them, but I gently take her hand again, and this time and she allows me.

The family comes toward the front of the shop, a large mass of unsettled children, overstuffed diaper bags, a wonky stroller with a sleeping baby, and a mom carrying lovies, sippy cups, and used napkins. She juggles her keys while still holding sticky hands, trying to keep all the treasures separate from the trash.

"She's so good," the mother says to me as she leads her kids to the door. "I'd give anything for mine to be that quiet, for even just a minute."

My mouth curves to an automatic, tight smile. I don't say anything. I don't trust my words.

They leave. I wait for them to pile into their minivan and drive away.

"Sylvie, let's go home." I toss our mostly untouched treats into the trash, and we walk, hand in hand, across the parking lot

227

to my car. As I buckle Sylvie into her seat, a breeze pushes through, and I smell the clean, chemical smell of Armor All. It's actually refreshing after the syrupy smell of the shop. I look around my car, and notice the winter dirt is gone from the floor mats, the white outlines of salty boots disappeared from the carpet. "Did Daddy take my car to get cleaned?" I ask Sylvie, who of course doesn't answer. Still, I smile. Eddie knows how I love an expertly detailed car. He's one of the good ones.

Sylvie and I go home.

25

SEPTEMBER, 1927

Hazel is kind enough—or maybe smart enough—to move us along to a different bench so the big white building and its barker aren't situated right in front of us. Now we sit next to the Galveston Flood show. The late show ends, and we're suddenly surrounded by spectators debating the merits of the phony flood, laughing and shouting and tossing their popcorn at each other. Hazel watches them, keeping an eye out for anyone who looks remotely connected to the entertainment industry. She straightens up and smiles when the midway photographer ambles past. He glances at us and lifts his camera but then he puts it down when he sees me. I must be a right chipper mess, crying into my hankie. He gives a little bow and walks away toward the Wonder Wheel. She flops back into the bench and blows her bangs off her forehead.

God bless her, she stays silent while I cry. She just holds my hand and doesn't tell me how I'm doing everything all wrong.

"Hazel…" I say quietly. I look up at her through wet eyes.

She turns to me. Squeezes my hand. Smiles.

"How did it feel?" I ask.

"How did what feel?"

"Your baby. When you…"

She pauses. "Hurt like hell. Nearly killed me," she says.

"No." I steady myself with a deep breath. "Not the procedure. The whole idea of giving up a piece of yourself."

"That's what I meant."

I smile through my tears. "You never told me."

"I never told anyone."

I nod. I understand. I look around at the people still spilling out of the theater. Farmers, children, couples. A young man with a somewhat mangled face limps out, followed closely by an old woman with a peaceful smile who drapes a jacket over his shoulders. They walk in a way that seems like they're supporting each other's steps. "I thought about ending it too," I say, "but…I don't know. I just…I couldn't. I was too scared."

"I know." Hazel says. "I was scared too."

The crowd dissipates a bit. She pats my knee, and we both stand to walk, taking each other's hand.

"I'm sorry, Hazel," I say. "I wish I could have helped you."

"I know, Jo. I just wanted to move past it." She shrugs.

"Okay." It's what I want to do, too, but I can't. My baby wasn't cut out of me—she's keeping warm in her purple frock just a block down, waiting for me.

But her sister…

"Honey, I'm glad I could be there with you—to see her. I know it was hard, but it will get easier." She kicks a wayward potato chip on the street. "One thing I can't get over is those little bags of ashes. Can you just imagine it?" Hazel asks, her free hand touching her cloche, adjusting its feather and preening her hair underneath. "A little bag, no bigger than a tobacco pouch, with all that's left of your child."

I don't respond.

"And then some people never even come back for it. Crazy. But, I suppose, what would the parents do? Buy a tiny plot at Green-Wood for a child that had only been in this world for a day or two, if that?"

"Haz…"

"I wonder if they get a discount since the plot would only need to be—"

"Hazel, please…"

"Well, if it were me, I'd make sure that baby went into a beautiful urn. Sit her up on the shelf next to old Aunt Matilda for all the world to see."

I stop, unable to take another step. "Hazel, one of those bags is mine."

Hazel's eyes widen. "What do you mean? Jo, we saw your baby. Violet is just fine."

"Hazel, there were two."

"Two? What do you mean?" She brings her hand to her mouth. "Is that why you asked about other girls admitted that day?" She sucks in a breath. "Twins?"

I nod.

"Oh, Jo." She shifts her weight and puts her hands in her pockets. She pulls out a cigarette, then shoves it back into the pocket and rubs her hands together. "When? Did you…was she…"

"She died in my arms, in the back of Barlow's flivver."

"My God." She pulls me into a hug. For a moment, it's just us, two girlfriends embracing in the dark on the midway. People break around us like we're a stone in a stream. She straightens and gently holds me at arm's length. She looks me in the eye. "You have a little bag. I wish I had that much." She smiles, but her smile is washed in a distant grief. "Your little Violet is fine. Beautiful. Never saw a prettier baby. She'll be home with you soon."

A roaring clatter fills my ears, and screams of terror break through my thoughts. I look up—we're under the Cyclone. We'd walked and walked and ended up here. I search for the peaceful man in his little house, but the house is dark. Nobody's home. Or he's asleep. Asleep with the noise of the world ending right over his head. I take a breath but nearly choke on the smells of hot grease, hot steel, and hot dogs. Even hot people, taking advantage of the cooler nighttime weather to pile on too many clothes and end up sweltering anyway.

The smell of rotten peas from Hazel's flask is still stuck in my nose, just like the image of a beautiful, tiny urn up on the shelf next to ol' Aunt Matilda.

"Jo." Hazel turns to me, lights the cigarette from her pocket. "You do plan to bring her home." It isn't a question; it's a demand. "No matter what Charlie says or does, you are still her mother."

"Charlie will never stand for it."

She lets out a stream of smoke. "Then fuck him."

"I need him. Mama and I both need him."

"You can't choose your mother over your child, honey."

Except when you've deceived your mother so horribly that you owe her everything to make it up. "Hot cotton, Hazel." I'm frustrated, and though Hazel doesn't deserve it, I feel myself heating up. I take a breath to calm down. "It's a sticky bit, okay?

So I choose my baby. I bring her home. Then what? I can't do it alone without a crumb of kale to pay the rent." I reach for Hazel's cigarette and take a drag on it.

"What about your Aunt Alice?"

I stare into the dark sky through the crisscross scaffolding of the coaster. I shake my head. Of course I'd thought of that, but Alice and Barlow made it clear that I had to make my own way. *Get on with things.* Still, maybe if they knew the truth of it…

I look up to the Cyclone. The cars whiz over the tracks, accelerating, zooming here and there, clanking and grinding, pulling everything and everyone into a wild vortex of screams and laughs. Scarves fly, gloved hands hold cloche hats to bobbed heads. Eyes are wide with excitement. And beneath it all sits the little house, quiet and dark. "There's no way to keep this baby and make it all work out," I say, my heart screaming as I speak the words. I feel defeated, smashed to bits. "The plan all along was to adopt the baby out to a good family. I guess that's just what I'll have to do, but I don't know how to go about that or who to talk to. Besides, what family would want a weakling who was born too early." I pass the cigarette back to her. "Hazel, I saw her. Now I just want to go home and sleep. I don't know what I'm going to do, but I can't make that decision now. I'm too exhausted."

"Jo." She pauses and purses her lips. "You're running out of time."

"I know."

A little girl is crying. Hazel and I watch as she's removed from the roller coaster car by a man with a curled mustache. The front of her dress is splattered with vomit. She can't be much more than five or six.

Poor thing.

Hazel puts her arm around me. I feel her warmth. All us girls are "poor things."

"Well," Hazel says, "giddy-up. Let's go home."

26

Beth

"Wine?"

I look up from the patio chair in the backyard to see Eddie standing over me with a bottle and two glasses. Out of habit, I glance over the top of my brand-new Autism Parenting Magazine I'm reading to check the baby monitor. Sylvie's sleeping soundly. As long as the video still works and Sylvie keeps getting up several times each night, that monitor will be a part of our lives.

"Hey, did you take my car in to get detailed?" I ask.

He gives me a wide grin. "I did it myself. Well, Sylvie and I did, the other day while you were sleeping after your shift. I had her do some little things while I vacuumed it out for you. She seemed to like helping."

"She did?" I log that idea in the back of my mind as a way to engage her. "Well, thank you. That was sweet."

"No problem. I know you've been stressed out, but I also know you feel better when things are clean." He smiles, shakes the wine bottle a bit. "Also, wine helps, right?"

"It does," I say, "but I thought you had to work on that project tonight. The packaging design for that all-natural shampoo?"

"Eh," Eddie shrugs. "It can wait. I'll pull some concepts together in the morning. Client meeting isn't until ten." He smiles and holds up the bottle. "If you're working nights all weekend and this is your only night off, then I want you all to myself."

I both admire and abhor Eddie's ability to procrastinate so diligently and still keep a decent job. "Oh, well, I was just going to go inside. Mosquitoes are getting bad."

"Bastards." He waves a bug away from his face. "Bummer. We haven't had much of a chance to use this new patio furniture yet. Summer is short enough anyway, and then the bugs ruin it." He lifts a cushion and sets it back down, off-center. "How is it?"

"Comfy," I say. I reach over and straighten the cushion.

"Outstanding. Well then, how about we go in and have wine and Scrabble?"

I look longingly at the magazine. "Well, I—"

"Beth." He sets the wine down on the table and plops down in the chair across from me. "Oh, wow. These *are* nice." He wiggles his butt in the seat, stretches his arms behind him, then leans over and takes the magazine out of my hands. "Listen, I miss you. I know all of this stuff with Sylvie is hard and everything, but I still want to keep us strong. You know, as a couple."

I flick the corner of the magazine, twist my hair up into a knot, and let it drop.

"Hey, what's up?" he says.

"Tomorrow is Patrick's memorial."

"The triplet?"

"Yeah. The family invited some of us from the NICU to attend, but I don't think I'm going to go."

"Why not?" He leans forward in his chair, his elbows on his knees, and watches me.

My cheeks flame. "I don't know. I guess, I feel like…" I realize I'm mumbling. I clear my throat. "I should have been there. I could have—"

"Stop, Beth," he says. "I'm going to stop you right there. You did your job. Sylvie and I know you're a superhero, but if the rest of your staff wasn't able to save that baby, there wasn't much more you could have done." He nods at me. "You should go. The family wants their baby to be known, remembered. You knew him. Not many people did."

He's right. Of course he's right. I smile and nod. "Okay, okay. I'll go. I'll also accept your Scrabble challenge," I point to the wine bottle, "as long as you don't mind the humiliation."

"You mean, when I humiliate you?"

I smile. It feels good to loosen up, to joke with Eddie. He stands and grabs the wine. "Uh, Ed?" I say.

"Hmm?"

"Maybe we should just put this stuff in the shed tonight." I wave my arm over the new furniture, then shoo a mosquito from my ear.

He looks confused. "Why would we put the furniture in the shed? It's waterproof."

"Hey, y'all!" Kirsten emerges from the trees and jogs past us. "Anyone seen a big, pink beach ball? We have a meltdown happening at our house."

"Sorry," I smile at her. She waves and continues on into the

237

next yard, calling for the ball like it's a puppy. I turn to Eddie. "Have you met the new neighbors?"

He shakes his head. "No, but sounds like they have kids. Maybe Sylvie can have a playmate."

I choose to gloss over that. "So, uh, the furniture. We opted for the lightweight set. If we get that bad weather they keep threatening us with, this stuff will be all over the neighborhood."

"Really?" His voice has a tinge of sarcasm, and he gives me that look that tells me I'm overreacting. I get that look a lot.

"This stuff was expensive." I wince at the whine in my voice.

"Beth, it's outdoor furniture, and we've got a line of trees back here. Where's it gonna go?" He looks to the sky, slaps a mosquito against his arm, and scratches at the itch. "Besides, should be okay tonight. Looks clear."

I stand. Start moving a chair. "But—"

"Beth. It's okay." He moves the wine bottle and both glasses to one hand and takes my hand with the other. "We can do it later. Tomorrow. Let's take some time for us."

"Umm…"

"Beth. Trust me, okay?"

I know I need to be better at that, but his artistic nature and scattered brain makes it hard. "Yeah. Okay. Tomorrow."

We go inside, and he pours the wine while I set up the Scrabble board. He sits down across from me and holds his glass out to clink. I touch his glass with mine and try not to look out the sliding doors at the furniture sitting so exposed, so unprotected. I keep my eyes on his. "Sorry I've been distant," I say. "I just want to help her, you know?" I tap the magazine that's sitting on the table next to us.

"I know. Me too. But sometimes I wonder if the best thing to do is just let her be."

Let her be. It sounds so simple. I pick my seven tiles and hand him the bag. "But, we—"

"Beth…" He lines his tiles up on his rack. "What happens when you can't fix her?"

I'm quiet for a minute. "You want to go first?"

"Nah. Go ahead."

"FIRS." I lay my tiles. "Seven points."

We play for a while in silence. Eddie plays FOX, I add GLUES. He lays down GUN, ZIP, and HEN, I play POX, RAVEN, and HOOF.

I relax at the casualness of it. We don't compete for the most obscure words; we just do what we can with what we have. Sometimes we play dumb little words like SAD and BIN. We certainly won't win any tournaments, but it's calming. It's nice to just be together.

"We should go out, Beth. God, it's been forever since we've been out for dinner. We could see who's playing at the Dakota. Have a…" Eddie gives me a suave, sleazy smile. "Date." He reaches over and plays WAGS for sixteen points. Double Word Score.

"Well, we'd need a babysitter. Cara isn't really available anymore." Cara was the only one I ever trusted to sit with Sylvie when Eddie and I had an occasional date night. Since Cara and I had our falling out, Eddie and I have stayed home.

"Maybe there's some teenager in the neighborhood?"

I cringe. No teenagers. No strangers. Absolutely not. "I can check into it. VIEW. Ten points."

"You know, Sylvie isn't going to break, Beth." Eddie is watching me; he must have picked up on my hesitation. I look up and meet his eyes. "But I'm afraid you might."

I look down and concentrate on my tiles to keep from crying.

239

"You're a good mom," he continues, "and you love her. That's all she really needs."

I feel the tears spill out of my eyes onto my cheeks.

"Hey, what's up?" he asks, his voice low.

I meet his eyes. "Eddie, I think that's the first time anyone has ever said that."

"Said what?" He wrinkles his forehead.

"That I'm a good mom."

"But you are. You know that." He reaches out and puts his hand over mine. "You don't need someone to tell you that."

Maybe I do, but I don't say anything. I take a sip of wine to stop the tears gathering behind my eyes. I use the sleeve of my hoodie to dab at the tears on my cheeks. "I'm afraid, Eddie." I work to keep the tremble out of my voice.

"Of what?"

I shake my head. "I don't know." But I do know. I know that if I'm not trying to heal her—*fix* her—that I just might…

That I just might leave.

I've done it before. Of course, he doesn't know that.

How can I trust myself to be Sylvie's mom? To *just* be Sylvie's mom? To love her, just as she is? Can I even let her just be herself?

"PUBS. Fourteen points." Eddie drains his wine. "I know it's been a hard year for you. Your mom, and all." He reaches his arms above his head to stretch. "I think you should call Cara. It would help. You need your sister. Bury the hatchet, whatever it is. It can't be so bad to tear you guys apart for this long. It's time."

It frustrated Eddie to no end when Mom died and my sister and I still weren't speaking. He doesn't know the details about our falling-out, and he also doesn't know about our run-in at Grandma Vee's nursing home the other day. I stare at the board, at the Triple Word Score that's just waiting for me to pull an M out of the bag. "Yeah. I know. I'm just not ready, I guess."

"What's it going to take, Beth?"

I look at him, and our eyes meet. He can see through me. I feel him reading my thoughts, recognizing my grief.

My cheeks blaze.

"Beth. Talk to me."

"I can't."

"You can. I'm your husband. I'm here. Whatever it is, I won't get mad."

Tears are streaming down my face. I reach for my wine glass, but my hand is shaking. "Eddie…"

"Beth. Tell me." He comes around to my side of the table and puts his arm around me.

"You're looking at my tiles, cheater." I smile at him through my tears.

"Here you have two *U*s, and I'm sitting there with a lonely Q."

"Sell one to you."

He pulls me close, and I lean against his shoulder. "Beth. Tell me. Let me help."

So I do.

I tell him everything, how I left Sylvie, but I came back. The relief at driving away. The despair in turning the car around and returning.

I sob into his shoulder while he hands me tissues to wipe my eyes and blow my nose. When I'm finished, he's quiet. I wait for his reaction. After what seems like forever, he speaks. "So, okay. Then what?"

"What do you mean?"

"Well, so, you took a drive, and you were late picking up

241

Sylvie. Then you came back and got her and brought her home. Do I have it right so far?"

"Well, yeah."

"And that's it?"

I sit up, look at him. "No."

"Okay, then what."

"Eddie," I reach for my wine glass, but it's empty. I set it back down again. "It wasn't so much that I left. I know that's not a huge deal. I get that. It was how I felt. It—" I stop. I can't look him in the eye. "It felt right. It felt really, really good to leave."

"Sure," he says. "I can understand that."

I look up. "You can?"

He nods. "So then you went to Cara looking for comfort, and when you confessed she chewed you out."

"Yes."

"Because she was also stressed out and grieving your mom, who was dying in hospice."

"Well…"

"Beth. Jesus Christ." He smiles at me, and I feel my shoulders relax. "First off, Cara is raising three boys, which is brutal. I have two brothers, so I know. My mom was a basket case when we were all home. Still is, to be honest. Remember how she flipped out over the scalloped potatoes at Easter? Cara just took everything out on you. Sure, it doesn't feel good, but that's life, I guess. We lash out at those we love. Secondly, you need to be better at forgiving yourself. That was a really stressful time for you, for both of you. The truth is, Sylvie was—is—a challenging kid, but you've been nothing but wonderful to her. She has no idea you were a couple of hours late picking her up one day."

"But it felt good to leave."

"Sure it did," he says. "Sometimes it feels good for me to leave too. I shouldn't tell you this, but some nights when I'm working late…" he leans in and whispers, "I don't really have to." He puts a finger to his lips.

"Yeah, I knew it. It's that new media buyer, isn't it? She's a hottie."

"She's twelve, I'm pretty sure. Nah, it's actually Yolanda in accounts receivable. I like my side action bitter and salty. And at least eighty."

I can't help but laugh. I dab at my eyes with a tissue. "I ran into Cara the other day, and she got all upset at me again."

"See? Like I said—basket case. Boys will do that to a mom. Shit, any kids will do that." He runs his finger along my cheek, and I see a shine in his eye. "I have a theory. I'm willing to bet that Cara attacked you about this whole thing because it hit a little too close to home. She'd probably been feeling the same way—I mean, Christ, three little boys—but you actually acted on it when she didn't have the courage to." He shrugs. "I think Cara needs your comfort and forgiveness as much as you need hers."

Courage. He thinks I have courage.

I nod, the lump still rising in my throat. "So you're not mad? About me leaving Sylvie?"

"What would I be mad about?" he says. "If anything, I'm mad that you had to pay such a hefty late fee, but eh, whatever. Shit happens." He looks me in the eye. "Beth, you didn't do anything wrong. The only person mad at you, is you."

"But…" I take a deep breath. "It runs in my blood." As soon as I say it, I feel my cheeks flush hot. What a stupid argument.

"What does?" His face twists in confusion.

"I shouldn't have brought it up. It's dumb."

"Well, now I'm curious."

I sigh. "Grandma Vee. Her mother abandoned her. She was adopted. I guess I feel like that tendency is there, like it's a part of me." I know it doesn't make any sense, yet I can't seem to shake the idea. I know something like this can't possibly be passed down, but maybe there's some underlying issue. Personality disorders, or narcissism…

Autism.

"When was that?" he asks. "The Depression?"

I shrug. "I guess. Maybe the Twenties? Vee is nearly ninety."

"A lot of sick shit went down back then. We don't know the full story." He refills my wine glass and hands it to me. "Don't make some random woman's story your story. You don't know what she was dealing with."

I sip the wine. I feel Eddie's fingertips gently tickle their way up my side under my shirt. My skin is hot where he touches me. I lean into him further. In minutes, I know the Scrabble game is over.

27

SEPTEMBER, 1927

"Mama?"

There's a long pause. Maybe she's asleep.

I look around. There's a light on in the bathroom. "Mama? Are you—"

"In here, Babydoll." She sounds resigned, tired. Maybe another headache.

I let her have her peace in the bathroom. I slip off my shoes, drop my pocketbook onto the sofa. Unpin my cloche and take it off, shaking out my bob underneath. Glance at the mail on the kitchen table and then at the clock. Nearly midnight. Hazel and I never did make it to Frank Shady's.

Maybe Mama would be well enough to care for a baby while I work serving coffee or connecting telephone calls. I could go out tomorrow and poke around at the phone company. They wouldn't care if a girl knew the difference between seal skin or calf skin or even moose skin. Maybe we don't need Charlie. Maybe we can raise this baby, just Mama and me. There has to be a way.

After so long thinking it would be only one baby and then to be surprised by two, it now chokes me up to know there's only one again.

I can't lose her too.

The kitchen is dark. I get myself a glass of water from the tap and plop down in a chair next to the table to enjoy the shadowy silence for a moment.

We can do this. Just us girls. But then I'll have to tell Mama that the wonderful Mirabelle and Henry don't exist. I'll have to tell her that no baby was ever adopted by anyone. I'll have to tell her why Charlie can't know about the baby.

I'll have to tell some more lies about the baby's father.

With a thousand tons on my shoulders, I drag myself out of the chair. Mama's still in the bathroom, so I wander in to check on her, dragging my feet.

She sits on the edge of the claw-foot tub, her pink-polished toes pressed into a shallow pool of water in the bottom of the basin. She has a towel wrapped around her and she holds her head in her hands, her dark curls falling over her fingers.

She looks defeated.

"Mama? Another headache?"

She doesn't look at me. She stares at her feet inside the tub as a small puddle of pink water gathers around her toes. I realize her toenails are not painted—it's blood.

"Jesus and Joseph, Mama. Did you step on a piece of glass?"

She still doesn't answer. I follow the faint stream of red up the porcelain curve of the tub to where it originates under her towel.

My insides quake and my mind clatters to life like the engine in Uncle Barlow's Ford. Things start adding up in my head: she's grieving her lover. She's worried about me, about us. She knows we're in a world of trouble.

Oh, God. She's hurt herself.

My body aches when I realize I'm holding my breath. What has she done?

I kneel next to the tub, beside my mother. "Mama, are you okay? What happened?" My mind races for a reasonable explanation. "If you're having your monthly, mama—"

"No." She shakes her head. "It's not that." She finally lifts her eyes to look at me. Her makeup is smeared. Her left eye is slightly droopy, dark.

"Mama?" My stomach tightens in panic. I feel sick. "What happened?" I take her hands, squeeze them. They're limp. I force myself to say the words I don't want to say. "Did you...Mama, did you do this? To yourself?"

"No, Josie." She shakes her head, pushes my bobbed hair behind my ear with her finger. She lets out a big, deep breath. She stares at the wallpaper in front of her for a minute before continuing. "It was Mr. Gillum, from down the hall."

My body recoils in disgust and confusion, but she doesn't seem to notice. "That pig in 411 who's always grabbing my rear end when we pass in the hall?"

"He does the same to me," she says.

"Did he attack you? What did he do?"

I stop. Stare at the white floor tiles.

I know what he did, what Mama did. And he was overly rough with her about it. I'm becoming like Hazel in being able to figure things out.

247

"Oh, Mama."

"Please, Josie. I don't need a lecture. I know what I did was wrong, but he gave me thirty dollars." Her face brightens as she looks at me. "Thirty! We can pay our rent this month. We'll be okay."

I slide back from my crouch next to her and sit on the tiled floor in front of the tub. We sit for a long time in silence. When Mama takes a breath, it trembles. Tears mix with the blood at her feet. "We need money," she says so quietly that it's barely a whimper.

I don't respond. I can't. I don't know whether to scream or to cry, to spit in disgust or even laugh at the absurdity of this horrible joke she must be telling.

It must be a joke. All of this. Yet here she is, bleeding into the bathtub.

I notice her flexing and wiggling her fingers, fighting off the numbness that vexes her. A dreamy look falls over her eyes, which often happens when a headache starts to clamp down on her.

"You…what…" I struggle to form a sentence.

Her eyes go even more hollow, and despair fills her face. She looks delirious. "I thought it might help."

"Help?" I struggle to keep my voice calm. "Mama, you let Mr. Gillum do this to you? I'd rather we live on the street." I take her hands. "Charlie will come through. Soon, Mama. It will be all right. You have to believe me. Don't…" I stop. Take a breath. She told me not to lecture her. Still, this is undeniably preposterous. I can't allow her to prostitute herself to the neighbors. It must be a dream. But no. We're here. I can smell the ammonia in the floor cleaner that scrubbed the tiles just yesterday, the sweat that clings to Mama's skin, leftover from

Mr. Gillum's entertainment. This is all real. "You don't have to do that, Mama. Ever. Please."

"Don't rush to marry Charlie if you don't want to, Babydoll. You're young; you should be having fun. Maybe you could get some training in those perfumes you like to mix. Is that why you got those chemistry books? Such a smart girl. You'll be so successful." Her lips arch into a Mona Lisa smile.

"Mama—"

Her smile falls. Her face is as pale as the porcelain tub. "It was Sergei," she says, "wasn't it?"

Oh, God.

She knows.

I'm sure my face has gone just as white as hers. I pick up a fresh towel to clean up the mess of ruddy water on the tile floor but then wonder if this busy work makes me look as guilty as I am. "Mama, what are you talking about?" I sop up a few small puddles and then force myself to look at her.

She's watching me. Her eyes float in pain and sadness. "Sergei had a wandering eye. I know he was with other women. Did he force you, Josie?"

Self-preservation pulls all of my lies out to my lips. "No, Mama." I say it emphatically, probably more so than I need to. I stay crouching next to her. "He never touched me. He was faithful to you. He was." I carry my heavy eyes up to meet hers. The look on her face nearly kills me. "And I would never do that to you. Or to Charlie."

My lies shred my throat. I have to make this up to her. If anyone should be selling their body to the man down the hall, it should be me.

She nods. "Okay." She wraps her arm around my head,

hugs me to her like she did when I was little and my height only reached her waist. "I believe you."

I can smell the Borax from the laundry in the bath towel she has wrapped around her. I can smell her warmth encircling me. I press my face into her as she holds me. My stomach bubbles with sickness. This is what we've become. This is what I've driven my mother to do. For us. This is what "okay" means—selling our bodies to pay the rent. Lying to save face. Putting babies in a sideshow.

I boost myself up and perch on the edge of the tub next to her. Then I pull her into an embrace. We hold each other for a long time. I release the sobs from my chest. I cry and cry, using the pink-stained towel I'd used on the floor to catch my tears.

It's all I can do.

"No one has to know, Babydoll. I won't do this again." Her slight body feels heavy in my arms. I keep my eyes on her, watching her. She rubs her hands, willing feeling back into her fingers. I know she's lying. When we run out of money—which we will, right quick—she'll do it again. And the next time, it just might kill her.

We are both liars.

I don't have time for Charlie to figure out what he wants. I also don't have the option to dream about bringing my baby home. I need to fix this. Now.

28

Beth

JUNE, 2017

"Funerals are for grandmothers and grandfathers," Kate Miller says. "Mothers and fathers, brothers, sisters, friends. They are all heartbreaking, but necessary. We lose people we love; it's just a part of life." She takes a deep breath. "We shouldn't have to lose those whom we've only just started to love. Funerals are not for children and babies. Yet, here we are."

Kate pauses a moment.

I've been to several funerals for infants. Some mothers are sobbing messes, and some respond to the stress by organizing and managing and controlling. Neither is wrong. At the moment, Kate's voice is gentle, but it carries easily over the group of mourners. There are about forty people here at the cemetery, all of us sweltering under the blazing sun and swimming in humidity. I shift my heels so they don't sink into the soft grass. I can feel droplets of sweat drizzle down my skin under my dress. Layana, next to me, clears her throat. Her forehead sparkles with moisture.

Kate is amazingly composed, but I know it's a veneer. I've seen her in the NICU visiting Paige and Phoebe. Underneath her poise and prepared words, she's a mess.

"A funeral is a place to grieve a life cut short or a life well lived," Kate continues. "Sweet Aunt Mildred who is remembered fondly or old Uncle Joe who was a miserable son-of-a-bitch. But still they're remembered, somehow, by someone. That's what a funeral is for. To remember.

"But Patrick won't be remembered by anyone other than Troy and me. There is very little to remember. Patrick spent seventeen days in the NICU. Outside of my womb, Patrick only ever existed inside a plastic box. His nurses and doctors spent more time with him then we did." She takes a deep breath, and I hear a tremble in it. She struggles to collect herself. "I never even held Patrick alive."

That thought alone makes me feel heavy. My eyes turn to the ground.

I sense some uncomfortable shifting in the group around me, but Kate quickly pulls herself together. "We still have two girls," she says, "and we're so thankful that they're healthy and doing well in the NICU. Still, I had dreams for my little boy. Hopes for him that now I'll never see fulfilled. I'll never watch him dig holes in my flower bed with his Tonka backhoe; I'll never adjust his bow tie as he dresses for his senior prom.

"But more than that, more than my own silly hopes and dreams, is that he would have had his own, too, and maybe they wouldn't have matched mine. Maybe we would have argued about it. Maybe I would have been disappointed. Maybe he would have rolled his eyes and slammed doors." She holds her fingers to her lips, her face reddening. "I'll take those irritations and disappointments over this any day."

I feel pins prick behind my eyes. I hear my own thoughts in her words: *My child will never struggle through algebra or debate books versus movies with me.*

My Sylvie won't fulfill my dreams. I'm awfully narcissistic to think she ever would have, anyway.

"You've all come today to help us grieve a baby that most of you never met. I can't tell you how much that means to me. I can't hold my baby. I can't watch him grow. Instead, we're putting him into the ground. But knowing that you are all here and that you all love Troy and me, then, in turn, you love Patrick too. You won't remember him, but please, just remember this day, and that will be enough."

Her husband gathers her into his arms, nearly knocking over one of the poster-sized photographs clipped to easels around the grave. A woman grabs it and rights it before it topples.

Those pictures are among the only mementos that Kate and Troy have—maybe one of the hospital-grade blankets or several videos of his first few days that they'll keep on their phones until the technology fails. But those things can never replace holding a child, feeling his skin, his soft, downy hair. Accepting who that child is, even if he doesn't speak and doesn't like ice cream and wants to play with wrapped tampons.

Reverend Dooley steps up next to give a eulogy, and I let my mind wander. I've heard the chaplain's preemie eulogy before; after about the fourth or fifth time I stopped listening. It's a lovely speech, but it's always the same. I envy people who know the right thing to say at the right time; I only ever get it wrong. Maybe that's why Reverend Dooley just sticks to his script.

I study one of the large photographs—the one that nearly fell. Patrick is in the middle, flanked by Paige on one side and Phoebe on the other. I know this picture was taken after his death because I'd helped remove the wires and tubes from Phoebe and Paige for a few minutes for the photographer. Three crocheted beanies, all lined up: pink, green, purple.

Of course Patrick's is green. Little leprechaun. But no number of lucky clovers could save the boy. I would not have been able to save him either, had I been there.

I keep telling myself that, but I'm not sure if I believe it yet.

When Reverend Dooley finishes, Layana takes my hand, and we line up to file past Patrick's casket. It's white, the size of a suitcase. This is never easy to see. Layana puts a handful of long-stemmed white roses on top of it. I follow her, resting a bouquet of colorful gerbera daisies next to the roses. Blue, green, orange, yellow, and red. It just seemed right for Patrick.

I swallow the lump in my throat. We go to Kate, and Layana gives her and Troy each a warm hug. I do the same, but I feel stiff, numb. I can't help but feel a crushing guilt that I did this. This is all my fault. If I'd just been there, maybe I could have saved him.

Layana and I move along to give others space to grieve. We meet up with Rita, who has her arm around a devastated Drea.

"How are you girls holding up?" Rita gathers us all in close for a hug.

Layana shrugs. "Shitty."

I nod. "Same."

Drea takes a deep, teary breath. Her eyes are red and her face is streaked with sweat and tears. I hand her a fresh tissue. "Drea, it's okay," I say. "These funerals are tough but necessary. The parents appreciate us being here."

"I failed," she says, her voice steady against her tears. "I couldn't save him. You put me in charge and I failed. I'm so sorry."

"Okay, you just stop right there, Missy." Layana leans over and pulls Drea into a strong embrace. "You did what you could. We all did. You're a good nurse, you hear me? I don't want to hear this failure talk."

"Drea, sometimes we have to let them go," Rita says, a little more gently than Layana. "I've spent thirty years as a neonatal nurse practitioner, and I've seen it all. It's tragic, but that's life in the NICU. With the good comes the bad."

The four of us—Rita, Layana, Drea, and I—stand in a close circle, sharing the pain of the people who were charged with saving Patrick but couldn't.

"Thank you for coming, ladies," a man's voice booms from behind me. Drea looks up, and her face pales. I turn, expecting to see Patrick's father Troy, or maybe one of the grandfathers.

It's Dr. Che. I hadn't seen him in the crowd or maybe I just didn't recognize him in a dark suit. He rarely comes to these.

He looks shaken.

"Good to see you, Dr. Che," Layana says, her voice soft and soothing.

He nods, his sleepy eyes only half open. He's less than a month from retirement. Maybe the finality of it all is making him sentimental. He pats me on the arm, gives Drea's hand a squeeze, then shuffles back to the lineup of cars parked on the cemetery road. We all watch him in silence.

One by one Rita, Drea, and Layana go back to their cars, but I linger a bit. After most of the mourners have gone, I walk in the opposite direction. Several yards away, behind a tree, I pick up a small bundle of pink roses that I'd left. Then I go for a walk.

29

It's Monday morning. I wait with three other girls in the lobby, our cloche hats all pulled low over our foreheads, the cigarettes in our hands not helping to keep us from fidgeting.

"Next please. Miss Trivelli?"

The young woman next to me stands. She stubs out her cigarette in the ashtray and adjusts her gloves before turning and following the woman with the clipboard. The rest of us watch over the glossy pages of our *McCall's* and *Modern Priscillas*, concealed behind our clouds of exhaled smoke.

Before the morning is over, one of us will be demonstrating and selling cosmetics at the brand-new Max Factor counter at Lord and Taylor. I did myself up as best as I could, but thank goodness I have a dancer for a girlfriend. Hazel rarely exists without her face fully made-up, so she came over early this morning, fixed my mistakes, and gave me a few pointers on what "in the know" words to toss around during the interview.

As I sit here waiting for my turn, I feel like a fraud. I glance over at the other women waiting and notice an air about them. They're fully comfortable with cosmetics and fashion. I pull my shoulders back and straighten my spine. I need to show that I am too.

I bet none of them can discern a *Rose Verite* from a *Rose L'Odeur*. I smile to myself.

"Miss Westley?"

I practically jump to my feet at the call of my name. I stand, smooth out my dress, touch the rim of my cloche, and paint on my winning smile.

The woman with the clipboard leads me up an escalator to a small, tidy desk at the back of the second floor. A mustached, portly man sits in a creaky chair behind it, his ankle crossed over his knee, a stack of papers lined up neatly in front of him. He leans on the desk with one arm as he studies a sheet of paper in his hand. A cigarette smolders in an ashtray just off his elbow.

"Mr. Childers. This is Miss Westley."

He looks up and arches his eyebrow at me. I watch his eyes take me in from head to toe. I feel a squeeze of disgust. Then I remember Mama and Mr. Gillum. Through a series of events that I started only because I didn't have the courage to say no to Sergei, my mother is now a prostitute.

I plant my feet on the terrazzo floor and give the lewd little man my most dazzling smile. His own grin widens into something that makes my skin crawl. He lets his eyes sweep over me again. I hitch out my hip. I hope my lavender shift dress delights him.

Thirty minutes later, with eyes dried out from fluttering

my lashes and my brain tired from describing cake mascara and plucked eyebrows just like Hazel described, I returned to the main level of Lord and Taylor. I don't know what did it—whether it was my full encyclopedia of fragrance knowledge that was, as the man said, "impressive though not useful, since we're not in the perfume business" or just the fact that the hem of my dress hit right at my knee. Either way, I'm now the new—and very surprised—Max Factor girl. I wander down to the scarf counter, where Hazel is wrapping herself in silk, waiting for me.

"Haz."

She turns, her neck covered in three different shades of purple. Her eyes are wide, questioning.

"I got it."

"Bees knees, Jo! You did it!" Hazel whoops, wrapping me in an exuberant hug. "Let's go celebrate, you and me!" She peels off her scarves and leaves them on the counter for the shop girl to sort.

We end up at the automat, which is fine by me since I'm starving. The place is packed with the lunch crowd, so much so that we have to reach between patrons to get our nickels in the slots.

"This is the start of something absolutely wonderful for you, Jo. I just know it." Hazel opens a little doorway and pulls out a ham salad sandwich. She balances it on her tray next to her coffee and pie. "Here, Jo. Get yourself dessert, on me." She hands me a nickel. I opt for pineapple upside down cake, and meet her in a tight little schmoozie booth in the corner.

"So tell me, what are you going to say to Charlie?" Hazel asks, sinking her fork into the high meringue of her lemon pie. Hazel always eats her dessert first, just in case.

I move the gravy around my Salisbury steak. Though I'm

hungry, I can't seem to bring the food to my mouth. The warm scent of Hazel's coffee drifts to my nose, making me wish I'd gotten one for myself. "I guess I'll tell him the truth. Mama and I need money, and since I don't have any marriage proposals filling up my dance card, I need to make do for myself." I force a bite into my mouth. It's warm, comforting. I chew it slowly.

Hazel smiles through her pie. "I like your moxie."

"Not moxie at all. It's the honest-to-God truth."

"Well, I, for one, think you are doing a capital thing." Hazel sits back in her seat, bringing her coffee cup with her. "Cosmetics counter. How very debonair. Just think of the celebrities you'll come across. Why, you may just be making up Mildred Davis before the end of the week!"

I push away my steak and stab at my cake with my fork. "Hazel, I don't know the first thing about applying cosmetics. If Mildred Davis comes to me for help with her look, then she's in bigger trouble than any of us."

Hazel laughs. "When do you start?"

"Tomorrow."

"Well, you better study up before then." She polishes off her pie. "This is going to be first-rate all around. And if it's still Charlie you're after, it may just set a flame to his feet."

We sit for a while, eating and gossiping. Being girlfriends. It feels so free, so wonderful, to just chew the fat like this.

After a while, Hazel stretches, then stands. "Honey, I hate to blouse, but I have an audition uptown at two o'clock, and I gotta go warm up the pipes." She puts her hand on my shoulder. "Jo, darling…" Her voice is warm and jubilant. "Congratulations. You did real good."

"Thanks, Haz." I watch her wiggle through the automat,

the eyes of nearly every man inside following her out the door. Near the front of the restaurant, her heel catches on a loose tile and she loses her balance. From where I sit, I see four different men jump up to catch her stumble. Without any of their help she rights herself, turns, and gives them all a wink. Then in a flash of sunlight hitting the revolving door, she's gone.

With a look like Hazel's, there's always someone to catch you when you stumble.

I smile to myself. I'm now one of those working girls. Like Hazel. Places to go, people to see. Pipes to warm up. Just last night, Mama confessed what she did to get us our rent. I had no prospects and was pinning all my hopes on an indifferent fella that cared more about his money than his Molly. Now, this morning, I've fixed it. I caught my own stumble. I smile. Things are high-stepping. We'll be okay.

Okay enough to bring home a baby? Maybe, but I can't think about that just yet. I still have time before the first of November, when the amusement park will evict my child. By then, I may have climbed us out of debt. I may have changed Charlie's mind about bringing home a helpless little urchin. And if I haven't? Well, maybe Mama and I can make do. I would miss Charlie— he's my guy, faults and all—but I have a baby now.

Well, anyway, so much can happen between now and then. I'll just have to wait and see. But somehow, everything is going to work out.

I will make this up to Mama. She deserves to be happy, and I've only caused pain. Now is the time to turn that around.

With fresh fortitude burning in my chest, I stand and carry my tray to the busser station. My lunch is mostly untouched, aside from the cake. I sneak my dinner roll into my pocket for the walk home. I can be a mother *and* a daughter. I'll be a wife when the time is right. But as of tomorrow, I'm a shop girl. I'm a…what did the man call it? *Cosmetologist.* Maybe I can segue it into being a perfumer.

There's a certain contentment that takes over as I walk home. Autumn is in full swing, and the cool breeze coming off the Hudson River is whisking away some of the stagnant, muggy air. The odor of wet leaves cooling on the streets is actually inviting, comforting. The fragrance of fall. For the first time in who knows how long, I feel a lightness in my step as I push open the door to our building.

We'll be okay.

There's mail in our box. I pull the envelopes out, shuffle through them one by one. Bills. But I don't have to be afraid of bills anymore. I drop them into my pocketbook and climb the steps, picking at my dinner roll. I pull off a piece of crust, pop it into my mouth. Wipe the crumbs from my fingers.

First floor. Second.

I come off the stairs on our floor and turn the corner down our hall. I can't wait to tell Mama. She'll find it all so chic. Maybe she'll come in and be one of my first customers. She won't mind if I make some mistakes with the kohl or the rouge. She'll be a good sport. I can practice on her at home.

There's a discarded coat piled in the hallway next to the phone.

I slow my step as I approach.

It's not a coat. It's a woman.

It's Mama.

My pocketbook hits the floor.

I kneel. Shake her. *Mama! Wake up! Mama!* Someone is yelling, howling. It's me, though the sound surprises me. I don't feel it coming out of my lungs, but I can hear it. It sounds wild.

No one else hears me. No one comes. The phone is on the floor next to her. I reach for it, beg for the operator. There's no sound. I follow the cord and find it pulled from the wall, severed from when she must have fallen on top of it. The weight of her slight body pulled the cord taut, breaking it.

I roll her over. Shake her. Rock her. Stroke her hair. Pull on her toes. Whatever I can think of to get her to respond.

Nothing.

I bury my face in her shoulder and search for some slight thumping of her heart, some warmth of blood making its way through her, a whimper at her throat. Something—*anything*—to tell me she's still here.

There's nothing.

She feels cool to the touch.

Just like Rose did.

30

Beth

I slip off my heels and feel the soft, manicured grass under my feet. I count off the gravestones while I walk about a half-mile to the northwest.

The Villanova marker, still waiting for Gladys to join her husband Anthony.

An obelisk-shaped headstone for Gareth Zillich, his birth unknown, died in 1916, the day and month worn off but it looks like *-uary* something.

The flat slab for Yury Orlovsky, born and died on March 4, 1983. A small teddy bear sits on the slab. I notice it's replaced with a new one every few weeks or so.

I try to stay in the shade of the trees, and when a breeze rustles the leaves, I lift my arms to let a little air underneath.

A quick pause at Michelle Craven, who was killed in a car

crash when we were in high school. "Hi, Michelle." I smile at her picture embedded into the stone. I keep moving.

Turn left at the stone bench that represents the wealthy McAffrey family.

Four plots past the massive oak tree with the unreadable, ancient marker under it.

Right at a pink, cast glass memorial carved with intricate Japanese characters.

Finally, I find her. I kneel next to her grave.

Andrea Jane Flaherty Milner. April 6, 1950 – December 22, 2016. I trace her name with my finger. Then I rest the roses beside the headstone, next to some other items that have been left.

A little yellow matchbox car.

A rock painted with swirls of blue and purple, and a crooked smiley face.

A bright green plastic triceratops.

And the red lid of a tub of ice cream. *Kemps Old Fashioned Maple Nut.* I pick it up. On the back, I recognize Cara's handwriting in thick, black Sharpie marker:

"Mom. Thought of you. Had your favorite in a waffle cone. Miss you so much. Miss the Three Little Kittens. Love you always."

I sit down in the sun next to Mom's grave marker, lean against the granite headstone, and cry.

31

SEPTEMBER, 1927

Lilies should have a wonderful smell. Dewy, snow-white petals painted with a dash of thick pink, orange flowers dotted with deep purples and reds—they're like royalty. They open themselves to the sky, spread their bodies to receive whatever the wind sends along, proud and fearless. They should smell of summer and charm and fortitude and all things wonderful and gay.

But they don't. By themselves, without a bit of citrus or a hint of vanilla to balance their scent, without the help of alcohol to diffuse, to soften, they smell like bologna.

I sit in the pew with my gloved hands tight against my stomach, pushing into the pain. I touch my handkerchief to my eyelid under my black veil, and when I close my eyes, I see Nathan's on the boardwalk. Hot dogs passing through an open window into the hands of the hungry. I see the Cyclone

266

sputtering and clanking overhead. I see the calm man, sitting in his tiny house with his newspaper. I see him crushed by a runaway coaster train that hurls through his front door.

I grip Charlie's hand next to me and squeeze. He pats my wrist methodically. I didn't want to wear gloves, but Charlie insisted. Proper, or something. I concentrate on the tight fabric stretching across my knuckles to keep my mind off that white building with the bright lights and the babies inside.

All the world loves a baby.

I didn't want roses. I'd told the undertaker, quite emphatically, no. I couldn't be surrounded by reminders of my dead child when I'm here grieving my dead mother. Charlie sat next to me on the uncomfortable wooden chairs reserved for the family of the recently departed and flipped through the mortuary paperwork. He only shrugged. The scent of a rose or anything else means nothing to him. Fine. No roses.

But roses would have been a hell of a lot better than this.

"Ah, yes, of course," the undertaker with the tailored suit and thin mustache had said, smiling as if he weren't selling me a profitable send-off for my loving mother. He gave me other choices: Gladioli. Chrysanthemums. Carnations. Lilies. Carnations seemed fine enough, but Charlie scoffed. Antiquated, he said. Old-fashioned. I was surprised he cared, until I learned later that they were the cheaper option. Charlie couldn't have his clients—his colleagues—seeing him surrounded by a bargain flower. I wondered how on earth he knew that. Charlie had never bought me flowers in the whole year we'd been courting. I would love a little bouquet of the cheapest blossoms on the planet, even those that grew in the cracks along the foundation of his apartment building. But I guess it doesn't matter much, anyway.

Now I wish I'd chosen the carnations. Their cost and their scent are both so subtle, I wouldn't be sitting here, sickened and indebted to the florist.

I'm anchored in the pew next to Charlie, surrounded by a smell I'm quickly coming to loathe. Charlie's leg bounces, shaking the whole length of the bench. It vibrates like the clanging of a roller coaster beneath me.

I will never mix another scent with lilies.

In fact, I have a very dark feeling that I'll never mix another scent at all. I don't know how I could, with the guilt of everything I've done, every lie I've told, pushing down on me and tainting my senses with grief. A grief that only I caused.

The brown box at the front of the church holds all that's left of my mother. Lilies sprawl over the top of the varnished wood, overthrowing everything, making their own presence the most important thing in the room. *Pay no attention to the woman in the box,* they say.

But a lily is nothing but a humbug. It likes to pretends it doesn't smell like a cheap slice of lunch meat.

The pastor is droning on about the valley of death. We all bow our heads to pray that my mother makes it into some kind of sparkling crystal kingdom in the clouds, so she can carry a harp and sit next to a bearded man with a visor of light encircling his head.

Another humbug.

My scalp tingles. Superstition leads me to make a quick sign of the cross, just in case.

I slide my fingers out of Charlie's grip and reach for a tissue in my pocketbook. I let my brain stumble over the forgotten words of the scriptures that have found little place in my memory.

After my father died, there wasn't anyone—or any real reason—to inspire Mama or me to follow the teachings of the Church.

And, well, look where that got us. Better say a few more Hail Marys, if I can remember how it goes.

Mama. She must have known something was wrong that day while I was out lollygagging after lunch. She might have gotten dizzy, felt the numbness in her hands, maybe come down with a banger of a headache that put all other headaches to shame. Whatever it was, she stumbled down the hall to the telephone. I can only assume she was trying to call for help. Or, maybe she had no warning. Maybe she was just calling her hairdresser, then halfway through negotiating a cut and a curl for a window washing or a toilet scrubbing, she just fell to the floor, dead.

I don't know. The doctor who had come after I finally got through to an operator on a downstairs telephone also didn't know. So her cause of death was listed as cerebral hemorrhage. Whether that's true or not, I guess it doesn't matter. Maybe it was Mr. Gillum's doing, or maybe it wasn't. Maybe it was connected to her headaches and her numb fingertips. Maybe it wasn't. I'll never know.

The service ends before I can remember any particular prayer in its entirety. I mutter a quick, "Help me, Jesus. It's all gone to hell," hoping it will be good enough. God is all-forgiving. He'll forgive me, even when no one else—including myself—will.

Right?

I follow the hired pallbearers who carry my mother's coffin to the back of the church, feeling Charlie's hand against the small of my back. As we enter the narthex, I can see Barlow's Tin Lizzy parked outside at the curb through the stained-glass windows of the church's front door. Uncle Barlow and Aunt Alice wait for me. I fall into Alice's arms while Barlow and Charlie shake hands and exchange pleasantries.

A scent breaks through the overwhelming lilies. *Tabac Blond.* I smile. Hazel's here.

"Jo. Goddamn. I don't know what to say." Hazel and Skip saunter over. She pulls me into a hug. I love her for not caring about using God's name in vain, even in a church. "You look good," she says in a conspiratorial whisper. "It fits like a glove."

"Thanks again, hon." I say. Since neither Hazel or I ever intended to spend any time mourning anyone, neither of us had a stitch of black in our closets. For this occasion, she nicked a couple of dark dresses from the Hudson Theater's costume department.

"Good of you to come, old man," Charlie reaches over and shake's Skip's hand. Skip stuffs his hands back into his pockets, looking as dazed as a fella would when he'd never even seen the inside of a church.

"Course. Least we could do." Skip fidgets. "Wouldn't miss it. Is there a going to be a luncheon?" He winces as Hazel elbows him in the ribs.

There's a moment of awkward silence. Finally, Barlow pulls in a billowing breath. "Well now," he says. He looks at Charlie. Looks at me. Shakes his head. "What an almighty shame."

"Yes. Yes it is," Charlie says. We all murmur our agreement. I see eyes flit around, chests heave with sighing lungs. We're all searching for something—anything—happy to say.

Barlow clears his throat. As the eldest man in our small group, he must feel compelled to speak, though I'd rather just enjoy the silent comfort of being with those I love. "So Charlie," Barlow says, "how are those lovely girls? Really something, aren't they? Been spending every day with them, I would imagine?"

"Girls?" Charlie freezes, his cigarette lighter poised unlit in his hand, ready to ignite the gasper between his lips.

My face goes cold, and I feel all of the blood rush out of it. I look at Hazel. She has the same panicked expression on her face.

Charlie slowly brings the lighter down and removes the cold cigarette from his mouth. "Which—"

"Oh, the dogs. I took them." Hazel says, flipping her hand like she's brushing away gnats. "Cutest darn little things you've ever seen. Pomeranians, I think. Those fluffy little cream puffs, both white as the driven snow. Yappy as a couple of mustard plasters, though." Hazel is talking fast. Only I know that means she's lying. Maybe Skip does too, but he doesn't have a rooster in this fight. He just watches her, amused. Looks like he's finally learned to keep his trap shut.

"Yes, the dogs," I say. "I couldn't keep them. Not allowed in our building, so I gave them to Hazel."

"And I couldn't keep them either. Damn allergies. Oops, sorry!" Hazel waves a finger around, gesturing to the statues and stained glass of the holy building. "I gave them to an old widow in our building. Darling lady, lonely as hell. Anyway, she adores them. Named them Sugar and Spice. I see her around." She fiddles for her cigarette holder in her pocketbook and nearly drops it. I notice a tremble in her hands. She lifts her head, her holder intact. "Seems happy," she says with a shrug, as if all of this talk about the dogs is boring and over with.

I look at Alice. Her bewilderment is plastered all over her face. She catches my eye, and I try to silently beg her to play along. I pucker my lips and raise my eyebrows. She gives the tiniest nod. My aunt understands. Barlow looks confused as ever, but I have Alice on my side.

"Dear, we don't want to be late." She pulls her veil down over her eyes and steers Barlow toward the front door. She tosses a glance back at me through the netting. I blink. I want to mouth a "thank you" to her, but I'm afraid of any more movement that could give away my lie.

I look at Charlie. He's lit his cigarette and looks calm. Still, I can't tell if he's bought our flimflam. "Alice is right," I say to him. "We don't want to be late getting to the cemetery. We should go."

"We can drive you," Hazel says.

"Dogs, Ducky?" Charlie squints at me. "I don't remember you ever mentioning dogs."

"Oh, I must have. Anyway, I didn't even bring them into the apartment. Hazel took them right away, and to be honest, I forgot about them."

"Why—"

"Charlie," Hazel glares at him. "Your girl's mother just died. We are at her funeral, about to drop her into the ground. And all you care about is a couple of worthless dogs? Come on, now." Hazel twists her face in annoyance and shakes her bobbed hair out of her face. "I didn't feature you bein' that kind of egg, Charlie."

Charlie stares at the ground. "You're right. I'm sorry, Ducky." He puts his arm around my waist. I play along and lean into him. I feel the indifference in his stance. "Let's go to the graveyard."

~

Within the hour, Mama is underground, and a couple of men in overalls are scooping dirt on top of her polished cedar casket. The pastor walks away, bible in hand. He pats me on the shoulder as he passes, shakes Charlie's hand and nods to Hazel, who hasn't left my side.

"God bless," he says. Then he looks to the heavens as if expecting God himself to open his hands. "At least it's a beautiful day."

I glance up to the cloudless blue sky. He's right; the air is comfortable around me, with just enough of a breeze to blow away the smells of death and lilies. A beautiful day to bury my mother. I wish for rain. Lightning. The crack of thunder. I wish for the ground to shake and pull open beneath my feet and eat me alive. The cheerful birds swooping overhead through the clear, early-autumn sky only make my heart break even more.

Mama died without ever meeting her granddaughter.

But then, she also died without ever truly knowing how I betrayed her with Sergei.

Tit for tot, I suppose.

I'm a monster.

Charlie ambles away from me toward a group of dark-suited men whom I don't recognize. He shakes hands all around and passes out his calling card. They do the same. I feel warm in the sun, so I remove my gloves. We're done here, anyway.

"Jo." Alice grabs my elbow and steers me behind a tree. I look around and see the small group of people who'd assembled to send Mama off are all breaking away to leave. Hands are stuffed in pockets and black veils are pulled up over the tops of hats. Party's over. Charlie's still busy, laughing with his new buddies.

Alice motions toward Barlow, who's stalking away toward the flivver parked on the dirt path. "Barlow is livid," she says. "I told him to keep his trap shut about your pregnancy around Charlie, but he doesn't understand. Frankly, I don't, either."

"Auntie." As soon as I look at her, all the emotion I'd been holding in all day spills out of my eyes and runs down my cheeks.

"So Charlie doesn't know? Why doesn't he know, Jo? Why are we making up stories about dogs? Why haven't you told him about his daughters?" She hands me a handkerchief from her pocketbook.

I wipe my eyes. I can't look up at her. Though my gloves are off, my hands still sweat with warmth and nerves. "Daughter. Just one."

"What?" Then her face falls. "Oh, Lord Jesus." She rubs my back in circles. "Honey. Which one?"

"Rose is gone."

She groans. "Poor thing." She makes a sign of the cross, then she puts her finger under my chin to lift my face. "Still," her eyes lock on mine, "that doesn't explain why Charlie's left out in the cold."

"Because this doesn't concern Charlie," Hazel says. She'd stayed within earshot, and now she's come up behind me. I feel her warmth and smell her perfume as her arm snakes around my waist.

Alice's hands plant onto her hips. "Well, I should say it does. After all—"

"We're all better off if we just leave this, Mrs. Owens," Hazel says to Alice.

My aunt's face hardens. "I think if there's anyone this doesn't concern, it's you, miss."

Hazel stiffens beside me—I can feel the heated rage course around her body through our borrowed dresses. I know what happens when Hazel feels slighted, and this isn't the place for that kind of brawl. I squeeze Hazel's arm. Then I look up at Alice.

"Charlie can't know I was pregnant or that there's any baby." I swallow hard. "Charlie wasn't responsible."

Fire flashes across Alice's eyes. "Miss Johnston," she turns her head toward Hazel but doesn't take her eyes off me. "I'd appreciate a word with my niece. Alone."

Hazel straightens even more beside me. Her grip on my waist tightens. I feel her strength, and I straighten as well. Together, we are a brick wall.

"No."

It's the simplest "no" I've ever heard Hazel say.

Alice nods, but she purses her lips and doesn't speak her part.

"Mrs. Owens," Hazel says, her voice firm, "there's much that happens in a girls' life that she has little control over."

"Jo," Alice says. "Are you saying that your pregnancy was the result of some man forcing himself on you?"

I lift my head and look her straight in the eye. "No." I keep my *no* just as straightforward as Hazel's.

Alice blanches. "Well then. I guess your uncle Barlow was right." She narrows her eyes. "You are a whore."

Before I realize my body is in motion, I feel my arm lift and my fingers open. The sting of flesh against my hand. Alice doubles over, her own gloved hand covering her reddening cheek. I hold my offending fingers to my shocked mouth. This was the woman who'd helped me when I needed it, who'd housed me when I was hiding from the world, who'd sopped the sweat from my brow as I pushed two humans out into life.

So now I'm not only a liar and a harlot, I'm an ungrateful, lying harlot.

"Auntie, I'm…"

My whimper trails off as she looks up. Her eyes flash between Hazel and me.

She turns and hurries toward her husband in his automobile.

"…I'm sorry." She doesn't hear my whisper. And even if she

did, she shouldn't turn around. I don't deserve her good will.

I've lost my mother, my aunt, and a daughter. I turn to Hazel, my eyes full.

She meets my gaze and gives me a brave smile. "Goddamn, Jo." She pulls me into a hug. Over her shoulder, I see Charlie shaking hands again, then turning to come collect me. Hazel and I break our embrace, and Hazel glances over her shoulder before she whispers in my ear. "We'll meet up later. At least you still have your job. You can tell me all about it."

She passes Charlie as she walks away, giving him a friendly squeeze on his arm.

Job. I have no job. In the flurry and confusion that took over after finding Mama in the hallway, I never showed up for work. I forgot I had a job at all. As a last-ditch effort, I called yesterday and tried to explain my case.

"Condolences, Miss Westley." Mr. Childers tone was impatient over the line. *"That is certainly bad news, but I'm afraid we hired one of the other ladies in your place. Best of luck to you."*

"Ducky," Charlie says, "let's get a cab. I'll take you home."

Home. To an apartment empty of everything.

32

Beth

I've spent the last couple of days finding excuses to not call Cara. I know she misses me—us—as much as I miss her.

My shift starts in about twenty minutes. I'm in my car in the hospital parking lot. The dust is all gone from the dash. There are no more candy wrappers stuffed between the seats. The cup holder is no longer sticky.

I have enough time to call her. I can do it right now. Just talk to her. If I can do that, maybe I can get my sister back. Then everything will be okay. Without her, I have an endless, empty hole in me. I replay what Eddie said in my head. He was right. She's human. We all are. I can show her that she's important to me. I can show some grace.

It's evening. They're in the middle of supper. Or at the boys' soccer game. She's busy. I shouldn't bother her.

This is dumb. She's my sister.

Call her. Just call her.

My hands shake. I stare at my phone, at my search window for *healing autism*. More ways to help Sylvie. More ways to know I'm not abandoning her.

No. Eddie said it's alright. I can forgive myself. It's okay.

Deep breath. Just dial her number, Beth.

I don't move. I need Mom. Her hug, her encouragement. Her smell. Then, I can call. With Mom here with me, I can do it. I'll be strong enough.

I lean over and open the glove compartment. Tiny paper scraps rain down to the clean floor mat as the door pops open.

Blue and white.

Foil. Cellophane.

Mom's empty cigarette pack. Torn to pieces.

I stare at the debris scattered across the clean mat. It was all I had that carried her scent. I reach out, touch one piece that is balanced on the open door. It flitters to the floor with the rest like the last autumn leaf.

It's gone.

My shift starts in fifteen minutes. I rest my head against the steering wheel, my fingers gripping it so tightly my knuckles hurt. I want to rip it out of the car, throw it out the window. I want to cry, thrash, scream.

But I can't.

Sylvie didn't know any better. Eddie wasn't paying attention. I can't blame them.

I can't. But I do.

My stomach clenches with nausea, rage, and grief. I feel my head tighten, feel the thickness at the back of my throat that signals an oncoming migraine.

No. I take a deep breath and pound my forehead against the steering wheel to relocate the pain, to give me control over it.

Pull yourself together, Beth. Time for work.

Clouds tower high into the atmosphere to the west. I open the door and let myself out into the sultry humidity of the evening.

I'm angry. They took her from me. The people I love most— my husband and my daughter—unknowingly took the only thing I had left that truly brought my mom back to me.

I slam the car door shut behind me. I lift my head and center my thoughts on my waiting patients.

I go through the sliding doors and leave my grief behind. I have a job to do.

33

SEPTEMBER, 1927

Charlie's hands are fisted deep into his pockets as we ankle along together in silence. We're still a good few blocks from my apartment; I had the taxi drop us early. I needed some air and to get my feet under me. To try to feel solid.

My apartment. No one else there, now.

I clutch my pocketbook; since he hasn't offered his arm for me to link with or even his hand to hold, I need something to grip, to make me feel solid. Mama's gone. I hadn't realized how she was my structure. My base.

"Awfully quiet, Jo?"

"Thinking about my mother." I look up to the clouds wisping slowly across the blue autumn sky. "I guess I never thought I'd be without her."

"She was young. In her prime. Shame."

"There's so much I never said to her. I guess—" I draw in a breath, "I guess I wish I could tell her I'm sorry."

"I'm sure she forgives you."

Not if she doesn't know. I stay quiet for a minute. At least he's trying. Right now, I feel like he's my old Charlie again, and it's comforting. "I guess you're right."

"I think there's a certain amount of cruelty that parents expect from their children. Isn't that the whole point of growing up?"

Cruelty. That's the best word to describe the situation with Sergei. I was cruel to Mama. He was cruel to her too. He was also cruel to me. He left me with the dream of a scent in my nose, and the seed of two helpless babies I could never care for.

"Your aunt Alice looked pretty sore at you when she left the graveyard," he says.

"Well, she'd just lost her sister. That's to be expected." I wasn't about to explain what happened while he was busy hobnobbing.

He shakes his head. "Not just sad," he says, his tone thoughtful. "She looked downright baked."

"Everyone's grief looks different."

"You're probably right." He looked up to the sky, his eyes following the rows of windows in the skyscrapers that line Manhattan's streets. "I would just hate to see you lose her too. She's all you have left."

It's a rare, tender moment from Charlie. I squeeze his arm. "I have you, Charlie."

"Sure do, Ducky." He looks down at his feet. Doesn't smile.

I know I don't have him. I'm just waiting to hear how he ends up spilling that to me. Or if he even tells me at all. Maybe we'll just end up one of those sad old married couples who never speak and can't stand each other.

Maybe we already are.

"Well, it was a nice service. The flowers worked well."

I don't respond.

"Those lilies were a good choice."

"Sure, Charlie." I bring myself to a stop. I'm not helping this at all by just going along with his flower choices, his dinner choices, his choices about our lives together.

He walks ahead a couple of steps before he realizes I'm not keeping up. He turns toward me and scrunches his face. "Hey, what's with the red light?"

"Listen, Charlie. Do you want me for your gal?"

"What?" He laughs. I don't.

"I'm not jingling for a line, alright? I need to know what you're thinking." I look into his confused eyes. He reaches into his pocket and pulls out a pack of Luckies. Offers me one. I take it. He lights mine, then one for himself. We stand, toe to toe, blowing smoke toward each other. Both of us clammed up. Not a damn thing to say.

I try again. "Charlie, I'm no nag, you know that. But be true with me, will ya? Are we ever going to get married?"

"Well that's the crop now, isn't it?" Charlie sucks on his gasper. "All you dolls are the same. Marry me, marry me, buy me a house, make me a baby." He shakes his head in disappointment. "I thought you were different, Jo, but of course you're not. You're just like all the rest, you know that?"

"No, I don't know that, Charlie. I just want to know what's in that head of yours."

"Now that your mother's gone and you don't have a foot to stand on, you want to know if ol' Charlie's gonna pick up the tab. Am I right?"

I feel a prickle in my spine. My vision closes in as my eyes narrow. "Mama and I haven't had any feet to stand on for some time now. Not that you're any help with that."

"So that's it, is it? It's my wallet you're after." He blows out a line of smoke, aiming it over my left shoulder. "Fine. You want to get married? We'll get married. We'll have a great big hullabaloo, and we'll be happy as a spring pig in a puddle." He flicks his ashes. "When? Tomorrow? Next week? You name the day. I'll be there in a morning suit. Hell, I'll wear tails if you want."

I step back from him. Now he's just making fun. I puff a good drag on my cigarette and pretend to look for something underneath my fingernail.

"And then what, Jo?" he goes on. "You can move in to my place, I suppose. And babies? Should we get started right away? Sounds like a right grand time to me." He tugs on his bow tie.

"Don't get sore, Charlie." I drop my cigarette and stomp it out.

We stay for a while on the sidewalk like that, not speaking. I want to walk away and leave him for good. Truth is, I'm not really sure where to go. Home is nothing but empty, and with Mama gone and Alice and Barlow sore at me, I don't have many options. "Hey," I reach out and touch his arm. He flinches. "Listen, everything's jake, okay? I'm just...it's been..."

He looks me in the eye, takes in a deep breath, and lets it out in a sigh. "I know. I'm sorry. You've had a hell of a day. Burying your mother—" He stops, shakes his head.

I nod. Look away.

"Listen. You're a modern gal, I know that. Now with your mother gone, you may want to get yourself a job or something. Something simple," He jumps in quickly, correcting himself.

"Not that chemistry nonsense you were talking about." He stifles a grin. He still thinks it's funny. "You know how I feel about all that. I don't like my gal working, but you've really got no connection to me as of just yet. All that will change once we're married, but that could certainly be a little while yet."

I frown. No connection? So I'm not his best gal?

"A while, Charlie?" I feel my heart skip. I have my answer.

"You want to be stable, don't you?" he asks. "I'll feel better bringing a wife into the mix when I'm a little closer to making partner at the firm. And losing the Shaws' account sure didn't help things."

"You lost their account, Charlie? I thought Julian said—"

"You don't know my business, Jo," he says. "I can't work with the likes of Julian and Mona and their liberal ways. He was actually proud of his wife's business sense; I found out he even finances her inane vanity projects. Then they bindled off before we even ordered dinner." He smirks. "What a mug. I'm having my assistant, Miss Fritzel, cancel everything."

He tugs on his bow tie again as I watch him. I don't remind him about the gift he scooted across the table that night, the one we all thought was an engagement ring. "Charlie," I say, "we'll never be married, will we?"

He doesn't meet my eye. He looks from the ground to the jalopy passing in the street to the rising lines of the towering buildings around us. "Tell me, Jo," he says, "if I were to ask you right now to marry me—and I'm not saying I am, I'm just asking—what would you say?"

I stay still.

The landlord was doing mama a favor by keeping us in our place at a reduced rent. He told me before I left for the funeral that he'll give me two weeks, then I gotta bindle.

I don't answer Charlie. I shuffle my feet.

I guess we both have our answer.

"This isn't the time, Charlie," I say. "Ask me again tomorrow."

Then he does something I would have never expected. Charlie pulls me into a strong hug.

34

Beth

I drop my bag in the locker room and swipe in with my badge. I place my chef salad in the fridge and congratulate myself for remembering it.

Mom's cigarette pack is in shreds on the floor of my Civic. I push it out of my head. My patients need my attention. Any distraction could mean life or death in the NICU. Besides, Sylvie didn't mean it.

She didn't mean it.

I'm destroyed.

Layana is at the desk, distracted by her phone. "Hey," I say, slightly irritated. So unprofessional.

"Hey," she says back. It takes her a second to look up. "Any action out there yet?"

I frown at her. "Action?"

She waves her phone at me. "Tornado watch. Didn't you get an alert?"

"Oh." Weather alerts had been coming daily. I'd stopped paying attention. Nothing but crying wolf.

I plop down in the rolling chair next to her and pick up the day's charts. "Some ugly clouds, but I doubt we'll get anything. Supposed to stay to the south." I drop the charts back on the desk and pull up the weather app on my own phone. To hell with acting professional. This is critical information. "Radar shows a squall line down west of Rochester. That's it."

"Yeah, I see that. Well, damn," she says. "Wouldn't mind a little excitement. Besides, I'm too lazy to water my tomatoes tonight." She stands, stretches, and pulls her tote bag from under the desk where she has it stashed. She tosses her phone into it and digs for her keys.

"You like tornadoes?" I ask.

"I said tomatoes," she says.

I smile. "I mean, you're all excited about tornadoes. You like the threat of mass destruction?"

"Honey," she says, "I work in a NICU. I thrive on widespread chaos." She winks and holds her keys up in triumph. "Found them!" She laughs. "Nah. I'm kidding about all that. Honestly, I don't like the twisters, but the thunder and lightning are damn sexy."

"God, you're strange," I say to her with a chuckle. I pick up the stack of patient charts again and look them over. "Anything of interest tonight?"

Layana nods toward the corner of the room where we have Carter situated. Gretchen stands next to Carter's isolette, staring at him through the plastic walls of his warm little vessel. She chews her thumbnail.

"Day ten," I say, looking at Carter's chart. "Off CPAP again?"

"Dr. Che wants to try it. Gretchen is terrified." Layana leans in close to me, dropping her voice. "Came in about an hour ago. She's still pretty shaken up about Carter's diagnosis. Still doesn't want to hold him. Afraid she'll hurt him."

"Mmm." I nod. Understandable, especially because she was here when Patrick died. She witnessed it all. That had to have been traumatic for her. NICU life is not for the faint of heart in the best of circumstances.

I watch Gretchen for a second and list off all of the possibilities for Carter in my head: seizures, cerebral palsy, brain damage. Or, a perfectly normal life.

Gretchen looks over at me as if she can feel my eyes on her. She wiggles her fingers in a shy wave, then sits in the recliner next to her son. I smile back. Layana looks at me with some kind of expectation in her eyes.

"Okay," I say with a grimace, "I'll talk to her."

I put the charts down and go over to where Gretchen sits, knowing full well that if Layana couldn't talk Gretchen into holding her baby, there's no way I'll get through to her. I probably should just let her be. It's okay to be scared.

Let her be.

Gretchen straightens herself in the chair as I approach. "Hi," she says.

"Hi. How are you doing?" I edge my butt up onto a stool.

"Okay, I guess."

"Carter's doing well."

"Yeah." She shifts in the chair.

"You know, he still may be just fine. Some babies come out of an IVH with little or no lasting effects." Or he might have severe brain damage. Or his hemorrhage could still kill him. I don't say any of that, though.

"Yeah."

"It's okay if you don't want to hold him today," I say. "Whatever you're comfortable with is perfectly fine. You won't hurt him, Gretchen, but I understand." I adjust the stool under me and get a better perch. "Sometimes it's just nice to sit and watch too. You can take all the time you need."

She turns to me with a quizzical look. "Oh. Yeah, okay." There's a long pause. She goes back to watching Carter, and I stay quiet. I'm not waiting; I guess I'm not really even thinking—just spinning the weather and Cara and Layana's tomatoes around in my thoughts, along with the song that's stuck in my head and whether or not Sylvie will eat her supper tonight.

After a minute or two, I stand. "I'm here if you need anything."

Gretchen looks up at me. She says quietly, "Well, maybe I could try." She nods her head toward her son, settles herself back into the chair, and puts a pillow on her lap.

Let her be.

I take Carter out of his isolette and place him into her arms, then cover them both with three blankets fresh out of the heater. He cuddles into her chest, and she rests her hand against the back of his head.

"Let me know if you need anything."

"Thank you, Beth." Gretchen's eyes shine.

I walk back to the desk where Layana waits for me, her eyebrows arched. "Nice work," she says.

I shrug. Smile. "What else is up today?"

Layana goes over the other babies in our care. Elaina. Trinity.

The remaining Miller girls. All the rest, all at different stages of maturing toward a day of birth that for them has already come and gone.

"You know," Layana says, fingering her bracelet. "That was really great, what you did there with Gretchen. God, girl. You just got that knack with the mamas, you know?"

I lock her warm, brown eyes with mine. "I didn't do anything," I say. "You don't know how wrong you are."

"Oh, honey. Don't—"

The rest of what she says gets lost in the screaming noise of Carter's alarms.

35

When I pass the spot in the hallway where I found Mama, I keep my eyes straight ahead, focused on the end of the corridor. Maybe it's a blessing that I'll be put out on the street in a couple of weeks; I won't ever have to walk these halls again, imagining her limp body slung across the spot on the floor where the floorboards are worn by the telephone, the curls in her hair sprawled out around her head like a tired halo.

I'm not sure how I'm ever going to be able to make a call here again.

There's a piece of paper stuck to my apartment door with a thumbtack. It's folded in half, and has "Miss Westley" scribbled on it in pen. The script is feminine but quickly scrawled. Someone expressing their condolences. That's nice. I pull it off the door and stick the tack back in between the grain of the wood, watching the worn wood separate to accept the sharp point. The paper trembles with me as I unfold it.

> *Your mother was a whore.*
> *She deserved what happened to her.*
> *Signed, Mrs. Francine Gillum*
> *P.S. She borrowed my cast-iron skillet.*
> *Please return it at once to 411.*

The paper crushes into a ball in my sweaty hand as I squeeze and squeeze and squeeze. No matter how tight I wring it, though, the words are still there. I can't see them but I know they're there. They tremble through my skin, into my core.

I have to destroy them, choke them. Render them to nothing more than dust and ash.

The door creaks as I lean into it to let myself into the apartment. I drop my pocketbook onto the floor. I'm shaking with rage. My knuckles are white around the note.

"Mrs. Gillum," I say out loud to no one, "you call my mother a whore, when it is your drifter husband who grabs our gams in the hallway whenever we pass? When he was the one who gave my mother money for a good time with her body?"

I look around. Mama's magazines are on the coffee table. Mama's favorite afghan is draped on the back of her favorite chair. Her favorite lighter sits next to the stove in the kitchen.

I reach for the lighter and flick it on. "A whore, Mrs. Gillum? Then what does that make you?" I unfurl the ball of paper from my grip and smooth it out just a bit, avoiding looking at any of the words. I hold the edge of the paper to the fire. It catches, sending a field of black across the page, the glowing orange edge eating up those words, erasing them forever.

Deserved.

Whore.

Mother.

Gone. All those dreadful words, gone. The sharp, pungent smell that the burning paper releases is a relief from the day full of lilies and sadness.

I could burn this whole apartment. Burn the whole building down. The whole block. The thought makes me feel free, giddy. In control. I can do that. Right now.

I hold the burning paper in front of me, watching with wonder. In this moment, it's all there is in the world. No infant baby in a sideshow. No Mama lying dead on the floor. No Charlie. No Mr. Gillum or his wife. No bills. Nothing. Just paper succumbing to a flame of my doing.

The page is about three-quarters burnt when I drop it into the sink and watch the flame gobble it up. As the fire spreads to the last fibers, it fizzles out, leaving smoke, wisps of blackened paper, and a smell that reminds me of last Thanksgiving in its wake.

It's gone. And I'm still here.

I run some water onto the paper, quelling any embers that may reappear.

The building still stands. Nothing burned but paper.

It was my chance. I was too scared.

Always too scared.

I feel calm, which is wrong. I'm far from calm. I don't know what this means. I should be screaming and crying and feeling a dark ball of dread flip around in my stomach. But I don't. I don't feel anything, except sorry that the flame is out.

Sitting next to me on the counter, right next to the sink, as if it were summoned there by Mrs. Gillum's letter, is a cast-iron skillet.

I wrap my fingers around the handle. Lift the skillet. It's heavy. So heavy. It weighs all of me down as I walk across the kitchen.

"Mrs. Gillum wants her skillet back," I say. I don't even mind that I'm talking to myself. It doesn't sound like me, anyway. The voice I'm hearing has been run across gravel, grated through razor wire.

Black. Rough against my throat.

Your mother was a whore.

"Lucky you, Mrs. Gillum. I found your skillet."

She deserved what happened to her.

"You want it back, Mrs. Gillum?" I lean into the window to open it. "Mrs. Gillum?" I yell out the window. "You want your skillet? Take it!" I rear back and throw the skillet out the window into the street. It makes an almighty clunk when it hits the pavement below. A few pedestrians hurry away from it, covering their heads with their arms and newspapers. They look up to my window where there's a crazy woman shouting at no one.

"Come and get your damn skillet, Mrs. Gillum!"

More. I need more.

I turn. On the table is Mama's azalea. Dead. It has been dead for a long time. Like me.

I pick it up and put my nose into its crusty stems, its dried leaves. It smells like rot and dust. I turn and heave it out the window too. People run as the pot hits the center of the road below and shatters in all directions. A delivery truck screeches to a halt, the driver yelling something unintelligible at me.

I stare at the explosion of dirt and shattered pottery in the street. A few feet away is the black skillet, resting where it bounced and tumbled to. People are stopped, peering up at my window, looking around, hovering under awnings.

I could have killed someone.

Jesus, Jo.

I shut the window. Though it's only late afternoon, I climb into bed with my clothes still on.

36

Beth

JUNE, 2017

For the first time in my professional career, I don't know what to do.

I want to go. Leave. Run away.

Carter's alarm is sounding. A monitor hooked up to another infant across the room is also going off urgently. The mobile phone of every nurse and visitor in the room is buzzing and binging with alerts. Gretchen is screaming. And then, the deafening emergency announcement over the PA nearly shakes the solid walls of the hospital:

"*CODE BROWN.*"

I squeeze my eyes shut and shake my head to clear it. The noise is extraordinary. It bounces off the walls, the glass doors, the equipment around me. It ricochets in my head with nowhere to land.

No.

I'm a nurse. It's my job to fix this.

The noise is overwhelming. Everyone in the NICU is frozen in place.

What is happening?

Through the chaos, my mind goes blank.

Layana and I stare at each other, her eyes reflecting the shock and panic that I'm feeling. Through my peripheral vision I see another nurse hurry to the other urgent infant.

"Nurse Beth!" Gretchen shrieks. I look over, and what I see on Carter's monitor from across the room frightens me.

"*CODE BROWN,*" the announcement demands again.

Code brown. Severe weather.

The sounding of the code can only mean that a dangerous storm is imminent. They don't sound a code brown for a passing thunderstorm. In my thirteen years here in the NICU, I've heard plenty of code reds and blues, a code pink once that was quickly resolved, and even a code silver. I've never had a code brown.

"*CODE BROWN.*" It will continue to repeat until the danger has passed. Or, until the building falls, taking the speakers and electrical system and all of us with it.

I glance at the clock, as we were trained to do at moments of urgency. Births. Deaths. Any sounding of any color code over the PA.

6:47.

37

Jo

SEPTEMBER, 1927

It's early as I walk toward the incubator exhibit. I'm not sure if the park is even really open yet, but I didn't give the ticket taker at the gate any opportunity to refuse me.

This time, I have to hold her. As hard as it is, I have to know her. I have to know what I'm giving up. I can't be afraid anymore.

I have to say goodbye to my daughter.

Now with Mama gone, and Charlie, well, with Charlie being Charlie, I know my chance of offering a comfortable life to a baby is slim. I'm not even sure how I can get myself a comfortable life, aside from saddling myself to my beau or finding myself a job I actually intend to show up for. Neither of these options will swiggle with a baby. I know that.

I know. I know. I keep saying that to myself.

Just once, I have to hold her. I have to see my baby and feel her skin again before I let her go.

Unfortunately, my feet have stopped responding. I'm standing still on the street, but in my head, I'm running. Running away, toward the ocean or the train or even back to the city to get lost in its bowels. Somewhere. Anywhere but here. But I can't. Not today. I have to do this. I have to stop running.

Before me, the Cyclone sits, waiting. Empty. Too early in the day for thrill riders. In the harsh light of morning, the dips and turns of the roller coaster look almost comical, like scaffolding holding up the backdrop of a sky, elaborately painted for the Hollywood cameras.

The house under the coaster is quiet. Everything around me is deserted. I feel alone. Of course, I am.

"Miss? Excuse me, miss?" A man's voice startles me. "Sorry to be a bother to you, but do you think you could you help us for a moment now?"

I turn. On my left stands a man in a crisp gray suit, his tie already askew for so early in the day. He looks vaguely familiar. I wonder if he is an associate of Charlie's, but his voice carries the slightest Irish lilt, and I'm pretty sure Charlie avoids working with any immigrants, especially the Irish.

He holds out his hand to shake mine. "Fionn O'Shea, ma'am. Please, call me Fionn. I'm running the photography exhibit." He waves his hand toward a small booth draped on three sides with a black curtain. Inside the booth, a boy of about twelve is standing on a stool, holding up a roll of canvas that's propped on one end with a wooden frame. His arms reach above his head, pulling his little-boy shirttails from his pants. Even from this distance, I see the strain turning his young face red.

I smile, nod, and follow Fionn. I'm just an extra set of hands. I can do that. There aren't t many others around to offer assistance. I can be useful. That's a rare occasion.

The boy releases a relieved puff of air as I climb onto a second stool next to his. The booth smells strongly of sharp chemicals and static electricity. I hold the other end of the canvas roll while Fionn twists a few screws into the framework.

"That should do it, sure. You can let it go." The boy and I both drop our arms, and the canvas unrolls to the ground, making me jump. Fionn beams—I guess it did what it was supposed to.

A mountain range is painted on the canvas, rendered only in shades of black, white, and gray. Several other sheets flap behind the mountains, suggesting other background options. Out of curiosity, I take a peek. Looks like Fionn offers a patron's likeness to be made not only in front of regal mountains but also on a lush tropical island, amongst Indian teepees, or even in front of the Eiffel Tower in Paris.

"Can I repay you then, miss?" His attention is elsewhere. I assume he hopes I demur and wave off any form of repayment. But he doesn't know my level of desperation.

I step down from the stool and am about ready to mention how ten cents would buy a decent lunch when I stop cold.

Clipped onto the opposite black-draped wall are several dozen photographs, all portraits of various people. Each of them had been taken right here at Coney Island just outside the photographer's booth, with the twinkling lights of the Cyclone looming in the background. A sign hangs above the photographs: "5¢ Each."

I take a few steps toward the wall of pictures. Some people look like they were asked to pose—or at least, they knew the camera was pointed toward them. They're doing a damn good impression of Hazel toward the lens. Others look as if they were caught off guard or not even aware that their photograph was being captured. My eyes scan the faces. Two young men hamming it up for the camera. A woman with black hair and a tall peacock feather in her headband caught mid-laugh. An old immigrant woman wrapped in a patterned babushka, intent on digging through the bag draped across her shoulder. A family with two young daughters who appear as not much more than a blur in the picture.

Then, in the middle of the field of photographs is one pensive young woman who grips her cigarette holder with trepidation. She's wrapped for the wrong season in a fur coat. She's wearing her favorite cloche hat with the rose brooch, and she's waiting. Waiting for her beau—the beau who doesn't know how she's betrayed him. How she's betrayed everyone. She stands under the Cyclone, her best friend out of focus behind her.

"Jesus," I whisper, choking on the smells of chemicals that swirl in the tight air around me. I take the photograph between my fingers.

"Miss, that's you, so?" The photographer smiles wide. "Well, you best have the photograph then. Only a nickel."

I look at him from under my cloche, my eyebrow arching toward my bangs. "Didn't you just ask how you can repay me?"

His face falls. "Well then, take it now."

"And ten cents for lunch."

"Now, a minute, there—"

"You took this picture of me with the intention of selling it to any old plug who came along." I cock my head. "I think you owe me lunch."

301

He shuffles his feet. I notice the boy behind him covers his mouth to hide a smile. "Cass," Fionn says to the boy through gritted teeth, "give 'er a dime from the cash register, then."

"Two nickels, please."

Fionn shakes his head, then nods to Cass. The boy scampers over and hands me the coins. I pocket them with the picture. My fingers brush the Chanel bottle, still hanging heavy in my jacket. I nod my goodbyes to the Irishman and the boy.

Not ten minutes later, I've paid my nickel, and I'm staring at my baby. I didn't expect to feel such a terrible yearning for this tiny infant. It feels like I'm being ripped in half from cloche to toe.

No. It's not possible. Charlie can never know about this, and I need Charlie, now more than ever. I can't make this my truth. There's no way.

I look around. No one recognizes me today at the exhibit, I'm just another gawker. The nurses must be on an opposite shift, and I never revealed myself as a mother when I pushed the nickel into the palm of this morning's barker—a portly man whose vest, littered with crumbs and ketchup from his breakfast, strained at its buttons. His oiled mustache curled upward as I passed the coin to him, his eyes yellowed from years under the sun and probably a host of other things.

But we forgot each other the minute I entered the curtained door.

This early, the room is mostly filled with anxious mothers in cloche hats and walking suits. Like me. The stuffy air holds a strong scent of ammonia and cold cream, which keeps my stomach from getting too comfortable. One woman hovers near infant number two, stoic except for the handkerchief gripped tightly in her palm, poised in front of her mouth.

My baby is still in number eight. It's strange to roll the name she's been given off my tongue. I tell myself I was the one who named her, but I don't know. It could have been Alice or Barlow. It could have been Nurse Ida. But since no one knows, I'll take the credit. I practice saying her name by barely moving my lips, carefully keeping any sound from escaping. As I press my teeth to my bottom lip to vibrate a V, I bite down instead, hoping to taste the salt of blood.

"Violet." I say it softly, a whisper.

Rose. My eyes burn.

"You." A strong voice sneaks up behind me, making me jump. "You're the new mother. The one who wanted a swim that night."

I turn. It's Mae. Little Trixie grips her hand, this time dressed in blue, a rag doll tight in her hand.

My teeth chatter as a shiver runs through me. I look down, unable to meet her eye. "I just needed some air. I wasn't going to…" To be honest, that night I wasn't sure what I was going to do. I'm still not.

Her voice softens. I feel her hand on my arm. "I'm glad you stayed dry."

I turn and look back at the steel box that holds my child, not even seeing it through the blur of tears that well in my eyes. I toughen my voice. "Why do you come here? Your child is healthy." I turn to her. I work to keep my eyes from leaking and drill my stare into her. "Are you and your daughter paid to mill about and peddle hope to grieving mothers?"

Mae's expression turns amused. She doesn't have to answer, because Trixie does it for her. "We're visiting Archie, my baby brother."

I feel everything in my body drop. "Oh." Shame burns my cheeks.

"Archie is fine, born at just under three pounds, much bigger than Trixie was. He'll be home before everything closes up for the season. Seems that my womb isn't as welcoming as one would hope." Mae gives a deep, defeated chuckle. "My babies are desperate to get out as quickly as they can."

"They just love you so much, they can't wait to meet you." A tall nurse with soft blond hair spun up in a bun floats over to us from the back room, a clipboard in her hands. I recognize her as Jane, the nurse who did the trick with the ring over the baby's wrist. "Archie is doing well, Mrs. Ross. Up to nearly five pounds now. He should be able to go home soon." The nurse looks at me. "You're Violet's mother, right?" Her face brightens. "What a lovely little teacup. I always have her in a purple bow, to match her name."

I cringe. Nod.

"Honey," Mae watches me with that concerned look of an experienced mother. "Have you held her yet?"

I can't form words, and luckily, I don't have to. Nurse Jane jumps in. "Oh, Violet is having a tough day. Maybe another time."

"Jane, you know better," Mae's voice turns to thick charm, rising just a bit. I get the idea that Mae isn't one to argue with. "These babies need the feel of their mothers' skin."

"Of course I agree, but that baby..."

"Now, Jane—"

"Mrs. Ross," Jane has gone from ethereal to stern in a snap. Like a mother. She's not afraid of Mae's austerity. "Please don't raise your voice at me. Our babies are sensitive. You, of all people, know that." She squares her shoulders. "That child is especially delicate today. I will not be told how to do my job."

The bickering between the women only sounds like noise to me. I'm instead taken with the baby through the glass window. She looks around her tiny metal room with eyes that don't yet know color, don't know shape. She doesn't understand where she is or why. She's oblivious to the turmoil around her—the arguing, the amusement, the lives she's turned upside down. She's surviving because that's all she knows how to do.

And she's the most beautiful creature I've ever seen.

"She's never even held her." Mae's voice turns pleading, arguing on my behalf. "You remember what happened with Beatrix. She was delicate too." Mae gently rests her hand on her daughter's shoulder. Trixie buries her face in her doll to disguise her displeasure.

"It's Trixie, Mama. Trixie," the girl whines.

Nurse Jane's eyes well. "That was different."

"No, it wasn't. That baby needs her mother. You know that."

That baby needs her mother. The words strike a sword through my heart.

The nurse makes a face but watches my reaction. I'm careful to control it. The truth is, I'm terrified to hold the child, but I know I need to. This may be my only chance. Nurse Jane checks over each shoulder. Finally, she opens the rope that spans the steel bar. "Come, sit here." She motions me to one of the rocking chairs hidden in the tiny back room. She opens my baby's incubator, and I crane my neck to see. Inside are tiny arms that wave at nothing in the air. "Open your collar slightly," Jane says as she approaches with the miniature human in her hands. "She'll like the smell of your skin." I untie the bow at my throat and unbutton the first two buttons of my blouse, comforted by the watchful eye of Mae just beyond the door and the successful incubator graduate beside her.

The nurse carefully hands me the tiny baby, resting her face against my neck.

The infant is the size of my childhood porcelain doll. Hazel and I had matching dolls, and she used to swipe her mother's old shoe boxes so we could make cribs for them.

Though this child may be as delicate as porcelain, she wiggles and flinches like she's alive. Because she is. She's here. She's soft and warm, her skin like down against my bare neck. She turns her face towards me, her slitted eyes searching for something familiar. Her mouth opens and closes, unsure of its use just yet. She rests her head back against my chest. Her smell—that familiar scent that mixed with Alice's bread only days before—fills my senses. It feels right in every way.

"Violet." The name falls out of my mouth as only a gasp.

The nurse nods. "You're a natural mother."

"Just look at her!" Mae beams. "You see?"

"Still, we must be careful." As if on cue, the baby arches her back and scrunches her face. Disquiet takes over. She's fighting. Fighting for breath. For life.

My body goes stiff.

The car ride. The dusty, hot backseat of Barlow's Ford. Rose against my chest, clinging to my warmth while hers drifts away. The muscles in her spindly limbs jittering, her breath weak and shallow. *Only seven more miles to the city*, Barlow had said. A shiver rushed through her, just like the one that courses through Violet now.

Rose didn't survive. And now Violet…

"No," I say in a breath, but no one hears me.

Mae steps aside so Nurse Jane can attend to us. "Violet." Jane calmly cups the baby's head with her palm. Flicks at her feet with her fingernails. "Come now, miss. Don't be a pill." She rubs the baby's back, tickles her hairless scalp.

Violet's body coils again. Her fingers pinch my skin with hardly any strength, groping for her mother to help her.

I can't.

"Take her," I say.

"Oh, I think she's fine—"

"No. Please—" I feel my heart failing me, racing and stumbling at the same time. This is too dangerous. I don't know how to hold them. I do more harm than good. This baby was fine until I entered the room.

I can't let Violet die like I did her sister.

I stand and pass the struggling baby carefully back to the nurse. "Please. Take her." I feel pressure behind my eyes, plugging my nose. The sensation of being underwater. I struggle for a breath, just like my child. The nurse takes the baby from me.

The crowd inside the Infantorium has thickened now, so I hurry past the line of incubators and fight my way through the people all craning to watch one of the other nurses slip a wedding band over a baby's wrist. I trip over oxfords and avoid the points of umbrellas. I slide through the curtained door out into the sunlight.

Then I do what I do best—the only thing I've ever done for anyone that has been useful. I run away, leaving them in the care of someone who knows, who can actually help.

But halfway down the midway I slow to a stop. I can't leave. Not yet. There's something I forgot.

38

Beth

"What's happening?" Gretchen tries to get up, but she's covered with too many blankets, too many tubes and wires that make tents of those blankets, and a baby arching and trembling in distress.

"*CODE BROWN.*"

"Take him. Please," Gretchen says, begging. "What is Code Brown? What does that mean?"

I rush to Gretchen's side. Carter's sats are falling. I can't think through the noise and the sudden panic. I scoop Carter out of Gretchen's arms, and she jumps to her feet, shedding blankets all around her. She stays knit to my side as I cradle her son. "Carter. Carter, honey." I run my fingers along his sides and across his scalp. "Come on, big guy. Nice, deep breath."

His eyes are fixed sideways. My stomach drops.

"CODE BROWN."

I turn and place him into his isolette. His body arches just a bit, and his foot shakes in a steady rhythm. It could just be a spell. It's likely just a spell. I know from looking at his chart that he's had sixteen significant apnea and bradycardia spells since his birth ten days ago. He's prone to them. He comes out each time just fine.

But this looks like more than a spell. It looks like a seizure.

"Beth, is he okay? What is Code Brown? Is it a tornado?" Gretchen pulls at my arm.

I don't look at her. I'm intent on Carter, on getting him breathing again, getting him comfortable. Figuring out what's happening. "Yes, most likely. But we're safe here. No external walls, no windows. All double-reinforced concrete. If anything, patients in the outside rooms will be evacuated into the NICU here with us."

I'm safe from the storm. We're all safe.

I concentrate on my job to keep my thoughts from wandering twelve miles away to my thin-walled, 1978-built house where Eddie is likely—hopefully—holding Sylvie under the stairs in the basement.

"I'm going to page the nurse practitioner," I say to Gretchen. I press a button clipped to my lanyard. "Dr. Rita Perez. Paging Dr. Rita Perez." I glance up at Carter's monitor. His sats are still dropping. Gretchen weeps next to me. Layana and the other nurses are comforting families, counting off the isolettes, and double-checking which infants are on life-sustaining equipment, in case there is an electrical blip between a potential power outage and the generators taking over. All the steps involved in a Code Brown. What we've trained for, over and over.

"I should have never held him." Gretchen says, hysterical. "I did this. This is my fault."

Rita bursts through the door, untwirling her stethoscope from around her neck. Her face is flushed and her scrubs are soaked at the bottom. She throws her stethoscope on the desk near Layana. "Pull all of the isolettes together as best you can," she says, the rigidity in her voice revealing her panic. "Get anyone who isn't on respiratory support into the southwest corner, by the stock closet. Thank God we don't have any on ventilators right now. Cannulas can be disconnected and moved. Anyone on CPAP, try to get them close to the walls and somewhat sheltered. Hurry!"

I grab her arm as she rushes by. "Rita, what—"

"It's coming this way, Beth. There's no time." Her eyes were wide enough to show the whites around her irises. "I was outside. I've never seen anything like it."

"Rita, I just paged you. This patient—"

"I didn't get it. Move. Now."

39

A few people are starting to mill about on the midway, but most of them are custodians and maintenance workers. One man empties garbage bins into a large wheelbarrow. Another fiddles with the bolts under a cotton candy machine.

I walk out to the boardwalk by the ocean. The warmth of summer is receding, so the vast beach is dotted with only a few early-morning sunbathers, each wrapped in towels to combat the chill. I look out on the Atlantic. The scent is nice, comforting. The sun peeks around the clouds over the water, casting my shortening shadow onto the worn boards behind me.

ClickClickClickClickClickClick.

I turn back toward the amusement park and slowly make my way down the street away from the ocean. I walk in the shadow of the coaster, watching the Cyclone's train of cars climb the first hill. At the top, instead of starting its thrilling drop down the ravine, it stops. Every seat is empty. The gears creak and moan, but they don't move forward.

Stuck. Nowhere to go.

Two men climb the wooden catwalk that runs next to the coaster rails. Each is dressed in overalls and carries a wooden toolbox.

I stop. My attention moves to the little house under the Cyclone. The door is open. The man stands on the front walk, holding his hat and a metal lunchbox. He shields his eyes and, like me, he looks up at the men working on the coaster. Then he adjusts his hat, shuts the door behind him, and makes his way down the walk. Off to work or wherever his day takes him.

Inside my jacket pocket, I grip the perfume bottle tightly in my sweaty hand. *Chanel No. 5*, the most modern scent for women and one of the most expensive. A man gives an intimate fragrance like this only to a woman he loves. To a woman he intends to marry.

Or, with a wealthy, sophisticated audience like Julian and Mona invited along to watch, a woman he wants the world to *think* he loves.

But no matter. Either way, he can't smell a damn thing. I look at the bottle of perfume. He'll never know if I never wear it.

I open the stopper and hover the bottle under my nose.

It smells rich. Elegant.

Sandalwood.

Vanilla.

Jasmine.

Rose.

Rose.

In a breath, my head feels disconnected from my body,

floating away like a child's helium balloon.

What did I do to Violet just now, when I held her? Did I kill my baby, just like I killed her sister? Rose died. I couldn't keep her alive. And now Violet. I couldn't carry them to term. I must have done something wrong. I didn't drink enough water. Or I drank too much water. I went on too many walks. Or I needed more exercise. I should have listened to Aunt Alice and had a brandy before bed each night to relax me. Or I spent too much time daydreaming and lounging about.

I didn't pray hard enough. Or at all.

I didn't do enough. I can't. I don't know how.

Rose. Violet. I'm so sorry.

40

Beth

I'm not leaving him.

He will not be another Patrick.

But Rita and Layana together are stronger than me. They had to physically drag me under the desk with them. Gretchen, too, although she'd been weakened by her fear.

Now I hold Gretchen in my arms under the wide Formica nurses' desk.

Carter's monitor is still sounding. Layana is on the floor next to me. She's praying. Over and over I hear her shaking voice: "Lord, protect us. In Jesus's name, amen. Lord, protect us, in Jesus's name…"

The Code Brown announcements have stopped. My phone has also stopped getting a signal. It's not reloading, only showing a spinning wheel over the weather radar map.

I feel every quiver of Gretchen's lungs as she cries and heaves. I hear every scuffle of a shoe and creaking of a rolling desk chair around me, crackling against the terrified silence. People are crying and sweating. Trinity's mother has vomited.

Still, I smell nothing.

We'd managed to push as many isolettes and monitors as we could to the corner of the NICU and got the families huddled together under the desk. Then we scooted in close around them, a fortress of scrubs protecting the families while leaving their delicate babies to sit exposed in their steel and acrylic crates.

Rita is next to me. I squeeze her arm. "Rita. Carter is having a prolonged apnea spell. His saturations are down—"

"Beth, we will attend to his spell when it's safe."

Spells are common in the NICU and most often rectify on their own. We intervene when we can, but in an emergency situation, they can be a lesser priority.

But with Carter, I know there's more to it. I never should have left his side, but Rita was panicked and not hearing me over the frenzy in the room. Now, I have her attention. I speak as quietly as I can, since I'm holding an already hysterical Gretchen. "I think he's also having a seizure."

Rita turns her head and looks at me. The shock in her eyes tells me she regrets not reacting earlier.

"His eyes are fixed up and to the left, his feet pedaling."

"Jesus," she says under her breath. "Okay." She searches the clump of isolettes in the corner. The monitors that tagged along with each child when we moved them are now all shuffled together. Carter's, though, is still beeping. Rita elbows me. "Come on." She and I crouch and make our way to the isolettes as if we were M*A*S*H nurses running to a helicopter. "Where is he?"

"Far corner."

"Of course he is." We shimmy and crawl under and between the units.

Then the lights flicker, and the hum of the generator kicks in.

The power blip has caused every alarm on every monitor to sound at a constant, insistent ring.

Rita and I stop and lock eyes under an isolette. We have no idea what's going on outside of our walls, but it can't be good if it's resulted in this level of chaos inside the well-protected NICU. We both stand and look around; every monitor, every digital readout seems normal. No real equipment failure aside from the deafening alarms. Over the noise, the terrified cries and sobs of the families rise up. The infants, oblivious to the trauma around them, seem stable.

Except Carter.

Rita and I hit the SILENCE buttons on the monitors as we pass them. One by one, the alarms stop.

"The patients are fine," I yell over to the group under the desk. "Everyone, stay down." I reach Carter's isolette and turn off his alarm too. "Here," I say to Rita. "He's coming out of it."

Rita slides in next to me. "Likely a subtle seizure, possibly clonic." She reaches through the armhole and places her gloved hand on his belly. His breathing has regulated and returned to normal. I glance up at his monitor and see his oxygen level rising again. "We won't know without further testing and monitoring, but I see his eyes fixed." She looks at me. "Good catch, Beth."

Though nothing in the room changes, the hairs on my arms suddenly rise; my skin tingles. I work to catch a breath; either the air has thinned or the anxiety that had been chasing me all evening has suddenly caught up with me and punched me in the chest. I keep my attention on Rita, who continues with her assessment, unaware of the shift in the room. She finally looks up at me when an odd creaking sound vibrates through the walls, like the doors in an old horror film.

Then, the freight train. It's muffled through the double-reinforced concrete that I'd been bragging about only a minute before, but it's there, unmistakable. It's exactly the sound that's mentioned when describing a tornado. Rita bends under the isolette, but I stay with Carter and keep my eyes on him and his monitor, figuring that if a tornado is going to rip through this building to get to me, putting a fragile infant between us isn't going to help. I keep my gloved hand covering his body. It's a small comfort I can offer in the most terrifying moment of my life.

Eighty-six percent oxygen. Eighty-nine. Ninety-three.

"My map updated," someone says from the huddle of adults on the floor. "Just passed over top of us, heading due east."

Due east. Toward home.

41

The mechanics high up on the Cyclone yell to each other as they hop around like crickets on the coaster.

"Hey you hose-sucking kidney cracker, toss the five-eighths ratchet, will ya?"

"That's what your mama said in the snag, you spinach-smelling peter-eater."

Some good-natured laughs, then one tosses a large wrench to the other, which he catches with the skill of Lou Gehrig completing a double play. Though they're eighty-some feet in the air, they work with the ease and comfort of being on the ground.

"Quite a thing, isn't it?" The man from the little house startles me. He's come down his walk and is passing me on the sidewalk. He tips his hat, a warm grin on his face. "Such a marvel, this is."

I want to reach out, to touch his shirt, to see if he's real.

Maybe to see if any of this is real. I want to ask him about everything—his life, his home, the decisions he made to land him in a house under a roller coaster at an amusement park. I want to know if he's married, if he has children, if he's lost children. If he's lost, himself.

But I don't. My fingers are numb and my shoulders are heavy; the massive weight of a roomful of steel incubators is piled on my conscience. I nod to him, barely smiling. "Yes." It's all I can squeak out.

I wrap my fingers around the bottle in my pocket.

It's quite a thing, isn't it?

It's the same thing Mae had asked me. And it is. It's quite a thing. All of this.

I watch the man amble down the street, swinging his lunchbox as he heads toward Stillwell Station. There's a lightness in his step that contrasts the heft of my own world. I can nearly hear the tune he whistles. Or maybe it's just the sparrows that have nested in the crosshatching of the coaster's frame.

My hand is cramped and tight in my pocket from squeezing the square vial of expensive perfume. I take the bottle out and hold it in front of me. Remove the stopper.

Then I slowly turn my wrist.

There is a pause as the liquid catches behind a bubble, but then it pours out of the bottle in tiny glugs. An ounce of *Chanel No. 5* waters the weeds that surround the Cyclone. Only an ounce—barely two spoonfuls—yet it feels like tidal wave washing over me.

I'm free of it.

The angry scent of wasted perfume wafts to my nose and mixes with the oil of the coaster and the salt of the sea. The skin

319

of my face stings; maybe Coco herself has slapped me across the cheek for my nerve.

I give the bottle a good shake to make sure every last drop is out, then I hold it in the air for a minute or two, letting the warm Atlantic sun evaporate any liquid left behind. I close my eyes and breathe in the smell. Elegant. Graceful. And, not for me. I return the stopper and place the bottle back into my pocket where its safe.

Through the weave of scaffolding that holds up the roller coaster, I watch the young sun sparkle across the ocean. My heart knows I'll never experience this view again. I stitch it into my memory. The whiteness of the morning sky, the crackling sound of the coaster's motor cranking up for the day's first runs, the clang of a wrench hitting the ground after it lost its battle with a stubborn bolt eighty feet overhead. The odors on the air as Coney Island opens for the day.

Each scent I breathe in—the days-old cooking grease thawing into another day's boil, the grinding metal of turning gears heating against each other, the fishy smell of the ocean welcoming the day—is stained by Chanel's wasted luxury now absorbing back into the earth. Vanilla, jasmine, rose, all returning to the soil from where they came.

One more moment, one more task left to do, and I'll go. I'll never come back. I turn and retreat down the street, away from the beach, away from the Cyclone. I have to go back to the incubators one more time.

This will be the last.

42

JUNE, 2017

The hospital stands. We're safe.

We, as a staff, all work together to rearrange the babies back to their places and console the parents back to some level of calm. Reset monitors, plug in lights and oxygen, fall back into our patients' routines of medicine, food, and sleep. Everyone is shaken, but no one is hurt.

Rita and I assess Carter as Gretchen hovers nearby. She rocks herself gently back and forth as she weeps into her phone, her husband on the other end.

Carter is responding well, acting normal.

"Beth."

I glance up at Rita across from me. "Yeah?"

"I shouldn't have dragged you away from your patient. You were right to stay with him."

I nod.

"I assume you've gotten ahold of your husband?" she asks. "Everything alright at home?"

I shake my head. "Couldn't get through. I'm sure towers are down all over."

"Try again."

"I will. In a minute."

"Beth. Try again. Now."

I keep my eyes on Carter. The truth is, I'm terrified to know the truth. I imagine our house flattened, my family dead. The longer I can bask in ignorance and concentrate on my job, the more I feel I have an excuse to suspend reality.

If Eddie's not answering, there's something very, very wrong.

I avoid looking at Rita, but she grabs my wrist over Carter. Squeezes gently. I finally look up and nod. I go to the desk and get my phone, then I call Eddie again. I return to Carter's isolette. "No answer," I tell Rita. I work hard to keep the tremble out of my voice.

"Then go home. Check on them."

I slide on new gloves. "Carter needs—"

"Carter's fine, Beth," Rita says. "We can handle it here. I'm having all of the nurses check in on their families, and you're the only one who hasn't heard. Go home. If all is well and you want to, you can come back and finish your shift."

"But—"

Rita slams her pen against her clipboard. "*Híjole*, Beth. Go. Be with your family. Your baby needs you."

My eyes gloss over. I can't cry in the NICU, I'm stronger than that. I peel off the gloves I'd just slipped on and grab my bag.

Minutes later, I'm fighting my way through the hallway

downstairs that leads to the Emergency Department, and I see a fragment of what really happened outside. The sliding doors don't even have time to close as people crowd in. Deep cuts, broken bones, children and adults crying.

I slide past a man holding a rag to a gash in his forehead and emerge into the parking lot.

The rain has stopped. And, I think, so has my heart.

The sun shines from beneath the clouds, lighting the world in an eerie brightness against the black clouds marching east. From what I can see, all of the buildings around the hospital are still standing. Then, across the parking lot, I notice the roof is gone on my favorite Starbucks. Plenty of tree branches litter the grounds, and the mobile mammography bus is tipped onto its side. Cars all over the parking lot sit up to their hubcaps in puddles. A vinyl banner snaps in the wind like a whip; I recognize it from the bar down the street. It catches on a streetlight that flickers against the black sheath of clouds marching away. The sign is torn on the end:

TWO-DOLLAR TUESD
DOS EQUIS AND CORO
ALL YOU CAN EAT TAC

I try Eddie's phone again as I run to my car.

Voicemail.

A sickening, electric buzz radiates from the overhead power lines. I can taste the electricity in the back of my throat. I instinctively duck my head as I jog to my Civic, as if that would protect me from falling live wires.

My socks are soaked inside my Crocs, but I don't feel it. My

323

purse bangs against my side, but I don't feel that either. I don't feel much of anything but the numbing tingle of panic surging through my body.

Whatever awaits me at home will change my life. I don't want that. I'm not ready for that.

My car is covered with wet leaves and a couple of branches. I wipe enough off the windshield to be able to see and get in behind the wheel. I don't even register the pile of torn-up cigarette packaging on the floor. I don't even notice that the rear window has a giant crack in it.

I keep trying Eddie. I keep blaming the downed cell phone towers. I hope that's it. I hope I get home and he meets me in the kitchen with a perplexed look on his face. *"Really? You've been trying this whole time? Huh. Well, we're fine..."*

My tires create a Moses-like Red Sea chasm in the parking lot puddles.

No answer.

No answer.

No answer.

It's the longest twenty minutes of my life. Traffic lights aren't working, so the lineup of cars creeps past each intersection, easing through flash-flood water and around downed oak trees like they have nowhere to be.

I finally toss my phone onto the seat next to me. Almost home. I'll know soon enough. I squeeze the steering wheel as tight as I can, willing feeling into my fingers. I'm not sure if I've even taken a breath since getting in the car.

I turn into our neighborhood, at the corner where the Andersens' house should be. It isn't there.

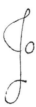

43

SEPTEMBER, 1927

"Nurse Jane?" My voice strains to stay clear, steady.

She comes to me, her eyebrows curved in sympathy. "I'm so glad you came back. I know it can be very emotional, dear, but you'll get used to caring for your baby very quickly. The more you hold her, the easier it will be. There will come a time when—"

"Is she okay?"

"Violet? Oh, of course." She takes my hand in both of hers. "Babies this small sometimes stop breathing, almost like they forget. But it's only for a moment, and they usually come around on their own. She's just fine. She's in her incubator now, happy as a lark."

"I have something," I say, shaking. "I have something to give you. For her."

She tilts her head, waiting.

I reach into my pocket and pull out the pink cut-glass perfume bottle. I run my fingers over the pink rose carved into the stopper.

Rose.

This was for my masterpiece. And that's what it will hold.

I hand it to the nurse, who takes it with a look of bewilderment. "This is beautiful," she says, "but—"

"This is for Rose."

"Rose?" She knits her eyebrows and hands the bottle back to me. "But dear, there is no Rose here. Violet—"

"No, not Violet." I gently push her hands back to her so the bottle is safe against her uniformed chest. I nod up to the shelf, where the row of tiny flour sack bags rest, piled against each other. "Rose. Her twin sister. She's dead. Please. This is for Rose."

Jane's face goes white. "My God. Twins. I didn't know there was a sister. No one ever told me." She looks around. "I don't think anyone here knew. Oh, dear God, it must have been Ida who took them in. Ida…Ida died…" she trails off.

Ida, Sweet as Apple Cider.

Nurse Jane turns, studies the shelf behind her. She boosts herself up onto her toes and collects the tiny packets from the shelf. She sorts through them, carefully reading the typed label pinned to each. Her face blanches further and her fingers freeze on a bag. "Rose. Of course." She says in barely a whisper. She takes the pink bottle from me. "Let me fill it for you. You can take it with you." She keeps her voice low as she speaks, careful to make sure none of the other hovering mothers hear.

"No," I say. "Rose needs to stay with Violet. Make sure they're never separated."

"But you—"

I shake my head. "Please." Then I reach in my pocket again. I pull out the now-empty *Chanel No. 5* bottle. Well, not completely empty. "This is in case you need it for Violet." I wrap Jane's hands around it, making sure she has it safe in her grasp. "And in case you don't, make sure it goes with her, wherever she ends up. There's something inside for her."

Jane gives me a confused look. "But when you take Violet home—"

"No." A sob catches in my throat. It takes everything in me to say the words, and to believe them. "Violet doesn't have a home. Please, make sure she finds one. A good one."

"Miss Westley—"

"Sing to her. Please. Sing to her often. Sing about, flowers, about beauty. Sing about Ida." I smile through the tears that have spilled onto my cheeks. "She'll love that. I know. Sing about Ida, sweet as apple cider."

44

Beth

JUNE, 2017

"Beth." Eddie's standing outside, his hair wet, sticking to his face. "Oh, God."

I run into Eddie's arms. Our house looks to be in good shape, aside from a few of the shingles missing. Our neighbors' houses next door and across the street are all standing. At the end of the road, a pile of splintered wood and siding sits where the Frasiers' shed used to be. The Estes' kids' trampoline is hanging off the Garcia's back deck. Somebody's grill is upside down in our front yard. The overpowering smell of leaking natural gas flavors the air.

All of the neighbors are outside. Some rush around, frantic; others are in a slow-motion haze. A few groups have clotted together here and there, talking and hugging. Two teenage boys pull a large piece of plywood across the street. A little girl sits on the curb, crying into a damp stuffed bunny. An older pre-teen girl sits next to her with her arm around her, rocking her gently.

Everyone is stooping and bending to the debris at our feet, but no one is actually picking anything up. Then my ears hone in on something that makes my stomach clench.

They are all calling my daughter's name.

"Eddie? Eddie, what's going on? Where's Sylvie?"

"She's missing. But Beth, listen—"

"What?" My breath chokes me. The stagnant sulfur air pushes in around me, burning my skin, buckling my knees. A tingle starts in my toes and slices through my body.

"She's fine. She's fine. She has to be fine." Eddie's voice is tight and rises as he talks to a level edging on shrill. "Beth, she has to be fine." He runs his fingers through his hair. His eyes have a wild look in them I've never seen before. "I've been on the phone with the police," he says. "They're sending a crew, they—"

"Sylvie is missing?" It takes a good minute for those words to fully absorb into my body, but when they do, they bring with them a violent quaking. I grab his T-shirt and pull as hard as I can. I lash at him. I hear my voice screaming, blaming him, blaming myself. I don't understand any words that either he or I are saying. All I want to do is hit and kick and bite.

My body has turned animalistic. Grizzly.

I see his mouth move, but my senses have stopped. I hear nothing but silence, and it's too loud; it overtakes me. I shove my hands against my ears, pushing.

Eddie's arms are around me. After a moment of fighting against him, he pulls me into a hug, and I collapse into him. He lowers me to the ground. Wrapped in his arms, I sit, not sure if

I'm comforted or if I want to use what little strength I have left to strangle him and destroy everything around me.

"We'll find her," he says. "I promise. We were outside, it was nice out before the storm moved in. She was in the sandbox. I was trying to get the patio furniture into the shed. She heard the sirens and she must have run."

Patio furniture. He was only doing what I'd asked. What I'd insisted.

"But, she's…" My mouth is so dry I can't speak.

"She was just…gone. In an instant." He squeezes me tighter. "I never expected that."

It's true. It's the last thing I would have expected from her too. Whenever we'd hear the civil defense tests on the first Wednesdays each month, she would freeze and look to me for reassurance. I never would have thought she'd run.

"You didn't go after her?" I'm baffled by all of this. If she's gone, why is Eddie still here? "Why didn't you go—"

"I didn't even see which direction she went. I thought she went inside. The patio door was open. I went in. Looked everywhere. The next time I looked outside…" Eddie squeezes his eyes shut, pauses for a moment. "It was black, Beth. Dark as night. But I went out. I tried to make it to the driveway, but I had to crawl. The wind was insane. There was no way I could scream her name out here. The noise. Jesus." Eddie drops his head. He's crying.

"Eddie." I put one hand on either side of his face, meeting his eyes with mine. "Eddie. What if—"

"No." Eddie says, his eyes rimmed red. "No. She's fine. She's safe. She has to be. We'll find her. We'll find her. We will. We have to. We'll…"

Emergency sirens wail in the distance. Ambulance. Fire. Police. Everything. People are hurt; buildings are on fire or flooded. I feel hysteria wash over me, taking over my thoughts, my actions.

I scream Sylvie's name until my vision blacks out.

45

SEPTEMBER, 1927

"You…but, dear, I…" Nurse Jane reaches over and hands me a tissue in a way that is as stiff and automatic as the Madame Vashti Fortune Teller machines down the midway. The nurse's eyes are wide; she seems mesmerized by me, by my words. I wonder if she hears any of it. "You are just nervous about having a baby. It will get better—"

"Please make sure my baby has a good life." I smile at the nurse and push against my eyes with the tissue.

I turn.

Walk out.

I hear the nurse calling behind me and spectators mumbling in confusion. I don't look back. I know I can't. My shoes click on the pavement. Now more people are at the park, filling in the spaces around me, readying for their day filled with jollies.

The morning sun warms my skin, but I feel cold inside with my soul ripped out of me. I head down the street and past the midway toward Stillwell Station. Inside, I stop and study the map on the wall, looking at all the lines and where they can take me.

I don't have the courage to be a mother to my baby girl. I don't have the courage to do much of anything right.

I have to stop being afraid.

Behind me, there is a pay phone on the wall. I lift the earpiece, drop in a washer to cheat payment. Ask to be connected.

"Honey." Hazel's voice comes through clearly. This time, she's expecting me.

I try to speak. I move my lips, nothing happens.

"Jo, you there?"

I clear my throat. "Hazel?"

"You okay, honey?"

I shake my head. She can't see me.

"I'm coming over," she says.

"No," I say. I pull in a deep, shaky breath. "I'm still here, at the Island. I don't... I don't know what to do."

"Yes, you do." Hazel's voice is as solid as the ground beneath my feet. I use it to lean against, to pull my shoulders back, to lift myself to my full height. I pretend I have a foundation to sink my heels into.

"Did you call?" I ask.

"Sure did. Called at four minutes before eight, like you said." Her voice changes over the line, suddenly sickly sweet. "Miss Fritzel, this is Miss Jones calling from Wilkshire Financial, downtown. I'm calling on behalf of my supervisor, Mr. Wilkshire himself, who spoke with one of your brokers about taking over a client's portfolio." Hazel's voice returns to normal. "I even

333

shuffled some papers around under my telephone, for the effect. I'll tell you, it sounded very official."

"You sound like a no-nonsense secretary, Hazel."

"The honorable—and very fictional—Mr. Wilkshire doesn't have time for skittish assistants." I hear the smile in her voice. "It was good practice for an audition later this week."

"Hazel, you're the best."

"You got a pencil?"

I scribble Hazel's pinched information down on the back of my day's admission ticket. Then I hang up. I stay for a minute in the phone booth, wondering what to do with what's in my hand. I feel an intense sadness in the pit of my stomach, but I feel something else that dizzies my head and tingles my fingers.

I'm not all that sure what hope feels like, but I'll go ahead and believe that's it.

The autumn sunshine seeps through the doors and falls across my feet, whitening the cement. It clears the way. I look in the direction it points me. I take a deep breath. I walk to the trains and find one to board.

The door pulls open in front of me. My feet hesitate.

Violet, forgive me, darling. Take care of your sister.

I step aboard the train.

46

JUNE, 2017

The smell of vomit and wet grass mingle in front of me. I open my eyes, surprised that I can actually smell anything. My face is slimed over with snot and tears, and I try to wipe at it with the short sleeve of my scrub shirt.

I have to pull myself together. I have to find her. I'll stand, as soon as I find my feet. "Eddie. Why haven't you found her?" I say, my face inches from the ground. I'm not sure if I'm even making any sound; it feels like my words are only gasps between my lips. "Why haven't you gone door to door, why are you just standing here…"

I feel a hand on my back. I cringe, and my voice snaps. "Don't touch me. Nobody touch me. Please."

The hand pulls away. I hear a familiar feminine voice.

"Beth. I'm so sorry. We're here to help."

335

I open my eyes. With all of the strength left in me, I pull myself to sitting. I'm looking into my sister's face.

Cara.

She gathers me into her arms. She holds me for a long time while I cry.

"Eddie called me, honey. I'm here. We're here." She nods toward Rocko. He's standing next to Eddie, staring at the ground while Eddie fills him in on what Sylvie's wearing and what happened. Cara's three boys hover nearby, waiting as quietly as I'd ever seen them with looks of terror on their faces. "We're going to help you," she says. "We'll find her."

I couldn't believe Eddie when he said those words, but from Cara's lips, they comfort me. "Cara," my voice is barely a whisper, "you came."

"Of course I came. I love you, stink butt. I'll always love you." She holds me firmly. I feel safe in her arms. "I'm so sorry, Beth. About everything. It's stupid, and I feel awful." She cups my face in her hands. "We're two halves of the same, remember?"

I look at her. "My baby is gone, Cara. She's my everything."

"I know."

"I was never going to leave her."

"I know." She holds me, rocking me like our mother used to. "I know. You came back. I know. You didn't do anything wrong."

In what I assume or at least wish to be a dream as thick as blood, I'm led to the front step of our house. They tell me to sit. Cara and Eddie. Rocko's there too. Some neighbors. There are hands patting my shoulders. I recoil from each touch.

"Don't move."

"Stay here."

"We'll find her."

This is a dream. This isn't real. This can't be real.

"She'll be okay."

"I'll get you some water."

I don't want water. I want to find my daughter. But I know I need to stay where they planted me. I guess maybe screaming at everyone didn't help my case, nor did that line of vomit I left across the driveway. But really, the look in Cara's eye tells me the real reason: If I was the one to find Sylvie dead under a pile of debris or in a runoff pond, it would kill me. After all this time, I can still read my sister like a book.

I look out toward the street. The rotten-egg smell of natural gas is dissipating. An elderly man works to right the mailboxes that are bent over while his wife collects whatever mail she can find stuck to the road. Two men and a woman all wearing work gloves are struggling a large tree trunk up over a curb. I hear the sound of a chainsaw in the distance. All this wreckage sits at my feet like offerings to an ancient goddess. Neighbors give me sad looks and toss over encouraging remarks as they pass the house. Someone hands me a cold, wet bottle of water. I hold it limply in my hand, squeezing it. The icy droplets slide off the plastic and onto my knee, making a dark pink spot on my scrubs. My skin feels numb under it.

Something in the yard glints in the golden post-storm sun, obscured by a splintered flower pot and broken hydrangeas.

Dropping the water bottle to the ground, I stand and reach for it.

The old *Chanel No. 5* bottle. I pick it up, sit back on the step, and look at it.

My breath wheezes. I struggle for air through sobs.

This damn perfume bottle. Heavy in my hand. Solid.

Unbroken. I don't know why it keeps clinging to me like a barnacle. I should just toss it, but for some reason, I can't. Even the tornado couldn't destroy it.

Mom didn't wear perfume. Neither did Grandma Vee with her sensitivities to smells. So who did this belong to? Great-grandma Jane? It seems unlikely, since she died so long ago. Why would anyone bother keeping this?

I remove the stopper and peer inside. What I thought was a moldy atomizer tube is actually something else. It looks like a joint. I could sure use that now, even if it's more than a decade old. I smile at the absurdity of it—good for Grandma Vee for finding innovative hiding places for her dope.

I try to shake it out, but it doesn't budge. I wander into the yard and find a thin branch taken down with the wind. With a little finagling, I pull the hidden item out with the stick. It's a rolled up, yellowed piece of paper. A message in a bottle.

No, it's heavier than that. Dense. It feels almost too stiff to unroll, but I put all of my concentration into it to avoid thinking about my lost child.

I carefully flatten the paper.

It's a photograph. In it is a sad-looking woman in a cloche hat and fur coat, smoke from her cigarette obscuring part of her arm. She wears what looks like a flapper dress under the fur, but it's much more modest than the Halloween costumes would have you believe. There's a tiny silver rose pinned to her hat. It looks remarkably similar to Grandma Vee's pin.

I gaze between the cracks in the photo. I don't know this woman. I'd seen photos of my grandmother from when she was a teenager in the Forties, and I know this can't be her. This style screams 1920s, and she really doesn't look much like Vee.

Plus, I'd never seen such a look of defeat on Grandma Vee. This woman is grieving something, and Grandma Vee has always been a firecracker. The woman's eyes in the photograph are set slightly closer together than Grandma's, and she has an oddly-placed dimple that punctures her upper cheek, even though she doesn't smile. Her expression is pensive.

I stare at her. I can't take my eyes away.

The look on her face. She's devastated. Something is destroying her.

That is the look of a mother grieving. That is the look of a mother who can't fix things, who can't save her child. One who can't do the right thing, even if she could figure out what that right thing is. I know that look. I recognize that look. I wear that look every day.

I see something else, something that makes my heart explode and fill every inch of me with sudden chills.

I see Sylvie's eyes.

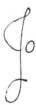

47

SEPTEMBER, 1927

She'll be six in 1933. I wonder where she'll go to school.
I step off the train.
She'll be eighteen in 1945. I wonder if she'll be in love.
I climb the stairs and emerge into the sun onto 23rd Street.
She'll be thirty in 1957. I wonder if she'll have children.
The Manhattan sky is a brilliant blue. I lift my face toward the sun. Pigeons swoop between the Flatiron Building and Madison Square Park across the street. A breeze rustles the leaves in the park. Soon, they'll all change to shades of red and brown. They'll all fall to the ground, submitting to the heaviness of a new season, leaving their branches empty. As empty as I feel now.

Commuters hurry past me toward the stairs that lead to the subway below, bumping my shoulders with an occasional "*'scuse me, miss.*"

Such a hurry. So many places to go.

She'll be seventy-three when the millennium turns in 2000. I wonder if she'll still be alive, if she'll be healthy for her age. I wonder if she'll be a grandmother.

I stop to check that the ticket with the scrawled notes is still in my pocketbook.

A small group of young girls gallops across the street to the park, eliciting honks from a Model T trying to make a turn. I watch them as they race into the park like sailboats, their hair bows like headsails in the breeze, their jump ropes are riggings that help steer their way.

I wonder if she'll be good at jump rope.

I wonder if she'll like sailboats.

I wonder if she'll ever know anything about me. I wonder if she'll wonder.

I know I'll go my whole life asking these questions. I know I'll never get any answers.

Slowly, I ease down the street, past the park, past Madison Avenue. The pigeons swoop over my head, free.

I have nothing. Yet, I also have nothing holding me back.

I turn a corner, then another toward my apartment.

I Stop.

Charlie.

He climbs out of a cab, his fist gripping a few stems of lilies. He goes straight for the door of my building without looking either way.

Goddamn lilies.

I don't have nothing; I have him.

I also have a small slip of paper with different future jotted on it. Memorized, from reading it over and over on the train.

341

I rest my fingers against my pocketbook and think about what's inside. I have Charlie. He's here. He brought flowers.

He also didn't see me.

I take a step backwards.

The girls are still jumping rope as I descend back down the stairs with the commuters.

48

Beth

"Lady, hey lady." A little kid runs up to me. Her hair is a mess, and it looks like she let a grape Popsicle melt all over her shirt.

"Bindi?"

"We found a little girl. Do you know her?"

"What? Show me!" I jump to my feet, and she points to two women hurrying down the sidewalk. Our new neighbors Kirsten and Olivia. Olivia carries a very upset little girl.

It's Sylvie.

I drop the Chanel bottle onto the driveway and it shatters. I run toward the women, stumbling over the muddy grass and downed tree branches.

"Sylvie!"

My little girl turns toward me. She stretches out her arms.

I run. I keep running until I practically bulldoze Olivia. I

343

gather Sylvie into my arms and fall to the wet ground. I hold her. She grips me tightly around my neck and presses her cheek against mine.

I hear people running, yelling. The yells turn jubilant. Eddie collapses on top of me and wraps us both in a tight hug. The crowd surrounds us.

"You saved her. Thank you," I hear Cara say. "Oh, dear God, thank you. What happened? Where did you find her?"

"I went outside to close my car windows. When I heard the sirens, I looked up and saw her running," Olivia says. "I didn't know who she belonged to, so we brought her inside and into the basement with us. We kept asking her who her mama was, but she wouldn't answer."

Kirsten puts her hand on my shoulder. "I'm so sorry, Beth. I thought your daughter was older."

"After the storm passed," Olivia continues, "she wouldn't come back up the stairs. She wouldn't let us hold her or hug her. She just sat at the bottom of the steps and rocked back and forth, staring at the wall, crying."

"She's autistic," Cara says. "She's mostly nonverbal."

Kirsten nods. "I figured. I've worked with some autistic kids about her age. Still, we knew someone out there was terrified that their child was missing, and we had to get her home."

"We finally got her up the stairs and outside. I had to carry her, and she cried and screamed the whole time. Poor thing," Olivia says. "We were hoping once she was outside, she could lead us home, but then she just stood there, looking all over the neighborhood at the wreckage." Olivia shakes her head. "Honestly, I did the same. This is devastating."

Kirsten knelt down to where I held Sylvie on the ground.

"I asked her one more time, 'Who's your mama, honey? Do you know her name? Anything about her?'"

"We've been trying so hard to get her to speak, to give her words," Eddie says, his voice choking, "But—"

"Well, you're doing something right because she finally told us." Kirsten stands. I look up at her, and then I stand, too, still holding Sylvie. I move Sylvie to my hip. She rests her head on my shoulder, dirty tears streaming down her face, a steady hiccup caught in her chest.

"What do you mean, 'she told you'?" I ask.

"She looked me right in the eye. She said, clear as day, 'Mama.'" Kirsten smiles. "Well, of course she wanted her mama, so I asked her if there was anything else. I used some hand gestures we use in pre-K classrooms, made it like a little game. It took a few minutes, but she finally said, 'Nurse. Mama. Nurse.'" Kirsten looks at me. "That's when I figured that maybe I misjudged what you'd said about your daughter, that maybe your girl was younger than I assumed. Bindi was so excited, she ran ahead and found you."

I look at Sylvie. She doesn't smile; in fact, she's still crying in fear. She has no idea what she's done.

She communicated.

I hold her tight. Eddie wraps his arms around us both again. All three of us sit on the muddy grass and cry.

Though I'm surrounded by chaos and destruction, my tears are those of joy.

Epilogue

"She's going to love this," Kirsten says as she slides onto the kitchen stool and takes the pink cut-glass bottle from my hands.

"I hope she does," I say. "Too bad about the Chanel bottle."

"Well, after that storm, I guess we should be thankful that anything is in one piece." Kirsten shrugs. "Anyway, I'm sure Aunt Linda already has several Chanel bottles. But this one is unique. She'll love it."

"Teacha." Sylvie says as she toddles over and pats her hand against Kirsten's knee.

"Sylvie, Sylvie, Sylvie! Hello, little girl!" Kirsten slides off her stool and crouches down to Sylvie's level. "Hello." She smiles.

Sylvie doesn't smile back, but she puts her hand on Kirsten's cheek. Then she turns to me. She pats my leg, her face still stoic. "Mama. Mama Mou."

That's the name she's given me. I'm not sure where it came from, but I'll take it. She can't quite say her *s* sounds yet, but I understand her—I'm Mama Mouse. It makes my eyes sting with tears. "Sylvie, my best girl," I say to her. Sylvie's lip twitches into the tiniest smile. Or maybe she's avoiding a sneeze, but I'll believe it's a smile. She turns and wanders back to her blocks in the living room.

"You're doing such amazing things with her," I say to Kirsten. "She's just blossoming."

"Well, she's as sweet as a rose. She should blossom, and bloom. She's wonderful."

Sylvie still has bad days. So do I. She'll crawl inside of herself and not speak, not react. Or she'll kick and scream and fuss. Then I'll blame myself. I'll cry all the way to work, or I'll climb into bed and lay there like a zombie. But those days are getting more manageable, and they're contrasted and balanced with real smiles and more words. We're getting through it. Sylvie, Eddie, and I are learning how to do this, together. And it feels right.

I smile at Kirsten. "Coffee? Cupcake?"

"Cupcakes? Oh, yes!" Kirsten says. "What's the occasion?"

"A baby was discharged from the NICU a few days ago. His mom and dad brought in cupcakes for the staff. They brought three dozen." I roll my eyes. "So sweet of them, but Mama Gretchen's a little over the top like that. There were only six of us on duty." I shrug. "Everyone took a bunch home. I brought some for Eddie and Sylvie."

Kirsten sinks her teeth into the cake and licks the frosting from her lips. "So what do I owe you for this?" She brushes her hands off, picks up the bottle and holds it up to the light.

"Take it," I say. "I'm happy that someone will appreciate it."

"Aw. Thank you. Linda's collection is amazing. Here, let me show you." Kirsten gets out her phone and opens Instagram while her coffee brews. She scrolls to find her aunt's profile and then shows me a picture of about forty vintage perfume bottles, all lined up and color coded from pinks and reds through to blues and greens, with clear glass bottles in the front and opaque black and metal in the back.

"Wow, that's beautiful," I say. "I can't say I care much for perfume, but her organization is fantastic. I love the rainbow effect." I study the picture. "Can I scroll?"

"Sure."

With Kirsten's blessing, I look through her aunt's posts. She'd taken pictures of some of the more unique bottles using artsy filters, and they're quite pretty. "She has a knack for photography," I say.

"It's what happens when you retire. You get to finally have some hobbies."

Kirsten and I both laugh. I land on one picture that's especially lovely. It's a small vial tinted slightly lavender, with a lovely stopper that looks like a swirled ribbon twisting and climbing out of the bottle. It reminds me of the Corkscrew roller coaster at Valleyfair. The bottle itself reflects this swirl, carrying the swooping curves. For a vintage bottle, it's actually very modern.

"*Violet Number Eight*, vintage 1933, from the perfumery Mona Jo." I read from Kirsten's aunt's caption. "Rose and violet, together with suggestions of sweet yet spicy apple cider, made this a unique debut in the early 1930's world of perfumes."

I stare at the picture for a minute taking in the beauty of the bottle, wondering what a mixture of rose, violet, and spiced apple cider would smell like. What a strange combination. It makes me think of Grandma Vee, singing that song about Ida and apple cider at the nursing home.

Grandma Vee—Violet—and her rose pin. Singing songs about apple cider.

"She had a lovely scent to her that seemed to hang in the air long after she was gone."

I feel a warm, comforting glow spread throughout my body. I hand the phone back to my friend. "I wonder…" I say to Kirsten as I reach for my own cupcake. "Do you think your aunt would ever consider a trade?"

ACKNOWLEDGMENTS

Many thanks to everyone who offered their valuable time, experience, and support to help bring this story together: Hannah Voermans and her amazing daughter, Ella; Becca Hillstead and the very lovely twins Layla and Olivia; and Rebecca Sedam and Gretchen Lyon, for your insider views on being a NICU nurse. Special thanks to Sarah Wolfe for reading an early draft (and for having such winning handwriting), my editor DJ Schuette for the thoughtful, detailed critique, and the very wonderful Minneapolis Mamas with Multiples Facebook group for answering my questions and offering support along the way. And of course, thank you always to Supergroup: Sean Beggs, Christine Brunkhorst, Coralee Grebe, Jana Hiller, Brian Rubin, Kate Schultz, and Kaethe Schwehn. You know I couldn't do this without you.

Thank you to my family: to Scott Bratberg for your love and support, to Luke and Eve for being an inspiration to me, and to my mom Janina Hanley for not only riding herd on the kids so I can work, but also for proofreading and being a generally awesome, supportive mom.

Last but not least, a heartfelt thank you to the NICU nurses of the world. You saved my babies, and so many others. I'm forever grateful.

SARAH HANLEY

Connect with me to learn more and
to be the first to hear about special events,
giveaways, and upcoming releases.

sarahhanley.com
Facebook.com/sarahhanleyauthor
Twitter: @sjhanley
Instagram: sarahhanleybooks

If you enjoyed this book, please consider leaving a review.
Every review means the world to me; I celebrate good reviews
and learn from the rest. Reviews never have to be long or detailed
to be helpful; any feedback or thought is encouraged.
Goodreads.com and Amazon.com are good places to start.

Thank you for reading and sharing!